GEORGETTE HEYER

April Lady

Pistols for Two

D1585521

ARROW

This edition published by Arrow in 1998
an imprint of The Ranodom House Group
20 Vauxhall Bridge Road, London SW1V 2SA

First published in Great Britain
by William Heinemann Ltd

Papers used by Random House UK Ltd are
natural recyclable products made from wood
grown in sustainable forests. The manufacturing
process conform to the environment regulations
of the country of origin.

A catalogue record for this book is available from
the British Library

Printed in Australia by McPherson's Printing Pty Ltd

ISBN 0 099 27942 8

April Lady

THERE was silence in the book-room, not the silence of intimacy but a silence fraught with tension. My lady's blue eyes, staring across the desk into my lord's cool gray ones, dropped to the pile of bills under his hand. Her fair head was hung, and her nervous hands clasped one another tightly. In spite of a modish (and very expensive) morning-dress of twilled French silk, and the smart crop achieved for her golden curls by the most fashionable coiffeur in London, she looked absurdly youthful, like a schoolgirl caught out in mischief. She was, in fact, not yet nineteen years old, and she had been married for nearly a year to the gentleman standing on the other side of the desk, and so steadily regarding her.

"Well?"

She swallowed rather convulsively. The Earl had spoken quite gently, but her ears were quick to catch the note of implacability in his voice. She stole a scared look up at him, and dropped her eyes again, colouring. He was not frowning, but there was no doubt that he meant to obtain an answer to the quite unanswerable question he had put to his erring bride.

Another silence fell, broken only by the ticking of the large clock on the mantelpiece. My lady gripped her fingers so tightly together that they whitened.

"I asked you, Nell, why all these tradesmen——" the Earl lifted the bills and let them fall again—"have found it necessary to apply to me for the settlement of their accounts?"

"I am very sorry!" faltered the Countess.

"But that doesn't answer my question," he said dryly.

"Well—well, I expect it was because I—because I forgot to pay them myself!"

"Forgot?"

1

Lower sank her golden head; she swallowed again.

"Under the hatches yet again, Nell?"

She nodded guiltily, her colour deepening.

His expression was inscrutable, and for a moment he said nothing. His gaze seemed to consider her, but what thoughts were running in his head it would have been impossible to have guessed. "I appear to make you a very inadequate allowance," he observed.

The knowledge that the allowance he made her was a very handsome one caused her to cast an imploring glance up at him and to stammer: "Oh, no, no!"

"Then why are you in debt?"

"I have bought things which perhaps I should not," she said desperately. "This—this gown, for instance! Indeed, I am sorry. I won't do so any more!"

"May I see your paid bills?"

This was said more gently still, but it effectively drove the flush from her cheeks. They became as white as they had before been red. To be sure, she had any number of receipted bills, but none knew better than she that their total, staggering though it might seem to the daughter of an impoverished peer, did not account for half of that handsome allowance which was paid quarterly to her bankers. At any moment now my lord would ask the question she dreaded, and dared not answer truthfully.

It came. "Three months ago, Nell," said the Earl, in a measured tone, "I forbade you most straitly to pay any more of your brother's debts. You gave me your word that you would not. *Have* you done so?"

She shook her head. It was dreadful to lie to him, but what else was to be done when he looked so stern, and had shown himself so unsympathetic to poor Dysart? It was true that Dysart's recurring difficulties were all due to his shocking luck; and it seemed that Cardross couldn't understand how unjust it was to blame Dysart for his inability to abandon gaming and racing. That Fatal Tendency, said Mama, with resignation, ran in the family: Grandpapa had died under a cloud of debt; and Papa, with the hopeful intention of restoring the fortunes of his house, had still more heavily mortgaged his estates. That was why Papa had been so over-joyed when Cardross had offered for her hand. For Cardross was as well-born as he was wealthy, and Papa had previously been obliged to face the horrid necessity of giving his eldest daughter to the highest bidder, even (dreadful thought!) if this should prove to be a rich merchant with social aspirations. He had done so with great fortitude, and he had had his reward: in her very first season—indeed, before she had been out a month—Cardross has not only seen the Lady Helen Irvine, but had apparently decided that she was the bride for whom he had so long waited. Such a piece of good fortune had never even occurred to Lord Pevensey. It was certainly to be supposed that Cardross, past thirty, and with no nearer relation than a cousin to succeed him, must be contem plating marriage in the not too distant future, but such was his consequence that he might have had the pick of all the damsels faithfully presented by their mamas at the Queen's Drawing-rooms, and thereafter exhibited by them at Almack's Assembly Rooms, and all the ton parties. Moreover, to judge by the style of the lady who was pretty generally known to be his mistress, his taste was for something older and by far more sophisticated than a child fresh from the schoolroom. Never had Papa thought to see his little Nell do so well for the family! In the event, her success, and Cardross's generosity proved to be rather too much for him: hardly had he led his child to the altar than he suffered a stroke. The doctors assured his lady that he had many years of life before him, but the visitation had rendered him so far incapable that he had had to abandon his usual pursuits, and to retire to the seclusion of his ancestral home in Devonshire, where, it was the earnest if unexpressed hope of his wife and son-in-law, he would be obliged to remain.

Nell did not know just what Cardross had done to earn her parents' gratitude. It all came under the vague title of Settlements, and she was not to bother her pretty head over it, but to take care always to conduct herself with dignity and discretion. Mama, declaring herself to be deeply thankful, had made quite plain to her what her duty henceforward would be. It included such things as always showing my lord an amiable countenance, and never embarrassing him by asking ill-bred questions, or appearing to be aware of it if (perhaps) he was found to have formed a Connection outside the walls of that splendid house of his in Grosvenor Square. "*One* thing I am sure of," had said Mama, fondly patting Nell's hand, "and that is that he will treat you with the greatest consideration! His manners, too, are so particularly good that I am persuaded you will never have cause to complain of the sort of neglect, or—or indifferent civility, which is the lot of so many females in your situation. I assure you, my love, there is nothing more mortifying than to be married to a man who lets it be seen that his affections are elsewhere engaged."

Mama should have known, for this had been her fate. What Mama did not know, and no one must ever guess, was that her carefully instructed daughter had tumbled headlong into love with my lord at their very first meeting, when Lady Jersey, one of the Patronesses of Almack's, had brought him across the room to be introduced to her, and she had looked up into his eyes, and had seen them smiling down at her. No, Mama had no suspicion of that. Mama was all sensibility, but she knew that marriage had nothing to do with romance. It had been her dread, she confided, that Nell would be married to a man whom she could not like, but she was quite sure that Nell must like so charming and so handsome a gentleman as Cardross. And, what was more, there could be little doubt that he was disposed to hold his bride in considerable affection. He had actually desired Lady Jersey to present him to her, on that memorable evening; and what he had said later to Papa, when he had made his offer, had quite soothed a mother's anxiety. Nell would meet with nothing but courtesy and consideration at his hands.

It hadn't seemed possible to Nell, lost in love, that Cardross could have proposed to her only because she was pretty, and well-born, and rather more pleasing to him than any of the other young ladies who met his critical eye, but Mama had been right. When Nell had met my lord's half-sister and ward, a vivid brunette, not then out, but hopeful of being presented by her sister-in-law, that impetuous damsel had exclaimed, warmly embracing her: "Oh, how pretty you are! Prettier by far than Giles's mistress! How famous if you were to put her nose out of joint!"

It had been a dreadful shock, but Nell had not betrayed herself, which was some small consolation; and she was thankful to have been made aware of the truth before she could render herself ridiculous by showing her heart to the world, or have become a tiresome bore to my lord by hanging on him in the doting way which one short season had taught her was considered by the modish to be not at all the thing. As for putting Lady Orsett's nose out of joint—it had not taken her long to discover the identity of my lord's mistress— that ambition probably belonged, like her earlier dreams, to the realm of make-believe, and certainly seemed very far from achievement today, when my lord was commanding her to account for her debts.

"Tell me the truth, Nell!"

His voice, quite kind, but unmistakably imperative, recalled her from her hurrying, jumbled thoughts. But it was impossible to tell him the truth, because even if he forgave her for having disobeyed him he was very unlikely to forgive Dysart, for whom, in his eyes, there could be no excuse at all. And if he refused to rescue Dysart from his difficulties any more, and made it impossible for her to do so either, what would become of Dy, or, for that matter, of poor Papa? Not so long ago he had said, a trifle grimly, that the best turn he could render Dysart would be to buy him a pair of colours, and pack him off to join Lord Wellington's army in the Peninsula; and it was all too probable that this was precisely what he would do if this fresh disaster came to his ears. Nor was there much doubt that Dysart would jump at the offer, because he had always hankered after a military career. Only Papa, with his next son a schoolboy still at Harrow, had refused even to discuss the matter; and Mama, at the mere thought of exposing her beloved eldest-born to the dangers and discomforts of a military campaign, had suffered a series of distressing spasms.

No, the truth could not be told, but how did one account for three hundred pounds with never a bill to show? There was no need for Lord Pevensey's daughter to cudgel her brains for more than a very few moments over that problem: few knew better than an Irvine how money could vanish without leaving a trace behind. "It wasn't Dysart!" she said quickly. "I am afraid it was me!" She saw his face change, an arrested look in his eyes, a hardening of the lines about his mouth, and she felt suddenly frightened. "Pray don't be angry!" she begged rather breathlessly. "I promise I will never do so any more!"

"Are you telling me you lost it at play?"

She hung her head again. After a pause he said: "I suppose I should have known that it would be in your blood too."

"No, no, *indeed* it isn't!" she cried, with passionate sincerity. "Only it seemed stupid and prudish not to play, when everyone else did so, and then I lost, and I thought that perhaps the luck would change, but it didn't, and——"

"You need say no more!" he interrupted. "There was never yet a gamester who didn't think the luck must change!" He looked frowningly at her, and added in a level tone: "I should be very reluctant, Nell, to take such steps as must put it wholly out of your power to play anything but silver-loo, or a pool at commerce, but I give you fair warning I will not permit my wife to become one of faro's daughters."

"Well, I am not perfectly sure what that is," she said naïvely, "but indeed I won't do it again, so *pray* don't do anything horrid!"

"Very well," he replied. He glanced down at the bills on his desk. "I'll settle these, and any others that you may have. Will you bring them to me, please?"

"Now?" she faltered, uneasily aware of a drawer stuffed with bills.

"Yes, now." He added, with a smile: "You will be much more comfortable, you know, when you have made a clean breast of the whole."

She agreed to this, but when she presently rendered up a collection of crumpled bills she did not feel at all comfortable. There could be no denying that she had been woefully extravagant. The allowance Cardross made her had seemed so enormous to a girl who had never had anything to spend beyond the small sum bestowed on her with the utmost reluctance by her papa for pin-money that she had bought things quite recklessly, feeling her resources to be limitless. But now, as she watched my lord glance through the appalling sheaf, she thought she must have been mad to have spent so much and so heedlessly.

For some moments he read with an unmoved countenance, but presently his brows knit, and he said: "A two-colour gold snuffbox with grisaille paintings?"

"For Dysart!" she explained apprehensively.

"Oh!" He resumed his study of the incriminating bills. With a sinking heart, she saw him pick up a document headed, in elegant scroll-work, by the name of her favourite dressmaker. He said nothing, however, and she was able to breathe again. But an instant later he read aloud: "Singing-bird, with box embellished turquoise-blue enamelled panels—— What the *devil*——?"

"It was a music-box," she explained, her voice jumping. "For the children—my sisters!"

"Ah, I see!" he said, laying the bill aside.

Her spirits rose, only to sink again an instant later when the Earl exclaimed: "Good God!" Peeping in great trepidation to see what had provoked this startled ejaculation, she perceived that he was holding another scrolled sheet. "Forty guineas for one hat?" he said incredulously.

"I am afraid it *was* a little dear," she owned. "It—it has three *very* fine ostrich plumes, you see. You—you said you liked it!" she added desperately.

"Your taste is always impeccable, my love. Did I like the other eight hats you have purchased, or haven't I seen them yet?"

Horrified, she stammered: "N-not *eight*, Giles, surely?"

He laughed. "Eight! Oh, don't look so dismayed! I daresay they were all quite necessary. To be sure, forty guineas seems a trifle extortionate, but it is certainly a charming confection, and becomes you delightfully." She smiled gratefully at him, and he took her chin in his hand, and pinched it. "Yes, very well, ma'am, but that is only the sop that goes before the scold! You've been drawing the bustle disgracefully, my dear. You seem not to have the smallest notion of management, and I should doubt whether you have ever kept an account in your life. Now, I am going to settle all these bills of yours and I am also going to place a further hundred pounds to your account. That should—indeed, it must!—keep you in reasonably comfortable circumstances until the quarter."

She exclaimed: "Oh, thank you! How *very* kind you are! I will take the greatest care, I promise!"

"I trust you won't find it necessary to exercise any very stringent economies," he said, with a touch of irony. "But if you have any more bills laid by, give them to me now! I won't scold, but I warn you, Nell, it won't do to keep your money safely in Childe's while you run up debts all over town! There are to be no bills outstanding at the quarter, so if you are concealing any from me now, make a clean breast of them! If I found that you had deceived me, then, indeed, I should be angry with you, and do much more than scold!"

"What—what would you do, if—if I did happen to owe any money at the quarter?" she asked, looking frightened.

"Give you only enough money for such trifling expenses as must occur from day to day, and arrange that all your bills are sent to me for payment," he replied.

"Oh, no!" she cried, flushing.

"I assure you I should dislike it as much as you, and feel as much humiliated. But I have seen something of what such reckless spending as you appear to delight in may lead to, and I am determined it shall not happen in my household. Now, think, Nell! Have you given me all your bills?"

The consciousness of having already deceived him, as much as his threat, coupled as it was by a certain look of inflexibility in his face, almost overpowered her. In suppressed agitation, which rendered calm reflection impossible, she said hurriedly: "Yes—oh, yes!"

"Very well. We shan't speak of this again, then."

The flurry of her heart subsided; she said in a subdued voice: "Thank you! Indeed, I am very much obliged to you! I did not mean to be such an extravagant wife."

"Nor I such a tyrannical husband. We could deal better than this, Nell."

"No, no! I mean, I never thought you so! You are most kind—I beg your pardon for being so troublesome: pray forgive me!"

"Nell!"

His hand was outstretched to her, but she did not take it, only smiling nervously, and saying again: "Thank you! You are very good! Oh, how late it is! M-may I go now?"

His hand fell; he said in quite a different voice: "I am not a schoolmaster! Certainly go, if that is your wish!"

She murmured something, in disjointed phrases, about his sister, and Almack's and fled out of the room. That gesture, coming as it did at the end of a scene during which he had indeed seemed to be more schoolmaster than husband, seemed to her rather the expression of kindness than of any warmer emotion, and, with her nerves already overset, she had not been able to respond to it as, in general, she had forced herself to respond to any advance made by him. That her retreat might offend him she knew; that it could wound him she had no suspicion, having, from the start of her married life, seen in his love-making only a chivalrous determination not to betray to her that although he had bestowed his name on her his heart belonged to another.

As for Cardross, he was left with some rather bitter reflections to bear him company, and the growing suspicion that all the well-wishers who had begged him not to marry Nell had been right after all: no good could come of an alliance with an Irvine. One of his cousins, that Pink of the Ton, Mr. Felix Hethersett, had put the matter to him with brutal frankness. "Nothing to say against the girl, dear old boy, but I don't like the stable," had said Mr. Hethersett.

Well, he had not liked the stable either. Nothing had been further from his intention than marriage with an Irvine; and nothing had seemed more improbable than a love-match. It was his duty to marry, but for some years he had enjoyed an agreeable connection with a fashionable lady of easy morals and skilful discretion, and that he should succumb to a pair of blue eyes and a mischievous dimple had been an event quite outside his calculations. But so it had been. He had first seen his Nell in a ballroom, and he had instantly been struck, not so much by her undeniable beauty as by the sweetness in her face, and the innocence of her enquiring gaze. Before he well knew what had happened, his heart was lost, and every prudent consideration thrown to the winds. She sprang from a line of expensive profligates, but he had been ready to swear, looking into her eyes, that she had miraculously escaped the Irvine taint.

She had been less than eighteen when he had married her, fourteen years younger than he, and when he found himself with a shy, elusive bride he handled her very gently, believing that tenderness and forbearance would win for him the loving, vital creature he was so sure lived behind the nervous child.

He had caught glimpses of that creature—or so he thought—but he had never won her; and the fear that he had deceived himself was beginning to grow on him. She was dutiful, even submissive; sometimes an entrancing companion, always a well-mannered one; but although she never repulsed his advances she never courted them, or gave any sign that she could not be perfectly happy out of his company. Once installed in Grosvenor Square she entered with apparent zest into every fashionable amusement, took her young sister-in-law into society, rapidly acquired a court of her own, and was by no means the sort of wife who constantly demanded her husband's escort. She was extravagant; he had today discovered that, like the rest of her family, she was a gamester; and what affection she had she appeared to lavish on her little sisters, and on her scapegrace of a brother. There had been plenty of people to tell Cardross that Nell had accepted him for the sake of his wealth. He had not believed them, but he was beginning to wonder. In her precipitate retreat from his book-room he saw only a spoilt child's desire to escape from a disagreeable schoolmaster, and never dreamed that she had fled because her feelings threatened to overcome her.

She made for the shelter of her own apartments, hoping, since she needed a little time in which to compose herself, that she would not find her dresser already there. She did not. She found her sister-in-law instead, blithely engaged in trying on one of those eight—no, *nine!*—modish hats.

The young Countess's apartments consisted of a spacious bedchamber, and an adjoining room, known to the household as her dressing-room, but partaking more of the nature of a boudoir. My lord had had both rooms redecorated on the occasion of his marriage, nesting his bride in a tent-bed with rose-silk curtains upheld by Cupids and garlands, and hanging her dressing-room with blue and silver brocade. In this frivolous bower, of which she was frankly envious, the Lady Letitia Merion was parading between various mirrors, very well-pleased with her appearance, but unable to decide on the precise tilt at which the hat should be worn. She hailed her sister-in-law light-heartedly, saying: "Oh, I am glad you are come! I have been waiting for ever! Nell, I do think this is a *ravishing* hat, only how should one wear it? Like this, or like *this*?"

"Oh, don't!" begged Nell involuntarily, unable to bear the sight of what had contributed to her late discomfiture.

"Good gracious, what's the matter?" demanded Letty.

"Nothing, nothing! I have the headache a little, that is all!" She saw that Letty was staring at her, and tried to smile. "Pray don't be concerned! It is only—I only——" She could not go on, her voice being totally suspended by the tears she was unable to control.

"Nell!" Letty flung off the ravishing hat, and ran across the room to put her arms round her sister. "Oh, pray don't cry! Has something dreadful happened?"

"No, no! That is—I have been so wickedly extravagant!"

"Is *that* all? I collect Giles has been giving you a scold. Don't regard it; he will come about? Was he very angry?"

"Oh, no, but very much displeased, and indeed it was unpardonable of me!" Nell said, drying her eyes. "But that was not the worst! I was obliged——" She broke off, flushing, and added in a hurried tone: "I can't tell you! I shouldn't have said that—pray don't regard it! I have been sadly heedless, but I shall hope to go on better now. Did you wish to speak to me particularly?"

"Oh, no! Only to ask you if I may wear your zephyr scarf this evening, if you shouldn't be needing it yourself—but if you are in a fit of the dismals I won't tease you," said Letty handsomely.

"Oh, yes, do wear it! In fact, you may have it for your own, for I am sure *I* can never bear to wear it again!" said Nell tragically.

"Never bear—Nell, don't be such a goose! Why, you went into transports when they showed it to you, and it cost you thirty guineas!"

"I know it did, and he saw the bill for it, and never spoke one word of censure, which makes me feel ready to sink!"

"For my part," said Letty candidly, "I should be excessively thankful for it! May I have it indeed? Thank you! It will be just the thing to wear with my French muslin. I *had* meant to try if I could persuade Giles to purchase one like it for me."

"Oh, no, do not!" exclaimed Nell, aghast.

"No, I shouldn't think of doing so now that he has taken

one of his pets," agreed Letty. "I'm sure I never knew anyone so odious about being in debt! What shall you wear tonight? You haven't forgotten that Felix Hethersett is to escort us to Almack's, have you?"

Nell sighed: "I wish we need not go!"

"Well, there's not the least occasion for you to go if you don't choose," said Letty obligingly. "You may send a note round to Felix's lodging, and as for me, I daresay my aunt Thorne will be very willing to take me with her and my cousin."

This airy speech had the effect of diverting Nell's mind from her own iniquities. Upon his marriage, the Earl had removed his young ward from the care of her maternal aunt, and had taken her to live in his own house. Mrs. Thorne was a goodnatured woman, but he could not like the tone of her mind, or feel that she had either the desire or the power to control his flighty half-sister. He had been startled to discover how casual was the surveillance under which Letty had grown up, how improper many of the ideas she had imbibed; and he was still more startled when she disclosed to him that young as she was she had already formed what she assured him was an undying attachment. Jeremy Allandale was a perfectly respectable young man, but although well-connected he could not be thought an eligible husband for the Lady Letty Merion. He was employed at the Foreign Office, and although his prospects were thought to be good his present circumstances were straitened. His widowed mother was far from affluent, and he had several young brothers and sisters for whose education he considered himself to be largely responsible. The Earl thought this fortunate, for although the young man conducted himself with the strictest propriety he was plainly infatuated with Letty, and no dependence whatsoever (in her brother's opinion) could be placed on her discretion. Could she but gain control of her fortune she was quite capable of persuading her lover to elope with her. In the event, he was wholly unable to support her, so that that contingency seemed unlikely. Mr Allandale received little encouragement to visit in Grosvenor Square, but, whether from wisdom or from a dislike of enacting the tyrant, the Earl had never forbidden his sister to hold ordinary social intercourse with him. She would incur no censure by standing up for two dances with Mr. Allandale; but Nell was well aware that under the careless chaperonage of her aunt she would not stop at that. She guessed from Letty's ready acquiescence in her own desire to remain at home that evening that Mr. Allandale would be at Almack's, and she at once shook off her megrims, and said that of course she would take Letty there.

Mr. Allendale was indeed at Almack's, and for the fiftieth time Nell found herself wondering why it was that Letty had fallen in love with him. He was a well-made man, he was even good-looking; but his manners were too formal for ease, and his conversation was painstaking rather than amusing. He was certainly solid: Nell found him a little dull. Mr. Felix Hethersett, not mincing matters, said: "Fellow's a dead bore. Shouldn't think the affair would last."

"No," agreed Nell, "but I must own that she has shown the greatest constancy, in spite of having been very much made up to, ever since she came out. I did venture once to suggest to Cardross that perhaps it would not be such a very bad match after all, but—but he cannot like it, and will only say that if she is still of the same mind when she is a few years older he will not then receive Mr. Allandale in an unfriendly spirit."

"Throwing herself away," said Mr. Hethersett disapprovingly. "Dash it, cousin, very taking little thing! Besides being an heiress. Not but what," he added, as a thought occurred to him, "very understandable you should wish to see her safely tied up to someone! I daresay she's the deuce of a charge,"

"Oh, no, indeed she is not!" Nell said, quite distressed. "How could you think I wished to be rid of her? I am only too happy to have her companionship!"

Much abashed, he begged pardon. His earlier strictures on her family notwithstanding he was one of her more faithful admirers, and was generally recognized to be her cicisbeo-in-chief. She had other and more dazzling followers, but he was certainly her favourite: a circumstance which presented an enigma to the worldlings who never dreamed that the beautiful young Countess had no taste for dalliance, but smiled on Mr. Hethersett because he was her lord's cousin. She treated him much as she treated her brother, an arrangement which suited him very well, since he was not, in fact, much of a lady's man, but attached himself to the court of some lady of rank and beauty as a matter of *ton*. A high stickler, Mr. Hethersett, precise to a pin, blessed with propriety of taste, an impeccable lineage, and a comfortable fortune. He was neither handsome nor articulate, but his dress was always in the first style of elegance; he could handle a team to perfection; was generally thought to be up to every rig and row in town; and had such obliging manners as made him quite the best liked of the Bond Street beaux. The gentlemen thought him a very good fellow; the ladies valued him for two very excellent reasons: to be admired by him added to any female's consequence, and to possess his friendship was to enjoy not only the distinguishing notice of a man of the first stare of fashion, but the willing services of one whose good-nature was proverbial. For the more adventurous ladies, the dashing chippers who damped their muslins to make them cling revealingly to their exquisite forms, painted their toe-nails with gilt, and lived perpetually on the brink of social disaster, there were many more attractive blades; but young

Lady Cardross was not a member of this sisterhood, and, while she naturally did not wish to be so unfashionable as to own no devoted admirer, she took care not to encourage the pretensions of any of the notorious rakes who courted her. Mr. Hethersett could be depended on to gallant one uncomplainingly to quite the dullest party of the season; and there was no need to fear that the abandonment of formality would lead him to encroach on his position. He was neither witty nor talkative, but a certain shrewdness characterized him, his bow was perfection, and his grace in a ballroom unequalled. Even Letty, who said that his notions of propriety were quite gothic, did not despise his escort when she went to Almack's. Almack's was abominably slow, of course, and its haughty patronesses by far too high in the instep; but any lady refused a voucher of admission to its sacred precincts must consider herself to be socially damned. To attend the Assemblies gallanted by Mr. Hethersett ensured for one the approval even of censorious Mrs. Drummond Burrell, and had been known to win for a perfectly insipid damsel a condescending smile from that odious Countess Lieven.

Nell was as much astonished as she was delighted to perceive, on arrival in King Street, that her graceless but beloved brother was rather inexpertly dancing the boulanger, with a quiet-looking girl for his partner. He explained to her presently that he had never been so taken-in before. "Ay, you may well stare!" he said, his angelic blue eyes kindling with indignation.

She could not help laughing, but she said: "Oh, Dy, what a wretch you are, when you wouldn't come with *me,* and said wild horses couldn't drag you here!"

"It wasn't wild horses," he replied darkly. *"They* couldn't have done it! It was old Mother Wenlock! Beckoned to me to come up to that antiquated landaulette of hers in Bond Street this morning, and said I must dine in Brook Street to meet her niece. Of course I said I was engaged with a party of friends, but I might as well have spared my breath. Of all the devilish things, Nell, these shocking old hags who are hand-in-glove with Mama are the worst! Mind, if I'd known she meant to drag me to Almack's she could have said what she chose, I wouldn't have budged! I ain't a dancing man, you can't get a thing to drink but lemonade and orgeat—and of the two, damned if I'd not as lief drink lemonade!—and this precious niece, whom she swore was a ravishing girl, is nothing but a dowdy!"

"Ought to have known she would be," said Mr. Hethersett, from the depths of his worldly wisdom.

"Why?" demanded the Viscount.

In other company Mr. Hethersett would have answered him with brutal frankness, but under Nell's innocently enquiring gaze his courage failed, and he said he didn't know. After all, one couldn't tell an adoring sister that no chaperon in her senses would invite Dysart to gallant a ravishing girl to a party. If the damsel in question seemed likely to attract his roving fancy she would be much more likely to forbid him the house. He might be the heir to an Earldom, but it was common knowledge that his noble father (until he had the good fortune to catch Cardross for his daughter) was all to pieces, having, in vulgar parlance, brought an abbey to a grange; and no one who had observed his own volatile career could place the slightest dependence on his setting the family affairs to rights by more prudent conduct. So far from being regarded as an eligible bachelor, he was considered to be extremely dangerous, for he combined with decidedly libertine propensities a degree of charm which might easily prove the undoing of the most delicately nurtured female. He was also very goodlooking, and although his critics unequivocally condemned the carelessness of his attire, it could not be denied that his tall person, with its fine shoulders, and its crown of waving golden hair, inevitably drew all eyes. He had an endearing smile, too, at once rueful and mischievous. It dawned now, for he was no fool, and he knew very well what Mr. Hethersett had meant.

"Craven!" he said challengingly.

But Mr. Hethersett refused to be drawn; and since Letty came up at that moment, under the escort of Mr. Allandale, Dysart allowed the matter to drop. He greeted Letty with the easy camaraderie of one who was in some sort related to her, and at once begged permission to lead her into the set which was just then forming. However unalterably devoted to Mr. Allandale Letty might be, she was by no means impervious to the Viscount's charm, and she went blithely off with him, leaving her swain to exchange civilities with Nell.

Her cousin Felix watched these proceedings with a jaundiced eye. It would have been hard to have found a greater contrast than that which existed between Lord Dysart and Mr. Jeremy Allandale. The one was a rather thick-set young man, whose grave eyes and regular features were allied to a serious mind, and solid worth of character; the other was a tall, handsome buck, bearing himself with careless arrogance, laughter never far from his lips, and in his gleaming blue eyes a reckless light which sprang from a disposition which was as volatile as Mr. Allandale's was dependable. But in one respect they were blood-brothers: as prospective bridegrooms each in his way was wholly ineligible. Mr. Hethersett, watching the start of a promising flirtation between Letty and his lordship, was much inclined to think that he had grossly failed in his duty towards Cardross. A quicker-witted man, he gloomily reflected, would have intervened before Letty had had time to accept Dysart's invitation.

Nell, too, was watching the couple on the dance-floor, not with misgiving (for although she knew that Cardross had no

great liking for Dysart she also knew that Letty had no
great liking for anyone but her Jeremy), but a little wistfully.
When she had seen Dysart she had known an impulse to
confide her troubles to him. She had no expectation of his
being able to give back to her the money she had so blithely
bestowed on him, but at least she might have warned him
not, in future, to depend on her.

There was no further opportunity offered her for speech
with Dysart. Her own hand was claimed; her place in the
set was far removed from Dysart's; and by the time she left
the floor he had restored Letty to Mr. Hethersett's protection,
and had returned to his own party.

He left it, on the flimsiest of excuses, ten minutes later:
a circumstance of which she was soon made fully aware by
his hostess, who sailed across the room for the express purpose
of favouring her with her opinion of his manners and upbringing. Mr. Hethersett could do nothing to spare her this
ordeal, but when one of his and Cardross's more formidable
aunts conceived it to be her duty to censure Nell for her
thoughtlessness in permitting Letty to dance with Mr. Allandale he came out strongly in her support, even recommending Lady Chudleigh to address her criticisms to Cardross
himself.

"Let me assure you, Felix," said the lady in quelling accents,
"that nothing is further from my intentions! Far be it from
me to seek to make mischief!"

"Just as well," responded the intrepid Mr. Hethersett. "Very
likely to give you one of his set-downs!"

Nell was quite overcome by such a display of heroism on
her behalf, but Mr. Hethersett disclaimed heroism. Having
watched through a quizzing-glass which hideously magnified
his eye the retreat of the dowager, he assured Nell that he had
spoken nothing more than the truth. "No need to fear
Cardross would listen to *her* tales," he said. "What's more, he

must know you couldn't stop Letty dancing with anyone. Doubt whether he could do it himself."

It seemed as though the Earl shared this doubt. He had not returned from a dinner given by the Sublime Society of Beefsteaks when the ladies were set down in Grosvenor Square sometime after midnight, but he visited his bride later in the morning. He found her with a breakfast-tray across her knees, the curtains of her bed drawn back in billowing folds of rosy silk. She was engaged, between sips of coffee and nibbles at a slice of bread-and-butter, in reading her correspondence. This seemed, from the litter on the counterpane, to consist largely of gilt-edged invitations, but there was a letter, crossed and recrossed, from her mama, which she was trying to decipher when Cardross came into the room. She put it down at once, and tried to tuck back the ringlets which had strayed from under her becoming night-cap of muslin and lace. "My lord! Oh, dear, I did not think you would be coming to see me so early, and I am dreadfully untidy!"

"Don't!" he said, capturing her hand, and kissing it. "You look charmingly, I assure you. Was it amusing, your party?"

"Yes, thank you. That is—it was just one of the Assemblies, at Almack's, you know."

"Not very amusing, then," he remarked, seating himself on the edge of her bed, and picking up one of the invitation cards. "Nor will this be, but we shall be obliged to accept it, I suppose. She is Letty's godmother. Did Letty behave with propriety last night, or did she hang on that fellow Allandale the whole evening?"

"No, indeed she did not! She stood up only twice with him."

"I am astonished to learn that she had as much moderation —and I make you my compliments: it must surely be your doing!"

"Well, of course, I should *try* to dissuade her from doing

what you don't like," said Nell doubtfully, "but it wasn't at
all necessary. Mr. Allandale's scruples are so *very* strict that
I am persuaded he would never ask her to do anything that
might set up people's backs."

"Good God!" said his lordship. "What a slow-top! My
dear, what *does* she see in him to hit her fancy?"

"I can't think!" said Nell candidly. "Though I am sure he
has many excellent qualities, and a most superior understanding."

"Superior fiddlesticks! I never found him to be anything
but a dreadful bore. I wish to God she would recover from
this green-sickness! It's quite impossible, you know: he has
neither fortune nor expectation, and I'll swear I never saw a
couple less suited to one another. I should be a villain to
countenance such an attachment. If his scruples are as strict
as you tell me I collect I've no need to fear he may run off
with her to Gretna Green?"

"Good gracious, no!" Nell exclaimed, startled.

"So much, then, for my aunt Chudleigh's croakings!"

"Your aunt Chudleigh! Oh, Giles, she was at Almack's
last night, and she gave me a terrible scold for permitting
Letty to dance with Mr. Allandale!"

"What impertinence!"

"Oh, no! Though that is what Felix said. And also he
told her to make her complaints to you, which was not very
civil of him, but excessively brave, I thought!"

"I wonder what she imagines I can do to stop Letty? Short
of incarcerating her at Merion—— By the by, I must go to
Merion next week. Useless, I suppose, to ask you to go with
me?"

She showed him a face of sudden dismay. "Next week!
But the Beadings' masquerade——!"

He raised his brows. "Is it so important? For my part,
masquerades at Chiswick——"

"No, indeed, but you did promise Letty she should attend it! It is the first she has ever been to, and she has had the prettiest domino made, and—and I must own I think it would be dreadfully shabby to tell her now that she cannot go!"

"Hang Letty! Can't she—— No, I suppose not. Very well: I won't tease you to go with me."

"I wish I might," she said wistfully.

He smiled at her, but rather quizzically, and picked up another of the invitation cards. "A quadrille ball at the Cowpers'! How dashing! It will be a horrible squeeze: must we go?"

The post had brought her ladyship a polite reminder from Mr. Warren, Perfumier, that a trifling account for scent, white nail-wax and Olympian Dew, was outstanding. It had lain hidden by Lady Cowper's invitation, and was revealed when the Earl picked this up. Only a few guineas were involved, but Nell instinctively put out her hand to cover it. The movement caught his eye; he glanced down, and she at once removed her hand, flushing, vexed with herself.

"What other delights are in store for us?" he asked, picking up another card. "Assemblies and balls seem to be in full feather: you will be knocked up by all this raking! Don't drag me to *this* affair, I beg of you!"

"That? Oh, no! It is to be a petticoat-party. You—you will be present at our own dress-party, won't you?"

"Of course."

There was a short silence. After that one glance the Earl had not again looked at Mr. Warren's account, but it seemed to his guilty wife imperative to divert his attention from it. She said a trifle breathlessly: "Cardross, what a very elegant dressing-gown that is! I think I never saw you wear it before."

"Ah, I hoped you would be pleased with it!" he replied blandly. "And with me for letting you see it."

"How absurd you are! It is certainly most handsome."

"Yes, and wickedly dear—as dear as your feathered bonnet, though not, I fear, as becoming. You see how I lay myself open to strong counter-attack!"

"Oh, Giles!"

He laughed, and tickled her cheek. "Foolish little Nell! Is it *very* shocking?"

She heaved a sigh of relief, smiling shyly at him. "No, indeed it isn't! Only it—it does chance to be a bill I had forgotten, and I was afraid you would be angry with me."

"What a disagreeable husband I must be!" he murmured ruefully. "Shall I pay that bill with the rest?"

"No, please! It is a *very* small one—look!"

She held it out to him, but he did not look at it, only taking her hand in his, the bill crushed between his fingers, and saying: "You mustn't be afraid of me. I never meant to make you so! I'll pay this bill, or any other—only don't conceal any from me!"

"Afraid of you? Oh, no, no!" she exclaimed.

His clasp on her hand tightened; he leaned forward, as though he would have kissed her; but her dresser came into the room just then, and although she quickly withdrew, the moment had passed. Nell had snatched her hand away, vividly blushing, and the Earl did not try to recapture it. He got up, his own complexion rather heightened, feeling all the embarrassment natural to a man discovered, at ten o'clock in the morning, making love to his own wife, and went away to his dressing-room.

SHORTLY before four o'clock that afternoon young Lady Cardross's barouche was driven into Hyde Park by the Stanhope Gate. It was a very stylish vehicle, quite the latest thing in town carriages, and it had been bestowed on her ladyship, together with the pair of perfectly matched grays that drew it, by her husband, upon her installation as mistress of his house in Grosvenor Square. "Slap up to the echo," was what Dysart called it: certainly no other lady owned a more elegant turn-out. To be seen in Hyde Park between the hours of five and six on any fine afternoon during the London season, driving, riding, or even walking, was de rigueur for anyone of high fashion; and before her marriage, when she had sat beside her mama in an öldfashioned landaulet, Nell had frequently envied the possessors of more dashing equipages, and had thought how agreeable it would be to sit behind a pair of high-steppers in a smart barouche, with its wheels picked out in yellow. She had been delighted with the Earl's gift, exclaiming naïvely: "Now I shall be all the crack!"

"Do you wish to be?" he had asked her, amused.

"Yes," she replied honestly. "And I think I ought to be, because although Miss Wilby—our governess, you know— says that it is wrong to set one's mind on worldly things, *you* are all the crack, which makes it perfectly proper, I think, for me to be fashionable too."

"I am persuaded," he said, his countenance admirably composed, "that Miss Wilby must perceive it to be your *duty,* even."

She was a little dubious about this, but happily recollecting that she was no longer answerable to her governess she was able to put that excellent educationist out of her mind. "You know how people talk of Lord Dorset on his white horse, and Mrs. Toddington with her chestnuts?" she said confidentially. "*Now* they will talk of Lady Cardross, behind her match-grays! I should not be astonished if my barouche were to draw as many eyes as hers!"

"Nor should I," agreed his lordship, grave as a judge. "In fact, I should be much astonished if it did not."

Whether it was the smart turn-out which drew all eyes, or its charming occupant, Nell had soon experienced the felicity of attracting a great deal of attention when she drove in the Park. She became a noted figure, and never doubted that she owed this triumph to her splendid horses until her more know-ledgeable sister-in-law remarked chattily, as she stepped into the carriage that day: "Isn't it a fortunate circumstance, Nell, that you are fair and I am dark? I don't wonder at it that everyone stares to see us: we take the shine out of *all* the other females! Mr. Bottisham told Hardwick so, and Hardwick says it is a compliment well worth having, because Mr. Bottisham is in general quite odiously censorious. I think," she added, dispassionately considering the matter, "that you are prettier than I am, but, on the other hand, I have a great deal of countenance, besides being dark, which is more in the mode, so I don't *excessively* mind your being beautiful."

Nell could not help laughing, but, with Miss Wilby's precepts in mind, she ventured to suggest to Letty that such candour was a trifle improper.

"That is the sort of thing Aunt Chudleigh says," observed Letty, unabashed. "For my part, I see nothing improper in speaking the truth. And you can't deny that it *is* the truth!" She made herself comfortable beside Nell, and unfurled a pink sunshade. "We make a perfect picture," she said complacently.

"I collect Lord Hardwick told you so!"

"*Everyone* tells me so!"

"Well, take care they don't next tell you that you are abominably conceited," recommended Nell.

"They won't," asserted Letty, with confidence. "No one I care a fig for, at all events. I daresay Felix might, for I never knew anyone so stuffy!"

However, when they presently saw Mr. Hethersett strolling in the Park there was nothing to be read in that stickler's countenance but critical appreciation. Nell directed her coachman to pull up his horses, and when Mr. Hethersett came up to the carriage leaned forward to give him her hand. "How do you do? I hoped we might see you. Do you mean to go to the Beadings' masquerade next week? Cardross has been obliged to cry off: isn't it infamous of him? Will you dine with us, and give us your escort in his stead?"

He looked regretful, and shook his head. "Can't," he said mournfully. "Excused myself to Mrs. Beading. Told her I had another engagement. Not the thing to go there after that. Pity!"

She smiled. 'You cannot hoax me into believing that you think so! Confess! You dislike masquerades!"

"Not trying to hoax you: happy to escort you anywhere! Not but what it ain't the sort of party I like. If I were you I'd cry off, because you won't enjoy it. Not just in your style."

"I declare, you are the stupidest creature, Felix!" Letty broke in. "Why shouldn't we enjoy it? It will be rare mummery, for we are all to wear masks, and——"

"Yes, a vast rout of people, and rompings!" interrupted Mr. Hethersett, in a tone of deep disapproval. "*You* may enjoy it: I never said you wouldn't. All I said was, Lady Cardross won't. Do you want a piece of advice, cousin?"

"No," said Letty crossly.

"Mistake," he said, shaking his head. "Not saying that ain't an elegant gown: it is. Not saying that hat don't become you: it does." He left an ominous pause, during which Letty eyed him uneasily. She might despise him for what she considered his antiquated notions of propriety, but no aspirant to high fashion could afford to ignore his pronouncements on all matters of sartorial taste. He delivered his verdict. "I don't like those pink ribbons. Or the feather. Insipid."

"*Insipid?*" she exclaimed indignantly. She cast a glance down at the double row of pink knots which ornamented her dress of delicate fawn-coloured muslin. They exactly matched the feather that hung down on one side of a little straw hat which was turned up on the other side, and worn at a dashing angle on her glossy black ringlets. French kid gloves of the same pink completed a toilet which she had thought to be, until this painful moment, in the first crack of the mode. Doubt now entered her soul; she turned her anxious gaze upon her cousin. "It isn't! You are saying it to vex me!"

"No wish to vex you. Just thought you wanted to be up to the knocker."

"I do—I *am* up to the knocker!"

"Not with those pink bows," said Mr. Hethersett firmly. "Quite pretty, but dashed commonplace! Ought to be cherry. Give you a new touch!"

With these words he made his bow to both ladies, and pro-ceeded on his way, leaving his cousin torn between wrath and a growing conviction that he was right, and Nell a good deal amused.

"If Felix were not related to me I should cut his acquaintance!" said Letty, glaring vengefully after him. "He is prosy, and uncivil, besides placing himself on *far* too high a form! And now I come to think of it I didn't above half like his waistcoat!" She transferred her gaze to Nell, as Mr. Hethersett's exquisitely tailored person receded in the distance. "If he thinks my ribbons insipid I am astonished that he hadn't the effrontery to say that *your* dress was commonplace!

Depend upon it, he thinks you would look more becomingly in purple, or puce, or scarlet! *Odious* creature!"

"Oh, he couldn't say that to me, when he told me weeks ago never to wear those strong colours!" said Nell, whose gown of Berlin silk was just the colour of her eyes. "That was when I was wearing that maroon pelisse. I promise you, he was quite as odious to me. Don't regard it!"

"I never pay the least heed to a word he says," replied Letty, in a lofty voice. She relapsed into thoughtful silence while the barouche proceeded on its way, but said after several minutes: "Do you think I should tell my woman to dye this feather, or purchase a new one?"

"Dye that one," responded Nell. "And also the ribbons. I wish he might have gone with us to the masquerade: it would have been much more comfortable! I suppose . . ." She hesitated looking doubtfully at Letty. "I suppose you would not like to go to Merion with Cardross instead?"

"Nell!" almost shrieked Letty, an expression of scandalized dismay on her countenance. "Go to Merion in the middle of the season? You must be out of your senses! And if that is what Giles wishes us to do I think it is the shabbiest thing I ever heard of, when he *promised* I should go to the masquerade! Yes, and after fobbing me off with this, when I particularly wanted to go to the Covent Garden masquerade!" she added indignantly. "Saying it was not the thing, and we should go to the Beadings' private masquerade instead! Just like him! I daresay, if I only knew——"

"It is *not* just like him, and I wish you will not fly into a pet for nothing!" said Nell, firing up. "*If* you only knew, he said not another word to persuade me to go with him to Merion when I reminded him that you particularly wished to go to the masquerade! And if Felix hadn't failed——"

"But, Nell, it's of no consequence!" Letty urged. "I am

sure quite fifty of our friends are going to it, and even if we found ourselves amongst strangers it still wouldn't signify, because Mrs. Beading is your cousin! I own, it would be more comfortable to take some gentleman along with us, but you may easily invite Westbury, or Sir George Marlow, or——"

"No!" said Nell emphatically. "*Not* to a masquerade!"

Letty uttered a tiny spurt of laughter. "Are you afraid they wouldn't keep the line? For my part, I think it would be very good fun if they did flirt outrageously with us! But you are the oddest creature! Not up to snuff at all, in spite of having come out a whole year before I did. Why, at my very first ball——" She broke off, as Nell nipped her arm, directing her eyes to the servants on the box of the carriage. "Oh, stuff! No, don't be cross: I won't say a word, I promise! How would it be if we took Jeremy with us? I daresay he would be very glad to go, and you may be sure he would conduct himself with all the propriety in the world, because even Giles owns that he is *perfectly* the gentleman!"

"Don't be so absurd!" begged Nell. "He told you himself that he hadn't received an invitation, and I can readily believe that he has too much propriety to go to the party without one. Besides, you know very well I wouldn't invite him when it is what Giles would particularly dislike."

Letty accepted this rebuff philosophically, saying in a resigned tone: "No, I didn't think you would. Well, what is to be done? *Pray* don't say you cannot go if Giles does not, for of all the dowdy notions——!"

Nell flushed. "No such thing! I mean, I haven't the remotest intention of saying such a thing! Only I can't immediately think of any gentleman whom I——" She stopped, as her troubled gaze alighted on two horsemen, riding easily towards them. Her eyes brightened; she exclaimed: "Dysart!"

"The very man!" declared Letty enthusiastically. "Now you may be easy!"

This optimism, however, seemed for several minutes to have been ill-founded. The Viscount, who was bestriding a nervous young blood-chestnut few men would have cared to exercise in the Park at an hour when it was thronged with traffic, responded readily enough to his sister's signal, bringing his reluctant mount up to the barouche, and holding it there with all the apparent ease of an accomplished horseman; but when she asked him if he had received an invitation to the Beadings' masquerade, he replied: "Ay, but I don't mean to go."

"Oh, Dy, you didn't refuse?" Nell said anxiously.

"No, I didn't *refuse* precisely," admitted Dysart, whose careless practice it was to leave all but a few favoured invitations unanswered. "Here, Corny! Don't have to introduce you to my sister, do I? Or to Lady Letitia?"

His companion, who had been holding coyly aloof, edged his horse forward, raising the low-crowned beaver from his head, and bowing slightly to both ladies. Mr. Cornelius Fancot was a chubby-faced young gentleman, slightly junior to the Viscount, whose devoted follower he had been ever since the pair had met at Harrow. There, he had been privileged to lend his aid to his dazzling friend in various hare-brained exploits; later, he had been of invaluable assistance in disposing suitably of the statue of Mercury in the Quad at Christ Church; and if he had never, either when up at Oxford or since both had come down from that seat of learning, contrived to rival Dysart's more celebrated feats, which included putting a donkey to bed with a complete stranger in an inn, and leaping one of his hunters over a dining-table equipped with a full complement of plate, silver, glasses, and chandeliers, he had won for himself, besides the reputation of being one who never refused a wager, considerable fame for having walked the length of Piccadilly on a pair of stilts; and for

having won a bet that he would journey to Dover and back
again to London before his too-hopeful challenger had made
a million dots on sheet after sheet of paper. Unlike his noble
friend, he was possessed of a handsome fortune, and was un-
encumbered by any kin more nearly related to him than
several aunts, to whose admonitions he paid no heed at all; and
various cousins whom he had no hesitation in condemning as
a parcel of slow-tops. His habit proclaimed the sporting man,
but a hankering after dandyism was betrayed by buckram-
wadded shoulders to his lavishly corded and tasselled Polish
coat, and a Brummell tie round his rather short neck. The
life and soul of a convivial party at Long's Hotel, or Limmer's,
he was apt to be tongue-tied in the presence of ladies, and
might be looked for in vain at Almack's Assembly Rooms. He
was sufficiently well-acquainted with Nell to feel no particular
alarm when she addressed him; but a quizzing glance from
Letty's mischievous eyes threw him at once into stuttering
disorder. Observing this, the Viscount, with his customary
lack of ceremony, recommended that enterprising damsel to
pay no heed to him. "Not in the petticoat-line," he explained.
"Are you going to this precious masquerade, Nell?"

"Yes, indeed we are, only we find ourselves in a little fix.
Cardross has been obliged to cry off, you see, and it is so disagreeable to go to such affairs with no gentleman to escort
one! And Felix cannot go with us either, so, if you please, Dy,
will you be so obliging as to——"

"No, dash it, Nell!" interrupted the Viscount hastily. "Not
to a masquerade out at Chiswick! Ask Marlow, or Westbury, or another of your flirts! The lord knows you've plenty
of 'em! Why choose me?"

"She is afraid they wouldn't keep the line," said Letty
demurely.

Before the Viscount could reply Mr. Fancot rather unexpectedly entered into the discussion. "Shouldn't wonder at

it if she was right," he said. "Masquerades, you know! Ramshackle! Ought to go with her la'ship!"

"What the deuce do you know about masquerades, Corny?" demanded Dysart. "You never went to one in your life!"

"Yes, I did," asserted Mr. Fancot. "I went with you, Dy! Well, I wouldn't let *my* sister go to one alone. What I mean is, I wouldn't if I had one. Had a sister, I mean," he added, becoming a little flustered, as Letty giggled.

"Covent Garden!" exclaimed Dysart scornfully. "I should think not indeed! But this affair will be quite another thing. Pretty insipid, I should think. Why do you go to it?"

"You see, it is the first masquerade Letty has attended, and so she wishes particularly to go," Nell explained.

"Yes, and, what is more, I am quite *determined* to go," corroborated Letty. "I collect you don't mean to be so obliging as to escort us, which doesn't surprise me above a very little, because of all imaginable persons I think brothers to be by far the most disagreeable!"

"Letty, that is not just!" exclaimed Nell. "*You* have no cause to say so, and I assure you I have none either!" She smiled lovingly up at the Viscount. "Don't come, if you had rather not! At my cousin's party I can't need an escort, after all."

However, the Viscount, either from perversity, or from a sense of obligation, said, with a darkling look at Letty, that if his sister was set on attending the masquerade he would certainly accompany her. He added, with an austerity which accorded ill with his rakish appearance, that if it suited Cardross's notions of propriety to allow Nell to go alone to such parties that was where he must join issue with his lordship. He then, most unhandsomely, rode off before either lady could counter this charge. Nell was merely distressed that he should think her husband neglectful, but Letty, who reserved to herself the right to criticize Cardross, was extremely incensed, and charged Mr. Fancot, lingering to make his adieux in form, with a rude message to him.

"Though, to be sure, I don't know why I should put myself to the trouble of fighting Giles's battles," she observed, as Mr. Fancot left them, and Nell told her coachman to drive on. "I am persuaded he would never fight *mine!*"

She encountered a very direct look from Nell's soft blue eyes. Nell said quietly: "You must not say so. It is quite untrue, and you know it!"

Letty sighed. "Well, I didn't mean precisely that, but you must own that no one was ever more unsympathetic than Giles. It is so unkind of him to take poor Jeremy in aversion! I had not believed he could be so proud, or care so much for consequence, or so little for my happiness!"

"It isn't that! Indeed, it is not, Letty! He doesn't dislike Mr. Allandale, and as for caring about his consequence you know he has said that if you are still of the same mind in a— in a year or two, he will not then refuse his consent. It *is* your happiness which he thinks of. I don't say that he *likes* the match, for although Mr. Allandale's situation in life is respectable, he is *not* your equal in station, and there is a disparity between your fortunes which makes the marriage even more ineligible."

"That is just what I have no patience with!" Letty said quickly. "If *I* were poor too it would be another matter! I don't mean to say that I shouldn't wish to marry Jeremy, for I should; but there would then be justice in Cardross's objection! It is a melancholy reflection, Nell, but I fear I shouldn't be a very good wife for a man in straitened circumstances. Of course I should endeavour to learn how to manage, but it is useless to deceive oneself: I don't think I have any turn for economy!"

"No, alas, nor I!" agreed Nell, with a wry grimace.

"The thing is, we were not bred to it" said Letty profoundly. "But what does it signify, after all, when I shall be the mistress of a substantial fortune as soon as I come of full age?"

"I think the thing is that Cardross feels you are too young to be making up your mind just yet," Nell said diffidently.

"Depend upon it, he would not say so if I wanted to marry a man of rank and fortune!" Letty said, her eyes kindling. "He did not think *you* too young when he offered for you, and I dare swear your papa did not either!"

"No," admitted Nell.

"No! But if he had *not* been Cardross, your papa *would* have said so, even though he came of a very good family, and was in all respects a most superior man! It is all pride and pretension, and for my part I think it is detestable!"

"No, no, not that—not *quite* that!" Nell said. "I suppose he would wish you to make what is called a good match, but he has told me himself that if you are still of the same mind in a year or two——"

"He knows very well that in a year or two—and probably much sooner!—Jeremy will have been sent abroad. Indeed, Jeremy has the greatest hope, if all goes as he has reason to expect—— But I mustn't tell you! Pray don't repeat it, Nell! He particularly desired me not to speak of it while nothing is yet settled." She hesitated, and then slid an impulsive hand into Nell's, and whispered: "*One* thing I must tell you! I believe—I hope—that he will shortly be calling in Grosvenor Square, to see Cardross. You may guess for what purpose! I should not be mentioning it to you, but oh, Nell, you will stand our friend, won't you?"

"Well, I might," said Nell, in whom a year's intimacy with her sister-in-law had engendered a good deal of caution. "But not if you mean to do something outrageous!"

"Nothing of the sort!" declared Letty indignantly. "Unless,

of course, Cardross drives me to it, and that I depend on you to prevent!"

"Oh, pray don't!" begged Nell, alarmed. "If he won't consent to your marriage, it is because he feels it would be wrong in him to do so, and how could I overcome such scruples, or—or even wish to overcome them? If only you will be a little patient! Once Cardross is satisfied that your affections are truly fixed——"

"When that day dawns, if ever it does, Jeremy may be thousands of miles distant!" Letty interrupted. "I shall have nothing to do then but to continue in patience until he returns to England—if he does return!"

"But naturally he will return!"

"Yes, but would you wager a groat on his doing so alone?" Letty retorted. "I would not! I don't mean to say that he does not love me as much as I love him, but if he does not set eyes on me for years, besides being made up to by I daresay a dozen girls, or more, it would be wonderful indeed if he escaped being snatched up into matrimony with Another!"

Nell could find nothing to say. Her imagination boggled at the picture of Mr. Allandale being courted by a dozen (or even half-a-dozen) girls, but she prudently kept this reflection to herself, only venturing to ask, after a slight pause: "What made you fall in love with him, Letty? I don't mean to say that he is not very amiable and civil, but—but——"

"I know precisely what you mean," said Letty, with unexpected cordiality. "And I haven't the smallest conjecture! If he had been like—oh, like your brother!—no one would have wondered at in the least: I shouldn't myself! I assure you, I am quite as much surprised as anyone, for it is not as if I had never met any other gentlemen! When I lived with my aunt I met everyone who came to the house, for she was not at all stuffy, you know, and didn't even *try* to keep Selina and me in the schoolroom. We knew *all* Maria's and Fanny's beaux, and some of them were pretty dashing, I can tell you! Only I never had the smallest tendre for any of them, until I met Jeremy. I don't know how it was: it has me quite in a puzzle!" She bestowed a dazzling smile upon a natty young gentleman in a sporting curricle who was trying to attract her attention. "Now, if I had formed an attachment to *him* Cardross would have had cause to be cross!" she observed. "In fact, when you consider, Nell, the *lures* that are for ever being thrown out to me by all the most shocking court-cards on the town, on account of my being an heiress, I think it astonishing that Cardross should not be thankful my interest has been fixed by a man of principle and character! And if he supposes that Jeremy loves me for my fortune he much mistakes the matter!"

Cardross did not suspect Mr. Allandale of fortune-hunting, but when the promised visit was paid him, a few days later, he received his sister's suitor with a cool civility that gave little promise of a yielding disposition.

Mr. Allandale was not a nervous man, but it was with considerable reluctance that he presented himself in Grosvenor Square. He prided himself on his level judgment, and although he did not set his own worth low every objection Cardross could raise to his pretensions was felt by him, and acknowledged to be just. His love for Letty bordered, in the opinion of his mother, on infatuation, but it had needed much persuasion from her to induce him to make Cardross a formal offer for her hand. The disparity between them of rank and fortune weighed heavily upon his spirit; he had felt from the outset that his suit was hopeless, and that his wiser course would be to keep out of Letty's way, and try to put her from his mind. Unfortunately, noble resignation was not a virtue which in any way attracted Letty. When he spoke of parting she first burst into tears, which unmanned him; and then accused him of wanting to be rid of her, which made him utter some very ill-advised vows of eternal fidelity. After that there was no more talk of renunciation. Mr. Allandale did indeed speak sometimes of waiting, but with this plan also Letty was out of sympathy; and since he had never desired anything so passionately in the whole of his well-ordered life as to marry her he allowed himself to become infected with her optimism, and even began to think that perhaps Cardross might not prove so inimical to his suit after all, if he were approached in a manly and straightforward way.

This confidence, never very strong, waned as he trod up the steps of Cardross House, and wholly deserted him while he waited for the Earl in the book-room. His appearance was always characterized by a neatness and a propriety of taste which struck the happy mean between the man of fashion and the man of affairs, and he had spent more time than usual that morning on the arrangement of his neckcloth. But as the clock on the high mantelpiece rather aggressively ticked away the minutes he became convinced that the faint stripe in his toilinette waistcoat made him look like a park-saunterer, that his coat of sober blue cloth was too tightly moulded to his form, and that by brushing his mouse-coloured hair into the Brutus style affected by Mr. Brummell he had committed a gross error of judgment: Cardross would probably suspect him of aping the fashions of the dandy-set.

However, when the Earl at last came into the room he did not appear to notice what by this time amounted in Mr. Allandale's mind to the blatant vulgarity of his waistcoat. On the other hand, his handsome, impassive countenance betrayed no sign of pleasure at sight of his visitor, and his greeting was courteous rather than cordial. Overcoming the sudden realization that his errand would certainly be regarded as a piece of presumption, Mr. Allandale opened the interview by saying with a stiffness engendered by his determination not to truckle to his siren's guardian: "You may wonder, my lord, why I am here."

"No," said the Earl.

There was nothing particularly daunting about this calm monosyllable, but it threw Mr. Allandale quite out of his stride. His carefully composed speech of explanation had to be abandoned, and he could not immediately decide what to say in its stead.

"Pray be seated, Mr. Allandale!" invited his host, himself strolling towards a chair.

Mr. Allandale hesitated. On the whole, he preferred to remain on his feet, but it was difficult to do so while the Earl sat at his ease, one leg, cased in an elegant Hessian boot, thrown over the other, and one hand even now raising his quizzing-glass to his eye. Mr. Allandale sat down, and cleared his throat. "I shall be brief," he stated. "It cannot, I fancy, be unknown to your lordship that I have been so fortunate as to engage the interest of Lady Letitia Merion."

A flicker of amusement crossed the Earl's eyes. "I understand that the violence of your mutual feelings is such as must melt all but the hardest of hearts. Mine, I am informed, is of marble."

Colouring, Mr. Allandale replied: "I am aware, my lord, that the affection I bear Lady Letitia must appear to you in the light of an encroaching fancy."

"Oh, no!" said Cardross. "I am really not as high in the instep as you seem to think. I don't deny that I should prefer her to make what passes in the world for a good match, but, I assure you, if your affections stand the test of time you won't find me ill-disposed towards you."

This very reasonable speech added nothing to Mr. Allandale's comfort. He said heavily: "I'm obliged to you, sir. I might remind you that the attachment between us was formed more than a year ago, and has but been strengthened by the passage of time, but I shall not do so."

"As we see," murmured Cardross dryly.

"The force of your objection is fully felt by me," continued Mr. Allandale, embarking on one of his rehearsed periods. "It might well be thought that Lady Letitia is as yet too young to be permitted to follow the dictates of her heart. Moreover, no one is more conscious than I that in so doing she would be held, in vulgar parlance, to have thrown herself away."

"Yes, well, do let us talk in vulgar parlance!" begged Cardross. "Not to wrap the matter up in clean linen, my sister is a foolish chit with a turn for the high-romantical; and you, my dear sir, are not very much wiser! Her fortune apart—and you need not tell me that you wish her fortune at Jericho, because I acquit you of hanging out for a rich wife—I can conceive of few more unsuitable partners for a man in your position. You have your career before you: I wish you very well, and in proof of this can only advise you not to saddle yourself with an extravagant and shatterbrained little puss for a wife!"

Considerably taken-aback by this forthright speech, Mr. Allandale could think of nothing better to say than: "Am I to understand, then, that you refuse your consent to our betrothal, sir?"

"For the present, most certainly you are!" returned the Earl. "You look to be a man of sense, so you will not, I hope, accuse me of cruelty. I have not said, nor shall I, that I will never give my consent; I don't even say that you must wait until Letty comes of age. But do, I beg of you, consider *my* position in this! Can you feel that I should honourably have fulfilled my charge if I allowed a chit who has not yet reached her eighteenth year to tie herself up in matrimony to a young man in your circumstances?"

"No," said Mr. Allandale bleakly.

The Earl was conscious of an impulse to retract, even to bestow his blessing on the lovers. He quelled it, saying cheerfully: "Of course you cannot! But if, in a couple of years' time, you are both still of the same mind, and you come to me again with this proposal, I must be hardhearted indeed to refuse my consent."

"I do not anticipate being in England in a couple of years' time," said Mr. Allandale, more bleakly still. "It was my intention to have explained to your lordship at the outset that I was emboldened to come to you today by the circumstance of my having been appointed to a very advantageous post. I owe this advancement in part to the kind offices of Lord Roxwell, who was formerly much attached to my father; and I have every reason to expect that it will lead, should I acquit myself creditably, to more rapid promotion than has hitherto seemed probable."

"I am sure you will acquit yourself admirably, and must beg leave to congratulate you on your good fortune. I collect that you are to join one of our embassies?"

"Yes, sir. I am appointed—that is to say, I shall, within the next three months be appointed to the staff of our minister at the Court of the Regent of Portugal."

"The Regent of Portugal?" repeated Cardross. "But he is in Brazil!"

Mr. Allandale inclined his head. "Just so, sir," he agreed.

"Good God!" ejaculated Cardross. "Were you proposing in all seriousness to take Letty to South America? You must be mad!"

"She assures me," said Mr. Allandale earnestly, "that she would like it above all things."

"And what the devil do you imagine she knows about it?" demanded Cardross.

"I am credibly informed," offered Mr. Allandale, "that the climate at Rio de Janeiro is salubrious."

"Oh, take a damper!" said Cardross impatiently. "Did this cork-brained notion come out of your head, or hers? Did she persuade you to come here today, or—— No, of course she did! You at least cannot have supposed that there was the least likelihood of my consenting to such a preposterous scheme!"

"No," said Mr. Allandale. "I must own that I had little hope of obtaining your lordship's consent. I am aware that in your eyes the scheme must seem preposterous."

"And how does it seem in yours?" enquired the Earl curiously. "You have been acquainted with my sister for more than a year, after all!"

"Were it not for your lordship's refusal to entertain my proposal, I should have no hesitation in asking Lady Letitia to accompany me, as my wife, to Brazil."

"The devil you wouldn't!"

"I believe her to be equal to anything," said Mr. Allandale reverently. "When I first learned of the appointment, I confess that the very natural feeling of delight I experienced was instantly tempered—I might almost say dissipated—by the same doubt of which your lordship is conscious. I could not believe that a delicately nurtured female—and one, moreover, of such tender years—could contemplate without dismay the several evils attaching to the appointment. The discomforts of a long sea-voyage! the going amongst foreigners! the separation from her relations! I promise you, sir, every disagreeable possibility that presented itself to my mind was at once communicated to her by me. But nothing was ever like her spirit! What inconveniences there may be she will not regard; and although I do not anticipate that there is any danger to be apprehended, *that* she would meet with the same trust and courage which she shows in being willing to bestow her hand upon one whose prosperity must depend upon his own exertions!"

The thought of this nobility overcame him so much that his voice thickened, and he was obliged to blow his nose. Its effect upon Cardross was to exasperate him into saying, with a snap: "I suppose she told you so!"

"Yes," replied Mr. Allandale simply.

"Did she also work on you to come here today with your fantastic proposal?"

"She certainly thought that with my advancement now secured we might hope for some relenting on your part," admitted Mr. Allandale.

The Earl looked him over somewhat grimly. "But you did not think so, Mr. Allandale, did you?"

"Well——"

"It appears to me, my dear sir, that you are as wax in my sister's hands! It is a reflection which fills me with deep misgiving. I know Letty to be as headstrong as she is bird-witted, and what she may next bully or bewitch you into doing there is no saying—though I might hazard a guess!"

"If you mean, sir, that I might be tempted to elope with Lady Letitia you may be easy!" returned Mr. Allandale, reddening. "Even if I were not a man of honour, my circumstances must forbid me to embark on anything of a clandestine nature." He drew a breath, and continued with a little difficulty: "You were kind enough, my lord, to acquit me of hanging out (as you phrased it) for a rich wife. That is true, for, in fact, I had not, until I met Lady Letitia, any thought of marriage at all. My widowed parent, though possessed of a respectable jointure, is quite unable to support the expense of educating my younger brothers and sisters without my assistance; and until they are established creditably I must not —indeed, I cannot!—marry a female who has no fortune of her own. Just a genteel fortune, to match my own. I never contemplated marriage to a great heiress—and, to own the truth, it is not what I like! However, I daresay it may be

possible to form some kind of a trust which would ensure that
I should not benefit by anything more than a reasonable
amount."

"The matter is not of pressing importance," said the Earl.
"Until she reaches the age of five-and-twenty my sister's
fortune is in my hands, and her allowance is at my discretion.
If I chose to do it, I could cut off every penny of it."

"I cannot believe, sir, that you would be guilty of
such inhumanity!" said Mr. Allandale, in a voice of strong
censure.

"There would be no inhumanity," replied Cardross coolly.
"Letty would merely be obliged to continue living in my
house, and her dress-bills would be paid by me. I may add
that I already pay quite a number of them. I am afraid you
would find her very expensive, for she never has a feather to
fly with, you know."

"I am aware that she has not been taught habits of
economy," said Mr. Allandale stiffly. "Indeed, she has told me
so herself, and has regretted it. She is very willing to learn,
and I hope to teach her to manage better."

"Yes, in my more optimistic moments I too indulge that
hope," agreed Cardross. "Go and take up this appointment of
yours, and I'll engage to do my best to instil some small knowledge of economy into her head while you are away. Who
knows? You may return to find her quite prudent!"

Mr. Allandale rose, and walked over to the window. He
said, staring out of it: "I do not imagine that it will be of any
use to return. Not, of course, that I contemplate passing the
rest of my life in Brazil, but——" He stopped, and cleared his
throat. "I cannot flatter myself that I shall find her still un-
attached. So much sought-after—and by men of far greater
address than will ever be mine—separated from me for a
prolonged period, and by such a distance—— No, it would be
too much to expect of her! She will wed another."

"The same fate may as easily overtake you, my dear sir," remarked the Earl.

"No," said Mr. Allandale baldly. He added, after a pause: "My feeling is unalterable. I am not subject to fits of gallantry, sir. I had even believed myself to be proof against—— But from the moment when I first saw your sister, I knew myself lost! I struggled against it, for the unsuitability of the match was as plain to me as it is to you. It was to no avail. I shall never marry any other lady."

"Ah!" murmured the Earl, looking amused. "I remember that I said much the same thing myself—a good many years ago. She was ravishingly beautiful—at least, I know I thought so, though, to own the truth, I can now only vaguely recall her face to my mind."

"I am happy to afford your lordship entertainment!" said Mr. Allandale, in rather less measured accents.

"No, you are not," replied Cardross, rising. "You would like to plant me a facer, and I'm sure I don't wonder at it. Nothing is more exasperating than to be obliged to listen to advice based on experience which is necessarily wider than your own—particularly when you have an uneasy suspicion that it may be good!"

"I have no such suspicion," instantly retorted Mr. Allandale. "I venture to think that my nature is more tenacious than your lordship's!"

"In that case," said Cardross, with unimpaired good humour, "I shall expect to see you again upon your return from Rio de Janeiro. In the meantime, accept my best wishes for your success in that salubrious locality!"

"Do you forbid me to hold further communication with Lady Letitia, sir?" demanded Mr. Allandale, somewhat reluctantly taking the hand that was being held out to him.

"My dear sir, do let me assure you that I am neither so gothic nor so cork-brained! I daresay you will meet Letty at any number of parties. As for clandestine meetings, I am persuaded that your sense of propriety must be safeguard enough."

"Anything of a clandestine nature is repugnant to me," stated Mr. Allandale. "I can only beg of you, sir, to consider well before you blight, perhaps for ever, the happiness of two persons, one of whom is—or should be—dear to you! I reject—indeed, I scorn!—your suggestions of inconstancy, but too well do I know the arts that are employed in the world of fashion to detach from an unworthy object the affections of such as Lady Letitia! All is sacrificed to pride and consequence! If I were in more affluent circumstances, I believe no considerations of propriety could avail to prevent me—— But it serves no purpose to continue talking!"

"None whatsoever," agreed Cardross, leading the way to the door. "It might even lead me to take you in dislike, and that, you know, would be fatal to your chances!"

ANY scheme of intercepting her lover on his way out of the house which Letty might have cherished was frustrated by the Earl's escorting him to the front-door, and seeing him safely off the premises. He strolled back to the library; and, after hesitating for a moment or two at the head of the stairs, from which post of vantage she had watched Mr. Allandale's departure, Letty ran lightly down, and herself entered the library.

Cardross was engaged in mending a pen, but he looked up, and, when he saw his half-sister backed against the door, an urgent question in her speaking eyes, abandoned this task. A laugh quivered in his voice as he said: "Letty, you goose! Did you really think that I should succumb to that unfortunate young man's oratory? Do forgive me! but surely he is a very dull dog?"

"I don't care for that," she said, swallowing a sob. "He is not dull to me. I love him!"

"You must do so indeed! I should have supposed him to be the last man to take your fancy, too."

"Well, he is not, and even if you are my guardian I won't submit to having my husband chosen for me by you!"

"Certainly not. It's plain I should make a poor hand at it."

Hope gleamed in her eyes; she moved towards him, and laid a coaxing hand on his arm. 'Dear Giles, if you please, may I marry him?"

He gave the hand a pat, but said: "Why, yes, Letty, when you are older."

"But, Giles, you don't understand! He is going away to Brazil!"

"So he informed me."

"Are you thinking that perhaps it might not suit me to live there? I believe the climate is *perfectly* healthy!"

"Salubrious," he interpolated.

"Yes, and in any event I am never ill! You may ask my aunt if it's not so!"

"I am sure it is. Don't let us fall into another exhausting argument! I have already endured a great deal of eloquence today, but it would take much more than eloquence to make me consent to your marriage to an indigent young man who proposes to take you to the other end of the world before you are eighteen, or have been out a year."

"That doesn't signify! And although I own it would be imprudent to marry Jeremy if I were indigent too I am *not* indigent, so that's of no consequence either!"

"I promise you I shan't refuse my consent on that head, if, when he returns from Brazil, you still wish to marry him."

"And what if some odious, designing female has lured him into marrying her?" she demanded.

"He assures me that his nature is tenacious, so we must hope that he will be proof against all designing females," he replied lightly.

"You don't hope that! You don't wish me ever to marry him!"

"No, of course I don't! Good God, child, how could I wish you to throw yourself away so preposterously, far less help you to do it when you are hardly out of the schoolroom?"

"If he were a man of rank and fortune you wouldn't say I was too young!"

"If he were a man of rank and fortune, my dear, he would not be taking up a post as some kind of secretary in Rio de Janeiro. But if it comforts you at all I don't wish to see you married to anyone for a year or two yet."

"Oh, don't talk to me as if I were a silly little child!" she cried passionately.

"Well, I don't think you are very wise," he said.

"No, perhaps I'm not wise, but I'm not a child, and I know my own mind! *You* aren't very wise either, if you think I shall change it, or forget Jeremy! I shall remember, and be unhappy for two whole years, and very likely more! I daresay you don't care for that, for I see that you aren't kind, which I thought you were, but, on the contrary, perfectly heartless!"

"Not a bit of it!" he said cheerfully. "With the best will in the world to do it, I fancy you won't fall quite into dejection. There will still be balls to attend, and new, and extremely expensive dresses to buy."

"I don't want them!"

"I wish I might believe you! Do you mean to abjure the fashionable life?"

She threw him a smouldering look. "You may laugh at me, but I warn you, Cardross, I am determined to marry Jeremy, do what you will to prevent me!"

He replied only with an ironical bow; and after staring defiantly at him for an instant, she swept from the room with an air of finality only marred by the unfortunate circumstance of her shutting a fold of her gown of delicate lilac muslin in the door, and being obliged to open it again to release the fabric.

Twenty minutes later Nell came softly into the room. The Earl looked up impatiently, but when he saw his wife standing on the threshold his expression changed, and he smiled at her, saying in a funning tone: "How do you contrive, Nell, always to appear prettier than I remembered you?"

She blushed adorably. "Well, I did hope you would think I looked becomingly in this gown," she confessed naïvely.

"I do. Did you put it on to dazzle me into paying for it?"

This was said so quizzically that her spirits rose. It had taken a great deal of resolution to bring her to the library that morning, for a most unwelcome missive had been delivered by the penny post. Since the Earl paid five shillings to the General Post Office every quarter for the privilege of receiving an early London delivery Madame Lavalle's civil reminder to her ladyship that a court dress of Chantilly lace was still unpaid for had lain on Nell's breakfast-tray. It was not an encouraging start to the day. It had quite destroyed Nell's appetite, and had filled her with so much frightened dismay that for an unreasoning hour she could think of no other way out of her difficulties than to board the first mail-coach bound for Devonshire, and there to seek refuge with her mama. A prolonged period of reflection, however, showed her the unwisdom of this course, and convinced her that since it was extremely unlikely that a thunderbolt would descend mercifully upon her head there was nothing for it but to make a clean breast of the matter to Cardross, devoutly trusting that he would understand how it had come about that she had forgotten to give him Madame Lavalle's bill with all the others which he had commanded her to produce.

But the more she thought of it the less likely it seemed that he could possibly understand. She felt sick with apprehension, recalling his stern words. He had asked her if she was quite sure she had handed all her bills to him; he had warned her of the awful consequences if he found she had lied to him; and although he had certainly begged her, later, not to be afraid of him, it was not to be expected that he would greet with equanimity the intelligence that his wife had overlooked a bill for three hundred and thirty-five guineas. It even seemed improbable that he would believe she really had overlooked it. She herself was aghast at her carelessness. She was so sure that she had given the bill to Cardross with all the others collected from a drawer crammed with them that her first thought on seeing Madame Lavalle's renewed demand was that that exclusive modiste had erred. But an agitated search had brought the previous demand to light, wedged at the very back of the drawer. It was by far the heaviest single item amongst her debts, casting into the shade the milliner's bill which had staggered Cardross. What he would say she dared not consider, even less what he might do. At the best he must believe her to be woefully extravagant (which, indeed, she knew she had been), and he would' be very angry, though forgiving. At the worst—but to speculate on what he might do at the worst was so fatal to resolution that she would not let herself do it.

With a childlike hope of pleasing him, she had arrayed herself in a gown which she knew (on the authority of that arbiter of taste, Mr. Hethersett) became her to admiration. It had instantly won for her a charming compliment, and she was now able to reply, not without pride: "No, no, it is paid for!" She added honestly, after a moment's reflection: "*You* paid for it!"

"It is a great satisfaction to me to know that I didn't waste my money," he said gravely, but with laughter in his eyes.

This was a much more promising start to the interview than she had expected. She smiled shyly at him, and was just about to embark on a painful explanation of her new embarrassment when he said: "Are you Letty's envoy, then? I own, I might listen with more patience to you than to her, but on *this* subject I am determined to remain adamant!"

Not sorry to be diverted from her real errand, she said: "Of course, I do see that it would be throwing herself away quite shockingly, but I believe you will be obliged, in the end, to consent. Well, I thought myself that it was just a fancy that would pass when she had seen more of society, and had met other gentlemen, but it isn't so, Cardross! She hasn't swerved from her devotion to Mr. Allandale, even though she has been made up to by I don't know how many others—and all of them," she added reflectively, "of far greater address than poor Mr. Allandale!"

"Nell!" he interrupted. "Can you tell me what she perceives in that dead bore to dote upon?"

She shook her head. "No, there is no accounting for it," she replied. "She doesn't know either, which is what makes me feel that it is a case of true love, and certainly no passing fancy."

"They are totally unsuited!" he said impatiently. "She would ruin him in a year, what's more! She is as extravagant as you are, my love!" He saw the stricken look in her face, the colour ebbing from her cheeks, and instantly said: "What an unhandsome thing to say to you! I beg your pardon: *that* is all forgotten—a page which we have stuck down, and shan't read again. My dear Nell, if you could but have heard that absurd young man addressing me in flowing periods this morning! Do you know that he proposed in all seriousness to carry Letty off to Brazil?"

Her thoughts were very far from Letty's affairs, but she answered mechanically: "Yes, she told me of his appointment."

He regarded her with a slight crease between his brows. "You are looking very troubled, Nell. Why? Are you taking this nonsense to heart?"

Now, if ever, was the moment to tell him that the page had not yet been stuck down. The words refused to be uttered. She said instead: "I can't help but be sorry for them. I know it is a bad match, and indeed, Cardross, I understand what your sentiments must be."

"I imagine you might! To be wishing Letty joy of a shockingly bad bargain would be fine conduct in a guardian! To own the truth, I wish I were not her guardian—or that I had never permitted her aunt to take charge of her. That woman wants both manner and sense, and, as far as I can discover, reared her own daughters as well as my sister in a scrambling way, encouraging them in every extravagant folly, and allowing them to set up their flirts when they should have been in the schoolroom!"

"Well, yes," admitted Nell. "I don't like to abuse her, for she is always very civil and goodnatured, but she does seem to be sadly shatterbrained! But I can't suppose that she encouraged Mr. Allandale, for she doesn't at all wish Letty to marry him, you know. She talked to me about it the other evening, at the Westburys' drum, and she seemed to feel just as she ought." She paused, considering this. "At least," she amended, "just as *you* think she ought, Cardross."

He was amused. "Indeed! But not as *you* think, I collect?"

"Well, not precisely," she temporized. "I must say, it has me quite in a puzzle to understand how it comes about that such a lively girl should fall in love with Mr. Allandale, for he is not at all sportive, and he doesn't seem to have more than common sense, besides having such very formal manners,—but —but there is nothing in his disposition to make him ineligible, is there? I mean, it isn't as if she wished to marry someone like Sir Jasper Lydney, or young Brixworth. And one wouldn't have felt the least surprise if she had, because they have both been dangling after her ever since she came out, and no one can deny that they have very engaging manners, in spite of being such shocking rakes! You would not have liked her to marry either of them!"

"I should not, but there is a vast gulf between Brixworth and Allandale, my love! As for eligibility, though there may be nothing in Allandale's disposition to dislike, there is nothing in his circumstances to recommend him. He has neither rank nor fortune."

"Letty doesn't care for rank, and she *has* fortune," Nell pointed out.

"Unequal marriages rarely prosper. Letty may imagine she doesn't care for rank: she doesn't know how it would be to marry a man out of her own order."

Nell wrinkled her brow over this. "But, Giles, I think she does know!" she objected. "For it is not as if she had been accustomed all her life to move only in circles of high fashion. Mrs. Thorne is perfectly respectable, but not at all exclusive, and you yourself told me that Letty's mama was not of the first rank."

"You are a persuasive advocate, Nell! But I must hold to my opinion—and to what I conceive to be my duty. I have said that I won't withhold my consent, if both are of the same mind when Allandale returns from Brazil, and that must suffice them. I shan't conceal from *you* that I hope Letty, by that time, will have transferred her affections to some more worthy object."

"You want her to make a *good* match, don't you?"

"Is that so wonderful?"

"Oh, no! Perhaps, if she doesn't see Mr. Allandale for some years, she will do so. Only—only—it would be so very melancholy!"

"My dear child, why?"

She tried haltingly to express the thought in her mind. "She loves him so much! And I cannot think that she would be happy if she married—only to oblige her family!"

His brows had drawn together. He said harshly: "As you did?"

She stared at him almost uncomprehendingly. "As—as *I* did?" she faltered.

A smile, not a very pleasant smile, curled his lips. "Had I not been possessed of a large fortune, you wouldn't have married me, would you, Nell?"

She was conscious of a pain at her heart, but she heard him without resentment. She thought of her debts, and of those mysterious Settlements, and could only be thankful that she had not disclosed to him Madame Lavalle's bill. Its existence weighed so heavily upon her conscience that she found herself unable to utter a word. A deep flush stained her cheeks, and her eyes, after a hurt moment, dropped from his.

"You must forgive me!" His voice had an ironical inflexion that made her wince. "My want of delicacy sinks me quite below reproach, doesn't it? I fancy it gave Allandale a disgust of me too."

She managed to say, in a stifled tone: "I didn't think—I didn't *know* about your fortune!"

"Didn't you?" he said lightly. "How charming of you, my dear! *Your* manners make *mine* appear sadly vulgar. Don't look so distressed! I am persuaded no man ever had so beautiful, so polite, or so amiable a wife as I have!" He glanced at his watch. "I must go. I don't know what nonsense Letty may have taken into her head, but I hope I may trust you not to encourage her in it. Happily, it appears to be out of Allandale's power to marry her without a substantial portion. She's under age, of course, but I'd as lief not be saddled with that kind of a scandal!"

A smile, a brief bow, and he was gone, leaving her with her brain in a whirl. There was little thought of Letty in it. For the first time in their dealings Cardross had hinted that he had looked for more than complaisance in his wife; and his words, with their edge of bitterness, had made Nell's heart leap. It was almost sacrilege to doubt Mama, but was it, in fact, possible that Mama had been wrong?

She went slowly upstairs, to be pounced on by Letty, bursting with indignation, and the desire to unburden herself. She listened with half an ear to that impassioned damsel, saying yes, and no, at suitable moments, but assimilating little from the molten discourse beyond the warning that her sister-in-law would be forced to take desperate measures if Cardross continued on his present tyrannical course. Before it had dawned on Letty that she had no very attentive auditor to the tale of her wrongs a message was brought up to the drawing-room that the Misses Thorne had called to take up their cousin on a visit to some exhibition.

Nell soon found herself alone, and at leisure to consider her own problems. These very soon resolved themselves into one problem only: how to pay for a court dress of Chantilly lace without applying to Cardross. If Cardross had offered for her hand not as a matter of convenience but for love, this was of vital importance. Nothing could more surely confirm his suspicion than to be confronted with that bill; and any attempt to tell him that she had fallen in love with him at their first meeting must seem to him a piece of quite contemptible cajolery.

No solution to the difficulty had presented itself to her by the time the butler came to inform her that the barouche had been driven up to the door, and awaited her convenience. She was tempted to send it away again, and was only prevented from doing so by the recollection that civility obliged her to make a formal call in Upper Berkeley Street, to enquire after the progress of an ailing acquaintance.

She directed the coachman, on the way back, to drive to Bond Street, where she had a few trifling purchases to make; and there, strolling along, with his beaver set at a rakish angle on his golden head, and his shapely legs swathed in pantaloons of an aggressive yellow, she saw her brother.

The Viscount had never been known to extricate himself from his various embarrassments, much less anyone else; but to his adoring sister he appeared in the light of a strong ally. She called to the coachman to pull up, and when Dysart crossed the street in response to her signal leaned forward to clasp his hand, saying thankfully: "Oh, Dy, I am so glad to have met you! Will you be so very obliging as to come home with me? There is something I particularly wish to ask you!"

"If you're wanting me to escort you to some horrible squeeze," began the Viscount suspiciously, "I'll be dashed if I——"

"No, no, I promise you it's no such thing!" she interrupted. "I—I need your advice!"

"Well, I don't mind giving you that," said his lordship handsomely. "What's the matter? You in a scrape?"

"Good gracious, no!" said Nell, acutely aware of her footman, who had jumped down from the box, and was now holding open the door of the barouche. "Do get in, Dy! I'll tell you presently!"

"Oh, very well!" he said, stepping into the carriage, and disposing himself on the seat beside her. "I've nothing else to do, after all." He looked her over critically, and observed with brotherly candour: "What a quiz of a hat!"

"It is an Angoulême bonnet, and the *height* of fashion!" retorted Nell, with spirit. "And as for quizzes—Dy, I never saw you look so odd as you do in those yellow pantaloons!"

"Devilish, ain't they?" agreed his lordship. "Corny made me buy 'em. Said they were all the crack."

"Well, if I were you I wouldn't listen to him!"

"Oh, I don't know! Always up to the knocker, is Corny. If you ain't in a scrape, why do you want my advice?"

She gave his arm a warning pinch, and began to talk of indifferent subjects in a careless way which (as he informed her upon their arrival in Grosvenor Square) made him wish that he had not chosen to walk down Bond Street that morning. "Because you can't bamboozle *me* into believing you ain't in a scrape," he said. "I thought you were looking hagged, but I set it down to that bonnet."

Nell, who had led him upstairs to her frivolous boudoir, cast off her maligned headgear, saying wretchedly: "I am in a *dreadful* scrape, and if you won't help me, Dy, I can't think what I shall do!"

"Lord!" said the Viscount, slightly dismayed. "Now, don't get into a fuss, Nell! Of course I'll help you! At least, I will if I can, though I'm dashed if I see—— However, I daresay it's all a bag of moonshine!"

"It isn't," she said, so tragically that he began to feel seriously

alarmed. She twisted her fingers together, and managed
to say, though with considerable difficulty: "Dysart, have
—have you still got the—the three hundred pounds I gave
you?"

"Do you want it back?" he demanded.

She nodded, her eyes fixed anxiously on his face.

"Now we *are* in the basket!" said his lordship.

Her heart sank. "I am so very sorry to be obliged to ask
you!"

"My dear girl, I'd give it you this instant if I had it!" he
assured her. "What is it? a gaming debt? You been playing
deep, Nell?"

"No, no! It is a court dress of Chantilly lace, and I cannot—
cannot!—tell Cardross!"

"What, you don't mean to say he's turned out to be a
screw?" exclaimed the Viscount.

"No! He has been *crushingly* generous to me, only I was
so stupid, and it seemed as if I had so much money that——
Well, I never took the least heed, Dy, and the end of it was
that I got quite shockingly into debt!"

"Good God, there's no need to fall into flat despair, if that's
all!" said the Viscount, relieved. "You've only to tell him
how it came about: I daresay he won't be astonished, for he
must know you haven't been in the way of handling the blunt.
You'll very likely come in for a thundering scold, but he'll
settle your debts all right and regular."

She sank into a chair, covering her face with her hands.
"He did settle them!"

"Eh?" ejaculated Dysart, startled.

"I had better explain it to you," said Nell.

It could not have been said that the explanation, which was
both halting and elusive, very much helped Dysart to a complete understanding of the situation, but he did gather from it
that the affair was far more serious than he had at first sup-

posed. He was quite intelligent enough to guess that the whole had not been divulged to him, but since he had no desire to plunge into deep matrimonial waters he did not press his sister for further enlightenment. Clearly, her marriage was not running as smoothly as he had supposed; and if that were so he could appreciate her reluctance to disclose the existence of yet another debt to Cardross.

"What am I to do?" Nell asked. "Can *you* think of a way, Dy?"

"Nothing easier!" responded Dysart, in a heartening tone. "The trouble with you is that you ain't up to snuff yet. The thing to do is to order another dress from this Madame Thing."

"Order another?" gasped Nell.

"That's it," he nodded.

"But then I should be even deeper in debt!"

"Yes, but it'll stave her off for a while."

"And when she presses me to pay for that I buy yet another! Dy, you must be mad!"

"My dear girl, it's always done!"

"Not by me!" she declared. "I should never know a moment's peace! Only think what would happen if Cardross discovered it!"

"There is that, of course," he admitted. He took a turn about the room, frowning over the problem. "The deuce is in it that I'm not in good odour with the cents-per-cent. I'd raise the wind for you in a trice if the sharks didn't know dashed well how our affairs stand."

"Moneylenders?" she asked. "I did think of that, only I don't know how to set about borrowing. Do you know, Dy? Will you tell me?"

The Viscount was not a young man whose conscience was overburdened with scruples, but he did not hesitate to veto this suggestion. "No, I will not!" he said.

"I know one shouldn't borrow from moneylenders, but in such a case as this—and if you went with me, Dy——"

"A pretty fellow I should be!" he interrupted indignantly. "Damn it, I ain't a saint, but I ain't such a loose-screw that I'd hand my sister over to one of those bloodsuckers!"

"Is it so very bad? I didn't know," she said. "Of course I won't go to a moneylender if you say I must not."

"Well, I do say it. What's more, if you did so, and Cardross discovered it, there *would* be the devil to pay! You'd a deal better screw up your courage, and tell him the whole now."

She shook her head, flushing.

"You know, it queers me to know what you've been doing," said Dysart severely. "It sounds to me as though you've had a quarrel with him, and set up his back. It ain't my business, but I call it a cork-brained thing to do!"

"I haven't—it isn't that!" she stammered.

"You must have done something!" he insisted. "I thought he doted on you!"

Her eyes lifted quickly to his face. "Did you, Dy? Did you *indeed* think so?"

"Of course I did! Well, good God, what would anyone think, when he no sooner clapped eyes on you than nothing would do for him but to pop the question? Lord, it was one of the on-dits of town! Old Cooling told me no one had ever seen him sent to grass before, no matter who set her cap at him. I thought myself he must be touched in his upper works," said the Viscount candidly. "I don't say you ain't a pretty girl, but what there is in you to make a fellow like Cardross marry into *our* family I'm dashed if I can see!"

"Oh, Dysart!" breathed Nell, trembling. "You're not—you're not *roasting* me?"

He stared at her. "Have you got windmills in the head too?" he demanded. "Why the devil should he have offered for you, if he hadn't been head over ears in love with you? You aren't going to tell me you didn't know you'd given him a leveller!"

"Oh——! Don't say such things! I did think, at first—but Mama told me—explained to me—how it was!"

"Well, *how* was it?" said the Viscount impatiently.

"A—a marriage of convenience," faltered Nell. "He was obliged to marry someone, and—and he liked me better than the other ladies he was acquainted with, and thought I should *suit!*"

"If that isn't Mama all over!" exclaimed Dysart. "It was a dashed convenient marriage for us, but if he thought it was convenient to be obliged to pay through the nose for you (which I don't mind telling you my father made him do!), let alone saddling himself with a set of dirty dishes who have been under the hatches for years, he must be a regular cod's head!"

"Dysart!" she cried, quite horrified.

"Dirty dishes!" he repeated firmly. "*I* can't remember when my father last had a feather to fly with, and the lord knows I've never had one myself! In fact, it's my belief we should have been turned-up by now if you hadn't happened to hit Cardross's fancy. It's the only stroke of good fortune that ever came in our way!"

"I knew—I knew he had made a handsome *settlement!*"

Dysart gave a crack of laughter. "Ay, and towed my father out of the River Tick into the bargain!"

She sprang up, pressing her hands to her hot cheeks. "Oh, and I have been so *wickedly* extravagant!"

"No need to fret and fume over that," replied Dysart cheerfully. "They say his fortune knocks Golden Ball's into flinders, and I shouldn't be surprised if it was true."

"As though that should excuse my running into debt! Oh, Dy, this quite overpowers me! No wonder he said *that!*"

He looked uneasily at her. "Said what? If you mean to have a fit of the vapours, Nell, I'm off, and so I warn you!"

"Oh, no! Indeed, I don't! Only it is such an agitating reflection—I didn't tell you, Dy, but he said something to me which made me think he believes I married him for the sake of his fortune!"

"Well, you did, didn't you?"

"No!" she cried hotly. "Never, never!"

"What, you don't mean to tell me you fell in love with him?" said the Viscount incredulously.

"Of course I did! How could I help but do so?"

"Of all the silly starts!" said his lordship disgustedly. "What the devil should cast you into this distempered freak if *that's* the way of it? What have you been doing to make Cardross think you don't love him, if you do?"

She turned away her face. "I—I was trying to be a *conformable* wife, Dy! You see, Mama warned me about not making demands, or—or hanging upon him, or appearing to notice it, if he should have Another Interest, and——"

"Oh, so the blame lies at Mama's door, does it? I might have known it! Never knew such a henwitted creature in my life!"

"Oh, Dysart, hush! Indeed, she meant it for the best! You will not repeat it, but she was so anxious I shouldn't suffer a mortifying disillusionment, as, I am afraid, she did!"

"Did she, though?" said the Viscount, interested. "I didn't know my father was pitching it rum in those days. I must say I should have thought even Mama could have seen that Cardross ain't a bird of that feather. Never been a man of the town from anything *I* ever heard. How came you to swallow all that humdudgeon, Nell? Dash it, you must have known he was in love with you!"

"I thought—I thought it was all consideration, because he is so *very* kind and gentlemanlike!" she confessed.

"Kind and gentlemanlike?" repeated Dysart, in accents of withering scorn. "Well, upon my soul, Nell, seems to me you're as big a ninnyhammer as Mama! To be taken in by one of her Banbury tales, when there was Cardross making a regular cake of himself over you! If that don't beat the Dutch!"

She hung her head, but said in a faint voice: "It was stupid of me, but there was more than that, Dy. You see, I knew about Lady Orsett. Letty told me."

"That girl," said the Viscount severely, "wants conduct! Not but what I shouldn't have thought you needed telling, because everyone knew she was his chère amie for years. And don't you put on any die-away airs to me, my girl, because, for one thing, it's no use bamming me you didn't know anything about my father's light frigates; and, for another, Cardross's way of life before you married him ain't your concern! Lady Orsett's got Lydney in tow now, so that's enough flim-flam about her!"

"Has she, Dy?" Nell said eagerly.

"So they say. *I* don't know!"

"Oh, if it were not for this dreadful debt how happy I should be!" she sighed.

"Nonsense! Make a clean breast of the whole to Cardross, and be done with it!"

"I'd rather die! Don't you *understand,* Dy? How could he believe me sincere, if I told him *now,* when I am in debt again, that I didn't care a button for his fortune?"

The Viscount checked the scoffing retort that sprang to his tongue. He did understand. After a thoughtful moment, he said: "He'd think it was cream-pot love, would he? Ay, very true: bound to! Particularly," he added, in a voice of censure, "if you've been treating him with a stupid sort of indifference, which I've a strong notion you have! Oh, well! we shall have to think of some way of raising the blunt, and that's all there is to it!"

Too grateful for his willingness to come to her aid to cavil at his freely-worded criticisms, Nell waited hopefully, confident that he would be able to tell her how to extricate herself from her difficulty. Nor was she mistaken. After a turn or two about the room, he said suddenly: "Nothing easier! I can't think why I didn't hit upon it at once. You must sell some of your jewellery, of course!"

Her hand went instinctively to her throat. "The pearls Mama gave me? Her very own pearls? I *could* not, Dysart!"

"No need to sell them, if you don't care to. Something else!"

"But I haven't anything else!" she objected. "Nothing of value, I mean."

"Haven't anything else? Why, I never see you but what you're wearing something worth a king's ransom! What about all those sapphires?"

"Dysart! Giles's wedding-gift!" she uttered.

"Oh, very well! But he's always giving you some new trinket: you must be able to spare one or two of 'em. He'll never notice. Or if you think he might, you can have 'em copied. I'll attend to that for you."

"No, thank you, Dy!" she said, with desperate firmness. "I won't do anything so *odiously* shabby! To sell the jewels Giles has given me—to have them copied in paste so that he shouldn't know of it—— Oh, how detestable I should be to deceive him in such a way!"

"Well, what a high flight!" said Dysart. "It's no worse than going to a cent-per-cent—in fact, it ain't as bad!"

"It *seems* worse!" she assured him.

"I'll tell you what it is, Nell!" he said, exasperated. "If you let this excessive sensibility of yours rule you, there will be no way of helping you out of this fix! If you don't care to have your trinkets copied, tell Cardross you lost them! I daresay you would not like to lose the sapphires, but you aren't going

to tell me your heart would break for every one of the trinkets
he's given you!"

"No, indeed it would not, if I really did lose them, but every
feeling revolts from the thought of selling them for such a
reason!"

She spoke with so much resolution that it seemed useless
to persist in argument. The Viscount, never one to waste his
time over lost causes, abandoned his promising scheme, merely
remarking that of all the troublesome goosecaps he had
encountered his sister bore away the palm. She apologized for
being so provoking, adding, with an attempt at a smile, that he
must not tease himself any more over the business.

But every now and then the Viscount's conscience, in a
manner as disconcerting to himself as to his critics, cast a
barrier in the way of his careless hedonism. It intervened now,
just as he was congratulating himself on being well out of a
tiresome imbroglio.

"Very pretty talking, when you know dashed well I can't
help but tease myself over it!" he said bitterly. "If there's one
thing more certain than another, it's that if I hadn't borrowed
that three hundred from you, you wouldn't be in this fix now!
Well, there's nothing for it: I shall have to get you out of it.
I daresay I shall hit on a way when I've had time to think it
over, but I shan't do it with you sitting there staring at me as
though I was your whole dependance! Puts me out. There's
no saying, of course, but what I may have a run of luck, in
which case the matter's as good as settled. I've got a notion I
ought to give up hazard, and try how it will answer if I stick
to faro."

He then took his leave, bestowing an encouraging pat on
his sister, and recommending her to put the whole business out
of her mind. There were those who would have taken the
cynical view that he would speedily put it out of his, but Nell
was not of their number: it did not so much as cross her mind

that her dear Dy, either from indolence or forgetfulness, might leave her to her fate. And she was quite right. There was an odd streak of obstinacy in Dysart, which led him, at unexpected moments, to pursue with dogged tenacity the end he had in view; and although his intimates considered that this streak was roused only by the most cork-brained notions, they were agreed that once such a notion had taken firm possession of his mind he could be depended on to stick to it buckle and thong.

Emerging from the house after a genial discussion with his brother-in-law's porter on the chances of several horses in a forthcoming race, he paused at the foot of the steps, considering whether he should summon a hackney, and take a look-in at Tattersall's, or stroll to Conduit Street, where, at Limmer's, he would be sure to encounter a few choice spirits. While he hesitated, a tilbury, drawn by a high-stepping bay, swept round the angle of the square, and he saw that the down-the-road-looking man in the tall hat, and the box-coat of white drab, who was handling the ribbons with such admirable skill, was Cardross. He had no particular desire to meet the Earl, with whom he knew himself to be no favourite, but he waited civilly for the tilbury to draw up beside him.

"Hallo, Dysart!" said the Earl, handing the reins over to his groom, and jumping down from the carriage. "Are you just going in, or just coming out?"

"Just coming out," replied Dysart, watching the tilbury being driven away. "That's a nice tit you have there: looks to be a sweet goer. Welsh?"

"Yes, I'm pretty well pleased with him," agreed Cardross. "Very free and fast, and has a good knee action. Oh, yes! pure bred Welsh: I bought him from Chesterford last week. Do you care to come in again?"

"No, I'm bound for Limmer's," said the Viscount. He eyed his brother-in-law speculatively. The Earl appeared to be in an amiable frame of mind; it was common knowledge that he was rich enough to be able to buy an abbey; and if there was the least chance of getting three hundred pounds out of him merely for the asking, the Viscount was not the man to let this slip. "You wouldn't care to lend me three hundred, would you?" he suggested hopefully.

"Three hundred?"

"Call it five!" offered the Viscount, recollecting certain of his own more pressing obligations.

Cardross laughed. "I'll call it anything you choose, but I shouldn't at all care to lend you money. And I'll thank you, Dysart, not to apply to Nell!"

"Nothing of the sort!" said the Viscount, repressing a strong inclination to tell him that the boot was on quite the other leg.

"Dipped again?" enquired Cardross. "You ought to be tied, you know!"

"I see no sense in that," returned Dysart. "Wouldn't do me a bit of good! The only way to come about is to make a big coup. I don't doubt I'll do it, for it stands to reason the luck must change *one* day! However, I've been thinking seriously of devoting myself to faro, and I believe I'll do it. The devil's in the bones, and has been, this year past."

The news that he was about to reform his way of life met with a disappointing lack of enthusiasm. "What other entertainments have you in store for us?" asked Cardross. "I didn't see you driving a wheelbarrow blindfold down Piccadilly last week, but I'm told you contrived to dislocate all the traffic for a considerable space of time. I must congratulate you. Also on your latest feat, of cutting your initials on all the trees in St. James's Park."

"An hour and fifteen minutes!" said Dysart, with simple pride.

"Very creditable."

"Oh, lord!" Dysart said petulantly, "what else is there to do but kick up a lark now and then?"

"You might see what can be done to put your estates in order."

"They ain't my estates," retorted Dysart. "I fancy I see my father letting me meddle! What's more, if there's anything to be done old Moulton will do it far better than I could. He's been our agent for years, and he don't mean to let me meddle either. Not that I want to, for I don't."

"I'll make you an offer," said Cardross, scanning him not unkindly. "I won't lend you three hundred pence to fling away at faro, but I'm prepared to settle your debts, and to buy you a commission in any serving regiment you choose to name."

"By Jove, I wish you would!" Dysart said impulsively.

"I will."

The Viscount's blue eyes had kindled, but that eager glow faded, and he laughed, giving his head a rueful shake. "No use! The old gentleman wouldn't hear of it. God knows why he's so set on keeping me in England, for putting aside the fact that I'm not his only son it don't seem to be any pleasure to him to have me at home. Fidgets him to death! I did go down to Devonshire after he had that stroke, you know. Went to oblige my mother, but the end of it was she was obliged to own it didn't answer. But he wouldn't let me join for all that."

"If you wanted it, I might be able to persuade him."

"Grease him in the fist, eh? Take my advice, and fund your money! Or wait till I do something so outrageous he'll be glad to see me off to Spain on any terms!" said Dysart, pulling on his gloves.

"Don't be a fool! Come into the house: we can't discuss it in the road!"

"If you're so anxious to waste the ready, lend me a monkey!"

mocked Dysart. "As for the rest—oh, lord, I don't know *what* I want, and it wouldn't be a particle of use if I did!"

He waited for a moment, and then, as Cardross made no reply, laughed rather jeeringly, and strode off down the flagway.

IT was almost with relief that Nell, a few days later, bade her husband a polite farewell. When he had asked her to accompany him to Merion, she had wanted very much to do so (though not with an indignant Letty in her train); but from the moment that Madame Lavalle's bill had arrived to blacken her life she had dreaded that he might renew his persuasions. There was now nothing she wanted less than to be in his company, for the sense of guilt, which already weighed heavily on her spirits, almost crushed her when he was with her. If he smiled at her she felt herself to be a deceiving wretch; if there was a coolness in his manner she fancied he had found her out, and was ready to sink. It did not occur to her, in this disordered state of mind, that the scruples which forbade her to let him see her heart were prompting her to pursue a course that might have been expressly designed to confirm him in his suspicion that she cared for nothing but wealth, fashion, and frivolity. There was no lack of parties, at the height of the season, to fill her days; and no lack of eager escorts for the beautiful young Countess, if the Earl had engagements of his own. It seemed to him that he never saw her except on her way to a review, or a ball; and he could scarcely doubt that she preferred the company of even the most callow of her admirers to his. "You know, my love," he said to her once, mocking himself, "I think fate must have thrown me in your way to depress my pretensions! Would you believe it?—I was used to think myself the devil of a fellow! I now perceive that I'm no such thing—almost a dead bore, in fact!"

She had not answered him, but the colour had flooded her cheeks, and as her eyes flew to his for a brief instant he thought that he caught a glimpse of the loving, vital creature he had once believed her to be. And a moment later she was gone, saying, with a nervous laugh, that he was absurd, that Letty was waiting for her, that she must not stay, because she had promised faithfully to attend Lady Brixworth's alfresco party out at Richmond.

Subjected to such treatment as this, it was hardly surprising that Cardross, far too proud to betray his hurt, retired behind a barrier of cool, faintly ironic civility, which effectually slew at birth Nell's impulse to fling caution to the winds, and all her doubts and difficulties at his feet.

To make matters worse, no word came from Dysart, and Letty, bent on achieving her own ends, wore her brother's temper thin by renewing her attacks every time she saw him. As she had been pledging his credit all over town for weeks past he was soon provoked into addressing a few shattering home truths to her, from which his unhappy wife, an unwilling third at this encounter, gathered that debt and dishonesty were, in his austere view, synonymous terms. Certainly no moment for the disclosure of her own embarrassments could be more unpropitious.

It was therefore with relief that she bade him farewell. He expected to be away for a se'enight, within which time she thought it not unreasonable to suppose that Dysart must have discovered a means of discharging her debt to Madame Lavalle. By way of recalling it to his mind (just in case, in the press of his sporting engagements, he had temporarily forgotten its urgency) she sent round a note to his lodging in Duke Street, inviting him to dine in Grosvenor Square on the night of the masquerade. Well aware of the fatal results of importunacy she resisted a temptation to ask him what progress he had made towards settling her affairs, and was soon rewarded for her restraint. The Viscount not only sent back a note accepting her invitation, but added, in a postscript, that she need not trouble her head more over That Other Matter.

This cryptic message sent her spirits up immediately. It would have been more satisfactory, perhaps, if Dysart had told her what expedient he had hit upon, but she knew him to be no ready letter-writer, and was content to trust that his third attempt at solving her difficulties would be more acceptable to her than his two previous suggestions. Except for one encounter in the Park, where it was impossible to hold private conversation with him, she did not meet him: a circumstance which led her to suppose that whatever plan he had evolved needed a good deal of preparation. This made her feel a trifle uneasy, but he nodded to her so reassuringly at the end of their one chance meeting that her misgivings were soothed. "I shall see you on Thursday," he said; and that, she thought, was his way of informing her that on Thursday, when he was to go with her to the masquerade, he would be able to tell her just what she must do to rid herself of her intolerable debt.

And then, on Thursday evening, when both the fair hostesses awaited his arrival in Grosvenor Square, he did not come.

Neither was surprised that he should be late in keeping his engagement, for his habits were known to be erratic; and for a full half-hour only the wizard belowstairs, with two capons roasted to a turn on the spits, fat livers in cases in imminent danger of becoming over-baked in the oven, and the caramel sugar spun over a dish of peu d'amours rapidly hardening, saw any cause for agitation. Letty, who had been in low spirits for days past, was wearing a new and extremely dashing ball-dress of white crape so profusely embroidered with silver spangles that when she stood in the light of the great chandelier in the drawing-room the effect was quite dazzling. Nell, less strikingly attired in satin and blonde lace, knew that if Lady Chudleigh should be at the masquerade she would unhesitatingly condemn this toilette as being totally unsuited to a young lady in her first season, for it was cut indecorously low, besides being worn over the most diaphanous of petticoats. Cardross would probably have insisted on its being changed for something more demure. He might even have considered that in his absence his wife should have done so, but Nell felt herself to be unequal to an exhausting and almost certainly losing battle; and assuaged her conscience with the reflection that the dress would be largely hidden by the domino of shimmering rose silk, which Letty had tossed across the back of a chair. Besides, Letty was so pleased with her appearance that it had put her into the sunniest of humours, which Nell, having endured a week of sulks and repinings, would not willingly upset.

"The worst of brothers is that they never think it is of the least consequence to keep one waiting," remarked Letty, spreading open a fan spangled to match her gown. "I only hope he may not be foxed when he does arrive! Look, do you think this is pretty?"

"Foxed! Why should he be?" demanded Nell rather indignantly.

"Oh! You know what men are, when they go off to watch a cock-fight!" said the worldly wise Letty. "There was one at Epsom today, I fancy."

"Good heavens, did he tell you he meant to go there?"

"No, but I heard Hardwick talking to Mr. Bottisham about it, and he said something about Dysart's taking him up in his curricle."

"Oh, dear!" said Nell, considerably dismayed by this most unwelcome intelligence. "If that is so—— Oh, I do hope he may not have forgotten he is to take us to Chiswick tonight!"

"What, you don't mean to say that you think he might?" exclaimed Letty, allowing her fan to drop into her lap. "Oh, it would be too infamous!"

Certain sinister memories flitted through Nell's mind. "Well,

I trust he has not, but he—he does sometimes forget his engagements—particularly when he doesn't like them excessively!" she said.

Letty controlled herself with a strong effort, but when, at the end of another ten minutes, there was still no sign of the Viscount, she could contain herself no longer, but said bitterly: "Even if he *is* your brother, Nell, I don't believe he ever meant to go with us, and he just said he would so that you shouldn't tease him!"

"No, no, he did mean to, for he said he would see me tonight when we met him in the Park that day! Besides, although I own he is shockingly careless, he wouldn't serve me such an unhandsome trick as that! I was wondering if I should perhaps send a note round to his lodging, to *remind* him. Only I daresay it would take my footman at least twenty minutes to reach Duke Street——"

"Yes, and ten to one he wouldn't find him at home when he did reach his lodging!" interrupted Letty. "For my part, I don't care a button whether he comes or not, for I am persuaded we shall do very well without him!" She looked at Nell with sharp suspicion. "You are *not* going to say we can't go to the masquerade unless he escorts us? Oh, Nell, you couldn't be so shabby!"

"No—that is, I know I need not scruple to go, when it is to my cousin's party, but I cannot like it! I wish you were not so set on it—and, to own the truth, I can't think why you should be, unless you have cajoled Mr. Allandale to go, and mean to spend the evening in his pocket! And mask or no mask, Letty, I can't and I won't permit it!"

"I did try to make him go," admitted Letty, quite unabashed, "but he holds to it that it would be improper, even if he slipped away before the unmasking, so you needn't be in a fidget! The thing is that I have never attended a masquerade, and if I don't go to this one I may not have the chance to go to one for years, for there's no saying that they have them in Brazil, after all."

Nell looked at her in concern. "No, but—— Dearest Letty, don't indulge your fancy with *that* thought! Cardross won't give his consent: it is useless to think he might!"

"I shall *compel* him!" Letty said, looking mulish.

"How could you possibly do that?"·

"Well, I don't know that yet, but you may depend upon it that I shall do it! Recollect that he said I shouldn't be presented till I was eighteen, or act in the theatricals at Roxwell, at Christmas, or drive his bays, or—oh, a hundred things! I can *always* get Giles to let me have my own way, in the end!"

Nell could not help smiling at the naïveté with which Letty classed these trivialities with her marriage, but before she could make any attempt to show her sister-in-law how the very fondness which led Cardross to indulge her in small matters would stiffen his resolve not to permit her (as he thought) to throw herself away in a marriage doomed to failure, Farley, her butler, had entered the room, bearing on a salver a sealed billet, and on his countenance the expression of one who not only brought evil tidings but had foreseen from the outset that this was precisely how it would be.

"My Lord Dysart's groom, my lady, has desired me to give this instantly into your ladyship's hands," he announced, proffering the salver.

"Only *wait* until I next see Dysart!" uttered Letty direfully.

Feeling as conscience-stricken as though she and not Dysart had been the culprit, Nell broke the wafer that sealed his note, and hastily unfolded the scrawled message. A sigh of relief escaped her, for although the news the message contained was bad, it was not as bad as it might have been. Dysart must certainly have lingered overlong at Epsom, but he had not forgotten that he was engaged to escort his sister to a masquerade. He begged her pardon for being unable to dine with her, but promised faithfully to pick her and Letty up in Grosvenor Square not a moment later than ten o'clock, unless (in a postscript) he should be unavoidably detained, in which case they were to set forward for Chiswick, and might be sure that he would meet them there, his mask in his hand.

"Ten o'clock! And we are invited for half-past nine!" said Letty wrathfully, when this was read to her.

A gleam of mischief shone in Nell's angelic eyes. "My dear, *surely* you would not be so *gothic* as to arrive at the very start of the party?"

"I daresay he won't come here at all!" said Letty crossly.

This seemed more than likely to Dysart's experienced sister, but loyalty as much as disinclination to drive out to Chiswick without male escort hardened her resolution not to order her landau to come round to the house a moment earlier than ten o'clock. The hour was by this time so far advanced that they had not very long to wait after dinner before Farley announced that the carriage waited for their ladyships. Dysart had put in no appearance, and although a loving sister would have given him a few more moments' grace she dared not, in face of Letty's kindling glance, suggest this. The dominoes, one rose-pink and the other sapphire-blue, were assumed; long gloves of French kid drawn on; loo-masks tucked into reticules; and evening mantles carefully donned over the silken dominoes. A final prinking, on tiptoe before the gilded looking-glass over the mantelpiece, and the ladies were ready to be escorted down the staircase, and handed up into the waiting carriage. Their respective women were in attendance, jealously arranging their delicate skirts, and laying shawls across their knees, Letty's Martha presuming on long service to warn her young mistress against adding any more Bloom of Ninon to an already perfect complexion; and Nell's lofty dresser reminding her to take care that her train of ivory satin did not brush the steps of the landau when she alighted from it.

Those steps were at last let up, and the door shut; the footmen nimbly mounted up behind; the coachman set his horses in motion; and the landau swayed forward over the cobbles.

It had not occurred to Nell, or, indeed, to any of her servants, that a drive to Chiswick could be attended by danger, so no one had thought it necessary to provide the equipage with outriders to protect her from possible highwaymen. But no one had foreseen that the Cardross carriage, instead of joining a procession of vehicles bound for Brent House, would be the last to arrive there by more than half an hour. There was hardly any traffic beyond the first pike off the stones. Kensington village seemed to be sleeping in the bright moonlight; only a post-chaise and an Accommodation coach were met in Hammersmith, coming in from the west; no other vehicle was seen except one of the mails, which swept past the Cardross carriage, its four fresh horses going along at a spanking pace, and its guard blowing a very loud blast of warning on his yard of tin. Shortly after this, the carriage turned off the high road towards Chiswick Mall; and then, just as Letty was saying: "Well, at all events it hasn't been nearly as tedious a drive as if we had been obliged to dawdle behind some rumbling coach!" both ladies were unpleasantly startled by a sudden pistol-shot, followed by a medley of alarming noises, in which the squeal of a frightened horse mingled with various rough voices upraised either in command or expostulation, and the trampling of hooves.

Letty uttered a whimper of fright, and clutched her sister-in-law, saying on a rising note of panic: "What must we do? What will happen to us? Oh, Nell, we are being *held up*! Why don't those *cowards* of footmen do something? This is all Dysart's fault! Will they murder us? Oh, I wish we hadn't come!"

Nell was not feeling very brave herself, but she was made of sterner stuff than this, and managed to reply with very creditable command over her voice: "Nonsense! Of course they will not murder us, though I am afraid they will take our jewels. Thank God I am not wearing the Cardross necklace, or my precious sapphires!"

"Give them *everything*!" begged Letty, her teeth chattering. "I feel sick with apprehension, and I am sure I shall faint! What is the use of taking footmen, when they do *nothing* to protect us? I shall tell Giles, and he will turn them off directly! He ought to be here: he had no *right* to go off to Merion, when he might have known——"

"Oh, do, pray, hold your tongue, Letty!" interrupted Nell, exasperated. "I wonder you should not have more pride than to let the wretches see you are afraid! And as for the footmen, what could the poor men do against armed ruffians? *They* are not carrying pistols! I don't suppose they ever dreamed we should be held up on the road to Chiswick, of all places! Oh, dear, it sounds as if there were several of them! I do hope they will be satisfied with our jewels, and not wish to ransack the carriage for a strong-box!"

This horrid thought made Letty shake with terror. Then she screamed, for a hideous figure, enveloped in a dark cloak, and with a mask covering his face, loomed up, and wrenched open the door of the carriage, presenting the barrel of a large horse-pistol, and growling in ferocious accents: "Hand over the gewgaws, and be quick about it!"

The moonlight glinted on the pistol, and the hand that held it. Letty cried: "Don't, don't!" and tried with feverish haste to unclasp the single row of pearls from round her throat.

"Not you!" said the highwayman, even more ferociously. "*You!*"

The pistol was now pointing straight at Nell, but instead of shrinking away, or making haste (as Letty quaveringly implored her to do) to strip off her bracelets and rings and the large pendant that flashed on her breast, she was sitting bolt upright, her incredulous gaze fixed at first on the hand that grasped the pistol, and then lifting to the masked face.

"Quick!" commanded the highwayman harshly. "If you don't want me to put a bullet through you!"

"Dysart!"

"Hell and the devil confound it!" ejaculated his lordship, adding, however, in a hasty attempt to cover this lapse: "None o' that! Hand over the gewgaws!"

"Take that pistol away!" ordered Nell. "How dare you try to frighten me like this? Of all the outrageous things to do——! It is a great deal too bad of you! What in the world possessed you?"

"Well, if you can't tell that you must be a bigger sapskull than I knew!" said his lordship disgustedly. He pulled off his mask, and called over his shoulder: "Bubbled, Corny!"

"There, what did I tell you?" said Mr. Fancot, putting up the weapon with which he had been covering the coachman, and riding up to bow politely to the occupants of the carriage. "You ought to have let me do the trick, dear boy: I *said* her ladyship would recognize you!"

"Well, I don't know how the devil she should!" said the Viscount, considerably put-out.

"Oh, Dy, how absurd you are!" Nell exclaimed, trying not to laugh. "The moonlight was shining on the ring Mama gave you when you came of age! And then you said, *Not you!* to Letty! Of course I recognized you!"

"Then you might have had the wit to pretend you didn't!" said the Viscount, with asperity. "Totty-headed, that's what you are, my girl! Hi, Joe! No need to keep those fellows covered any longer! I've lost the bet."

"Dysart, how abominable of you!" Nell said indignantly. "To bring your groom into this is utterly beyond the line!"

"Fiddle!" said the Viscount. "You might as well say it was beyond the line to bring Corny in! I've known Joe all my life! Besides, I told him it was for a wager."

"I *do* say it was beyond the line to bring Mr. Fancot in. And I should have supposed he would have thought so too!" added Nell, with some severity.

"No, no! Assure you, ma'am! Always happy to be of service," said Mr. Fancot gallantly. "Pleasure!"

Letty, to whom relief had brought its inevitable sequel, said in a furious undervoice: *"Idiot!"*

"Nothing of the sort!" said the Viscount, overhearing. "In fact, if we're to talk of idiots——"

"I think you are detestable! You broke your engagement with Nell in the rudest way, just that you might play this odious trick on her, and frightened us to death for sport! *Sport!*"

"What a hen-hearted girl you are!" remarked his lordship scornfully. "Frightened you to death, indeed! Lord, Nell's worth a dozen of you! Not but what *she's* got more hair than wit! Of course I didn't do it for sport! I had a devilish good reason, but one might as well try to milk a pigeon as set about helping a female out of a fix!"

Letty was so much intrigued by this cryptic utterance that her wrath gave place to the liveliest curiosity. "What can you mean? Who is in a fix? Is it Nell? But how—— Oh, do tell me! I'm sorry I was cross, but how could I guess it was a plot, when no one told me?"

"Ask Nell!" recommended Dysart. "You'd best be on your way, if you don't wish to be late. I'll follow you presently."

"Dysart!" said Nell despairingly. "It must be nearly eleven o'clock already! How can you possibly follow us? You cannot attend a masquerade in your riding-dress, and by the time you have returned to town, and——"

"Now, don't fly into a fidget!" begged Dysart. "I'm not going all the way back to London! You must think I'm a gudgeon!"

"Oh, I *do*!" she interpolated, on a quiver of laughter.

"Well, that's where you're fair and far off," he told her severely. "I've got all my toggery waiting for me at the Golden Lion here, and a chaise hired to bring me on to Brent House. Yes, and when I think that I never planned anything so carefully in my life, only to have it overset because nothing would do for you but to show how clever you are by screeching that you knew me, I have a dashed good mind to wash my hands of the whole business!"

"Good God, dear boy, mustn't say things like that!" intervened Mr. Fancot, considerably shocked. "*I* know you don't mean it, but if anyone else heard you——"

"Well, there isn't anyone else to hear me," said the Viscount snappishly, walking away to where his groom was holding his horse.

Mr. Fancot, feeling that it behoved him to make his excuses for him, pressed up to the carriage, and bowed again to its dimly seen occupants, saying confidentially: "He don't mean what he says when he gets in a miff—no need to tell you so! *I* know Dy, *you* know Dy! *He* won't buckle!"

"Mr. Fancot," said Nell, almost overcome by mortification, "I am persuaded *I* have no need to beg you not to tell anyone why Dysart tried to hold me up tonight!"

"I shouldn't dream of it!" Mr. Fancot assured her earnestly. "Wild horses couldn't drag it out of me! Well, it stands to reason they couldn't, because, now I come to think of it, I don't know."

"You don't know?" she repeated incredulously.

"Forgot to ask him," he explained. "Well, I mean to say— no business of mine! Dy said, Come and help me to hold up m'sister's carriage! and I said, Done! or some such thing.

Nothing else I could say. Dashed inquisitive to be asking him why, you know!"

At this moment Dysart called impatiently to him, so he made his bow, and went off. Nell sank back into her corner of the carriage, exclaiming: "Thank heavens! I was ready to sink!" She became aware of her footman awaiting orders, and said hastily: "Tell James to drive on, if you please! His lordship was—was just funning!"

"I should think he must believe his lordship to be out of his mind," observed Letty, as the carriage moved forward. "Why did he do it, Nell?"

"Oh, for a nonsensical reason!"

"Very likely! But what nonsensical reason?"

"I wish you will take a leaf out of that absurd Fancot's book, and not ask inquisitive questions!"

"I daresay you do, but I shan't! Come, now, you sly thing!"

"No, pray don't tease me!" Nell begged.

"Oh, very well! I wonder what Giles will say to it?" said Letty, all sprightly innocence.

"Letty! You wouldn't——!"

"Not if I were in your confidence, of course!" replied Letty piously.

"Really, you are the most unscrupulous girl!" declared Nell.

Letty giggled. "No, I am not, for I never betray secrets! I shan't rest till I know this one, I warn you, for I cannot conceive what was in Dysart's head, unless he was just knocking up a lark, and that I know he was not."

"Well, pray don't think too badly of him!" Nell said, capitulating.

But Letty, listening entranced to Nell's story, did not think at all badly of Dysart. She said handsomely that he had far more wit than she had ever guessed, and was much inclined to join him in blaming Nell for not having held her peace. "For if only you had pretended not to recognize him everything would now be in a fair way to being settled. And you can't deny that if you had truly not known him you wouldn't have cared a button for your jewels. I suppose you might have guessed how it was, when he brought you the money, but that wouldn't have signified!"

"How can you say so? My peace would have been utterly cut up! I *must* have told Cardross—yet how might I have done so, when already he thinks Dy too—too rackety? Oh, it would have been worse than anything!"

"I declare you are the oddest creature!" Letty exclaimed. "For my part, I think you should have sold some of your jewels, and I don't wonder at it that Dysart is out of all patience with you! I suppose you may do what you choose with what is your own!"

She continued arguing in this strain until Brent House was reached; and when Dysart presently joined his sister, in something very like a fit of the sullens, did much to restore him to good-humour by heartily applauding his ingenuity, commiserating him on the mischance which had brought his scheme to nothing, and abusing Nell for having such stupid crotchets. For once they found themselves much in sympathy, but when the Viscount said that if Nell made such a piece of work over a little necessary deception she had better screw up her courage and tell Cardross she was under the hatches again, agreement was at an end between them. Letty strongly opposed this suggestion. In her experience, Cardross, in general so indulgent, was abominably severe if he considered one had been extravagant; and if confronted by debts (however inescapable) he became positively brutal. She spoke with feeling, her last encounter with her exasperated brother still vivid in her mind. "Only because I purchased a dressing-case, which *every* lady must have, and desired him in the *civillest* way to pay for it, for how could I do so myself on the paltry sum he allows me for pin-money—he *sent it back to the shop*!

I was never so mortified! And, would you credit it, Dysart?—
he promised me that if I again ran into debt he would send
me down to Merion in charge of a strict governess! A
governess——!"

The Viscount was not much impressed—and, indeed, he
would have been still less impressed had he been privileged to
set eyes on the necessary adjunct to a lady's comfort in question. A handsome piece of baggage, that dressing-case, with
every one of its numerous cut-glass bottles fitted with gold
caps, embellished with a tasteful design in diamond-chips. It
had made the second footman, a stout youth, sweat only to
carry it up one pair of stairs; and when it was flung open it
had quite dazzled the eyes of all beholders. It had dazzled
Cardross's eyes so much that he had closed them, an expression
on his face of real anguish.

"That has nothing to say to anything. I daresay he thought
it not the thing for you," said the Viscount, with unconscious
shrewdness. "But everyone knows court dresses cost the deuce
of a lot of money, and I shouldn't wonder at it if——"

"When Giles discovered that Nell was so monstrously in
the wind he said such things as cast her into the greatest affliction!"

"Were you there?" demanded the Viscount suspiciously.

"No, I was not there, but I saw her directly afterwards, and
she was quite overset! She cried in the most affecting way, and
ever since she has been subject to fits of sad dejection. If you
abandon her, it will be the most abominable thing I ever heard
of!"

"Who said I meant to do so?" retorted his lordship. "All
I said was—— But it ain't to the purpose! It's a pity tonight's
affair came to nothing, but I shall come about. And I'll thank
you not to start meddling!" he added, in a very ungallant way.

"I have not the remotest intention of *meddling*!" said Letty,
rigid with wrath.

"Well, see you don't!" recommended Dysart. "And don't go blabbing either!"

These ungentlemanly words brought to an abrupt end the excellent understanding which had seemed to be flourishing between them. Letty, in freezing accents, requested his lordship to restore her to her chaperon, and his lordship did so with unflattering alacrity. Finding that Nell was attended by a great many of her friends he did not feel that it behoved him to remain at her side, but went off to amuse himself in his own way. Since he was, regrettably, one of those dashing blades who could not be trusted to keep the line at a masquerade he managed to do this tolerably well by flirting outrageously with any lady obliging enough to encourage him. By the time that had palled he had been so fortunate as to have rubbed against a crony, in whose company, and that of several other bucks of the first head, he spent the remainder of the evening, rejoining his sister finally in very merry pin. He was not precisely castaway (as he would himself have phrased it), and only a high stickler could have found anything to object to in the affable, not to say rollicking, mood engendered by champagne punch; but it was evident that he had temporarily banished care, and could not be expected to bend his mind to the solving of Nell's difficulties. Instead, he entertained the ladies during the drive back to town with snatches of song, delivered in a fine, forceful baritone.

IN spite of the absence from it of Mr. Allandale Letty had much enjoyed the masquerade. Like the Viscount, she had indulged in a good deal of flirtation, allowing her vivacity to carry her to lengths only possible under the disguise of a mask and domino; she had received a great many audacious compliments; and her spangled gown had been much admired. Her giddiness added nothing to Nell's comfort, but she was powerless to check the liveliness that several times put her to the blush. A gentle admonition was met merely with a laugh, and a toss of the head; and when she ventured to say: "Letty, if you won't keep a proper distance for your own sake, do so for mine, I beg of you!" her wilful sister-in-law replied: "Oh, fudge! You place yourself on too high a form! There's no harm in romping a trifle at a masquerade: everyone does so! It is all just fun and gig!"

"It is unbecoming," Nell said. "Bath miss manners! You wouldn't behave with so little particularity if Mr. Allandale were here!"

"*Dear* Jeremy! No, indeed! I should flirt with him instead. But he is not here, and I've no notion of being moped and die-away at *such* an agreeable party, I can tell you. I think we are having a splendid night's raking, don't you?"

It was useless to persist; useless too to hope that Letty would not be recognized. At midnight there would be a general unmasking, when disapproving eyes would see that the fast girl in the shimmering domino and the spangled gown was none other than Cardross's little half-sister. Youth and a naturally volatile disposition led Letty, carried away by excitement, into behaviour that was beyond the line of being pleasing. The evils of her former situation in her aunt's house were never more clearly shown: she had neither precept nor example to guide her, her aunt being both indolent and shatter-brained, and her cousins over-bold young women with nothing in their heads but finery and dalliance.

Having perceived Lady Chudleigh amongst the gathering of unmasked chaperons, Nell braced herself to meet the inevitable strictures which she did not doubt her husband's most formidable aunt would feel it her duty to address to her. In the event, however, Lady Chudleigh was surprisingly gracious. She certainly condemned the spangled dress, and was thankful that she had no cause to blush for her own daughter, but she said that she did not blame Nell for Letty's want of conduct. "It is much to be regretted that Letitia does not take a lesson from you, my dear Helen," she said majestically. "I shall not deny that I have been used to think that Cardross made a great mistake when he chose to offer for you. I always speak my mind, and I told him at the time that he would do better to ally himself to a female nearer in age to himself. But I must own, and do not hesitate to do so, that I have been agreeably surprised in you. It is a sad pity that Letitia has neither your discretion nor your good taste."

With these measured words of approval she moved on, which was just as well, since Nell could think of nothing whatsoever so say in reply to them. Her daughter, a rather angular girl, unkindly described by her cousin Felix as an antidote, lingered to exclaim: "Only fancy Mama's saying *that* to you! She does not often praise people, I can tell you, Cousin Helen!"

The congratulatory tone in which this was uttered was a little too much for Nell. She said tartly: "I am sure I ought to be very much obliged to her!"

"I knew you must feel it so. Do you know, she said to me yesterday that you were a very pretty-behaved young woman? There!"

"Did she indeed? Well, don't repeat any more of her compliments, for they might puff me up too much in my own conceit!"

Miss Chudleigh tittered. "That is precisely what Mama said! At least, I mean she said that it was a wonder your head was not turned by all the compliments you receive. But I quite expected her to censure you for permitting Letty to wear such an improper gown. I can't think how she can do so without blushing. *I* could not!"

"No, and I must own that I think you would be very unwise to attempt anything in the same style," instantly retorted the pretty-behaved Lady Cardross. "But Letty, you know, has so perfect a figure that she can carry off anything! For my part, I never saw her in greater beauty!"

"And I hope she told her detestable mother!" Nell said, when later recounting this exchange to Letty.

"Well!" said Letty, giggling. "What a bouncer! When you took one look at my dress, and said you had never seen anything so improper!"

"Yes, but I didn't say it was not *becoming*! And in any event it was a great piece of impertinence for Miriam to criticize you. Or for Lady Chudleigh to do so either, for now I come to think of it she is not your aunt, but only Giles's!"

"*Dear* Nell!" gurgled Letty.

Nell submitted to an enthusiastic embrace, but said, in rather a conscience-stricken tone: "But I must tell you, Letty, that I agreed with every word they said! It is a *shocking* dress, and don't say you didn't damp your petticoat, for I know you did! Nothing else could have made it cling so! What Cardross must have said, had he seen it——"

"You sound *just* like a governess!"

"So I do!" Nell said, much struck, and looking quite aghast. "Oh, what an odious girl you are, Letty, to put me to that necessity! You make me *feel* like a governess!"

"*I* did not purchase a lace gown for more than three hundred guineas," said Letty, folding her hands, and gazing piously at the ceiling. "*I* am not in a quake lest my husband should discover it!"

Quite confounded, poor Nell remained speechless for several moments. She made a gallant recover. "No, *you* bought a dressing-case for five hundred pounds, didn't you? And you are not in debt because Cardross sent it back! At least *that* has not happened to me!"

"I hoped you wouldn't remember that," said Letty candidly. "Oh, Nell, it *has* put a famous notion into my head! Send the gown back to Lavalle! You may say that it is not in the least what you wanted, and doesn't become you!"

"Well, if that is your famous notion I never heard anything so unscrupulous in my life!" gasped Nell. "Besides, I tore it a little at Carlton House that night, and Lavalle would instantly see where Sutton darned it!"

"What a pity! There is nothing for it, then, but to order another dress from the horrid creature," said Letty, unconsciously echoing Dysart. "That is what my aunt does when her dressmaker duns her. And if you keep on sending it back, saying it does not fit, or that you prefer a floss trimming instead of lace, or some such thing, it won't be finished until the quarter, and then you may pay for both the gowns! Why, in less than two months it *will* be quarter-day, and you will find yourself in funds again! I see no difficulty."

The suggestion found no favour with Nell, but since Madame Lavalle had followed up her bill with a polite letter, drawing my lady's attention to it, and trusting that my lady would find it convenient to defray it within the immediate future, she felt her case to be desperate, and resolved on a course which, disagreeable though it might be, seemed to hold out more promise of success than any scheme Dysart was likely to evolve. She would pay Madame Lavalle a visit, not to bespeak another expensive dress, but to explain with what dignity she could muster that although it was not at all convenient to her to pay the account in the immediate future she would faithfully do so at the end of the following month. That this would dig an uncomfortably large hole in her next quarter's allowance Nell realized, but decided, with the optimism of youth, that with a little economy she would contrive to scrape through the summer months.

She had been startled to receive Madame's letter, and shrewd enough to perceive, underlying its smooth civility, a threat; but she was as yet too inexperienced to know that some unusual circumstance must lurk behind it, or that no *modiste* of high fashion would dream, for the paltry sum of three hundred and thirty guineas, of alienating a patroness of such rich promise as the young Countess of Cardross. But after a very few minutes in Madame Lavalle's company she learned that the circumstances governing Madame's action were very unusual indeed. Madame, after a long and lucrative career in Bruton Street, was about to retire from business. She was, in fact, returning to her native land, but this she naturally did not disclose to Lady Cardross, preferring to say with a vagueness at odd variance with her sharp-featured face, with its calculating sloe-eyes and inflexible mouth, that she would henceforward be out of the way of collecting debts. Lady Cardross was certainly an *innocente,* but even a bride from the schoolroom might wonder how it would be possible for Madame to return to France in time of war. It was possible, if one had money and time to spend on the journey, influential connections to assist one over the obstacles in the path, and, above all, relations well-placed in Paris. From England one might still travel to Denmark, and after that—*eh bien,* the matter arranged itself!

On the whole Madame had done very well out of her last London Season, but this was now in full swing, her most valued clients had purchased quite as many gowns as they were likely to need, and it was time to close her accounts. She had several bad debts: that went without saying; it was not worth the pain of attempting to recover those losses; but she knew well that although Lady Cardross might be at a temporary standstill her lord was as wealthy a man as might be found, and would certainly pay his wife's debts. The sense of this she managed to convey to Nell in the most urbane manner conceivable, not an ungenteel word spoken, the sugared smile never deserting her lips.

"Oh, if it is the case that you are retiring from business——!" said Nell, shrugging her shoulders with splendid indifference. "I had not perfectly understood: naturally you will wish to be paid immediately! Rest assured that I will attend to the matter!"

She then sailed away, her head high, and her heart cowering in her little kid shoes. Madame, having curtseyed her off the premises with the greatest deference, rubbed her hands together, and said: "She will contrive, that one!"

That she must somehow contrive, and without Cardross's knowledge, was by this time a fixed determination in Nell's mind. Every day that had passed since the first appearance of Madame's account had added to her dread that he would discover the debt; reason was lost sight of; the debt, and Cardross's sentiments, if he should be called upon to pay it, assumed grotesque proportions, until it seemed to her as though it might wreck her life. No sobering counsel was at hand to cast a damper on lurid imagination, and give her thoughts a saner direction. Letty, exaggerating her own experiences, recommended her at all costs to settle the matter before Cardross got wind of it; and Dysart, knowing how much his own depredations on her purse were responsible for her present predicament, was apparently prepared to go to extraordinary lengths for the furtherance of this end. But Dysart had shaken her faith in him. Letty might applaud his scheme for her relief: she could not. It seemed to her a shocking thing to have attempted; and the thought of what next his wild humour might prompt him to do put her in a quake of apprehension. There must be no depending on Dysart; and there was no one else to whom she could turn.

Such a reflection as this was scarcely soothing to nerves already irritated. The conviction that she was friendless, and hunted into the bargain, began to take strong possession of Nell's mind. She sank into a slough of self-pity, seeing her debt as a sum large enough to have ruined a Nabob, and her husband as a miser with a heart of flint.

It was in this mood that she presently stepped down from her barouche, and it was her coachman who rescued her from it, by desiring to know whether she would be requiring the carriage again that day. The very mention of it dispelled that unjust vision of Cardross. Just because she had once admired a friend's barouche he had given her one for her very own, and with a pair of horses that took the shine out of every other pair to be seen in town. She had not liked the famous Cardross necklace, an awe-inspiring collection of emeralds and diamonds heavily set in gold, and instead of being offended he had told her to keep it for state occasions, and had given her the most charming pendant to wear in its stead. "For everyday use!" he had said, with the smile that had won her heart in his eyes.

Self-pity turned in an instant to self-blame. From being a tyrannical miser Cardross became the most generous man alive, and quite the most ill-used; and she the embodiment of selfishness, extravagance, and ingratitude. And, if Dysart were to be believed, she had added blindness and stupidity to these vices. It now seemed to her wonderful that Cardross should have remained patient for so long. Perhaps he was regretting the impulse that had made him offer for her; perhaps, even, disgust at her coldness and depravity had already driven him back to Lady Orsett.

A year earlier Nell, instructed by Mama, had steeled her-self to accept the fact of Lady Orsett as one of the inescapable crosses a wife must bear with complaisance; but between the girl who had supposed herself to be making a marriage of convenience and the bride who had been brought to realize that hers was a love-match there was a vast difference. Mama would scarcely have recognized her docile, beautifully man-nered daughter in the bright-eyed young woman who uttered between clenched teeth: "She shan't have him!"

This determination, excellent though it might be, only strengthened her resolve to settle Madame Lavalle's account without applying to Cardross. In her view nothing could more surely jeopardize her whole future than to cast out lures to her husband while presenting him with yet another debt. He must certainly believe her to be hoaxing him, playing off a detestable cajolery that could only disgust a man of sensibility.

Her thoughts flickered to the second of Dysart's suggestions, that she should sell some of her jewellery. Not, of course, Cardross's gifts, but perhaps the row of pearls Mama had given her? But every feeling revolted. They were Mama's own pearls, jealously preserved by her for her eldest daughter, and bestowed upon her with such affecting tenderness. Stress of circumstances had obliged poor Mama to sell nearly all her jewellery, but her pearls she had clung to through the direst of her straits, and for her daughter to sell them only to pay for an extravagant gown must sink her for ever below reproach.

A very little reflection convinced Nell that there was only one way in which she could raise three hundred pounds. It must be borrowed. Dysart had rather unexpectedly condemned this expedient, but Nell knew that even Mama had had deal-ings with a moneylender, so that borrowing upon interest, though it might be an expensive practice, could not be a crime. Papa, of course, had carried it to unwise lengths: Nell perfectly understood how ruinous continued borrowings could be, but it was surely absurd to suppose that anything very dreadful would happen if one borrowed three hundred pounds only for a few weeks. It would be paid back at the end of June, and no one need ever know anything about it.

The more she considered it, the more Nell liked the scheme, and the more she was inclined to attribute Dysart's severe attitude to some antiquated notion of propriety. Even the most careless of brothers could be amazingly stuffy on any question of conduct affecting the ladies of his family: that was one of the incomprehensible things about men. To hear Papa, in the bosom of his family, one would suppose that modesty and discretion were the two virtues he considered most indispensable in a female. But there had been nothing in Papa's career to suggest this: indeed far otherwise! Dysart, warmly approving the generously displayed charms of a certain actress, almost in the same breath could speak censoriously of his sister's gown, if it were cut rather lower than usual, or clung too closely to her form for his suddenly austere taste. Even Cardross suffered from this peculiarity. He had not criticized her raiment, but he made no secret of the fact that he expected from his wife and sister a degree of decorum which he did not practise himself. "I will have no scandal in *my* household," said Cardross inflexibly, just as though he had not been creating scandal in Lord Orsett's household for years. Nell didn't doubt that he would disapprove strongly of his wife's patronizing a moneylender, but she didn't allow it to worry her very much. Imprudent it might be, but what Mama had done could not be a crime.

Nell gave Dysart a day's grace, and when he neither came to see her nor wrote to tell her what next he meant to do, set forth, not without some inward trepidation, on a visit to Mr. King, in Clarges Street. It had been Mr. King who had enjoyed Mama's custom.

There were certain difficulties in the way of setting forth

from Grosvenor Square alone and on foot, but she overcame these by ordering her carriage round to take her to the Green Park, where (she said) she was going to walk with some friends. At the last moment Letty nearly spoilt this careful plan by going with her, but she had the happy thought of saying that she had arranged to meet in the park two ladies whom Letty violently disliked, so Letty decided instead to go with her maid on a shopping expedition. Nell might tell herself that there was no harm in her projected errand, but she could not tell herself that it would be proper to take Letty into her confidence, for, oddly enough, although it might be allowable for herself to seek relief from her difficulties with Mr. King, for Letty to do the same thing would be quite shocking. And she could not help feeling that that was just what Letty would do, once the idea had been put into her head, for she was never out of debt, and had lately been warned by Cardross that he was not going to encourage her extravagant habits by continuing to defray all the totally unnecessary expenses she incurred.

Nell dressed herself with great care for her expedition, choosing from the formidable collection of walking dresses in her wardrobe one of cambric, made high to the neck, and with long sleeves, and only a border of cable trimming to relieve its austerity. For some reason which she could not have explained she felt that when one visited a moneylender one's habit should be as modest as possible, so she added a sarsnet pelisse of dark blue to her ensemble. This lent her an undeniable note of sobriety, but when it came to the selection of a hat the only one she possessed that approached sobriety was made of olive brown silk. No exigency could induce her to wear this with a blue pelisse, so she was obliged to choose instead a frivolous bonnet that matched the pelisse but was trimmed with lace and flowers. A thick veil served the double purpose of providing a disguise and a touch of rather dowdy respectability. It also staggered her dresser, and certainly made her suspicious; but Nell said glibly that the dust from the streets had slightly roughened her cheeks, an explanation which seemed to satisfy Miss Sutton.

Set down at the Bath Gate, Nell entered the Green Park, and strolled for a little while beside the Basin, trying to recruit her ebbing courage. Two unwelcome thoughts had occurred to her: Mama, when she had turned in desperation to Mr. King, had employed a go-between; and would not Mr. King wish to know her identity? She had not previously considered this possibility, but as she rehearsed, during the drive from Grosvenor Square, what she must say at the coming interview she realized that not the most obliging moneylender was in the least likely to advance a large sum of money to an unknown and heavily veiled lady. Not only would he wish to know what were the circumstances of his client, but no doubt he would demand a note of hand from her. One might, of course, sign this with a fictitious name, but that would hardly satisfy Mr. King. Nell was quite shrewd enough to know that an obscure Mrs. Smith of no address would find it very much harder to borrow money upon interest than would the wife of an extremely wealthy peer.

A good deal daunted, it was with lagging steps that she left the Park, and crossed the ruts and cobbles of Piccadilly. Her errand no longer seemed so innocuous, for while it would be a simple matter, and surely quite unembarrassing, to arrange a loan under a cloak of anonymity, it was another matter altogether to be obliged to announce: "I am Lady Cardross."

She turned into Clarges Street, and was soon abreast of the discreet-looking house in which Mr. King carried on his business. She hesitated, saw that a man on the opposite side of the street was looking at her, and walked on, blushing under her veil. When she ventured to look round, he had disappeared from her view, so she turned, and began to walk back. By this time she was wishing herself a hundred miles away, dreading what lay before her, no longer sustained by the comforting reflection that it was not so very wrong, after all. A small but insistent inner voice told her that on this occasion Mama would not wish her example to be copied; and again she walked past Mr. King's house.

From a window in a house on the other side of the street Mr. Hethersett had for several minutes been observing these vacillations through his quizzing-glass. The particular crony whom he had come to visit, having addressed several remarks to him without receiving any other answer than an absent-minded grunt, at last demanded if anything was amiss, and came to see what was claiming his attention. Mr. Hethersett, letting his glass fall on the end of its ribbon, ejaculated: "Good God!" and hastily picked up his hat and gloves. "Can't stay!" he said. "Remembered something important!"

His astonished friend protested, but Mr. Hethersett, in general polite to a point, did not stay to listen. He was out of the house in a matter of seconds, and crossing the street with long strides.

Nell, drawing a resolute breath, had mounted the first of the steps leading to Mr. King's front door when she heard herself accosted in slightly breathless accents.

"Cousin!" said Mr. Hethersett.

She jumped, and looked round. Mr. Hethersett raised the hat from his head and executed the bow for which he was famous. "Very happy to have met you!" he said. "Beg you will allow me to escort you home!"

"Sir!" uttered Nell, in what she hoped was the outraged voice of a stranger.

Apparently it was not. "Can't hope to deceive me in that bonnet," explained Mr. Hethersett apologetically. "Wore it the day I drove you to the Botanic Gardens." Acutely aware of the goggling gaze fixed on him from a window across the

street, he added: "Take my arm! George Burnley has his eye
on us, and it won't do for him to recognize you. Not that I
think he will, but no sense in running the risk."

"I am very much obliged to you, but pray don't stay for me!"
Nell said, trying to speak in a careless way. "I—I have some
business to transact!"

"Yes, I know. That's why I came across the road."

"You *know*?" she repeated, rather scared. "But you cannot
know, Felix! Besides——"

"What I mean is, know whose house this is," he explained.
"It ain't any concern of mine, but it won't do for you to be
doing business with Jew King, cousin. What's more, if
Cardross knew——"

"You won't tell Cardross?" she cried involuntarily.

He was just about to refute with considerable indignation
the suggestion that he was a tale-bearer when prudence intervened. He temporized. "I won't tell him if you let me escort
you home. If you don't, nothing else for me to do."

"Felix, I never thought you could be so ungentlemanly!"

"No," he agreed. "To tell you the truth, I didn't either. But
the thing is it would be a dashed sight more ungentlemanly to
go off and leave you to get into a pickle. Jew King! Lord,
cousin, do you know the fellow owns an ornamental villa on
the river? Slap up to the nines—never saw such a place in your
life!"

"No, and I don't see what that has to say to anything!"
retorted Nell crossly.

"Point is, where did he find the blunt to pay for it? From
people like you, cousin! Take my word for it!"

"Yes, yes, but I only wish for a loan for a particular reason,
just—just a very temporary one!"

He drew her hand through his arm, and obliged her to walk
with him up the street. "Believe me, fatal!" he said earnestly.

She sighed, but attempted no further argument. After a

pause, Mr. Hethersett coughed, and said delicately: "Very reluctant to offend you—awkward sort of a business! Thing is, might be able to be of service. Tolerably plump in the pocket, you know."

She was a good deal touched, but said at once: "No, indeed! I am sure there was never anyone half as kind as you, Felix, but *that* would be the outside of enough! And you mustn't suppose that I am in the habit of borrowing money: this—there are reasons—why I don't wish to apply to Cardross for this particular sum! Don't let us talk about it! It is of no moment, after all."

"Certainly not: shouldn't dream of prying into your affairs, cousin!" he replied. "Only wish to say—at least, I don't, but must!—feel myself obliged to ask you to give me your word you won't come running back here as soon as my back's turned!"

She sighed, but said submissively: "No, I won't do that, if you think it so very bad."

"Worst thing in the world!" he assured her.

"I don't see why it should be. After all——"

"You may not see why, but it ain't a bit of use telling me you didn't know it, because I've been watching you," said Mr. Hethersett severely. "Going backwards and forwards like a cat on a hot bake-stone!"

"Oh, how can you say such an uncivil thing?" she protested. "I did *not*!"

"That's what it looked like to me," he said, with great firmness. "Not the moment for civility, either. Got a great regard for you, cousin. Dashed fond of Giles, too. Wouldn't wish to see either of you in a tangle. Thing is—nothing he wouldn't give you! Officious thing to do—giving you advice—but if you're in a fix you tell him, not Jew King!"

She said unhappily: "There are circumstances which—— Oh, I can't explain it to you, but he musn't know of this!"

To her relief he forbore to press her. She would have been dismayed, however, had she known the construction he had put on her words.

Mr. Hethersett, who had so strongly disapproved of his cousin's alliance with any member of Lord Pevensey's family, had now the doubtful felicity of realizing how just had been his objections to the marriage. If Nell had incurred a debt she dared not disclose to Cardross, it was as plain as a pikestaff that she had embroiled herself in her brother's chaotic affairs. In Mr. Hethersett's view that was almost the only form of expenditure Cardross would not tolerate in his wife. Probably he would not take gaming debts in good part either, but Mr. Hethersett did not think that Nell was a gamester. He had once struggled to support her through several rubbers of whist, an experience which had left him in doubt of her ability to distinguish spades from clubs.

He had made his offer to rescue her from her embarrassments in good faith, but he was considerably relieved by her instant refusal of it. He enjoyed a considerable independence, but the last settling-day at Tattersall's had not been happy, and to have advanced what he feared must be a very large sum of money to Nell must have left him in uncomfortably straitened circumstances. It might also, if the truth leaked out, have involved him in a quarrel with Cardross, who would certainly feel that he had behaved in a very improper way. Cardross was a man of calm judgment, so it was perhaps unlikely that he would suspect his cousin of having formed a warmer attachment for Nell than was seemly. At the same time, there was no predicting what crackbrained notion a man deeply in love might take into his head; and Mr. Hethersett was uneasily aware that by assuming the rôle of Nell's cicisbeo-in-chief he had certainly laid himself open to attack. Nor had he the smallest desire to contribute towards Dysart's relief. Mr. Hethersett, a gentleman of the first respectability, and a high stickler in all matters of taste and conduct, disapproved unequivocally of such dashing blades as Dysart. Such feats as jumping one's horse over a loaded dinner-table awoke no admiration in his breast, for anything that set people in an uproar was bad ton, and to be in bad ton was to be beyond pardon. The world of fashion might embrace all manner of men: the Out-and-Outers, the Tulips, the Dashes, Tippies, and Bloods: but the first style of elegance could only be achieved by those whose dress and deportment were characterized by an exquisite moderation. Dysart was never moderate. In the saddle he was a hard-goer; on the road his ambition was to give the go-by to every other vehicle; in the gaming-room, not content, like Mr. Hethersett, to sport a little blunt on the table, he played deep. He engaged in hare-brained pranks; and the chances were that if you met him any time after noon you would find him ripe already. None but the very strait-laced objected, of course, to a man's becoming foxed during the course of a convivial evening; but either Dysart had an uncommonly weak head, or he was carrying his drinking propensity beyond the line of what was acceptable. As for his debts, he had been monstrously in the wind at the time of his sister's marriage, and he had had ample time, since being relieved by Cardross of his more pressing obligations, to run himself to a standstill again. It would be typical of him, Mr. Hethersett considered, to apply to his sister for succour; and ridiculous to suppose that she could bring herself to deny him. He did not blame her in the least, but he was strongly of the opinion that such reckless generosity ought to be checked before it had run to such lengths as must put her as well as Dysart heavily in debt. A hazy recollection of the appalling load of debt under which Devonshire's mother had died flitted through his mind. Astronomical figures had been whispered: probably false, for no one knew the exact truth, but it must have been a monstrous sum. It was said she had lost a huge fortune at play: queer sort of fellow the old Duke must have been, not to have known what his wife was about, thought Mr. Hethersett. Things would never get to that pitch of disaster in Cardross's household, of course; still, they might become pretty bad before he discovered what was happening. He was rich enough to be able to stand the nonsense, but Mr. Hethersett had a very fair idea of what his feelings would be if he found Nell out in such deception. Someone, he decided, ought to drop him a hint now, before any serious mischief had been done, and while he was still so much in love with Nell that he would find it easy to excuse her folly. He was inclined for a moment to regret having promised Nell he would not betray her to Cardross; but as soon as he played with the notion of making such a disclosure to his cousin his imagination boggled at it. Under no circumstances could he have done it. The proper person to intervene was Lady Pevensey, and had she been in town he might, he thought, have contrived to hint her on to the trouble. Only she was miles away, tied to that ramshackle husband of hers, and there was no saying, after all, that she would see the matter as she ought: she had never seemed to Mr. Hethersett to have much more wit than a pea-goose; besides, she doted on Dysart so fondly that she might possibly think his interests of more importance than Nell's.

Nell's voice, would-be cheerful, but decidedly nervous, intruded on these ruminations. "You are very silent!" she said.

"I beg pardon!" he said. "I was thinking."

"About—about *this*?" she asked anxiously.

"No," he said unblushingly. "Thinking we should take a look-in at Gunter's. You'd like an ice, I daresay. Just the thing!"

She thanked him, but declined the treat. She would have

declined the offer of a chair to carry her home, too, but on this point Mr. Hethersett was firm, knowing well what was due to her consequence. To be strolling through the streets of London with only himself as escort would not do for Lady Cardross. So he beckoned to a couple of chairmen before suggesting to her that he should do so, handed her into the chair, and completed his politeness by walking beside it to Grosvenor Square, and engaging her in a commonplace conversation that gave her to understand that he had dismissed the episode in Clarges Street from his mind.

RESCUED from the perils of Clarges Street, and restored to the shelter of her own house, Nell hardly knew whether to be grateful to Mr. Hethersett for having thrust a spoke in her wheel, or resentful. When the moment had come for knocking on Mr. King's door she had certainly been extremely reluctant to do so, and had suffered very much the same sensations as if she had been about to have a tooth drawn; but her dependance now was all on Dysart, whom she had not seen since the night of the masquerade, and who might, for anything she knew, have taken a pet at having his ingenious plot frustrated, or (which was even more likely) have forgotten all about her troubles. She and Letty were going to the Opera that evening, where it was extremely improbable that she would meet him; so she wrote a letter to him, telling him how urgent her need had become, and begging him he would call in Grosvenor Square.

She had hardly despatched this missive, by the hand of her footman, when Letty came in. In general, when Letty went shopping, she returned laden with parcels, and eager to display to her sister-in-law a collection of expensive frivolities which had happened to catch her eye; but on this occasion she had nothing to show but a disconsolate face. She said she had had a stupid morning, but when Nell asked if she had been unable to find a muslin she liked, she replied; "Oh, yes! Martha has it. I met my cousins, and went with them to Grafton House, all amongst the quizzy people. Selina *would* have me go, because she said there were amazing bargains to be had there. I must say, they had a great many muslins. I chose a checked one, but I daresay I shan't like it above half when it is made up. It cost seven shillings the yard, too, and I don't consider *that* a bargain, do you?"

"No, but checked muslin is always dearer than the plain colours. I hope the Miss Thornes are quite well?" Nell said politely.

"Yes—at least, I didn't enquire. Selina seemed pretty stout. Fanny was gone with my aunt to Mrs. Mee, to arrange to have her likeness taken. They are persuaded Humby means to come to the point, and Selina says my aunt and uncle are in transports, though I can't think why they should be, for he presents a very off appearance, don't you think? besides having some odd humours."

"I don't know that. I believe he is very respectable," Nell responded, wondering whether her cousin's approaching betrothal was accountable for the clouded look on Letty's vivid little face. "I collect it was Mrs. Thistleton, then, who was with Miss Selina Thorne?"

"Yes, and I can tell you I was soon wishing her at the deuce!" said Letty, with a disgusted pout. "She is increasing, and bent on telling the whole of London! You would suppose no one had ever before been in her situation, for she can talk of nothing else! And then what must we do but walk into Lady Eastwell! *She* expects to be confined next month, and nothing could be like her simperings and sighings and affectations! Sir Godfrey is *aux anges* over the *petit paquet* she means to present to him. *Petit paquet! Un très grand paquet,* I should think, for I never saw anyone so large! I was vexed to death, dawdling along in her company, and being obliged to listen to such insipid stuff! And Maria at least was used to be the most entertaining creature! I do hope *you* won't turn into a bothersome bore when you start increasing, Nell!"

The colour rushed up into Nell's cheeks; she said: "I hope not, indeed!" but in a constricted voice, for Letty's careless words had touched her on the raw. It was some months since Lady Pevensey, tearing herself away from her stricken lord to visit her daughter, had soothed an anxiety which was even then teasing Nell. "Think nothing of it, dearest!" she had said, adding, with simple pride: "You are like me, and you know I had been married for three years before dear Dysart was born."

Nell had been comforted; and although the prospect of being obliged to wait for three years before she gave Cardross an heir was dismal, it was permissible to indulge the hope that she might find herself in an interesting situation considerably earlier than had Mama. And since Cardross, neither by word nor by look, gave the least sign of disappointment, and her mind was pleasantly occupied with the manifold gaieties of fashionable life, she had not thought very much about it. But Letty's petulant remark was ill-timed: her quite uninteresting situation now seemed to Nell of a piece with all the rest of her iniquities. She was proving herself to be in every way a deplorable wife: foolish, deceitful, spendthrift, and barren!

Fortunately, since her deep blush betrayed her, Letty had picked up the latest number of the *Ladies' Magazine,* and was contemptuously flicking over the pages, and commenting disparagingly on the fashions depicted in this valuable periodical, so that Nell had time in which to recover her countenance.

"Good heavens, I never saw anything so dowdy! . . . Slate-coloured twilled sarsnet, lined with white—*what* a figure to make of oneself! . . . Do these new Bishop-sleeves hit your fancy? I don't think them pretty at all, and as for this evening gown, with French braces over the bodice——!"

"I liked the picture of the pelisse, with the round cape," Nell said, trying to infuse her voice with interest.

"For my part, I think it no more than tolerable. Unless one is a regular Long Meg, those capes make one appear positively *squat*! Hair-brown merino, too! Horridly drab!" Letty cast the *Ladies' Magazine* aside, and, after hesitating for a moment, said, in a voice whose carelessness was a little studied: "By the by, I shall have to cry off going with you to Somerset House tomorrow, Nell. Selina has been telling me that my aunt is hipped because I have not been to visit her quite lately, and is saying she had not thought I could show such a want of affection, or have my head turned so utterly that I don't any longer care to be with her. You know how it is with her! She is cast into raptures, or down in a minute. So, if you do not very particularly wish to look at pictures tomorrow—I daresay they will be a dead bore, too!—I think I should go to my aunt's, and make her comfortable again."

Nell agreed to it, though she might, had she been less preoccupied, have wondered at Letty's sudden concern for Mrs. Thorne's comfort. That Mrs. Thorne might be piqued by a lack of proper observance could surprise no one who knew Letty, for without having the least ill-nature, or want of disposition to render attention where it was due, she had never been taught to consider the feelings of others, or to consult any convenience but her own. Having so easily won Nell's acquiescence, she took herself off to her own bedchamber, there to peruse for the third time the very disturbing letter she had received from Mr. Allandale.

Nell waited in vain for Dysart to put in an appearance that afternoon. Her footman brought back no answer to her note, his lordship having gone out. No, his lordship's man had not been able to say when he expected him to return.

His lordship did not return to his rooms, in fact, until an advanced hour of the day; and since he was engaged to dine at Watier's, with a select company of his intimates, and afterwards to try his luck at that most exclusive of gaming-clubs, it was rather too much to expect him to keep the best dinner in town waiting while he danced attendance in Grosvenor Square. A fortunate bet had (as he phrased it) brought the dibs into tune again, and encouraged him to think that a long run of bad luck had come to an end. With a little ready to sport on the table there was no saying but what he might by the end of the evening be in a position to settle any number of damned dressmakers' bills, and through no more exertion than was required to cast, instead of the worst chances in the game, a few winning nicks. Inured by custom to all the stratagems known to creditors, he considered that Madame Lavalle's story of being about to put herself out of the way of collecting the monies due to her was a piece of gammon. In his experience, no creditor ever put himself out of the way of collecting money. Having pursued a precarious course for some years, he was not at all alarmed by duns, and thought that Nell was being more than commonly gooseish. However, he was fond of her, and if she was as sick with apprehension as her letter seemed to indicate he would not, on the following morning, grudge an hour spent in soothing her alarms. Moreover, the morning might find him out of ebb-water, and hosed and shod again, for it was nothing for a man enjoying a run of luck to win three or four thousand pounds in one night's sitting at the Great Go.

It might have been thought that a club where the minimum stake was double the sum fixed at any other gaming establishment, and the play was known to be tremendous, was scarcely the place for a young blood, living on an inadequate allowance and a grossly encumbered expectation. The Viscount's well-wishers shook their heads over it, but they could scarcely blame him for playing there, since he had become a member of the club under the auspices of his own father. In general an indifferent parent, Lord Pevensey every now and then awoke to a sense of his responsibilities. Finding that his heir, after an adventurous period at Oxford, had established himself in London and was about to make his début in fashionable circles, he had felt that it behoved him to do what lay within his power to launch him into society. He introduced him to White's and to Watier's; franked him into the subscriptionroom at Tattersall's; pointed out to him certain individuals whose business in life it was to diddle the dupes; recommended him to let none but Weston make his coats; advised him to purchase his hats at Baxter's, and to have his boots made by Hoby; and warned him of the dangers of offering a carte blanche to too high-flying an Incognita. He was obliging enough to instruct his son in some of the signs by which he might recognize, amongst the muslin company, those prime articles who might be depended on to ease a protector of all his available blunt; and to counsel him strongly not to visit any but the highest class Academies. After that, and feeling that he had left nothing undone to ensure for the Viscount a prosperous career, he cast off his parental responsibilities, which had by that time begun to bore him very much, and left his son to his own devices.

Watier's, which was situated on the corner of Bolton Street and Piccadilly, in an unpretentious house which had once been a gaming establishment of quite a different order, was generally supposed to owe its existence to the Prince Regent. Watier had been one of his cooks, but the Prince, upon learn- nig from some of his friends that a good dinner was not to be had at any of the London clubs, had conceived the benevolent notion of providing gentlemen of high ton with a dining-club not just in the common style, and had suggested to Watier that he was the very man to carry out this pleasing design. The idea took; in partnership with two other of the royal servants Mr. Watier embarked on the venture, and prospered so well that within a very few years he was able to retire from active participation in the business of running the club. By that time what had begun as a dining-club, with excellent cooking, carefully chosen wines, and harmonic assemblies as its attractions, had blossomed into the most exclusive as well as the most ruinous of all London's gaming clubs. The dinners, under the surveillance of Mr. Augustus

Labourie, continued to be the best that could be had in town; it had a bank of ten thousand pounds; Mr. Brummell was its perpetual president; and to be admitted to membership was the object of every aspirant to fashion. Play began at nine o'clock, and continued all night, the principal games being hazard, and macao: a form of vingt-un introduced into England by the emigrés from France, and still enjoying a considerable vogue.

The Viscount, after an evening devoted to faro, had not found that this alteration in his habits answered as well as he had hoped it might; and when he rose from a very convivial dinner he resisted all attempts to lure him into the macao-room. He would give the bones another chance, he said, for he had a strong presentiment that fortune was at last about to favour him. So, indeed, it seemed. Being set twenty pounds, and naming seven as the main, he threw eleven, nicking it, which promised well for the night's session. Even Mr. Fancot, who had been trying to lose money to him for months and had begun to despair of achieving his ambition, felt hopeful.

From the circumstance of the Prince Regent's holding one of his bachelor parties at Carlton House that evening, the club was rather thin of company. Mr. Hethersett, strolling in at midnight, found the macao-room deserted by all but a collection of persons who figured in his estimation either as prosy old stagers or tippies on the strut. He took a look-in at those intent on hazard, but here again the company failed to attract him, and he was just about to leave the premises when he was suddenly smitten by an idea. It was not a very welcome idea, nor did he look forward with the least degree of pleasure to the putting of it into action, but it was the best that had occurred to him during the course of a day largely devoted to wrestling with the problem of Lady Cardross's financial difficulties.

The more he considered this matter the greater had grown his uneasiness, for the mild *tendre* he felt for Nell did not lead him to place any very firm trust in her promise to keep away from usurers. A just man, he was obliged to own that if she dared not confess her debts to Cardross no other solution than to borrow upon interest suggested itself. In his opinion, she was magnifying Cardross's wrath rather absurdly. It was unlikely that he would hear the confession with complaisance, but he was not only a man very much in love; he was also a man of generous temper, and a good deal more than common sense. No one would be quicker to make allowance for youth and inexperience; and although there could be little doubt that he had forbidden Nell to keep her brother in funds Mr. Hethersett had still less doubt that he would understand, and even sympathize with, the very natural feelings which had led her to disobey him. He would know how to put a stop to such practices, too; and that was something that ought to be done immediately, if Nell was not to founder at the last in a morass of debt and deception. Cardross would pardon her now with no loss of tenderness, but if he discovered in the future that she had been playing an undergame with him, perhaps for years, the very openness of his disposition would cause him to regard her with revulsion.

Mr. Hethersett, gloomily pondering, had reached the conclusion that although it would be of some advantage if his cousin were to be put in possession of the facts by almost any agency, the only happy outcome to the affair would be for Nell herself to make the disclosure. But when he had urged her to do so she had recoiled from the suggestion, and had begged him in considerable agitation not to betray her to Cardross. The suspicion had crossed his mind that all might not be so well with that marriage as appeared on the surface. Thinking it over, it occurred to him that the couple were not as often in company together as might have been expected. It was not, of course, in good *ton* for a man to live in his wife's pocket; but the cynicism which had prompted the higher ranks of the previous generation to regard marriage as a means of advancement or convenience was going out of fashion. Amongst his father's contemporaries, Mr. Hethersett knew of more than one man who could never be sure how many of his lady's offspring had been fathered by himself; while the number of middle-aged couples of the first stare who never willingly spent as much as half an hour together was past counting. But that sort of thing was going out of fashion. Love-matches were being indulged in by persons of consequence; and public signs of affection, instead of being thought intolerably bourgeois, were even smiled on. Mr. Hethersett, whose fastidiousness had lately been offended by the sight of a newly-married pair seated side by side on a small sofa with their heads together at an evening party, was inclined to think that the pendulum was swinging too far, and he certainly did not expect Cardross to behave with such a want of breeding. At the same time, he did sometimes wonder that Nell, married to a man who had not only chosen her, for love, from amongst a dozen more eligible ladies, but was also possessed of a charm which made him generally fascinating to females, should so frequently appear in public either unescorted, or with some quite inferior gallant at her side. There was nothing to take exception to in that, of course; and never anything in her manner towards her admirers to encourage the most inveterate seekers after crim. cons to suspect her of having formed a guilty attachment. Mr. Hethersett was pretty well persuaded that she had no eyes for any man but Cardross: he had seen them light up when his cousin had unexpectedly entered a room where she was sitting. No: he did not think that if anything had gone amiss with the marriage it arose from any lack of affection. He recollected having heard it said that in love-matches even more than marriages of convenience the first year was often one of tiffs and misunderstandings, and decided that so much profound cogitation was leading him to refine too much upon the couple's public conduct. But if there had been disagreements, Mr. Hethersett, knowing just how formidable his cousin could be when he was angered, could readily understand the reluctance of his very young bride to confide her sins to him. It would be useless to press her to do so, he thought; but having reached this conclusion he found himself at a stand, for there was no one other than herself who could tell Cardross of the fix she was in without setting up his back.

But just as he was about to leave the hazard-room, Dysart, who had been too deeply concerned with the fall of the dice to notice his entrance, happened to look up, and to see him. He called a careless greeting, and on the instant Mr. Hethersett was smitten by his idea.

If he could be persuaded to do it, Dysart was the one person who could tell Cardross, unexceptionably, even, perhaps, with advantage, the truth. Mr. Hethersett had no doubt at all that Nell's debts had been incurred on his behalf, and very little that a frank confession made by him of the whole would win plenary absolution for Nell, and in all probability pecuniary assistance for himself. It would be an easy matter for him to convince Cardross that Nell had yielded only to his urgent entreaties; and Cardross would be swift to recognize and to appreciate the courage that enabled him to perform so un-pleasant a duty. Only, did he possess that courage? Mr. Hethersett, joining the scattering of lookers-on gathered round the table, glanced speculatively at him, considering the matter. Physical courage he certainly possessed to a pronounced degree; but in spite of taking a perverse pride in being thought a Care-for-Nobody he had not as yet given anyone reason to suppose that he had any strength of moral character. Mr. Hethersett, several years his senior and a man of a different kidney, was not one of his friends, and even less one of his admirers, but he did him the justice to acknowledge that although he was a resty young blade, decidedly loose in the haft, incorrigibly spendthrift, and ready at any moment to plunge into whatever extravagant folly was suggested to him by his impish fancy, he had never been known, even in his most reckless mood, to step over the line that lay between the venial peccadilloes of a wild youth and such questionable exploits as must bring his name into dishonour. He was both generous and goodnatured, and Mr. Hethersett rather thought that he held his sister in considerable affection. He knew, too, that Cardross, better acquainted with him, and increasingly exasperated by his starts, by no means despaired of him. Without going to the length of forecasting for him a future distinguished by sobriety or solvency, he said that if a cornetcy could but be provided for him he would find an outlet for his restless energy, and might do tolerably well.

"He may be a scamp," said Cardross, "but there's no sham in him—nothing of the dry-boots! It would give me great pleasure to go sharply to work with him—but he's pluck to the backbone, and I own I like that."

Mr. Hethersett had a great respect for his cousin's judgment, and, remembering these words, he made up his mind to have at least a touch at Dysart. Since the task was not one he looked forward to with relish, he thought that the sooner it was accomplished the better it would be, and decided that unless Dysart arose from the table a loser he would broach the matter that very day. From the flush in the Viscount's cheeks, and the over-brightness of his eyes, he had at first glance supposed him to be a trifle foxed; but he soon realized that for once he had wronged him. The Viscount, whose exuberance could lead him to become top-heavy at almost any hour of the day, was by far too keen a gamester to join a gaming-table when in his altitudes. There was certainly a glass at his elbow, but the brandy it held sank hardly at all during the time Mr. Hethersett stood watching the play, and from time to time making his bet on the odds monotonously declared by the groom-porter.

The table broke up at a comparatively early hour, even the Viscount agreeing, after a series of throw-outs, that the game had become languid and boring. He did not rise a loser, but his winnings were not large. However, when one of the company joked him about his uncertain luck, saying that he would be obliged to go back to faro after all, he replied cheerfully that only a muttonhead could have been blind to the signs of reviving fortune that night. "Not a vowel of mine on the table!" he said.

"And upwards of forty guineas in your purse!" added Mr. Fancot encouragingly. "To my mind, that clinches it, Dy: stick to the bones!"

"Yes, I think I shall," agreed Dysart. "Dashed if I won't try my luck at this new house Jack was talking to me about! I remember my father's telling me once that he often found it answered to shift one's ground."

Lord Pevensey's notorious unsuccess as a gamester notwithstanding, everyone, except Mr. Hethersett, thought that the Viscount could hardly do better than follow his advice, only one slightly muddled gentleman demurring that no one should play at a hell who was not up to the sharps. But as he became hopelessly incoherent in his subsequent attempt to illustrate this remark by recounting the sad history of a flat who went from a nibble at a club to a dead hit at a hell, no one paid any heed to him.

The morning light was faintly illumining the scene when the party dispersed on the steps of the club. Mr. Hethersett, who knew that it might be days before he again found the opportunity to approach Dysart, considerably surprised him by suggesting that they should bear one another company on the way to their respective lodgings. "Duke Street, isn't it?" he said. "Take a look in at my place, and play off your dust! All on our way, and the night's young yet."

Dysart looked at him, suspecting him of being slightly mellow. He showed no sign of it, but Dysart, perfectly well aware of his disapprobation, could think of no other reason to account for his sudden friendliness. Before he had had time to answer him, Mr. Fancot, who lived in St. James's Square, and had sent the porter out to procure a hackney, generously offered to take both him and Mr. Hethersett up, and to set them down again at their lodgings.

"Very much obliged to you," responded Mr. Hethersett, a shade of annoyance in his face. "Think I'll walk, however. Devilish stuffy in the club tonight: need a breath of air!" He met the Viscount's alert, speculative gaze, and said curtly: "Got something to tell you!"

"Have you though?" said Dysart, considerably intrigued. "I'll go along with you, then!"

They left the club together, but were overtaken almost immediately by a gregarious gentleman, who fell into step with them, saying chattily that since his destination was in King Street he would walk with them. His company was accepted cheerfully by Dysart, and by Mr. Hethersett, who foresaw that he would be difficult to shake off, with resignation. It would be a hard task to avoid the necessity of including him in his invitation to Dysart, but he was determined to do it, however much it went against the grain with him to appear inhospitable.

He managed to perform this feat at the cost of standing patiently at the corner of Ryder Street and St. James's, while the Viscount and Mr. Wittering maintained for twenty minutes an argument which had been started before the party had crossed over to the south side of Piccadilly. It was pursued with considerable animation, and it afforded Mr. Hethersett, mildly contributing his mite whenever he was granted the opportunity, with a novel view of the Viscount. The victory of Bonaparte at Lützen over General Wittgenstein, commanding the combined forces of Russia and Prussia, had not long been known in London, and was still being much discussed. Shaking his head over the disaster, Mr. Wittering expressed the opinion that there was no doing anything against Boney, and never would be. Since this pessimism was shared by many, such remarks having been heard for years past at any social gathering, Mr. Hethersett did not think it worth while to reply. It was otherwise with the Viscount. He was ready to agree that none of the foreign generals could have the smallest hope of defeating Boney, but he recommended Mr. Wittering to wait and see how quickly Wellington would knock him into flinders. Mr. Wittering said disparagingly that a victory or two in Spain made no odds; the Viscount instantly offered to bet a monkey that the English army would be over the Pyrenees before the year was out; and the argument rapidly became heated. Mr. Wittering, no supporter of the Wellesleys, was unwise enough to say that Wellington's victories had been exaggerated; and within a very few minutes was not only being dragged relentlessly through the previous year's campaigns, but was being given a lesson in strategy into the bargain. To Mr. Hethersett's surprise, the Viscount, whom he had always supposed to be perfectly feather-headed, not only appeared to be passionately interested in the subject, but had very obviously studied it with some thoroughness. Mr. Wittering, on the retreat, acknowledged that Wellington was a good defensive general, but added that he was too cautious, and had no brilliance in attack.

"No brilliance in attack?" demanded the Viscount. "*After Salamanca?*"

"Well, I don't know about Salamanca," said Mr. Wittering unguardedly. "All I say is——"

But the Viscount cut him short. Mr. Hethersett, standing in patient boredom while armies manœuvred about him, and the Viscount drew invisible lines on the flagway with the point of his cane, reflected that it would henceforward be impossible for Mr. Wittering to say (if there was any truth in him) that he didn't know about Salamanca. When Dysart, passing from the general to the particular, spoke of Le Marchant's charge, he did so with so much enthusiasm that Mr. Hethersett was moved to say that he seemed to know as much about it as if he had taken part in it.

'By Jove, don't I wish I had!" Dysart said impulsively.

"Well," said Mr. Wittering, preparing to take his leave, "what you ought to do, Dy, is to join! I shouldn't wonder at it if you got to be a general. You go and tell old Hook-nose what you want him to do! There's no saying but what it *might* make him break up from cantonments before the summer's over!"

With this Parthian shot, he went off down the street, leaving the Viscount to explain to Mr. Hethersett that the lack of news from Wellington's headquarters undoubtedly presaged some brilliant move, probably in an unexpected direction. "Everyone thinks he means to march on Madrid again, but you mark my words if he don't strike north! He's kept his plans mighty dark this time, but I've been talking to a cousin of mine. You know my cousin Lionel?" Mr. Hethersett believed he had not that pleasure. "Been serving on one of our frigates," said the Viscount. "Sent home a month ago, on sick-furlough. Plain as a pikestaff all those fellows have been warned to keep their mummers dubbed, but one thing he did let slip: we've been landing stores along the northern coast. You can say they're for that guerilla-fellow, Longa, if you choose, but it don't look like it to me. No need to keep the thing so dark if that's all it is."

Mr. Hethersett did not avail himself of this permission, but said instead, glancing curiously up at his tall companion's profile: "Why *don't* you join?"

"Oh, I don't know!" replied Dysart, with a return to his customary insouciance. "I rather thought I should like to at one time, but I daresay I shouldn't. Anyway, my father won't hear of it."

Mr. Hethersett did not pursue the matter. He could only be thankful that his question seemed to have cast a damper over the Viscount's desire to fight past battles again. They had by this time reached his lodging. He ushered his guest into the comfortable parlour he rented on the entrance floor of the house, begged him to take a chair, and produced from a large sideboard a bottle of smuggled French cognac. "Eye-water?" he enquired. "Mix you a Fuller's Earth, if you like it better; or I've got a pretty tolerable madeira here."

The Viscount said he would take a drop of eye-water. He watched Mr. Hethersett pour some of the cognac into two heavy glasses, and remarked with engaging frankness that he was damned if he knew what Mr. Hethersett wanted with him. "Thought at first you must be a bit on the go, but you don't seem to be," he said.

Mr. Hethersett handed him one of the glasses. "Got something to tell you," he replied briefly.

"You haven't had a tip for the Chester races, have you?" asked Dysart hopefully.

"No: nothing like that." Mr. Hethersett took a fortifying sip of brandy. "Awkward sort of business. Been teasing me all day."

"It sounds to me like a dashed havey-cavey business!" said Dysart, eyeing him in astonishment.

"No, it ain't exactly that, though I don't mind telling you I'd as lief not break it to you," said Mr. Hethersett, who was finding his self-imposed task even more difficult to accomplish than he had foreseen.

"Good God, you ain't going to tell me you've been set on to tell me my father's slipped his wind?" exclaimed Dysart, sitting up with a jerk.

"No, of course I haven't!" said Mr. Hethersett, irritated. "Is it likely that I'd be the man to break that sort of news to you?"

"No, but if it comes to that you ain't the man to invite me at half-past four in the morning either!" retorted Dysart. "It's no use bamming me you've got a sudden fancy for my company, for I know dashed well you haven't."

"Never said anything of the sort. No objection to your company, mind, but it wasn't that I wanted. The thing is, it's a deuced delicate matter!"

"Well, I can't guess what the devil it can be, but there's no need to skirt around it!" said Dysart encouragingly. "In fact, I'd lief you cut line: I can stand a knock or two!"

Mr. Hethersett tossed off the rest of the brandy in his glass. "Concerns your sister," he said.

The Viscount stared at him. "Concerns my sister?" he repeated. "What the devil——?"

"Didn't think you'd like it," said Mr. Hethersett, with a gloomy satisfaction in the accuracy of his prognostication. "Don't like it myself. You know George Burnley?"

"*What?*" thundered the Viscount, setting his own glass down with such violence that he nearly broke it.

Mr. Hethersett winced, and protested. "No need to bellow at me!"

"No need to—— What has that ginger-hackled court-card to do with my sister?" demanded the Viscount, a very dangerous light in his eyes.

"Hasn't anything to do with her," replied Mr. Hethersett, faintly surprised. "What's more, though I don't say he ain't ginger-hackled, he ain't a court-card. Friend of mine. Dashed if I know why you should get into a miff just because you're asked if you're acquainted with him!"

"You said it concerned my sister Cardross!"

"Didn't say anything of the kind. At least, not about poor George. And if you weren't the biggest gudgeon on the town you'd know I wouldn't have said a word about it, if he *had* been concerned with her!" he added severely.

"Well, what has Burnley to do with it?" asked the Viscount, mollified, but impatient.

"Gave him a look-in this morning. He lives in Clarges Street."

"Yes, I know he does, and if that's all you wanted to tell me——"

"Got a house opposite Jew King's," said Mr. Hethersett, contemplating his elegant snuff-box with rapt attention.

There was a momentary silence. "Go on!" said Dysart grimly.

Mr. Hethersett glanced up at him. "Well, that's it," he said apologetically. "Saw Lady Cardross. Recognized her bonnet. Heavily veiled—no need to fear George knew her!"

"Are you saying she went into Jew King's place?"

"No. Meant to, but I stopped her."

"I'm much obliged to you, then! Bird-witted little fool!" said Dysart savagely.

"Don't have to be obliged to me: got a great regard for her! Besides, related to Cardross, you know! Dashed well had to stop her. Seemed to be all in a pucker. Very anxious I shouldn't blab to Cardross. Well, stands to reason I shouldn't!"

"No, my God! What did she tell you?"

"Just said she wanted a temporary loan. Something she was devilish anxious Cardross shouldn't discover. Told her I wouldn't say a word to Giles if she promised to give up the notion of borrowing from a cent-per-cent. So she did, but I ain't easy. Made up my mind the best thing to do was to tell you, Dysart."

The Viscount nodded, and got up. "Much obliged to you!" he said again. "I'll give her pepper for this. I told her that was no way to raise the recruits—damme, I forbade her to, now I come to think of it! Promised her I'd see all tidy. I might have done it, too, if she hadn't taken a distempered freak into her head. And why she should be cast into high fidgets only because she's a trifle scorched I'm damned if I know. Anyone would think Cardross was going to discover it tomorrow! Unless I miss my tip, there's no reason why he should ever know a thing about it, but it's no use expecting me to raise the wind in the twinkling of an eye. But that's women all over!"

He turned to pick up his great-coat. Mr. Hethersett watched him shrug himself into it. He was strongly tempted to let him go, but although he was not very hopeful of being able to prevail upon him to approach Cardross, he felt that it behoved him to make the attempt.

"Been thinking about it all day," he said. "Seems to me Cardross ought to know of it."

"Well, he ain't going to," replied Dysart shortly.

"Wouldn't do if he were to get wind of it," insisted Mr. Hethersett. "Wouldn't like it, if he found her ladyship had been hoaxing him."

"Now, don't you start fretting and fuming!" begged Dysart. "I told my sister I'd settle it, and so I will!"

"No business of mine, of course, but how?" asked Mr. Hethersett.

"By hedge or by stile," replied Dysart flippantly.

"It won't fadge. All to pieces yourself. Daresay you're thinking of a run of luck, but it ain't when one's run off one's legs that one gets the luck: more likely to be physicked! Ever noticed that it's pretty near always the best-breeched coves who win? Seems to me there's only one way you can help Lady Cardross."

Dysart looked at him with a slight frown creasing his brow. "Well, what is it?"

Mr. Hethersett took snuff with deliberation. "Best way out of the fix is for her to tell Cardross the whole. Tried to get her to do it, but she wouldn't hear of it. Seemed to be in the deuce of a quake. No use telling her not the slightest need. Got the notion fixed in her head. *I* can't tell him. The thing is for you to do it."

"*I* tell Cardross my sister's swallowed a spider, and is trying to break shins with Jew King?" gasped the Viscount. "Well, I thought you must be a trifle disguised when you asked me to come home with you, but I can see now that you're either ape-drunk, or touched in your upper works!"

"No, I ain't," replied Mr. Hethersett stolidly. "I know it's a dashed difficult thing to do: in fact, it needs a devilish good bottom, but they say you've got that."

"Bottom! A damned whiddling disposition is all I'd need, and I'll have you know that's something I've *not* got!" Dysart shot at him. "Cry rope on my own sister? By God, if I hadn't been drinking your brandy, damned if I wouldn't tip you a settler, Hethersett!"

Mr. Hethersett was thrown into disorder. It was not that he particularly feared the Viscount's fists, both of which were suggestively clenched; but that, in face of that fiery young man's quick wrath, the horrid suspicion assailed him that he had been doing him an injustice. This was a breach of *ton* the very thought of which made him turn pale. He hastened to make amends. "Beg you won't give the brandy a thought!" he said. "Not that I wish to sport a painted peeper, but shouldn't like you to feel yourself at a disadvantage. Boot might be on the other leg, too. What I mean is, not a thing I'm partial to, but I can mill my way out of a row."

"I should like to know what the devil you mean by thinking I'm the sort of rum touch who——"

"Spoke under a misapprehension!" said Mr. Hethersett. "Took a notion into my head! Stupid thing to do!"

"What notion?" demanded the Viscount.

Mr. Hethersett, much embarrassed, coughed. Upon the question's being repeated, with a good deal of emphasis, he said: "Couldn't think why Lady Cardross should be afraid to tell my cousin she was in debt. Very well acquainted with Cardross, you know. Boys together. Ready to swear he'd give her anything she wanted. Might be in a tweak if she'd taken to gaming, but it can't be that. I mean, she don't know one card from another! Occurred to me that perhaps it was something Cardross wouldn't allow." He once more studied the design on his snuff-box. "Might even have forbidden it. Mind you, very understandable thing for her to do! Persuaded my cousin would think it so, too. Natural affection, I mean."

"Are you saying you thought she was under the hatches because she'd lent her blunt to me?" demanded the Viscount.

"Only thing I could hit on!" pleaded Mr. Hethersett. "See I was mistaken, of course."

The Viscount was just about to tell him extremely forcefully that so far from being responsible for Nell's difficulties he had had nothing whatsoever to do with them when he suddenly remembered his own obligation to her. It was true that this had not put her in debt at the time; but it was equally true that it had made it impossible for her to pay, later, for a Chantilly lace court dress. For a moment he felt abominably ill-used. She had assured him that she was flush in the pocket; and it was rather too bad of her subsequently to run into debt, instead of exercising a little economy.

He eyed Mr. Hethersett smoulderingly. He had never liked the fellow above half, and to be unable to refute his ignoble suspicions made him seethe with rage. He wanted more than anything to plant him a facer, but since that also, under the circumstances, was impossible, he had to content himself with saying in a voice of ice: "Accept my thanks for your kind offices! And rest assured that you have no need to tease yourself further in the matter! I wish you good-night!"

With these dignified words he picked up his hat and cane, bowed stiffly to his host, and departed. Mr. Hethersett, closing the front door behind him, was left to mop his brow, and to wonder what would now be the outcome of the affair. Convinced of Dysart's innocence, he was still profoundly sceptical of his ability to rescue his sister from the River Tick.

NOT very many hours later Nell was surprised and gratified to receive a visit from her brother. She had been hopeful that he would call that day, but since his habits were by no means matutinal she had had no expectation of seeing him until after noon. She and Letty had returned to Grosvenor Square at eleven o'clock, after spending more than an hour walking in Hyde Park, and the Viscount reached the house just as they were rising from the breakfast-table. He declined an offer of breakfast, saying that all he wanted was a word with his sister. From his tone Nell was not encouraged to hope that he had hit upon a solution to her problem; and the look on his face warned her that something had happened to put him out of humour. Letty, with deplorable want of tact, informed him that he looked to be as cross as a cat, and demanded to know the reason. He replied that he was not at all cross, but wished to be private with his sister. Since this could only be regarded as a heavy set-down, Letty instantly took umbrage, and a very spirited dialogue ensued, during the course of which several personalities of an uncomplimentary nature were exchanged. The Viscount emerged victorious from the engagement, taking unhandsome advantage of his greater years, and informing Letty, with all the air of a sexagenarian, that pertness was neither proper nor pleasing in chits of her age. Unable to think of anything crushing enough to say in reply, Letty flounced out of the room, slamming the door behind her.

"How could you, Dy?" exclaimed Nell reproachfully. "I never heard anything so uncivil! And if we are to talk of impropriety, you know it is quite improper for you to be scolding Letty! *You* are not her brother."

"No, and thank God for it!" he returned. "If she don't take

care she'll grow into one of those hurly-burly women there's no bearing."

"But, Dy, why are you so out of reason cross?"

"I'll tell you!" he said awfully. "And don't put on any innocent airs, my girl, because you can't gammon me, or turn me up sweet by making sheep's eyes at me! You've been playing an undergame, and well you know it! What the devil did you mean by going off to Jew King after I'd told you I wouldn't have you dealing with a cent-per-cent?"

She looked a little conscience-stricken, but demanded hotly "Did Felix tell you that? I had not thought he could use me so shabbily!"

The Viscount was incensed with Mr. Hethersett, but he informed his erring sister, in a few pithy words, that she might think herself much obliged to him. He then drew a picture of the horrifying fates that overtook persons so corkbrained as to walk into the clutches of usurers; moralized in a very edifying way on the evils of improvidence; and demanded from Nell a solemn promise that she would never again try to visit Jew King, or any other moneylender. "And if you think jauntering to ruin is something to go into whoops over," he added wrathfully, "let me tell you that you much mistake the matter!"

"Oh, no, indeed I don't!" Nell said, trying to speak soberly. "It—it was just that I c-can't help laughing when you talk like that about being improvident, and careless, and—and all the things you are yourself, Dy!" She saw that this remark had had anything but a softening effect, and said contritely: "I will never do so again! Of course it would be very bad if I were to *continue* borrowing, but *that* I had not the least intention of doing. I should have paid the money back after quarter-day, I promise you!"

"I daresay! And have found yourself in the basket again before the cat had time to lick her ear! Don't I know it!"

returned the Viscount, with feeling. "And why the devil you had to meddle, when you knew I had the business in hand, the lord alone knows!"

"Yes, but I thought perhaps it would be better if I did the thing myself," said Nell frankly. "In case you did anything dreadful!"

"Oh, you did, did you? Coming it too strong, Nell! What the deuce should I do, pray?"

"Well, to own the truth," she confessed, "I was afraid you might hold someone up!"

"Afraid I might hold someone up?" gasped Dysart. "Well, upon my soul! A pretty notion you have of me, by God!"

"You held me up!" Nell pointed out. "And if I hadn't recognized you you would have robbed me—you know you would!"

"If that doesn't beat all hollow!" ejaculated Dysart. "When all I meant to do was to have sold your curst jewellery *for* you! If you think I should have kept a groat of the ready for myself, you're fair and far off, my girl!"

"No, but it *was* a desperate thing to do, Dy, and it quite cut up my peace. I can't but wonder what next you may do, which puts me in high fidgets. Because——"

"Gammon!" interrupted Dysart. "Why, I wasn't even going to take Letty's trinkets! What's more, this is all humdudgeon! You wouldn't have cared a button for losing your jewels—now, would you?"

"N-no, but——"

"And you'd have been devilish thankful *not* to have recognized me, if I'd handed over the dibs to you next day. And it's my belief," pursued the Viscount relentlessly, "that you'd have taken good care not to have asked me how I'd come by them!"

Stricken, she said: "Oh, Dy, I am sadly afraid that that is true! It is the most mortifying reflection, too!"

"Stuff!" said the Viscount contemptuously. "Now, there's

no need for you to sit there looking as blue as a razor, Nell! I don't mean to leave you in the lurch, I promise you. I've got one or two capital notions in my head, but I can't raise the wind all in a trice, so it ain't a bit of use fretting like a fly in a tar-box, and wanting to know every time you see me what I've been doing! Give me a week, and see if I don't have the business blocked at both ends!"

She regarded him in some apprehension. "*What* notions have you in your head, Dy?"

"Never you mind!" he replied crushingly. "*One* notion I've got is that the less you know about it the better!"

Her apprehension grew; she said: "I won't tease you, but I think I would *rather* know!"

"Yes, I daresay, but you can't expect me to pull you out from under the hatches if you turn maggotty every time I hit on a scheme," said the Viscount. "And that's just what you would do, for you seem to me to be regularly betwattled!"

"I am very sorry!" she said humbly. "I do try to take it with composure, but it is excessively hard to do so when one is in such affliction, Dy! Every time I hear the door-knocker I think it may perhaps be Lavalle, coming to demand her money from Cardross, and alarm suspends all my faculties!"

"Now, don't be such a goosecap, Nell!" recommended the Viscount, putting his arm round her shoulders and giving her a slight hug. "She won't do that. Not for a week or two, at all events. You may depend upon it she knows, if you don't, that it must take you a little while to raise the ready. Ay, and unless she's as big a greenhead as you are yourself, which it stands to reason she can't be, she knows you will pay her," he added shrewdly. "All she meant to do was to frighten you into paying down the dust as soon as possible. She'll give you a week's grace at the least, and very likely longer. When does Cardross come back to town?"

"On Monday, I think. I am not perfectly sure, but he said

that he would be away for a se'enight." Nell was silent for a moment, and then said, turning her face away: "I quite dread his coming, and *that* is more lowering than all the rest!"

He was spared the necessity of answering her by Letty's coming back into the room at that moment. She was wearing her hat, and a light shawl, draped gracefully across her elbows; and she had come merely to take leave of Nell, and to inform her that she should send the carriage back immediately from her aunt's house, in case her sister should be needing the services of the coachman. She pointedly ignored the Viscount, but kissed Nell's cheek very affectionately, and told her not to dream of sending the carriage to fetch her away from Bryanston Square, since her aunt would undoubtedly provide for her safe return.

"All that finery just for an aunt?" said Dysart, critically surveying her. "I must say, that's a deuced fetching bonnet!"

Becoming aware of his existence, Letty raised her brows as haughtily as she could, and said in freezing accents: "You are too kind, sir!"

"Silly chit!" said Dysart indulgently.

Her eyes flashed, but Nell intervened hastily, before she could again cross swords with her incorrigible tormentor. "You look charmingly," she assured her, edging her towards the door. "I will come and see you into the carriage. Will you be warm enough, do you think, with only that shawl?"

"No, I daresay I shan't be," Letty replied candidly, "but it is so dowdy to wear a pelisse!" She paused in the hall to draw on her gloves, and said in a brooding tone: "I don't wish to distress you, Nell, but I think Dysart is the most odious, uncivil person I ever met!"

Nell laughed. "Yes, indeed! I am sure you must. The thing is, you see, that because you are my sister he treats you as though you were his as well."

"*My* brother has a great many faults, but he doesn't use me in *that* fashion!"

"No, for he is so much older than you. If you had had one of your own age you wouldn't be such a goose as to let Dy put you in a miff," Nell said, smiling.

"I am excessively thankful that I have *not* one, and I assure you, Nell, I *feel* for you!"

"Thank you! Mine is a hard case indeed," Nell said, her eyes brimful of amusement. "You nonsensical creature! There, don't take me in aversion as well! Good-bye: you will say everything from me to your aunt that is proper, if you please. I fear she may hold me to blame for your neglect of her, but I hope she may give me credit for sparing you to her today."

She spoke lightly, but she was very sensible of Mrs. Thorne's claims on Letty. Cardross, believing that Letty's faults were to be laid at the poor lady's door, might wish to detach her from that household, but Nell could never bring herself to promote this object. Indeed, she had more than once suggested to Letty that she should pay her aunt a morning visit. It did not surprise her to learn that Mrs. Thorne thought herself ill-used, for she too thought that Letty showed sadly little observance to one who had stood to her in place of her mother. She would, in fact, have been very much surprised had she known that so far from begging her niece to visit her that morning Mrs. Thorne had not the smallest notion that she was to receive this treat, and had gone out with her daughter Fanny on a tour of the silk warehouses.

It was Miss Selina Thorne who awaited Letty; and as soon as she saw the carriage draw up outside the house she came running down from the drawing-room to greet her, which she did with every manifestation of surprise and delight, whispering, however, in a very dramatic way, as she kissed her: "Have no fear! All is safe!"

She then said, for the benefit of the servant who had admitted Letty into the house: "How glad I am I didn't go with Mama and Fanny! Come upstairs, love: I have a hundred things to tell you!"

She was a fine-looking girl, a little younger than Letty, but very much larger. Beside her exquisite cousin she appeared over-buxom, a little clumsy, but she did not resent this in the least. She was as good-natured as her mother, liked to think that she had a great deal of sensibility, and had so romantic a disposition that she was inclined to think real life wretchedly flat, and to fancy that she would have found herself very much more at home in one of Mrs. Radclyffe's famous novels. Having swept Letty up to the drawing-room, she shut the door, and said, lowering her voice conspiratorially: "My sweetest life, such a morning as I have had! I thought we must be wholly undone, for Mama almost commanded me to go with her! I was obliged to prevaricate a little: I said that I had a head-ache, and so it passed off at at last, though I was frightened almost out of my senses by her dawdling so much that it seemed she and Fanny would not be gone before you reached the house! How delightfully you look! Mr. Allandale will be in raptures!"

"If he doesn't fail!" Letty said. "I begged him most particularly to meet me here today, but it might not be possible, perhaps. If there is a press of business, you know, he might be detained all day at the Foreign Office. Only would he not have contrived to send me word?"

Miss Thorne was strongly of the opinion that the violence of Mr. Allandale's feelings would outweigh all other considerations. She drew Letty to the window, to watch for his arrival, for she had formed the intention of running down to admit him into the house before he could advertize his presence to the servants by knocking on the door. "For it would be *fatal* if Mama were to discover that he had been here! If her suspicions were aroused, depend upon it, she would instantly go to your brother, for she likes the connection as little as he does. She was talking about it only yesterday, calling it a shockingly bad match, and wondering that Mr. Allandale should be so *encroaching*! I kept my eyes lowered, and my thoughts *locked* in my bosom, but you may guess how I *felt,* on hearing such words from one whom I had believed to be all sensibility! Oh, my dearest Letty, I vowed to myself that if any exertion on my part could save you from the misery of being sacrificed to pride and consequence it should not be lacking!"

Letty thanked her, but said in a more practical spirit that since it was very unlikely that Cardross would listen to her advice there was really nothing that she could do to achieve this noble end. Miss Thorne, who had embraced with enthusiasm the rôle of go-between so suddenly thrust upon her, was daunted. Upon reflection, she was obliged to own that the ways in which a young lady in her seventeenth year could aid a pair of star-crossed lovers were few. In the fastness of her bedchamber it was possible to weave agreeable romances in which she played a leading and often heroic rôle. "Noblest of girls! We owe it all to you!" declared Mr. Allandale, having been joined in wedlock to Letty upon the eve of her marriage to a nobleman of dissolute habits (chosen for her by her brother), by a clergyman smuggled into the house at dead of night through the agency of her devoted cousin. In these romances, Selina overcame all difficulties by ignoring them, but in the cold light of day she was not so lost in dreams as to be unable to perceive that in a world depressingly humdrum certain insurmountable obstacles stood in the way of her ambition, not the least of which was Mr. Allandale himself. Though Letty would perceive in a flash the beauty of that marriage-scene in a dim room lit by a single branch of candles held up by her cousin, it would probably take a great deal of persuasion to induce the ardent lover to lend himself to such an improper proceeding. As for the indispensable cleric, not the wildest optimist could suppose that the Reverend William Tuxted, who happened to be the only clergyman with whom Selina was well acquainted, could be suborned by any means whatsoever into performing his part in the affair.

Melancholy though they were, these considerations had not the power to depress Selina for long. Letty's love affair might not attain the heights of drama, but it was still a very romantic story; and there was comfort in the thought that without her cousin's assistance she would have been hard put to it to have contrived a clandestine meeting with her suitor. Selina's good offices had not been required to promote her elder sisters' espousals; and nothing, in her opinion, could have been more insipid than Maria's marriage to Mr. Thistleton unless it were Fanny's betrothal to Mr. Humby: an event which had taken place on the previous evening. Neither lady had encountered the least opposition, each gentleman being possessed of a genteel fortune, and a situation in life which made him a very eligible suitor. Fanny's betrothal was perhaps more tolerable than Maria's, Mr. Humby having been unknown to the Thornes until he began to dangle after her. This, it must be allowed, was less deplorable than Maria's marriage to John Thistleton, whom she had known all her life; but Miss Selina Thorne was going to think herself pretty hardly used if Fate did not provide for her a dashing lover of such hopeless ineligibility as must assure for her the most determined parental opposition, accompanied by persecution, which she would bear with the greatest heroism, and culminating in an elopement. Pending the appearance on the horizon of this gentleman, she was prepared to throw herself heart and soul into Letty's cause. She found no difficulty in crediting Cardross with all the attributes of a tyrant; and if Mr. Allandale's propriety seemed at first to indicate that there was little hope of his engaging on any desperate action she soon decided that this was the expression not of an innate respectability, but of interesting reserve.

She was giving Letty an account of the degrading congratulations which had greeted the news of Fanny's betrothal when she caught sight of Mr. Allandale approaching the house. She at once put her plan into execution, flying with such swift feet down the stairs that she reached the front door considerably in advance of him, and found herself inviting only the ambient air to come in and fear nothing. However, Mr. Allandale soon arrived; and from having rehearsed (though involuntarily) her speech of welcome she was able to improve on it. "I knew you would not fail!" she uttered. "I will lead you to her immediately. Do not fear that you will be interrupted! Not a soul knows of your coming! Hush!"

Mr. Allandale, already surprised to find the front door being held open by one of the daughters of the house, blinked at her. "I beg your pardon?" he said.

"Do not speak so loud!" she admonished him. "The servants must not suspect your presence."

"But how is this?" he demanded. "Is not Mrs. Thorne at home?"

"No, no, you have nothing to fear!" she assured him. "She and my sister are gone into the City. If they should return, you may depend on me to warn you of their approach!"

"I should not be here," he said, looking vexed. "It is quite improper for me to be visiting the house in Mrs. Thorne's absence."

She was somewhat daunted by this prosaic attitude, but she made a gallant recover. "This is no time to be considering the proprieties!" she said earnestly. "Your case is now desperate, and strive though she may to support her spirits under this crushing blow, my cousin is in the greatest affliction! You must come to her immediately!"

The thought of his Letty's agony made Mr. Allandale turn

pale; but still he hung back. "I had not supposed that the assignation was of a clandestine nature," he said. "I cannot think it right! I assured Lord Cardross that such conduct was repugnant to me, and to be visiting your cousin behind his back, and in such a way, cannot be thought to be the part of a man of honour!"

None of Selina's romantic schemes had included a lover who had to be urged into the presence of his inamorata, and could she but have found a substitute to take his place in the drama she would then and there have thrust Mr. Allandale out of the house. But since she knew of no substitute, and was rather doubtful of Letty's willingness to accept one, she was obliged to make the best of the unpromising material to her hand. "I am persuaded you will not permit such trifling scruples to keep you from Letty's side!" she said. "Only consider her agitation! She is quite worn down by despair, and I should not wonder at it if her mind were to become wholly overset!"

Mr. Allandale was but human. The dreadful picture conjured up by these words took from him all power of resistance, and without further argument he followed Selina up the stairs.

"I have brought him to you, dearest!" announced Selina, throwing open the door into the drawing-room.

Mr. Allandale's afflicted love, who had been trying the effect of a slightly different tilt to her fetching new hat, turned away from the looking-glass, and showed him a countenance glowing with health and beauty. "Thank goodness you are come!" she said. "I have been quite in a worry, thinking that perhaps you might not be able to. To be sure, I should have known that you would contrive it by some means or other. *Dear* Jeremy!"

Selina could have improved upon this speech, but she had no fault to find with the way in which Letty cast herself upon Mr. Allandale's broad bosom, and flung both arms about his neck. This was a spectacle which might well have impelled Cardross to have consigned his ward to a strict seminary for young ladies of quality, but it afforded Selina intense, if vicarious, gratification. Lingering for long enough to see that Mr. Allandale, his propriety notwithstanding, was returning this artless embrace with a fervour that made Letty squeak, and protest that he was crushing her ribs, she withdrew reluctantly, to take up a post of vantage on the half-landing.

Mr. Allandale, casting an uneasy glance over his shoulder, was relieved to see that she had left the room. Relaxing his hold on Letty, he said seriously: "You know, my love, this is not at all the thing! That cousin of yours——!"

"Oh, do not mind her!" Letty said. "She will never betray us!"

"No, but for a girl of her age—why, she is not yet out, I believe! It is very shocking."

"Fiddle!" said Letty, drawing him to the sofa, and sitting down beside him there. "We have so much to discuss, Jeremy! This dreadful news which you sent me! Six weeks! Oh, dearest, *pray* tell them you won't go!"

Mr. Allandale was by this time pretty well acquainted with his love, but this ingenuous plea startled him. "Not go! But, my sweetest life——!"

"It is too soon!" she urged. "If you are to sail in six weeks' time, only consider the difficulties that confront us! I have the most melancholy persuasion that I can never, in so short a time, prevail upon Giles to consent to our marriage."

He possessed himself of her hands, and sat holding them in a close grasp. "Letty, you will never prevail upon him to do so," he said heavily.

She stared at him, her eyes round in astonishment. *"Never?* Oh, how absurd! Of course I shall! It is merely that this comes so suddenly, before he has grown *accustomed* to the notion, you know!"

He shook his head. "He will do everything that lies within his power to prevent our marriage. I have been as sure as a man may be of that ever since the day I called in Grosvenor Square. Nor can I blame him. From the worldly stand-point——"

"Well, I *can* blame him!" Letty interrupted, her eyes flashing, and her colour considerably heightened. "If I do not care a fig for worldly considerations I am sure he need not! And if my happiness means so little to him I shall think myself perfectly justified in marrying you in despite of anything he may say!"

He got up, and began to pace about the room, kneading one fist into the palm of his other hand. "If it were only possible! I do not know but what, with this appointment and my prospects, which I do not scruple to say are excellent, I too should think myself justified—— But it is to no purpose! Circumstances have placed us wholly in his power."

"What?" cried Letty. "No such thing! I am not in *any-one's* power, and I hope you are not either!"

"You are under age," he said gloomily.

"Oh, well, yes!" she conceded. "But if we were to be married he would be obliged to countenance it, because he would dislike excessively to make a scandal."

He was silent for a moment. When he did speak it was in a voice of deep mortification, and as though the words were forced from him. "In his power—because I am unable to support a wife. *That* is what renders my position so hope-less!"

"I would *try* not to be expensive," offered Letty.

He threw her a warm look, but said: "You are used to enjoy the elegancies of life. As my affairs now stand I cannot even offer you its comforts. To remove you from the protec-tion of your brother only to place you in a situation where you would be obliged to practise the most stringent economy would be the action of a scoundrel! I must not—indeed, I *will* not do it!"

"No, for I don't think I could practise *stringent* economies," agreed Letty, considering the matter in an impartial spirit. "But we could live upon my expectations, couldn't we?"

"*Borrow* on your expectations? No!—a thousand times no!" declared Mr. Allandale, with every evidence of repulsion.

"Well, it is what Nell's brother does," argued Letty. "I don't know precisely how he contrives to do it, but if *he* can I am persuaded I could too, for mine are much better than his, you know."

"Put it out of your mind!" begged Mr. Allandale, blanching visibly at the appalling vision of debt conjured up by her artless suggestion. "Nothing shall prevail upon me to take Lord Dysart for my model!"

"No, very true!!" she replied, recalling his lordship's unamiable behaviour. "I am sure he is the most ramshackle person—besides being excessively disagreeable! Only what is to be done, if you don't think my allowance sufficient? I have five hundred pounds a year, you know, and I need spend very little of it on my dresses, because I have a great many already." She stopped, and her eyes brightened. "Yes, and besides that I have suddenly had an excellent notion! I can very well buy *hundreds* of ells of silk, and muslin, and cambric—enough to set me up for *years,* I daresay—and tell all the mercers to send their bills to Giles!"

"Good God!" ejaculated Mr. Allandale, pausing in his perambulations to gaze upon her with starting eyes.

She perceived that her suggestion had not found favour. "You don't think that is what I should do? But consider, Jeremy! Even if he refused to pay—and I don't think that in the least likely—they couldn't dun me, because I should be in South America, and so all would be well."

It spoke volumes for the depth of Mr. Allandale's love that

after the first stunned moment he recovered from an involuntary recoil, and realized that this ingenious solution to their difficulties arose not from depravity but from a vast and touching innocence. "That," he said gently, "would be dishonest, my dearest."

"Oh!" said Letty.

It was plain that she was unconvinced. Mr. Allandale was aware that it behoved him to bring her to a more proper frame of mind, but he felt, at this present, unequal to the task, and merely said: "Besides, if I were to marry you out of hand there can be little doubt that Cardross would discontinue your allowance."

She was quite incredulous. "No! He would not be so shabby!"

"He warned me that your fortune remains in his hands until you attain the age of twenty-five. How much of its income you may enjoy is at his discretion. I could not mistake his meaning."

"Twenty-five?" gasped Letty. "Oh, of all the *infamous* things! Why, I shall be quite old! I declare I am excessively thankful that I can't remember my papa, for if he served me such a trick as that he must have been a most detestable man! You would think he *meant* Giles to chouse me out of my inheritance!"

"No, there is no question of such a thing as that," said Mr. Allandale painstakingly. "It is only——"

"Well, I don't mean to be worsted by either of them, and so I promise you!" Letty said briskly. "Depend upon it, I shall hit upon a way of bringing Giles about. But I must own, love, that it makes it very hard if you must sail so soon. Jeremy, pray do not!"

"You don't understand," he said. "I could not refuse such an adventitious appointment! You would not have me do so."

"Oh, no! Not refuse it, but could you not tell them that

it is not perfectly convenient to you to go to Brazil so soon? Tell them that you will go in three months! I am persuaded we shall have come about by then."

This drew a slight, melancholy smile from him, but he shook his head. "No, indeed I could not do such a thing! Consider, dearest, how unwise in me it would be to offend my kind patron! I owe this advancement to Lord Roxwell, you know, and to give the least appearance of ingratitude——"

"I have been thinking about that," she interrupted. "I daresay he was anxious to oblige you, only the thing is that he has quite mistaken the matter."

"How so?" he demanded, looking bewildered. "He was good enough to say that he had my advancement very much to heart, certainly. I believe I told you that he held my father in great affection."

"Yes, you did, and it has given me a very good notion. You must go to him instantly, and tell him that you would prefer to be made ambassador!"

"Tell him that I would prefer to be made ambassador?" repeated Mr. Allandale, in a bemused voice.

"In a very civil way, of course," she urged, seeing that her notion was not having that success with him which it deserved. "You could say that now you have had time to consider the matter you feel that it would be better if you became an ambassador; or—— But you will know just how to say it in an unexceptionable way!"

"No!" said Mr. Allandale, with a good deal of conviction. "I do not know! My dearest life, you don't know—you have not the least conception——! It will be many years before I can hope to be so elevated. As for asking Lord Roxwell—— Good God!"

"Should you prefer it if I were to ask him?" enquired Letty. "I am not particularly acquainted with him, but Giles knows him, and we meet him for ever at parties."

Mr. Allandale sat down again beside her, and grasped both her hands. "Letty, promise me you will do no such thing!" he begged. "It is not to be thought of! Believe me, it would be quite disastrous!"

"Would it? Then I won't, of course, and I expect it will answer best for you to approach him, after all," said Letty sunnily. "The only thing is that perhaps you might not like to tell him that you would make an excellent ambassador, while for me there could be nothing easier."

Much moved, Mr. Allandale pressed several kisses on to her hands, ejaculating in a thickened voice: "So sweet! so innocent! Alas, no, my love! it cannot be! I must be content with what is offered to me—and, indeed, it is more than ever I expected!"

"Well, I am sure it is not more than you deserve," said Letty warmly. "However, if you believe it would be useless to apply to Lord Roxwell, I won't tease you. We must think of some other scheme."

She spoke with optimism, but Mr. Allandale sighed. "I wish we might! But my thoughts lead me only to the melancholy necessity of waiting. If your present allowance were secured to you I should be *tempted* indeed, though I trust I should find the strength to withstand the impulse of my heart. Situated as we both are—you dependent upon your brother's caprice, I with such charges upon my purse as I cannot but consider sacred—our case is hopeless. *One* of my sisters is on the point (I hope) of contracting an eligible marriage; my uncle has always promised to present Philip to a living, as soon as he shall have been inducted into Holy Orders, which, I trust, will be this year; but Edward is still at school, and Tom must be sent to join him in September. I could not reconcile it with my conscience, love, to leave my widowed parent to bear, without assistance, these heavy charges."

Letty agreed to this, but without enthusiasm. She ventured

to say: "You don't feel that perhaps Tom would as lief not go to school?"

Mr. Allandale dismissed unhesitatingly a tentative suggestion which would have won for Letty her future brother-in-law's esteem and approval.

"Perhaps your uncle would pay for Tom?"

He shook his head. "I fear—You must know that he has himself a numerous progeny, and has, besides, been responsible for a part of Philip's education. Philip is his godson, but it would not be right to expect him to provide for Edward or Tom."

A depressed silence fell. Mr. Allandale broke it, saying with a praiseworthy attempt to speak cheerfully: "We must be patient. It will be very hard, but we shall have the future to look forward to. Cardross has said that if we are of the same two minds when I return from Brazil he will not then withhold his consent. I believe him to be a man of his word; and that thought, that hope, will help us to bear with fortitude our separation. I do not consider him unfeeling, and I trust he will not forbid us to correspond with each other."

"He may forbid it if he chooses, but I shall pay not the least heed!" declared Letty, her voice trembling. "Only I am not a good hand at letter-writing, and I don't *wish* to correspond with you! I wish to be with you! Oh, don't talk of our being separated, Jeremy! I can't bear it, and I won't bear it! Cardross must and *shall* continue to pay my allowance!"

He could not feel hopeful; nor did he think well of a scheme for Cardross's subjection which depended for its success on her ability to bring herself to the brink of a decline by refusing to let a morsel of food pass her lips. Letty then broke into a passion of weeping, and by the time he had soothed and petted her into a calmer state he was obliged to tear himself from her side. His haggard countenance, when he emerged from the drawing-room, did much to restore Selina's good opinion of him; and when she found her cousin still hiccuping on convulsive sobs she felt that matters were progressing just as they should. It now only remained for Letty to suffer abominable persecution at the hands of her cruel guardian.

"Well, I had as lief not be persecuted, I thank you!" said Letty crossly. "Besides, he *is* persecuting me!"

"Not enough!" declared Selina positively. "Do you think, if you threatened to run away, that he would lock you in an attic at the top of the house?"

"No, of course he wouldn't, you silly creature!"

"They do in general," argued Selina. "If only you could prevail upon him to, you could throw a note down from the window to me, and I would instantly deliver it to Mr. Allandale. He would feel himself bound to rescue you, and then you could fly to the border."

"That only happens in novels," said Letty scornfully. "I should like to know how Jeremy could possibly rescue me! Why, he could not even enter the house without knocking on the door, and what, pray, would you have him say to the porter?"

"I suppose there isn't a secret way into the house?" asked Selina, rather daunted.

"Of course not! You only find them in castles!"

"No, that is not true at all!" Selina cried triumphantly. "Because I have seen a secret way into quite a commonplace house! I don't precisely remember where it was, but I drove there when Mama took Fanny and me to stay with my uncle, in Somerset!"

"It's of no consequence *where* it is, because there are no secret doors in Grosvenor Square."

"No," agreed Selina regretfully. Another idea presented itself to her, but although her eyes brightened momentarily they clouded at the thought of Mr. Allandale gaining an entrance to Cardross House in the disguise of a sweep.

"And now I come to think of it," said Letty, clinching the matter, "the attics are all as full as they can hold with servants. I wish you will stop talking nonsense, like a goose!"

"It is not nonsense! *You* did not think it so, when we read that capital story about the girl who was imprisoned by her uncle, so that she should consent to wed his son—the one that had a villainous aspect, and two savage mastiffs, and——"

"Books!" cried Letty impatiently. "But this is *real*!"

LETTY remained in Bryanston Square all day; and great was Mrs. Thorne's delight to find her there when she returned from a protracted shopping expedition with Fanny. Silks and muslins for the making of Fanny's bride-clothes had been their object; and while the tour of the warehouses had been in the nature of a preliminary skirmish so much had been bought, and so many patterns had been brought home to be studied at leisure that little else was talked of during the remainder of Letty's visit. Mrs. Thorne did indeed notice that she was rather languid in spirit, but this circumstance she ascribed to pique, and paid no heed to it, beyond remarking, not very felicitously, that in spite of her three years' seniority she had never expected Fanny to go off before her cousin.

Nell, meanwhile, spent an unexceptionable if rather dull day, and since such sedentary occupations as netting, tatting, knotting a fringe, or trying to bring to a successful conclusion a game of Patience, a new form of recreation which the Prince Regent had been so condescending as to explain to her, left her mind rather too much at liberty to fret over her troubles, she soon began to be sorry she had refused even so mild a form of entertainment as an invitation to practise French country-dances at a select morning-ball. In general, there never seemed to be enough time into which to fit her various engagements, for once the season was in full swing every sort of amusement offered, from Venetian breakfasts to Grand Balloon Ascensions; and in brief respites from these she was either submitting to the ministrations of Mr. Blake, who combined a laughable coxcombry with a positive genius for cutting ladies' hair; or sitting for her portrait to Mr. Lawrence. Cardross had commissioned this full-length likeness of his lovely bride, and since Lawrence had become, since Hoppner's death, the most fashionable portrait painter in England it was going to cost him not a penny less than four hundred guineas. But Mr. Blake had given her a smart new crop only a week earlier; Mr. Lawrence's work on the portrait had had to be suspended until he had recovered from an indisposition. She did not care to visit the Royal Academy's exhibition at Somerset House alone, for that would not only be dull work, but might render her an easy prey to some other unaccompanied lady: probably Miss Berry, whom one ought to admire, but could not contrive to like. London was overfull of elderly ladies who were Mama's dear friends, and Somerset House was just the place where one might be sure of meeting them. So after knotting a few inches of fringe, reading three pages of *Corinne,* rather wistfully watching some children playing at battledore and shuttlecock in the Square-garden, and trying to make up her mind to write an overdue letter to Miss Wilby, she decided that the day was too fine for such sedentary pursuits, and determined, in default of livelier amusements, to drive to Chelsea, on a visit to Tubbs' Nursery Garden, in the King's Road, and to select there such plants as would transform the ballroom at Cardross House into a fairyland of flowers.

This lavish scheme had its birth in Letty's desire to hang the ballroom with pink calico. She had seen this novel form of decoration at one of the first balls of the season, and it had instantly hit her fancy. Hundreds of ells of calico had been gathered to form the likeness of a huge tent: everyone had exclaimed at it, and had complimented the hostess on such a charming notion; and Letty, convinced that it would shortly become all the crack, had been alternately hectoring and cajoling Cardross for weeks past to have his own ballroom turned into a pink tent for the grand dress-party to be held there at the end of the month. Unfortunately Cardross had not admired the effect of pink calico; and upon Letty's agreeing that to be sure calico was shabby, and it would be far more elegant (besides going one better than Lady Weldon) to use silk, he had expressed himself so unequivocally on the subject as to confirm her in her belief that his taste was as old-fashioned as his disposition was mean. She had not scrupled to tell him so, and his way of receiving this terrible indictment did him no honour at all. "I know it," he had said sympathetically. "I assure you, Letty, it astonishes even *me* that I could be such a hog-grubber as to grudge the expenditure of I daresay not much above a few hundred pounds on the suitable decoration of the ballroom to set off your charms." He had cast a laugh-ing glance towards Nell, and had added provocatively: "Now, had you asked me for *blue* hangings——!"

Letty had been perfectly willing to compound for blue, but had met with no support from Nell. Nell, quite as desirous as she to cut a dash, had no notion (she thanked Letty) of imitating Lady Weldon, or any other fashionable hostess. If Cardross approved, she would make the ton exclaim much more loudly by creating a flower-garden in her ballroom. It had often astonished her that hostesses made such meagre use of flowers: they should be made to gnash their teeth with envy at the result to be achieved by taste, ingenuity, and the services of a first-rate florist. Cardross promptly gave her carte blanche; and Letty, having rather reluctantly listened to her scheme, was obliged to own that it would be at once pretty, and quite out of the ordinary way.

So off Nell went to Chelsea. No sooner did Mr. Tubbs, greeting her ladyship with flattering deference, grasp the pur-pose of her visit than he became an enthusiastic supporter of it, summoning up his chief minions, and rapidly devising several alternative plans for the tasteful decoration of her ball-room. They differed in many respects, but in one they were alike: they were all extremely costly. But since Cardross had said Nell might do anything she chose, provided she didn't drape his ballroom in pink calico, this consideration was of no moment. In choosing the flowers and the ferns, and discussing with Mr. Tubbs the rival merits of garlands, hanging-baskets, and a trellis-work set against the walls and covered with greenery, out of which flowers could be made to appear as if growing, she passed an agreeable hour, her cares for the time being forgotten. She parted from Mr. Tubbs on the most cordial terms, that excellent horticulturist begging her to do him the honour of accepting a bouquet composed of all the choice blooms she had particularly admired during her tour of the garden. It was such a large bouquet that it had to be laid on the floor of the barouche, but Mr. Tubbs did not grudge a single blossom in it: it was not every day of the week that he received so magnificent an order as Lady Cardross had given him. He assured her ladyship that she might repose the fullest confidence in his ability to achieve a result that would hold her guests spellbound with admiration; and no sooner had her barouche driven away than he took his foreman apart, and exhorted him to put forth his best endeavours. "For mark my words, Andy," he said earnestly, "if this does not set a fashion! I shouldn't wonder at it if we were soon turning orders away!"

Nell was rather hopeful, too, that she might be starting a new mode. There had been a number of parties at Cardross House since her marriage, but this would be the first grand ball she had held, and she wanted people to say something more of it than that it had been a dreadful squeeze.

Letty had not returned from Bryanston Square when she reached home again, so after putting off her hat and her gloves she occupied herself with the arrangement of her bouquet in several bowls and vases. She was trying the effect of one of these on a pie-crust table in a corner of the drawing-room when a voice said behind her: "Charming!"

It was fortunate that she was not holding the bowl, for she must certainly have dropped it, so convulsive was the start she gave. She gasped sharply, and turned, to find that Cardross had come quietly into the room, and was standing by the door, quizzically regarding her. He had shed his driving-coat, but he had plainly but that instant arrived in town, for he was still wearing a country habit of frock-coat, buckskins, and top-boots.

The shock of hearing his voice when she had believed him to be a hundred miles away was severe, and her first sensation was of consternation. She made a quick recover, but not before he had seen the fright in her eyes. The quizzical look faded, to be replaced by one of searching enquiry. She exclaimed a little faintly: "Cardross! Oh, how much you startled me!"

"I appear, rather, to have dismayed you," he said, making no movement to approach her, but continuing to watch her face with hard, narrowed eyes.

"No, no! How can you say so?" she protested, with a nervous laugh, and reddening cheeks. "I am so glad—I did not expect to see you until Monday, and hearing you speak suddenly—made me jump out of my skin!"

"I beg your pardon," he replied, unsmilingly. "I should, of course, have warned you of my arrival. You must try to forgive my want of tact."

"Giles, how absurd!" she said, holding out her hand.

He strolled forward, and took it, bowing formally, and just touching it with his lips. He released it immediately, saying: "Yes, in the manner of the farce we saw at Covent Garden, and thought so stupid. I shall stop short of searching behind the curtains and under the furniture for the hidden lover."

The chilly salute he had bestowed on her hand had both alarmed and distressed her, but this speech fell so wide of the mark that she laughed. "In the expectation of finding your cousin Felix? It is a *most* improper notion, but how very funny it would be to discover him in such a situation!"

He smiled slightly, and some of the suspicion left his eyes.

He still kept them on her face, and she found it hard to meet them. "What is it, Nell?" he asked, after a moment.

"But indeed it is nothing! I—I don't understand what you can mean! Are you offended with me for having jumped so? But that was quite your own fault, you know!"

He did not answer for a moment, and when he did at last speak it was in a colourless voice. "As you say. Which of your many admirers bestowed that handsome bouquet on you? You have arranged it delightfully."

"None of them! At least, I don't flatter myself that he admires me precisely!" she replied, thankful for the change of subject. "I had it—but this is only a part of it!—from Tubbs, the nursery-man! I have been there today, to order the flowers for our dress-ball, and at parting he begged me to accept the most enormous bouquet imaginable!"

"Did he indeed? Then it seems safe to assume that you've lodged a very handsome order with him."

She looked a little anxious. "Well, yes," she admitted. "But it will be the prettiest ball of the season, and—and you *did* tell me I might spend as much as I wished on it!"

"Certainly. I wasn't criticizing you, my love."

She felt impelled to justify herself, for in spite of this assurance there was an alarming want of cordiality in his voice. "It is the first ball we have held here—the first *grand* ball," she reminded him apologetically. "You wouldn't wish it to be talked of as just another jam—nothing out of the common style!"

"My dear Nell, you have no need to excuse yourself! By all means let it be of the first stare. Shall we give our guests pink champagne?"

"Are you joking me?" she asked cautiously. "It *sounds* excessively elegant, but I think I never heard of it before."

"Oh, no, I'm not joking you! I assure you it will lend a great *cachet* to the party."

"More than pink calico?" she ventured, a gleam of fun in the glance she cast at him.

That did draw a laugh from him. "Yes—or even pink silk! Where is Letty, by the by?"

"She has gone to visit Mrs. Thorne. She will be back directly, I daresay." She fancied there was a frown in his eyes, and added: "You don't like that, but indeed, Giles, it would not be right to encourage her to neglect Mrs. Thorne."

"Very true. Tell me, Nell, what does my aunt Chudleigh mean by writing to inform me that Letty's conduct at that masquerade you took her to set everyone in a bustle?"

"If your aunt Chudleigh would be a little less busy we should go on very well!" cried Nell, flushing with wrath. "She is never happy but when she is making mischief! Pray, has she any animadversions to pass on me?"

"No, she exonerates you from all blame."

"Obliging of her! I hope with all my heart that you will give her a sharp set-down, Cardross!"

"I probably shall. What, in fact, did Letty do to bring this scold down upon me?"

"Nothing at all! That is to say, nothing to make a piece of work about! You know how it is with her, when she is in high gig! She allows her vivacity to carry her beyond the line of what is pleasing, but she is so young that it is only people like Lady Chudleigh who don't know that it is all done in innocence."

"And want of upbringing," he said, with a sigh. "I can blame no one but myself for that. You didn't, in sober truth, let her wear an improper gown, did you?"

"No—oh, no!" she replied guiltily. "Not—not *improper* precisely! I own it was not just the thing for a girl of her age, but—well, she won't wear it again, so pray don't mention it to her, Cardross!"

"If it made her look like a class of female which my aunt

prefers not to particularize, she most assuredly won't wear it again!" he returned.

"Nothing of the sort! Lady Chudleigh knows very well that such gowns are worn by women of the first consequence. Do, pray, let the matter rest! To scold Letty will only set up her back—and it was my fault, after all."

"I don't mean to scold either of you, but I must own, Nell, that I could wish you had put your foot down," he said, looking displeased.

"Perhaps I should have done so," she replied, in a mortified tone. "I am very sorry!"

"Yes—well, never mind! I don't doubt that it is very hard for you to check Letty's starts. And while we are speaking of the masquerade, what, in heaven's name, is this extraordinary story I have been hearing about Dysart's holding you up on the road to Chiswick?"

"Oh, good God, Lady Chudleigh knows nothing of *that*, surely?" she exclaimed, rather aghast.

"No, I had it from your coachman. According to him, your carriage was stopped by Dysart and two companions, all of them disguised as highwaymen. It seems quite incredible, even in Dysart, but I can hardly suppose that Jeffrey would entertain me with a Canterbury story. Do you mind explaining the matter to me?"

She had forgotten that her servants would be very likely to tell him of Dysart's strange exploit, and for an ignoble moment wished that she had had the forethought to have bought their silence. She was instantly ashamed of herself, and said, her colour rising: "Oh, it was one of Dy's mad-brained hoaxes, and a great deal too bad of him! I must own that I hoped it wouldn't come to your ears."

"That, Nell, is patent!" he said.

"Yes—I mean, I knew you would be vexed! There was no harm in it—it all arose out of a—a stupid wager—but of course it was a most improper thing to do, and so I told him."

"All arose out of a *wager*?" he repeated incredulously. "With which of his associates did Dysart see fit to make you the subject of a wager?"

"N-not with any of them!" she stammered, frightened by the look on his face.

"Then what the devil do you mean?" he demanded.

"It was with me!" she said, improvising desperately. "We— we were talking about masquerades, and I said it was nonsense to suppose that one wouldn't recognize somebody one knew well just because they wore a mask. Dy—Dy said that he would prove me wrong, and—and that was how it was! Only I did recognize him, so I won the wager."

"Gratifying! Did you also recognize his companions?"

"No—that is, it was only Mr. Fancot!" she said imploringly. "Oh, and Joe, of course—Dy's groom! But he doesn't signify, because he has always been with us, ever since I can remember! *Pray,* Cardross, don't be vexed with Dy!"

"Vexed with him! I am very much more than vexed with him! To be giving you such a fright for the sake of a prank I should find it hard to pardon in a schoolboy goes beyond anything of which I believed him to be capable!" he said wrathfully.

"I wasn't frightened!" she assured him. "Only a very little, at all events!"

"Oh?" he said grimly. "What, then, made you scream?"

Her eyes sparkled with indignation. "I did not scream! I would *scorn* to do anything so paltry! It was Letty who screamed."

"How chicken-hearted of her, to be sure!" he said sardonically.

"Well, that's what I thought," she said candidly.

"Are you quite blinded by your doting fondness for Dysart?" he demanded. "He is fortunate to possess a sister who can find excuses for his every folly, his every extravagance, and for such *larks* as this latest exploit! I am aware—I have for long been aware!—that he holds a place in your affections that is second to none, but take care what you are about! Encourage him to think he may turn to you in any extremity! smile upon kick-ups unworthy of a freshman! You will not smile when the *high spirits* you now regard with such indulgence carry him beyond the line of what even his cronies will pardon!"

She shrank a little from the harshness in his voice, but she was quick to recognize the note of jealousy in it. She heard it with a leap of the heart, and it took from his words all power of wounding. Instead of flying to Dysart's defence, she said merely: "Indeed I didn't smile upon such a prank! It was very bad—quite unbecoming! But it is unjust in you, Cardross, to say that his wildness will lead him into doing anything *wicked*! You dislike him very much, but that is going too far!"

"No, I don't dislike him," he replied, in a more moderate tone. "On the contrary! I like him well enough to wish to be of real service to him. You think me unjust, but you may believe that I know what I am saying when I tell you that his present way of life is ruinous."

She said, in swift alarm: "Oh, pray, pray don't thrust him into the army!"

"I have no power to thrust him into the army. I own I have offered to buy him a commission, and I have not the smallest doubt that there is nothing I might do for him which he would like better, or which would be of more benefit to him. If the only bar in the way of his accepting it is your father's dislike of the project I will engage to make all right in *that* quarter."

"No, it is not that. I should not say such a thing, but I am afraid Dy doesn't care much for what poor Papa wishes. But Mama made him promise he wouldn't do it, and however ramshackle you may think him Dy doesn't break his promises!"

"If that is how the case stands," he said, "I recommend you, my dear, to use your best endeavours to persuade your mother to release him from a promise which I don't scruple to tell you should never have been extracted from him!"

"I could not! Oh, she would sink under the very thought of his exposing himself to all the dangers of war!" She hesitated and then said, with a little difficulty: "Mama has had so many trials to bear. Poor Papa, you know . . ."

"Yes, I know," he replied. "For that very reason I am persuaded that if she was aware of the truth she would think the hazards of war less perilous than those of the metropolis. Living, as she now must, so far from London, I fancy she cannot know how closely Dysart is following an example she must dread."

She looked a little frightened, but said: "I know he is sadly wild, and—and expensive, but surely—no worse than that?"

"Well, that is bad enough," he replied. He saw that she was inclined to question him more closely, but he was already vexed that he had allowed his irritation to betray him into saying so much. Before she could speak again he had turned the subject; and very soon after he left her, saying that he must change his habit. Whatever bitter feelings he might cherish he could not shock her by disclosing the full sum of Dysart's folly. She probably did not even know of that little narrow pink room behind the stage at the Opera House, where the dancers practised their steps in front of long pier-glasses, and any buck in search of amatory adventures could have his pick of the west-end comets. Dysart was a familiar figure in that saloon, and so was his latest chère amie. Nell had certainly seen him driving with this article of virtue—a dasher of the first water, too!—reflected Cardross—but what she had made of her one couldn't tell. She had asked no questions, so perhaps she had guessed. But she didn't guess that Dysart frequently sallied forth with the Peep o' Day boys, starting the evening with a rump and dozen at Long's, and gravitating thence to a less respectable world of which she was wholly ignorant. It diverted the wilder blades to mix on equal terms with the roughest elements of society; buttoning up, they would plunge into the back-slums of Tothill Fields, rubbing shoulders (and often falling into a mill) with all-sorts, from honest coal-porters to petermen. They saw badger-baiting in the reeking squalor of Charles's, where a man must be a very fly-cove to avoid having his pockets picked; they rubbed shoulders with bing-boys and their mollishers in the sluiceries; became half-sprung on blue ruin in these gin shops, and, wandering eastward, deep-cut at the Field of Blood. The night music of the watchmen's rattles marked their progress through the sleeping town; often a drowsing Charley was overturned in his box, and sent sprawling into the kennel; many were the respectable householders brought down to their doors on false alarms of fire, or thieves. Sometimes these larks ended in a roundhouse, with its sequel of Bow Street, a false name, and a fine; sometimes a blade, fortunate enough to be numbered amongst Mother Butler's favourites, sought refuge at the Finish, and spent what was left of the night snoring on a settle beside the dying embers of the fire in the tap. No, Nell knew nothing of such exploits as these, and no prompting of jealousy was going to seduce her husband into enlightening her. The shock would be severe, and her innocence as much as her affection for Dysart would lead her to regard his excesses in a far more serious light than that in which they appeared to her husband. He was vexed by them, and he viewed their continuance with grim fore-boding; but he believed that they sprang from the boredom of idleness rather than from any ingrained depravity. What disturbed him far more was the suspicion he had formed that Dysart, in his restless quest for novelty and excitement, had lately become enrolled as a member of the Beggars' Club.

This decidedly unsavoury institution had its locality in a

cellar at the back of Broad Street, and was generally presided over by the Earl of Barrymore, with Colonel George Hanger as his Vice. It was patronized by all the raff of town, and such persons as those who thought it amusing to eat their suppers out of holes carved in the long table, and with knives and forks that were chained to their places. There was no particular harm in this, but the evils that could accrue from a young man's getting into Barrymore's set were grave enough, Cardross knew, to alarm even so casual a parent as Lord Pevensey. Old Georgie Hanger, for all his eccentricities, exercised little influence over the younger men. He was over sixty; and after a varied career, which began at Eton, rose to a commission in the 1st Footguards, reached its nadir in the King's Bench prison, and included an excursion into trade (when, upon his discharge from the Abbot's Priory, he set up as a coal-merchant), he had contrived to get himself restored to full-pay, and was now living rather more moderately. His age and his oddities caused him to be tolerated by society, but his manners were too coarse to render him an attractive figure; and, to do him justice, he had not the smallest desire either to figure as the leader of a set or to corrupt the morals of its members.

The noble Earl of Barrymore was a bird of another feather. Neither his rank nor his achievements on the box or in the saddle sufficed to make him acceptable to the ton. He had been one of the founders of the Whip Club; he had introduced the fashionable practice of driving with a small Tiger perched up beside him; his colours were to be seen on any race-course; but society, with the exception of the Prince Regent, who too often appeared to have a strong predilection for disreputable company, was obstinate in avoiding him. An Irish peer, he had inherited the title from his brother, who had earned for himself the unenviable nickname of Hellgate. This circumstance, coupled with the possession of a club-foot, naturally led to his being dubbed Cripplegate. A younger brother, in orders, was known as Newgate, from having (according to his boast) been imprisoned in every gaol in the country; and an excessively foul-mouthed sister became, inevitably, Billingsgate. Cripplegate, with his fame as a Nonesuch, his cool daring in the saddle, and his dark reputation, constituted a real danger to such reckless young bloods as Dysart; and if the hint dropped in Cardross's ear held so much as a grain of truth neither Lady Pevensey's maternal fears nor Nell's distress at being separated from her brother was going to prevent his putting a summary end to that troublesome young man's career as a town buck of the first cut. The demon of jealousy apart, he liked Dysart well enough to make a push to save him from the consequences of his own folly; for Nell's sake he was prepared even to undertake the disagreeable task of disclosing to Lord Pevensey the exact nature of the course his heir was treading. He could only hope that the news would not prove fatal to his lordship's shattered constitution, but he thought it extremely probable that a second stroke might result from it, and could only trust that it would not prove necessary for him to approach his father-in-law. Lord Pevensey might shrug up his shoulders at a tale of fashionable dissipations, but in his day not the most dissolute rake amongst the Upper Ten Thousand sought diversion in the back-slums. Unless the stroke he had already suffered had rendered him very much more incapable than Cardross had reason to suppose, he could be trusted to overbear his lady's opposition the instant he received the intelligence that Dysart was not only associating on the friendliest terms with scamps, pads, and drivers, but was also in a fair way to becoming a boon companion of one whom his lordship had been amongst the first to ostracize.

CARDROSS feared that his unguarded words would lead Nell to enquire more particularly into her brother's mode of life, but in point of fact she was less disturbed by them than by the possible consequences of the story she had fabricated to account for his holding up her carriage. She had certainly been startled by what he had said, but a few minutes' reflection led her to think that the jealousy she had so clearly perceived in him had led him to exaggerate. That he had so abruptly turned the subject seemed to her to lend colour to this belief; and since her own troubles were looming large she thought very little more about the matter.

Her encounter with him had quite overset her; it was a struggle to support her spirits, for never before had he treated her with such cool reserve of manner, or looked at her with such hard, searching eyes. The fault was her own: that frightening expression had not been in his face when first he had entered the room. She had been terrified that he might demand an explanation of the dismay she had betrayed, but when he had refrained, as though in disdain or indifference, she had found his cold forbearance more alarming than any display of wrath. She felt herself to have been set at a distance, and although his voice had been kinder when he had asked her what was the matter she had not been conscious of any impulse to confide in him. In her view no moment could have been more unpropitious for confession. Rendered suspicious by her reception of him, vexed with her for not having taken better care of his sister, and his temper dangerously exasperated by Dysart's conduct, the disclosure that his wife was again badly in debt, and had been putting forth her best endeavours to deceive him, could only be expected to act on him like a match to gunpowder. Nor did it seem at all probable that the knowledge of Dysart's motive in holding her up would lead him to regard him with more lenient eyes. In fact, far otherwise, she thought: for if she had been shocked by the scheme it seemed safe to suppose that Cardross would utterly condemn it. Once the truth was out Dysart would be more than likely to tell him that he had had three hundred pounds from her, and then, surely, the miserable tangle would be past unravelling.

This melancholy conviction at once put her in mind of the immediate necessity of conveying a warning to Dysart. Cardross plainly meant to call him to book, and it would never do for him to tell a different story from hers. She sat down to dash off a note to him then and there, but she was obliged to pause several times to wipe the blinding tears from her eyes. Try as she would to compose herself, they would keep welling up, because it was so very dreadful to be plotting with Dysart against Cardross.

She had just given the sealed billet to her footman when Letty came in, and at once it occurred to her that she too must be warned to say, if Cardross should question her, that Dysart had held them up for a wager. She could feel herself blushing as she told Letty what she had said to Cardross, but Letty was not at all shocked. "Oh, certainly!" she said, taking it as a matter of course. Nell hardly knew whether to be glad or sorry.

"So Giles is come home!" Letty remarked, slowly pulling off her gloves. "Well! I am positively *glad* of it!"

"Oh, yes!" Nell murmured. "Of course! I mean——"

"Because," pursued Letty, a martial light in her eye, "my affairs have now reached a Crisis!"

"Good God!" exclaimed Nell, quite alarmed. "What in the world, love——?"

"In six weeks—in *less* than six weeks!—Jeremy sails for South America!" announced Letty, in a voice of doom.

"Oh, dear!" said Nell. "As soon as that! I am so very sorry!"

"Well, you need not be," said Letty. "Though I own I had rather not be married in such a scrambling way. However, I don't mean to repine, for that is a small thing, after all."

Nell regarded her uneasily. "But, dearest, there is no question—— You cannot suppose that Cardross will permit it!"

"And neither he nor you," flashed Letty, "can suppose that *I* will permit my adored Jeremy to leave England without me! Unless he has a heart of stone, Giles cannot now refuse his consent."

Nell was unable to perceive why the imminent departure of Mr. Allandale should be supposed to melt Cardross's heart, and ventured to say as much. It was ill-received. Letty broke into an impassioned diatribe. This was not very coherent, but one plain fact emerged from it: Cardross was to be given a last chance to rehabilitate his character.

As far as Nell was concerned, this supplied all that was needed to set the crown on a singularly disastrous day. She begged Letty with great earnestness not to attempt to argue her case that evening; and when Letty, with a toss of her head, declared that *she* was not afraid of Cardross, warned her that his back had already been set up by Lady Chudleigh's letter.

A thoughtful silence descended upon Letty. After a few moments she said, with a nonchalance that would have deceived no one: "It is not of the least consequence. I shan't regard it if he does give me one of his scolds. Is he very angry, Nell?"

"No, but—oh, a good deal displeased, I fear! I believe he won't speak of it to you, if only you won't vex him!"

"Well, I won't say anything to him tonight," Letty decided. "What a fortunate thing it is that we are going to the play! I had meant to ask you if we need, because I haven't any inclination for it. Still, it won't do to fall into a lethargy, even though Cardross is determined to break my heart. He will be very well served if I go into a decline, for although I daresay he doesn't care a button what becomes of me I shall leave a letter to be opened after my death, saying that it was all his doing, and he won't like *that*!"

Slightly heartened by this reflection, she then went off to change her dress. With rare tact she selected from her wardrobe a very demure half-dress of French muslin, and further heightened its modesty by arranging round her shoulders a lace fichu. This led her adoring abigail to look upon her with anxious concern, but upon the matter's being explained to her Martha entered at once into the spirit of the thing, and contributed her mite by substituting a pair of silk mittens for the elegant kid gloves she had previously laid out. Letty eyed them with disfavour, but consented to wear them; and presently burst upon her half-brother's sight as the embodiment of virtuous maidenhood. The effect of this modest ensemble, though not what she had expected, was good. When she entered the drawing-room Cardross was looking stern, but after one glance at his pious little sister his countenance relaxed. He put up his glass, the better to study her appearance, and said dryly, but with a quivering lip: "Doing it rather too brown, Letty!"

Her saintly expression melted into one of engaging mischief. She twinkled roguishly, and stood on tiptoe to kiss his cheek. "*Dear* Giles! What an agreeable surprise, to be sure!"

"Turning me up sweet, my pet?"

She giggled. "No, no, it is the luckiest chance that you have come home, because the case is that we mean to go to the play tonight, and have no one to escort us!"

"What an abominable girl you are!" he remarked.

"Yes, but don't be cross!" she begged.

"It would be a waste of time. I entertain serious thoughts, however, of sending you to stay with Aunt Honoria. She *may*

take you to the Assemblies at the Upper Rooms now and then
—by the by, they end punctually at eleven!—but only if you are
excessively well-behaved."

"Oh, what a horrid notion!" cried Letty, shuddering. "*Aunt
Honoria!* Bath, too, of all places! But of course I should run
away—to become an actress, I daresay, just to serve you out!"

"Nonsense! She will have you in subjection within a week!
She frightens *me* to death!" he retorted.

"Very likely! There is more steel to *my* nerves, I promise
you!"

He laughed, and upon dinner's being just then announced
bowed both ladies out of the door, and followed them downstairs to the dining-room. Bent on charming him into an
acquiescent mood, Letty kept him amused by a good deal of
nonsensical raillery, in which Nell took little part, merely
smiling mechanically at Letty's more outrageous absurdities.
Her spirits were oppressed; and she was on tenterhooks lest
Letty, encouraged by her brother's indulgent mood, should
think the time opportune to broach the subject of her marriage.
Dinner seemed interminable, though it was, in fact, shorter
than usual, his lordship not having been expected. The artist
belowstairs had had time only to fling together the merest
travesty of a second course, supplementing the soup, the
pigeons, the poulard à la Duchesse, and the morels of the first
course with a grilled breast of lamb with cucumber, prawns in
a wax basket, and some cheese-cakes. This very commonplace
repast had not escaped censure from the steward; and Farley,
who maintained a guerrilla warfare with the Gallic ruler of the
kitchens, prophesied that his lordship would send a pretty
sharp message downstairs. His lordship, however, made no
comment; and as for her ladyship, although she rejected most
of the dishes, and ate very sparingly of the others, this
abstinence seemed to arise from loss of appetite rather than
from any particular distaste of what was offered her.

When they rose from the table the Earl, who had glanced rather narrowly at his wife several times during the course of the meal, asked her quietly if she was feeling quite the thing.

She said hurriedly: "Yes—oh, yes! A little tired, but nothing to signify!"

Letty, interposing in a helpful spirit, said that they were both of them quite fagged with balls and routs; and when Cardross suggested that they should remain at home, instead of going to Drury Lane, she at once lent her support to the scheme, reminding Nell that there had been no play put on for months that had been worth seeing. For her part, she said, she would as lief stay at home, and enjoy a comfortable coze. But as Nell was well aware that her comfortable coze would speedily develop into an extremely uncomfortable altercation with her brother, she said that she wanted very much to see the play. Cardross at once bowed his acquiescence, but gone was the gentler note in his voice when he replied, with civil indifference: "As you wish, my love."

The play was neither better nor worse than any other that had been performed at Drury Lane that year, and even Letty, who was young enough to think herself hardly used if brought away from a theatre before the final curtain, greeted with approval Cardross's suggestion that they should not stay to see the farce. London was passing through a dramatic doldrums, and with the exception of an occasional appearance of Mrs. Siddons, in charity performances, and the promise of a new melodrama by Charles Kemble, to be produced at the end of the month, under the intriguing title of *The Brazen Bust*, there was really nothing in prospect to lure the most inveterate playgoer into any of the theatres. The Haymarket Theatre being closed, owing to the preoccupation of the management in the Court of Chancery, the Surrey, on the south bank of the river devoting itself to *burlettas* that were not at all the thing for ladies, the Regency fast sinking into decay, and both the Lyceum and the Olympic staging displays that resembled Astley's circuses, lovers of the drama were obliged either to stay at home, or to attend a succession of indifferent plays put on at Drury Lane, or at the Sans Pareil.

"I can't think what made you wish so particularly to see such a stupid piece!" said Letty frankly, when Cardross, having conveyed his ladies back to Grosvenor Square, had gone off to spend an hour or two at White's Club. "I did my best to save you from it, too, for I could see you were not in spirits."

"I didn't wish to see it," replied Nell, rather wearily. "I said so only because I was in such dread that you would begin to tease Giles about your marriage, and I thought that anything would be better than that!"

"How can you be so nonsensical?" demanded Letty, quite astonished. "Why should you care if I did tease him? He would not blame *you* for that!"

"No, very likely he would not—until you had dragged me into the quarrel, which you would have, if I know you! And in any event I can't bear to be obliged to listen to you driving Cardross into losing his temper, which no one can wonder at his doing, for you must own, Letty, that as soon as you are cross you express yourself in the most improper way to him!"

"Pooh! why shouldn't I say what I choose to him?" said Letty scornfully. "He is not my father, after all! I don't wish to distress you, Nell, but I warn you I mean to speak to him tomorrow morning, before he goes out. And, what's more, I shall continue to press the matter every time I see him, until he yields, which I don't doubt he will, because I have frequently observed that gentlemen dislike excessively to be continually teased, and will do almost anything only to win peace again!"

Upon hearing this pleasing programme, Nell expressed the fervent hope that providence might see fit to strike her down with influenza during the night, so that she would be obliged to keep her room for several days, and went off to bed, a prey to what her sister-in-law was uncivil enough to call the blue devils.

There was no intervention by providence, but Nell very prudently put in no appearance at the breakfast-table. Since it was Sunday, and she liked to breakfast before attending Morning Service, this was served earlier than on weekdays: early enough to afford Letty ample time to launch her preliminary skirmish.

That she availed herself of the opportunity Nell soon knew. She was seated before her dressing-table, while Sutton arranged her shining ringlets in a fashionable mode known as the Sappho, when Letty erupted into the room, out of breath from having rushed upstairs in pelting haste, and with her eyes and cheeks blazing. *"Nell!"* she uttered explosively.

Well aware that she would not be deterred from pouring forth the tale of her wrongs by Sutton's presence, Nell at once dismissed her stately dresser. She would probably learn the whole from Martha presently, since that devoted and un-critical abigail was deeply in her mistress's confidence, but that couldn't be helped, and at least Nell would be spared the embarrassment of her presence while Letty gave rein to her first fury of indignation.

Hardly had the door closed behind Miss Sutton than the storm broke. Pacing about the room in a fine rage Letty favoured her sister-in-law with a graphic and embittered account of what had taken place in the breakfast-parlour. The preliminary skirmish had clearly developed rapidly into a full-scale attack. Equally clearly Letty had been beaten at all points. Her recital was freely interspersed with animadversions on Cardross's character, cruel, callous, tyrannical, and odious being the mildest epithets she used to describe it. After one quite unavailing attempt to check her, Nell resigned herself, listening with half an ear to the various measures (most of them, happily, impossible) Letty was prepared to resort to if Cardross should persist in his uncompromising attitude; and wondering whether either of them would be in time for Morning Service. Not surprisingly, considering the overwrought state of her nerves, Letty's diatribe ended in a flood of tears, violent enough to make Nell entertain serious fears that she was about to fly into a hysterical fit. This danger was averted by a mixture of hartshorn and common sense, and the sufferer from fraternal persecution presently subsided into milder weeping. Nell had just succeeded in soothing her, and was bathing her temples with Hungary water, when Cardross, after the curtest of knocks on the door, walked into the room. At sight of Letty, languishing upon the sofa, he stopped short on the threshold, and said cuttingly: "An affecting spectacle!"

"Oh, Giles, pray hush!" begged Nell.

The stricken maiden on the sofa bounced up, and in a husky voice of loathing promised to go into strong convulsions if Cardross did not instantly leave the room.

"By all means do so if you have a fancy to be well slapped!" retorted Cardross, looking as though it would give him considerable satisfaction to carry out his threat. "If you have not, stop enacting Cheltenham tragedies, and go to your own room!"

"Do you imagine," gasped Letty, "that you can order me to my room, as though I were a child?"

"Yes, and carry you there, if you don't instantly obey me!" he said, pulling the door open again. "Out!"

"For heaven's sake, Cardross!" expostulated Nell, in the liveliest dread that Letty would relapse into hysterics. "Do, pray, go away, and leave her to me! This is *my* room, and really you have no right to order Letty out of it!"

"You have an odd notion of my rights," he said grimly. "I don't question that she is more welcome in your room than

I am, but you will own that I at least have the right to be private with you when I choose!"

She whitened, but said quietly: "Most certainly, and if it is the case that you wish to speak to me, shall we go into my dressing-room?"

"You need not put yourself to so much trouble!" declared Letty, trembling with anger. "I would not for the world, love, expose *you* to the sort of ill-usage *I* am compelled to suffer, and to spare you I will go!"

This very noble speech wiped the thunderous look from Cardross's face, and made him burst out laughing: an un-looked-for event which exacerbated Letty, but considerably relieved Nell. Letty, pausing only to inform her brother that his manners were as disgusting as his disposition was malevolent, swept out of the room, sped on her way by a recommendation to go and take a damper. Cardross then shut the door, saying: "Little termagant! I shall be sorry for Allandale, if ever she does marry him."

"She is very much overset by this news that he must leave England so soon," Nell replied excusingly. "One cannot but feel for her, and for my part—— But I don't wish to tease you any more."

"Thank God for that! I have had as much as I can support in one day, I assure you. At breakfast, too!"

"I must say, I think that was a very foolish time to choose," admitted Nell.

"Very! But she would not have found me more persuadable at any other hour." He added, as she sighed: "Yes, I am aware of what your sentiments are, but I didn't come to enter into argument with you over this lamentable affair. What I did come for was to discuss with you what will be the wisest course to pursue now. We may be sure of one thing: until that regrettable young man is out of the country there will be no peace for either of us. I shall no doubt be subjected to endless repetitions of today's scene; and you, I suppose, will be obliged to sustain the exhausting rôle of confidante. Well, I know of no reason why you should be called upon to endure Letty's tantrums, so tell me frankly, if you please, if you would wish me to pack her off to Bath?"

"Upon no account in the world!" she said quickly. "Surely you were only funning when you made that threat?"

"I was, but I didn't then know that Allandale was to leave England so soon."

"No, no, don't think of it! It would be so dreadfully unkind to send her out of town when she has so little time left before Mr. Allandale sails! I am persuaded, too, that she would run away—perhaps to Mrs. Thorne, and you would very much dislike that. Only think how it would look!"

"If I know my Aunt Honoria, she would be given no chance to run away," he said, with a wry smile. "Don't imagine, however, that I wish to send her there! She's a tiresome little wretch, and when she starts brangling and brawling I could willingly wring her neck, but so much must be laid at the door of her upbringing that I can't feel she deserves quite such a fate as to be delivered up to that dragon of a female. But I don't wish you to be worn to a bone by her nonsense."

"Indeed I shan't be, and I beg you won't dream of sending her to Lady Honoria! *One* thing you may be sure of: you have no need to fear an elopement."

"No, very true!" he agreed. "Allandale's inability to support a wife must put that disaster beyond the range of possibility!"

"Yes, but that is not quite just, Cardross!" she said reproachfully. "He may be an ineligible match for poor Letty, but you cannot doubt that his principles are high, and his sense of propriety too great to allow of his entertaining the thought of an elopement, whatever might be his fortune!"

"His principles and his propriety may be as high as the

moon, but I have no great opinion of his resolution!" Cardross replied. "Had that been on the same level he would never, as his affairs stand, have allowed his fancy for Letty to carry him to the length of applying to me for her hand! She can be an engaging little devil when she chooses, and I will own myself astonished if he is not being led about with a ring through his nose, like a performing bear. My dependence is all upon his straitened circumstances. We will keep Letty in London, then —and you won't blame me if she drives you to distraction!"

He left the room on these words, and after a discreet interval Miss Sutton returned to it, to complete, with lofty dignity, her task of presenting her mistress suitably coiffed and gowned for an appearance in the Chapel Royal.

In the event, Nell decided that the hour was too far advanced to admit of her making anything but an undesirably spectacular arrival at the Chapel Royal; and she presently dismissed her carriage, setting out on foot for the Grosvenor Chapel, which place of worship, though frequented by persons of ton, was hardly worthy of Miss Sutton's best efforts. She was accompanied by Letty, having coaxed that injured damsel to go with her in the hope that religious exercise would bring her to a more proper frame of mind. Unfortunately, the officiating cleric announced as the text for his sermon a verse from the Epistle to the Philippians. *"Let nothing be done through strife or vainglory,"* he pronounced sonorously, *"but in lowliness of mind let each esteem other better than themselves."* Nell felt Letty stiffen.

Nor was there anything in the discourse that followed to produce in either lady any thoughts suitable to the Sabbath. So apposite to the events of the morning was the sermon that Nell, far from being edified, was hard put to it to stifle a shocking fit of giggles; while Letty, swelling with wrath, could not afterwards be persuaded that Cardross had not suborned the blameless cleric into choosing a text aimed directly at herself.

Upon their return to Grosvenor Square Nell found a note from Dysart awaiting her. No, the porter informed her: his lordship had not called in person, but had sent it by the hand of his groom. Nell bore it upstairs to her dressing-room to peruse it in private, but its contents were disappointing. The Viscount had scrawled no more than a couple of lines to say that he had received her warning, and would take care to keep out of Cardross's way. He remained her affectionate brother, Dysart. It was only by the exercise of all the resolution at her command that she was able to refrain from despatching another letter to him then and there, reminding him of the urgency of her need. Lady Sefton called during the course of the afternoon, and stayed for an hour, uttering cryptic remarks, and peeping at Letty through her fingers as she did so in a roguish manner that caused that young lady to apostrophize her later as a nasty creature, which was unjust, since beneath her tiresome affectations she was the kindest of creatures. From having been acquainted with Mrs. Allandale for many years she was pretty well aware of the state of affairs in Grosvenor Square, but even Nell, who liked her, could not acquit her of having come to discover, if she could, any interesting circumstances which had not reached Mrs. Allandale's ears. Hardly had she departed than a much more unwelcome visitor arrived, in the person of Lady Cowper, who came with the ostensible object of begging dear Lady Cardross to lend her support to a charitable organization of which she herself was a leading patroness, but lost little time in trying to ferret out, in the most caressing way possible, all the details of Letty's romance. Nell was mortified indeed to realize that her lord's little sister had become one of the on-dits of London, and, glancing towards her, thought that she too looked to be rather struck. Lady Cowper, like all the Lambs, was possessed of a degree of charm that too often lured the unwary into reposing confidences in her which would later provide her with matter for her witty tongue; but her insinuating manners won her nothing from the two Merion ladies but a stoney stare from Letty, and from Nell a gentle civility that rebuffed all hints and enquiries, and caused her later to tell her numerous acquaintances that it was a sad pity that so beautiful a creature should be so insufferably insipid. As for her hostesses, no sooner had she taken herself off than they spent an agreeable half-hour abusing her, and in trying to decide whether her worst fault was cutting at people behind their backs, or paying visits in dresses trimmed with positively dirty lace.

The evening was enlivened by a spirited attempt made by Letty to convince her brother that in withholding her fortune from her he was guilty of embezzlement. He refused to be drawn into altercation, and even listened to her with great patience when, abandoning this unpromising line of attack, she expatiated on the manifold, if somewhat nebulous, advantages of life in Brazil, and the miseries she would undergo if separated by thousands of miles and an æon of time from Mr. Allandale. He even tried to coax her into viewing her circumstances with rather more moderation, representing to her in a little amusement, but with a good deal of kindness, that two, or even three, years could hardly be thought an æon of time; and that the possibility of Mr. Allandale's being snatched into marriage by a designing female of Portuguese extraction was too remote to be worthy of consideration. "Don't put yourself in this passion, my dear little sister!" he said, taking her hand, and giving it a squeeze. "You might be so very much worse off, you know! If I were the unfeeling tyrant you believe me to be, I should have told Allandale never to think of you again—and that is certainly what the world will say I should have done! I haven't said it, and I shall not. But you must not expect me to allow you, at seventeen, to throw yourself away on a young man who has neither birth nor position, and stands as yet only on the threshold of his career. I shan't do it, so stop coming to cuffs with me, like a good girl, and try to be a little wiser!"

She stared bleakly up into his face, her own very set. "You wouldn't talk so if you had ever loved anyone as I love Jeremy. You cannot know what it is to form a lasting passion!"

He dropped her hand. "You are mistaken," he said, in an even tone, and turned away from her to address some light commonplace to his wife.

Letty flushed vividly, and said: "I am not mistaken! You may think you have a heart, but you haven't! You don't like to be told that, but it's true!"

He said, over his shoulder: "Letty, you are not only becoming a dead bore, but you want manner as well as sense! Let me tell you that until you learn to behave with propriety you will make the worst wife imaginable for a diplomat!"

"Jeremy," said Letty, her bosom heaving, "thinks me *perfect!*"

"Which," remarked Cardross, as she slammed herself out of the room, "gives me no very high idea of his understanding."

Nell smiled, but said only, as she rose from her chair: "I think I should follow her. She has been very low and oppressed all day, and you know how it is with her! When she is happy I never knew anyone whose spirits mounted so high, but they can be all dashed down in a minute, and then she knocks herself up with one of her fits of crying."

"I have very little patience to waste on such distempered freaks," he replied. "The truth is that she has been spoilt to death, and cannot endure to have her will crossed!"

"Oh, yes!" she agreed. "But you would not wish her to cry herself into a fever."

"Nonsense!" he said irritably, adding, however, after a frowning moment: "I don't wish her to wear *your* spirits down, at all events! I suppose she will make us endure weeks of sulks. There's no doing anything until Allandale has sailed, but how would it be if I took a house in Brighton, after all, instead of going home to Merion at the end of the season? Do you remember how cross she was when I refused to take her there? I had nothing but scowls from her for a full week! Well! Prinney's parties are not what I would choose for her, but if it would divert her to go there——?"

"Perhaps it would divert her a little," she answered. She raised her eyes, and added, after a moment's hesitation: "Not very much, however. I don't mean to vex you, Cardross, but I think you don't perfectly understand. You hope that Letty will forget Mr. Allandale, but she won't. You see, she *loves* him!"

"A child of her age! What does she know of the matter?"

She coloured faintly, and managed to say, though not easily: "I was not very much older—when you offered for me."

His eyes turned towards her, an arrested expression in them. He did not answer her immediately, and when he did speak it was with a certain deliberation. "No. You were not, were you?" he said.

THE following day was one of gloom, relieved only at nightfall, when the guests began to arrive for a loo-party. It began inauspiciously, with a further reminder from Madame Lavalle, which threw Nell into such a fever of apprehension that she could no longer forbear to plague Dysart, but sent round a letter to his lodgings immediately, imploring him either to tell her what she must do, or to negotiate a loan for her "with a respectable usurer". Hardly had this been despatched than Martha came to her with a message from her mistress. Letty, it appeared, had awakened with a toothache, after a troubled night, and begged to be excused from accompanying her sister to North Audley Street, on a morning visit to the Misses Berry.

Nell found the sufferer still abed, a trifle heavy-eyed, but looking remarkably pretty, and without the vestige of a swollen jaw. This seemed to indicate that at least there was no abscess; but when Letty announced in the voice of one dwindling to decay that she thought perhaps the pain would go off if she remained quietly in bed, Nell was resolute in insisting that she should visit the dentist. She was not surprised by Letty's reluctance to do so, for the prospect of having a tooth drawn was not one which she herself could have faced with equanimity; but when Letty said at last that she would go, and that Martha should accompany her, so that Nell need not postpone her duty-call in North Audley Street, she began to suspect that the tooth-ache was not unconnected with this call. The late Lady Cardross had been a close friend of both the Berry sisters, but her daughter, ungrateful for the kindly interest they took in her, could be depended on to find ingenious excuses for not visiting them. She said that Miss Berry was quizzy, and Miss Agnes cross, and nothing bored her more than to be obliged to drive down to Little Strawberry to spend the day with them. Indeed, she had brightened so perceptibly when Miss Berry, on the occasion of her last visit to the Merion ladies, had confided, with a sigh, that she was compelled to find a tenant for Little Strawberry, that Nell had been positively ashamed of her, and had later taken her severely to task for heartlessness and incivility. So she now eyed the spoiled beauty measuringly, and said that she would herself take her to visit Mr. Tilton. Had she been feeling less oppressed she must have laughed at the smouldering look of resentment cast at her from beneath Letty's curling eyelashes.

Happily for Letty, who, by the time she was handed into the sinister chair in Mr. Tilton's room, was in a quake of fright, that worthy practitioner could find nothing amiss with her teeth. In his opinion, the pain she was enduring so bravely was due to a nervous tic. He recommended bed, and a few drops of laudanum as a composer: a prescription which Nell inexorably forced her unwilling sister to carry out, with the result that by four o'clock Letty announced herself to be perfectly cured, and got up to array herself for the evening's party. She was not in spirits, but somewhat to Nell's surprise, and greatly to her relief, she had made no further reference, after a bitter outburst on the previous evening, to Cardross's cruelty. She seemed to have realized that there could be no moving him; and while the droop to her mouth, and the brooding look in her eyes, held out every promise of a fit of the sullens, Nell could not but feel she could bear this better than the exhausting and quite fruitless discussions she had lately been compelled to enter into.

Dysart did not come, but as the retired gentleman's gentleman, in whose establishment he resided, rather thought that he had gone out of town to see a prize-fight, this was not wonderful. Nell could only hope that he would find the time to send a written answer to her letter, since, if he were to call in person in Grosvenor Square on the following day, he would not find her at home. She was engaged to take Letty to an al fresco party at Osterley.

There was no letter from him in the morning; and had her hostess been any other than Lady Jersey, whom it would be very dangerous to offend, she would have been much inclined to have cried off from the party. It was impossible to do so, however, without giving grave offence, for Lady Jersey had been one of the guests at her loo-party, and would certainly not believe any tale of sudden indisposition.

"Oh, no!" Letty agreed. "It would be quite shocking if you did not go! But I am sure I need not, for I have not the least heart for it, besides being teased by this horrid tic. I mean to stay at home, with a shawl round my head."

"And Paley's *Sermons* in your hand, I daresay!" exclaimed Nell. "For shame, Letty! You have no more tic than I have!"

"Even if I have not I won't be forced to go to parties when I am in the deepest affliction!" said Letty, flushing. "I don't doubt it would suit Cardross very well to be able to say that if I continue to do so it is plain he has not done his best to break my heart, but he shan't have *that* satisfaction, and so you may tell him! I won't go!"

"Indeed, Letty, you must go!" Nell said earnestly. "You cannot, surely, wish to have your affairs made the subject of gossip! Think how vexed you were when Lady Sefton and Lady Cowper came here on Sunday to try if they could discover what truth there is in the rumours that are going about! Pray do not wear your heart on your sleeve, my dear! it is so very unbecoming!"

"I won't go!" Letty reiterated mulishly.

"Won't go where?" asked Cardross, coming into the room in time to hear this declaration.

"I won't go to Osterley with Nell! And I don't care if people do gossip!"

"Of course you will go to Osterley!" he said calmly. "What excuse could you possibly offer for crying off?"

"I have already told Nell I have the tic, and if she doesn't choose to believe me she need not, but you can neither of you force me to go!"

"Doesn't Nell believe you? How unfeeling of her! *I* believe you, my pet, and I will send a message round to Dr. Baillie, desiring him to call." He added, the glimmer of a smile at the back of his eyes: "My own engagements are of no particular moment, and I will promise to remain at home with you."

"Rather than endure *your* company I will go to Osterley!" said Letty, quivering with suppressed fury.

"Yes, I thought you would," he observed, holding the door for her to pass out of the room. He raised an eyebrow at Nell, and said, as he shut the door again: "What mischief is she plotting? A clandestine meeting with Allandale?"

"I don't know," Nell said worriedly. "I *hope* not, but I own I can't feel easy about her: I do most sincerely sympathize with her, but it will not *do* for her to be meeting him in such a way. You won't mention this to her, but I fear she has let her partiality for him be too clearly seen, and there is already a little gossip about her, in a certain set."

"The devil there is! Take care, then, she doesn't give you the slip! Secret meetings I will not endure!"

"No, indeed! But I have been wondering, Cardross, if you would permit me to invite Mr. Allandale to dine with us before he leaves England. Poor Letty! it is very hard if she is not even to be granted the opportunity of taking leave of him."

"Lending my countenance to an engagement of which I disapprove?" he said quizzically.

"Not more than you have done already, in saying that they may be married when he returns from Brazil!" she urged. "I am persuaded she would be very sensible of your kindness in granting her that indulgence; and then, you know, there would be no need for her to meet him without our knowledge."

He looked sceptical, but shrugged, and said: "Very well: you may do as seems best to you."

"Thank you! I will tell her, and I do hope it may comfort her a little."

But Letty, informed of the treat in store, betrayed no enthusiasm for it; nor, when Nell represented to her the impropriety of her meeting Mr. Allandale in secret, did she return any very satisfactory answer. She sat beside Nell in the carriage looking the embodiment of discontent, but grew rather more cheerful at Osterley. She was always susceptible to admiration, and she received so many compliments on her appearance in a new and dashing dress of pale lemon-coloured crape worn over a slip of white sarsnet, that Nell soon saw, to her relief, that she had abandoned her die-away air, and was prepared to enjoy herself.

Shortly after noon the porter at Cardross House opened the door to the Viscount Dysart. His lordship, who was dressed for travel, in breeches and top-boots, trod briskly into the hall, and demanded his sister. Upon learning that she had gone off on an expedition of pleasure with the Lady Letitia, he looked first thunderstruck, and then wrathful, and exclaimed: "Gone to Osterley? Well, hell and the devil confound it! Did she leave any message for me?"

No, the porter said apologetically, he did not think her ladyship had left a message, unless, perhaps, with Farley.

The Viscount turned an impatient and an enquiring look upon Farley, who had appeared from the nether regions, and was bowing to him with stately civility. "Did her ladyship say when she would be back?" he demanded.

"No, my lord—merely that she had no expectation of being late. I understand it is an al fresco party: something, doubtless, in the nature of a pic-nic."

"Well, if that don't beat all hollow!" said the Viscount involuntarily, and in accents of disgust.

"I fancy that his lordship has not yet gone out, my lord, if you would care to see him? Mr. Kent *was* with him, but——"

"No, no, I won't disturb him, if he's got his man of business with him!" interrupted Dysart, with aplomb. "In fact, there's no need to tell him I called: came to see her ladyship on a private matter!"

"Just so, my lord," said Farley, accepting with a wonderful air of unconsciousness the handsome douceur which the Viscount bestowed on him.

"I'll step up to her ladyship's dressing-room, and write a note to her," said Dysart. "And you'd better give me my hat again! I don't want his lordship to catch sight of it."

However, the porter undertook to keep the hat hidden from his master's eyes, so Dysart, quite unembarrassed, told him to see that he did, and, declining escort, went off up the broad stairway.

"As bold as Beauchamp, that's what he is," remarked the porter, carefully setting the hat down under his huge chair. "Down as a hammer, up like a watch-boy! Got some new bobbery on hand from the look in his ogles. Ah, well! he ain't one of the stiff-rumped sort, that's one thing, and it don't matter to him if he's swallowed a spider: you won't catch him forgetting to tip a cove his earnest! There's plenty as wouldn't give me more than a borde for hiding their tiles, but you mark my words if he don't fork out a hind-coachwheel! What did he drop in *your* famble, Mr. Farley?"

But Farley, revolted by such vulgar curiosity, merely withered him with a stare before retiring again to his own quarters.

Twenty minutes later the Viscount came lightly down the stairs again, pausing for a moment on the half-landing to make sure the coast was clear. Encouraged by a nod and a wink from the porter, he descended the last half-flight, and handed over a sealed billet. "Give that to her ladyship, will you, George?"

"Yes, my lord. Thank *you*, my lord!" said the porter, as a large and shining coin followed the billet.

"And if you want a sure thing for the King's Plate at Chester tomorrow," added the Viscount, setting his high-crowned beaver on his head, and pulling on his gloves, "put your blunt on Cockroach!"

The porter thanked him again, but with less fervour. A keen student of the Turf, he perceived that his lordship had taken to betting the long odds, and he could only regret his imprudence: if that was his new lay there would be a sad dwindling of the stream of heavy silver coins that fell from his hand.

Nell, eagerly deciphering the scrawl some hours later, in the privacy of her bedchamber, no sooner made herself mistress of its contents than she read it a second time, more slowly, and with a knit brow, unable to decide whether she ought to be consoled by its message, or alarmed.

"*What the devil*," wrote Drysart, without preamble, "*is the use of setting up a squawk for me to come and see you if the next thing you do is to go jauntering off to a pic-nic? I can't wait to see you, for I'm going out of town for a day or two, but you may as well stop fretting and fuming, because I have hit on a way of setting all to rights, and more besides. I shan't tell you what it is, because ten to one you would not like it, for I never knew anyone with more buffleheaded scruples. I daresay you would have tried to throw a rub in the way, had you been at home, so I am just as glad you are not. If that hog-grubbing mantua-maker of yours starts dunning you again before I get back to town tell her she shall be paid before the week's out. Now, don't be in a pucker, my dear Sister, for we shan't fail this time, and don't get to wondering if I've sold your precious sapphires, or anything else you doat on, for I have not. Your affectionate brother, Dysart. P.S. I greased Farley in the fist not to tell Cardross I was in the house, and your porter too— at least, I shall—so don't go blurting it out to him like a ninny-hammer."*

Having read this twice, Nell's spirits rose a little. There seemed to be no doubt that Dysart really had discovered a way of paying her debt, though what it could be she had not the remotest guess. It made her uneasy to read that she would not like it; but since he had been indignant with her for supposing that he would play the highwayman in earnest, and had now assured her that he had not taken her jewels, she did not think it could be anything very bad. He wrote with such certainty that her first sharp fear died: even Dysart would not have stated so positively that they would not fail this time had the matter rested on the turn of a card, or the fall of the dice. The worst would be if he had backed himself to perform some crazy exploit, and his going out of town made this appear rather probable. Nell knew that he had jumped his horse over that famous dinner-table because someone had betted heavily against his being able to perform the feat. She knew also that no dependance could be placed on his refusing a dangerous wager, because he was so much a stranger to fear that his anxious relatives had more than once entertained the unnerving suspicion that he was incapable of recognizing peril, even though it stared him in the face. Vague but hideous possibilities began to suggest themselves to her, but before she had made herself quite sick with apprehension common sense reasserted itself, and she thought what a fool she was to suppose that even the most totty-headed of his cronies would offer him a wager the acceptance of which would put him in danger of breaking his neck.

For twenty-four hours she hung between hope and fear, and then a blow more crushing than any she had thought possible almost annihilated her. She had come in to find a message awaiting her that called for an immediate answer, and taking it upstairs with her, sat down at the tambour-top writing-table in her dressing-room to scribble a reply before ringing for Sutton to dress her for dinner. She had just signed her name and was about to shake the pounce-box over the single sheet of paper, when the door opened behind her, and Sutton's voice said: "Oh, my lady!"

Sutton sounded agitated. Thinking that she must suppose herself to have been sent for long since (for the only thing that ever ruffled her stately calm was the degrading suspicion that she had fallen short of her own rigid standard), Nell said cheerfully: "Yes, I am come home, but I had not pulled my bell, so don't be thinking you are late! The India mull-muslin with the short train will do very well for tonight."

"It's not that, my lady!" Sutton said. "It is the necklace!"

"The necklace?" Nell repeated uncomprehendingly.

"The necklace of diamonds and emeralds which your ladyship never wears, and which we placed for safety in this very cupboard!" said Sutton tragically. "Between the folds of the blue velvet pelisse your ladyship wore last winter, where no one would think to look for such a thing! Oh, my lady, it is more than an hour since I made the discovery, and how I have found the strength to keep me on my feet I know not! Never in all my years of service has such a thing happened to any of my ladies! Gone, my lady!"

Nell sat turned to stone. As the appalling implication flashed into her brain she found herself unable to move or to speak. The colour drained away from her very lips, but her back was still turned to her dresser, and Sutton did not see how near she was to fainting.

"I took your ladyship's winter garments out to brush them, and be sure there was no moth crept in, which is always my practice, for too often, my lady, and particularly when a garment is trimmed with fur, will it be found that camphor does not prevail! The case the necklace was laid in was there still, but when I lifted it I thought it felt too light, and the dreadful suspicion came to me—— My lady, I opened it, and it was empty!"

A voice which Nell knew must be her own, for all it did not seem to belong to her, said: "Good God, what a fright you put me into, Sutton!"

"My lady?"

Sutton sounded startled. Nell set the pounce-box down with a shaking hand, her underlip gripped between her teeth. She had overcome her faintness: one must not faint in such an extremity as this. "But surely I told you, Sutton?" she said.

"*Told* me, my lady?"

She was beginning to see her way: not more than a few steps of it yet. "Did I not? How stupid! Yet I thought I had done so. Don't—don't be afraid! It hasn't been stolen."

"You have it safe, my lady?" Sutton cried eagerly.

"Yes. That is—no, it—— I took it to Jeffreys."

"You took it to Jeffreys, my lady?" Sutton repeated, in an astonished tone. "Indeed you never told me! And to remove it from the case——! Never say you stuffed it into your reticule! My lady, it is not my place to say so, but you should not! Why, you might have dropped it, or had it snatched from you! It gives one palpitations only to think of it!"

"Nonsense! It was safer by far in my reticule. I hope you may not have told anyone—any of the other servants—that it was stolen? If you have, it must make them very—very uncomfortable—in case they should be suspected of having taken it!"

"Not to a living soul have I opened my lips!" declared Sutton, drawing herself up rather rigidly. "I should think it very improper, my lady, to make such a disclosure to anyone other than your ladyship."

"I am so glad! The thing is, you see, that I have some notion of wearing it—at our own ball here. I thought, perhaps, with the pale green gauze I might not dislike it. So—I put it on, to see how it would be—yes, on Thursday last, when you went to visit your sister!—and it seemed to me that the clasp was not quite safe. That is why I took it to Jeffreys."

"Well, my lady," said Sutton, rapidly recovering her poise, "it is a prodigious relief to me to know that my alarm need not have been. I am sure I was never nearer in my life to suffering a spasm."

She then folded her lips tightly, dropped a stiff curtsey, and wihdrew to the adjoining room to lay out the evening-gown of India mull-muslin.

Nell tried to rise from her chair, found that her knees were shaking, and sank back again. She had staved off immediate discovery, but what to do next she had no idea, nor could she, for many minutes, force her stunned mind to think. Only pictures as useless as they were unwelcome presented themselves to her: of herself, taking the necklace from its hiding-place to show it to Dysart—oh, months ago! of Dysart, seated at this very desk, and writing to tell her that he had not taken her sapphires, or anything else she doated on; of Cardross's face, when he had spoken to her so harshly about Dysart, and then, quite suddenly, had checked himself. She uttered a stifled moan, and covered her eyes with her hand. Dysart knew she didn't like the Cardross necklace, but how could he have supposed that it was hers to dispose of at will? Or didn't he care?

It was fruitless to ask herself such questions as that: no answer could be forthcoming until Dysart himself gave it to her. And that at once raised another question, and a far more urgent one: where was Dysart? It seemed to her at first incomprehensible that he should have left London; but presently it occurred to her that it might be very dangerous to sell the necklace to any London jeweller or pawnbroker. She knew very little about such matters, but she believed it was quite a famous piece; and certainly there could be no mistaking it, if once one had seen it. It had been made a long time ago, in the time of Elizabeth, as a wedding-gift from the Cardross of that age to his bride, and it figured in more than one family portrait. It was, moreover, of unusual workmanship, for the jewels were set in the semblance of flowers and foliage, and every flower trembled on the end of a tiny spiral of gold. Nell had worn it once only, at a Drawing-Room, but although it had excited a good deal of admiration, and not a little curiosity (for no one could imagine what held the jewel-clusters quite half an inch clear of Nell's breast, or what caused them to nod and quiver with every movement she made), she knew that it did not really become her; there were too many clusters, too much twisted gold in the foundation from which they sprang, too many leaves of flashing emeralds. She had once told Cardross that he ought to lend it to a museum, but although he had agreed that the proper place for it was in a glass case he liked her to wear it on state occasions, and so it had never gone to a museum. But even though it had not been publicly shown she supposed it must be well enough known to make Dysart seek a buyer for it in the provinces. She wondered hopelessly how he expected her to conceal the loss, whether he had found some craftsman skilled enough to copy the necklace, or whether (and this was the best she could hope) he had not sold, but pledged it.

She became aware of Sutton, coughing discreetly in the adjoining room. It was growing late, and though one might stand on the brink of a deep chasm of disaster one was still obliged to dress for dinner. She got up, steadier now, but with so white a face and such a look of strain in her eyes that Sutton, when she saw her come into the bedchamber, exclaimed that she was ill. She glanced at her own reflection in the mirror, and was startled to see how hagged she looked. She forced up a smile, and said: "Not ill, but I have had the head-ache all day. You must rouge my cheeks a little."

"If I may say it, my lady, I had as lief see you laid down in your bed. I am sure none knows better than I what it is to have the migraine."

Nell shook her head, but she consented to swallow a few drops of laudanum in water, feeling that even though she had no migraine she had never stood in more urgent need of a composer.

The finishing touches had just been put to her toilette when Cardross sought admittance to the room. A sudden terror that Sutton might mention the disappearance of the necklace to him darted through Nell's mind, and made her tongue cleave to the roof of her mouth; but Sutton did not speak. Her face was always rather immobile, and in Cardross's presence it became mask-like. She dropped a slight curtsey, and at once withdrew, according to her correct practice. Nell remembered that she held men in abhorrence, and could breathe again.

Cardross was still habited in his morning-dress, and the sight of his blue coat and tasselled Hessians made Nell recollect, with relief, that he was not dining at home that evening. She said, with an effort at lightness: "Ah! Daffy Club, I collect!"

He smiled. "No: Cribb's Parlour! You have no engagement for tonight?"

"No, none. I am quite thankful for it! I have had the head-ache all day, and am not rid of it yet."

"For several days, I think."

Her eyes flew to his, at once startled and wary. "No—but I own I am worn to a bone with dissipation!"

"By something, at all events." He spoke very evenly, but his expression alarmed her. "I could almost suppose you to be love-lorn—as love-lorn as Letty!"

She looked rather blindly at him. A tragic little smile

wavered on her lips, but she turned her head away, not answering.

"I can only wish you a speedy recovery," he said. "Who is the man so fortunate as to have hit your fancy? No doubt some dashing sprig of fashion?"

"I think you must be trying to joke me," she said, her face still averted. "It is not kind—when I have the head-ache!"

"You must forgive me." After a slight pause, he added: "I came to tell you—and I trust it may relieve your head-ache—that I learned today that Allandale has gone into the country for a couple of nights, on a visit to an uncle, or some such thing. You may relax your vigilance—and I would he might remain out of town until he sets sail!"

"I can't blame you for that. I know you have had a great deal to vex you."

"Do you?" he said. "Well! it is something that you should own it, I suppose!"

CHAPTER XI

THE night, though she spent the better part of it in desperate thought, brought Nell no counsel, and certainly no comfort. While Dysart remained out of her reach there seemed to be nothing she could do. There was no way, even, of finding him, for though they might know, at his lodgings, where he had gone, she could not follow him. Yet of all things that was the most important, to find Dysart before he had sold the necklace. She wondered, since that could not be done, whether he would be able to recover it for her. Lavalle's bill suddenly became a matter of little significance: so much so that she was vaguely surprised she should have thought it so impossible to tell Cardross about it. It seemed a trivial thing, set beside the loss of the necklace, and far too trivial a thing to have led to the disaster which now confronted her. The maxims of her childhood reproached her; almost she could see Miss Wilby's grave countenance when she lectured her charges on the awful consequences of trying to conceal a fault. Miss Wilby had had plenty of examples to cite, but not even the awe-inspiring tale of the abandoned character whose dreadful end upon the scaffold could be traced back, through a series of crimes, to the fatal day when he had stolen the jam from his mother's cupboard, and denied it, was more terrible than the consequences of Nell's attempt to deceive Cardross. She had been afraid that confession would make it impossible for him to believe that she had married him for love, and not for his fortune; and now it seemed dreadfully probable that he would not care any longer whether she loved him or not. She had made him suspicious of her; there was a hard look in his eyes; and not once, since his return from Merion, had he attempted to do more than kiss her hand. If his love were not already dead, the discovery of her black wickedness would surely give it its *coup de grâce*.

She fell asleep with the dawn, but suffered uneasy dreams, and woke to full sunlight with heavy eyes, and a heavier heart.

She received no morning visit from Cardross, and he had left the house before she emerged from her room, looking, according to his sister, a perfect quiz, in a blue and yellow striped waistcoat, and a spotted cravat. From this unflattering description Nell realized that it must be one of the days when the Four-Horse Club met in George Street, and drove out to dine at Salt Hill. "Very likely!" said Letty. "Though why they have to make such figures of themselves I cannot conceive!"

She then informed Nell that her cousin Selina had sent a note round to beg her to go with her in her mama's carriage to choose a wedding-gift for Fanny. She added, with the light of battle in her eyes, that she supposed there could be no objection to that scheme.

Nell was glad to be able to acquiesce. She had no great liking for Miss Selina Thorne, but if Mr. Allandale had gone into the country it was hard to see what harm could come of allowing Letty out of her sight for an hour or two. She did indeed suggest, when she saw that Mrs. Thorne had not sent a maid with her daughter, that Martha should accompany the young ladies, but Letty scoffed at her for a prude; and Selina exclaimed rather pertly that of all odious things a servant listening to one's private conversations was the worst. Nell had a momentary vision of the cousins with their heads together, giggling over secrets, and thought, not for the first time, that Selina would have been the better for a course of Miss Wilby's discipline. She said no more, however; and after arguing for a few minutes about the nature of the gifts to be chosen, the girls went away, their first objective, Nell guessed, being the Pantheon Bazaar, in which fascinating mart, though they might not discover a suitable wedding-gift, they would certainly fritter away a good deal of money on ingenious trifles for themselves. Nell was too glad to see Letty in better spirits, and too anxious to be left to the indulgence of some quiet reflection, to raise any objection to this programme.

Her quiet reflection did nothing to raise the tone of her own spirits; but when Letty returned, much later in the day, she was seen to be in a sunnier humour than she had been for some time. As Nell had expected, she was laden with parcels, most of which were found to contain such doubtful purchases as a pair of perkale gloves, which it had seemed a pity not to buy, since they were so cheap, but which, on second thoughts, Letty thought she would give to Martha; a stocking-purse; several faggots of artificial flowers, one of which she generously presented to Nell; a gauze apron; two muslin handkerchiefs; a box of honeysuckle soap; and a Turkish lappet, which had hit her fancy at the time, but which, now that she saw it again, was quite hideous. For Fanny she had purchased a gold armlet and ear-rings, a handsome gift which made Nell exclaim: "Good gracious! I had not thought you could afford anything so dear!"

"No, but I asked Giles, and he said I might purchase what I liked," replied Letty unconcernedly.

This seemed to indicate that a truce had been declared. The impression was strengthened by Letty's next words, which were uttered after a thoughtful pause. "He says it is true that he told you that you might invite Jeremy to dine here."

"Of course it is true!"

"Well, I thought very likely it was a hum, but if it was not I expect it was your notion, and you coaxed him into it. I am very much obliged to you! When will you write to Jeremy?"

"Whenever you wish," Nell replied. "Now, if you desire me to."

"Oh, no, there is no occasion for you to do so now! He is

gone to visit his uncle, you know, and he did not expect to
be in London again until tomorrow evening. I was thinking,
love, that if we were to go to Almack's on Friday I daresay we
should meet him there, and then, don't you think? we
could discover when it would be convenient for him to come
to us."

It was evident, from this speech, that an assignation at
Almack's had already been made. Nell did not feel equal to
giving a promise that she would attend the Assembly, but she
said that she would do so if she felt well enough, and with this
Letty, after a little more coaxing, was obliged to be content.
In the state of wretchedness she was in Nell could not think of
taking part in such a frivolous entertainment without a
shudder, but she did manage to extract a grain of comfort from
the reflection that the first fury of Letty's passionate despair
had worn itself out, and she was not contemplating any
immediate act of imprudence.

The more compliant mood lasted. Letty was able to see
Cardross again without ripping up; and although her spirits
were languid, and her manner lacked its usual liveliness, there
could be no doubt that she was making a serious endeavour to
mend her temper.

The hope that Dysart would come to her kept Nell at home
on the following day. Cardross was to have escorted both his
ladies to a Review in Hyde Park, but in the end only Letty
went with him. She had said at first that she was in no
humour for it, but upon Nell's appealing to her to bear
Cardross company so that she herself might nurse a head-
ache at home she at once agreed to go. She was too much
absorbed in her own troubles to perceive that her sister-in-law
was looking far from well until her attention was directed to
this circumstance, but when Sutton told her that she was
quite in a worry over her mistress, she was instantly ready not
only to do what was asked of her, but a great deal that was not

asked, such as placing cushions behind Nell's head, a stool under her feet, and a shawl across her knees, bathing her brow with vinegar, offering her all manner of remedies from hartshorn to camphor, and enquiring every few minutes if she felt a degree better. Nell endured these ministrations patiently, but Cardross, coming to see how she did, exclaimed: "Good God, Letty, don't fidget her so! Enough to drive her into a fever!"

Letty was inclined to take affront at this, but he pushed her out of the room without compunction, telling her to go and put her hat on, since his curricle would be at the door in five minutes. "And if you want me to let you handle the ribbons, take that pout from your face!" he recommended. He turned, and went back to Nell's chair, and held her wrist in his hand for a moment. Under his fingers her pulse was flurried enough to make him say: "If you are not better by the time we return I'll send for Baillie."

"Oh, no, pray do not! Indeed I am not ill! Only I still have the head-ache, and it seems foolish to go out in this hot sun," she replied quickly. "I shall be perfectly well presently."

"I hope you may be," he said, laying her hand down again. He glanced at Sutton. "Take care of her ladyship!"

An extremely dignified curtsey was all the answer vouchsafed to this behest. From the dresser's downcast eyes and lifted brows he might have inferred that she was deeply offended, but he did not look at her again. His gaze had returned to his wife's face; his expression seemed to her to soften; and after hesitating for a moment he bent over her, and lightly kissed her cheek. "Poor Nell!" he said.

He was gone before she could say a word, leaving her with an almost overpowering inclination to cry her heart out. She managed to overcome it, and to assure Sutton, with very tolerable composure, that she was already better, and needed nothing to restore her to her usual health but to be left to rest quietly for an hour or so. She believed that she might fall asleep if no one came to disturb her.

It would have been well for her had she done so, but sleep had never been farther from her. She tried to interest herself in a new novel, and discovered that she had read three pages without taking in the sense of one word; every vehicle heard approaching in the square below brought her to her feet and hurrying to the window; and when she took up her embroidery, determined to employ herself rather than to pace about the room, a prey to most harrowing reflections, she found that her hands were so unsteady as to make it impossible for her to set a stitch.

Dysart did not come, and so severe was her disappointment that it took all the resolution of which she was capable to enable her to meet Cardross upon his return with a calm countenance. Her training stood her in good stead: no one could have supposed from her demeanour that her brain was in a turmoil; and when it was suggested to her that she might prefer not to go to the Italian Opera that evening she laughed away this solicitude, telling her husband and sister-in-law that they must not try to wrap her in cotton.

Dysart walked in on her, unannounced, just before noon on the following morning. She was sitting with Letty in the drawing-room, endeavouring to soothe feelings very much ruffled by a visit from Miss Berry. The good lady had called a little earlier to enquire after her state of health, but upon Letty's coming into the room had speedily infuriated that injured damsel by entering with great earnestness into a discussion of her affairs. What she said held excellent common sense, and did honour to her heart as much as to her judgment, but her manner was unfortunate. A trick she had of repeating over and over again some catch-phrase could only irritate; she had a way of talking in a hurried, over-emphatic style; and the caresses and exaggerated terms of affection she employed in trying to win more confidence than was voluntarily reposed in her served only to set up Letty's back. She had not long left the house when Dysart entered it; and when he walked into the drawing-room the angry flush had not faded from Letty's cheeks.

"Dysart!" Nell cried, springing up from her chair.

"Hallo, Nell!" he responded, with cheerful nonchalance. "I hoped I should find you at home." He looked critically at Letty, and enquired in a brotherly fashion: "What's put *you* in a miff?"

"If nothing else had *you* would!" retorted Letty, with spirit, but a distressing want of civility. "No doubt, dearest Nell, you would like to be private with your detestable brother! *I* would as lief converse with the muffin-man, so I will go and sit in the library until he has gone away again!"

"Well, if ever I saw such a spitfire!" remarked the Viscount, mildly surprised. "What have *I* done to set you up on the high ropes?"

Deigning no other answer than a withering look of scorn, Letty swept out of the room with her head in the air. He shut the door behind her, saying: "Too hot at hand by half!"

"Oh, Dy, thank God you are here at last!" Nell uttered, with suppressed agitation. "I have been in such distress—such agony of mind!"

"Lord, you're as bad as that silly chit!" said Dysart, diving a hand into his pocket, and bringing forth a roll of bank-notes. "There you are, you goose! Didn't I promise you I wouldn't make a mull of it this time?"

She would not take the roll, almost recoiling from it, and crying with bitter reproach: "How *could* you? Oh, Dy, Dy, what have you done? You cannot have supposed that I would accept money obtained in such a way!"

"I might have known it!" ejaculated Dysart disgustedly. "In fact, I did know it, and I took dashed good care not to tell you what I meant to do! When it comes to flying into distempered freaks, damme if there's a penny to choose between you and Mama!"

"Distempered freaks!" she repeated, gazing at him in dismay. "You call it that? Oh, *Dysart!*"

"Yes, I dashed well do call it that!" replied his lordship, his eye kindling. "And let me tell you, my girl, that these Methody airs don't become you! Besides, it's all slum! I may have to listen to that sort of flummery from Mama, but I'll be damned if I will from you! What's more, it's coming it a trifle too strong! Let me tell you, my pious little sister, that if Felix Hethersett hadn't thrown a rub in your way you'd have borrowed the blunt from that Old Pope in Clarges Street!"

"But, Dy——!" she stammered. "The cases are not comparable! Perhaps it was wrong of me—indeed, I know it was wrong!—but it was not—it was not *wicked!*"

"Oh, stop acting the dunce!" he said, exasperated. "Of all the fustian nonsense I ever heard in my life——! What the devil's come over you, Nell? You were never used to raise such a breeze for nothing at all!"

"I can't think it nothing! *Surely* you do not?" she said imploringly. "I had rather have done anything than lead you into this! I never dreamed—— Oh, if I had but told Cardross the truth!"

"Well, if you meant to kick up such a dust as this I'm dashed sorry you didn't tell him!" said Dysart. "I always knew you had more hair than wit, but it seems to me it's worse than that! Queer in your attic, that's what you are, Nell! First you plague the life out of me to raise the recruits for you—and where you thought I could lay my hand on three centuries the lord knows! Then, when I hit on a way of doing the thing neatly you've no more sense in your cock-loft than to cry rope on me; and now, when I hand you a roll of soft you ain't even grateful, but start reading me a damned sermon! And when I think that I came posting back to town the instant the thing came off right because I knew you'd fall into a fit of the dismals, or go off on some totty-headed start, if I didn't, I have a dashed good mind to let you get yourself out of your fix as best you can!"

"It is all my fault!" she said mournfully, wringing her hands. "*I* was in such desperate straits, and begged you so *foolishly* to help me——"

"Now, don't put yourself in a taking over that!" he interrupted. "I don't say I was best pleased at the time—and now that all's right I don't mind owning to you that there was a moment when I thought I was at a stand—but *I'm* not complaining. There's no saying but what if you hadn't kept on teasing me to dub up the possibles I mightn't be standing here today pretty well able to buy an abbey!"

"Dysart, *no!*"

"Well, no, it ain't as much as that," he acknowledged. "As a matter of fact I had thought it would be more. Still, it's enough to keep me living as high as a coach-horse for a while, and that will be a pleasant change, I can tell you! Lord, Nell, I was so monstrously in the wind that I'd not much more than white wool left to play with! Six thousand and seven hundred pounds is what I've made out of it! And that's not counting my debt to you, and the monkey I owed Corny!"

She grasped the back of a chair for support, for her knees were shaking under her. From out a white face her eyes stared up at her beloved brother in horror; she felt as though she were suffocating, and could only just manage to say: "Don't! Dy—oh, Dy, you *could* not! Not money gained in *such* a way!"

The thought of his sudden affluence had banished the frown from his brow, but at this it descended again. "Oh?" he said ominously. "And why could I not?"

"Dysart, you must *know* why you cannot!" she cried hotly.

"That's where you're out, my girl, because I don't know! And there's something else I don't know!" he said grimly. "Perhaps you'll be so obliging, my lady, as to tell me what you did with the blunt you won at Doncaster last year? Very pretty talking this is from a chit who backed three winners in a row! You weren't blue-devilled then, were you? Oh, no! you were in high croak!" He shot out an accusing finger at her. "And don't you try to tell me you didn't go to Doncaster, because I was there myself! Cardross took you to stay at Castle Howard, with the Morpeths, and you drove over from there with a whole party of people! It's no use denying it: why, I remember how you told me that the only thing you didn't like at Castle Howard was the old Earl, because there was so much starch in him that he frightened you to death! Now, then! How do you mean to answer that, pray?"

Utterly bewildered, she stammered: "But—but—I don't understand! What has that to say to anything? I remember perfectly! But——" She broke off suddenly, and gave a gasp. "Oh, can it be possible that——? Oh, Dy, dearest, *dearest* Dy— did you *win* that money?"

"Well, of course I did!" he replied, in the liveliest astonishment. "How the devil else was I to do the trick?"

She sank down on the sofa, wavering between tears and laughter. "Oh, how *stupid* I have been! I thought—— Oh, never mind that! Dy, has the luck changed at last? Tell me how it was! Where have you been? How—— Oh, tell me *everything*!"

"Chester, for the King's Plate," he replied, eyeing her uneasily. She seemed to him to be in queer stirrups, and he was just about to ask her if she felt quite the thing when a happy explanation occurred to him. "I say, Nell, you haven't sprained your ankle, have you?" he demanded, grinning at her.

"Sprained my ankle? No!" she answered, a good deal surprised.

"What I mean is—in the family way?"

She shook her head, colouring. "No," she said sadly.

"Oh! Thought that must be it." He saw that her face was downcast, and said bracingly: "No need to be moped! Plenty of time yet before you need think of setting up your nursery. I shouldn't wonder at it if you were like Mama."

"Yes, that is what she thinks, but—— Oh, never mind that! Tell me how this all came about!"

He sat down beside her. "Lord, it was the oddest thing! A fifteen to one chance, Nell! And I'd no more notion of laying my blunt on it than the man in the moon! Well, I didn't know the horse existed, and as for backing it——! Anyone would have laid you odds there was only one horse entered that could beat Firebrand, and that was Milksop. But what do you think happened to me?" She shook her head wonderingly, and he gave a chuckle. "Sort of thing that only comes to a man once in a lifetime. It was on Saturday night that it started. I thought I might take a look-in at the—well, it don't signify telling you the name of the place: you wouldn't know it! It's a club I go to now and again. Anyway, I called for a tankard there, drank it off, and damme if there wasn't a great cockroach in the pot!"

"Ugh!" exclaimed Nell, shuddering.

"Yes, I didn't like it above half myself," agreed the Viscount. "But the queer thing about it was that it wasn't dead! Seemed a bit lushy when I tipped it out on to the table, but, dash it, what could you expect? It got quite lively after a while, and so we matched it against a spider that—a friend of mine—picked off its web."

"Cockroaches and spiders?" interrupted Nell, aghast.

"Oh, lord, yes: dozens of 'em! The place is full of them!"

"But, Dysart, how *very* shocking! It must be a sadly dirty house!"

"Yes, I expect it is," he agreed. "In fact, I know it is, but

that don't signify! The thing is, most of the company fancied
the spider. Well, I did myself, to tell you the truth, for it was
a stout-looking runner, with a set of capital legs to it. I didn't
back it, of course, because the cockroach was my entry, but I
never thought to see the cockroach win."

"And it *did*?" Nell asked anxiously.

"Won by half the length of the course!" said the Viscount.
"That was the table. We had 'em lined up, and I must say I
thought my entry was still a trifle bosky, and I daresay he was,
but no sooner did I give him the office—with a fork—than off
he went, in a fine burst, straight down the course for the
winning-post! Mind you, the spider had it in him to beat him:
devilish good mover, I give you my word! The trouble with
him was that he was a refuser. If he didn't fold his legs up
under him, he went dashing off in circles. Now, young Johnny
Cockroach jibbed a trifle, but every time I used my persuader
on him, off he went again at a slapping pace, and always
straight ahead! You wouldn't have thought, to look at
him, that he was such a good mover. A daisy-cutter, is
what *I* thought, and so he was, but a regular Trojan, for all
that!"

"Oh, Dy, how absurd you are!" Nell exclaimed, laughing.
"And you won all that money on the creature?"

"No, no, of course I didn't! That was only funning! I didn't
win much more than a pony on him."

"What happened to him?" Nell could not help asking.

"How should I know? Went back to his stable, I daresay:
I wasn't paying much heed to him. Or to any of it, if it comes
to that. Well, what I mean is, never thought another thing
about it, once the race was won. There wasn't any reason why
I should. *But,* Nell, when I went to bed on Sunday night, I
pulled back the clothes, and damme if there wasn't a cockroach
right in the middle of the bed! How I came to be such a
gudgeon as not to see *then* what it meant still has me in a

puzzle. I didn't. It wasn't till Monday that it fairly burst on me. I went just to see how they were betting their money at Tatt's, and who should be there but old Jerry Stowe? No, you don't know him—not the kind of fellow you would know, but he's a mighty safe man at the Corner, I can tell you. Did him a trifling service once: no great matter, but to hear him you'd think I'd saved his life! Well, the long and short of it was that he told me in my ear to put all my blunt on Cockroach for the King's Plate at Chester! That fairly sent me to grass, I can tell you! I hadn't even heard of the tit: didn't mean to bet on the race at all, because I've no fancy for an odds-on chance, and to my mind there wasn't a horse entered, barring Milksop, that could beat Firebrand. But, of course, as soon as Jerry tipped me the office that settled it: taking one thing with another, I could see Cockroach was a certainty. The only trouble was, how the deuce was I to raise enough mint-sauce to make the thing worth while?" He paused, frowning. The amusement was quenched in Nell's eyes, which were fixed on his face in painful enquiry. "Did something I've never done before, and never thought I should do," he said, shaking his head. "Too damned ramshackle by half! Mind, if I hadn't known the horse *couldn't* lose I wouldn't have done it!"

She smiled faintly: "What did you do, Dy? Tell me—pray!"

"Borrowed a monkey from Corny," he replied briefly.

"O-h-h!" It was a long sigh of unutterable relief. "Is that all? I thought you meant you had done something—something shocking!"

"Well, if you don't know that it's shocking to go breaking shins amongst your friends it's time someone told you!" said the Viscount severely. "What if the horse hadn't won? A pretty Captain Sharp I should have looked!"

"Yes, yes, but I am persuaded Mr. Fancot wouldn't have thought so, or cared a jot!"

"No, of course he wouldn't, but that don't make it any better! Worse, in fact. I don't mind owing blunt to the regular brags, or to a parcel of tradesmen, but I'm not the sort of rum 'un that sponges on my friends, I'll have you know!"

She was abashed, and docilely begged his pardon. He regarded her frowningly, and suddenly said: "If you didn't kick up all that dust because you knew I'd won the money at Chester races, how *did* you think I'd come by it?"

She hung her head, blushing. "Oh, Dysart, I have been so foolish!"

"I daresay, but that don't tell me anything! What made you fly into that odd rage? You aren't going to tell me you thought I'd held up a coach and robbed some stranger?"

"No—worse!" she whispered, pressing a hand to one hot cheek.

"Don't be such sapskull! I should like to know what you imagine would be worse than that!" he said impatiently.

"Oh, Dysart, forgive me! I thought you had taken the necklace!"

"No, you didn't. I particularly told you I hadn't made off with your precious jewels, so stop bamming me!"

"Not *my* jewels—the Cardross necklace!"

"*What?*"

She quailed involuntarily.

"You—thought—I—had—stolen—the Cardross necklace?" said the Viscount, with awful deliberation. "Are you run quite mad, girl?"

"I think I m-must have run m-mad," she confessed. "It was because you held me up! I never should have thought it if you hadn't meant to seize my jewels, and sell them for me! I thought——"

"I want to hear no more of what you thought!" interrupted Dysart terribly. "Good God, are you going to sit there telling

me you believed me capable of making off with something that
don't belong to either of us?"

"No, no! I mean—I wondered if perhaps you thought it *was*
mine! And you knew I didn't care for it, so——"

"—so I prigged it while you were out of the way—a thing
worth the lord only knows how many thousands of pounds!"
he cut in wrathfully. "Just to pay your trumpery debt, too!
Oh, no! I was forgetting! *Not* just to pay your debt, was it?
I gave you three centuries—devilish handsome of me, by God!
—and pouched over seven thousand! Do you happen to know
what I did with the thing? Did I sell it to some fence or other,
or did I lodge it with a spouter? I don't wonder at it that I
found you in such a grand fuss! The only thing that I wonder
at is how I've contrived to keep out of Newgate!"

He had sprung up from the sofa, and was striding about
the room, in a black rage that made her quake. She dared not
approach him, but she said imploringly: "It was very bad of
me, and indeed, I *beg* your pardon, but if you knew how it
was—oh, Dysart, don't be so angry with me! Everything has
been so dreadful, and I fear my mind is less strong than I had
believed it! I knew how much I had teased you, and when I
read your letter my first thought was that you had backed yourself to win some reckless wager. I didn't entertain the least
suspicion *then*! It was when I knew the necklace had gone—
and you had written the letter in the very room where it was
hidden, and I remembered that I had shown you once—Oh, it
was unpardonable of me, but——"

He had stopped his pacing, and was standing staring down
at her, an arrested expression in his eyes. "Just a moment!" he
interrupted sharply. "You don't mean that, do you? That the
necklace has gone?"

"Yes, I do mean it. That was what overthrew my mind, Dy!"

"My God!" he ejaculated, turning a little pale. "When did
you discover this?"

"The next day—on Tuesday. It wasn't I, but my dresser who discovered it. She told me immediately, and that was when it flashed into my mind that—If I had had time to think, perhaps I should not—But I hadn't, I hadn't!"

"Never mind that! What did you say to your woman?"

"That I had taken the necklace to Jeffreys to have the clasp mended. She assured me she hadn't spoken of the loss to a soul, and I told her not to do so, and I am persuaded she has not."

"Cardross doesn't know?"

"No, no! How could you think I would tell him when I thought it was you who had taken the necklace?"

He drew an audible breath. "*That's* the dandy, isn't it?" he said with blighting sarcasm. "It's been missing for three days, and your damned dresser knows it, and you haven't seen fit to tell Cardross or to make the least push to recover it! Famous! And *now* what do you mean to do, my girl?"

FOR perhaps half a minute Nell sat staring up at the Viscount, the colour slowly draining from her face. In the flood of relief that had swept over her her only thoughts had been of thankfulness that Dysart had not taken the necklace, and of remorse for having so misjudged him. But his words brought her back to earth with a jarring thud. She lifted a hand to her brow. "Oh, heavens!" she said, in the thread of a voice. "I hadn't considered—Dysart, what must I do?"

"*I* don't know!" he replied unhelpfully.

"Someone did indeed steal it. But who? This is dreadful! It must have been one of the servants. Someone who knew where it was hidden, and how can I tell who may have known of it? The chambermaid whom Mrs. Clopton turned off a month-ago? I cannot think it!"

"Oh, can't you?" said his lordship acidly. "Much obliged to you, my lady!"

"Don't Dy!" she begged. "If you had taken it I knew you had done it only for my sake! But *now*——! It might have been any one of them, at any time! It was not necessary to know where it was kept: it must be known to them all that I have it, and never wear it, and only think how many opportunities there must be for persons living in this house to search for the hiding-place! And when they had found it they would guess that I should not discover the loss for months, perhaps. Had it not been for Sutton's care, in taking out my winter clothes to brush them, I might have known nothing!"

"It ain't a bit of use talking about what *might* have happened," said Dysart. "It's what *did* happen that has put you in the basket. Unless you can stop your dresser's mouth, it's bound to come out that you knew the necklace had been stolen three days before you said a word about it to Cardross. Well, you know the woman better than I do! Can you bribe her to tell the same story you mean to tell?"

"I don't know," she said slowly. "It's of no consequence, however: I will not do it!"

"I daresay you're right," he agreed. "Too damned risky! She'd be bound to guess there was something havey-cavey afoot, and once she knew you was scared of Cardross's getting wind of it she'd very likely bleed you white! Lord, there'd be no end to it!"

"I don't think it. It is not for that reason! Dysart, all this trouble has come upon me because I set out to deceive Cardross, and it has grown and grown until——" She broke off with a shudder. "I must tell him the truth. I must tell him *immediately*!"

She got up as she spoke, but the Viscount said dampingly: "Well, you won't do that, because he ain't in. Told Farley he wouldn't be back till five or thereabouts."

"Not till five! Oh, if my courage does not fail!"

"Do you want me to see him with you?" he demanded.

"You? Oh, no! I must see him alone."

"Well, it's my belief the thing will come off a dashed sight better if you do," he said frankly. "It ain't that I mind seeing him, because now the dibs are in tune again there's no reason why I should, but for one thing I'm pledged to Corny, and for another Cardross won't like it if you take me along, like a dashed bodyguard! That's the way to get his back up at the very start. Besides, you don't need a bodyguard. I don't say he isn't going to be devilish angry, because it stands to reason he's bound to be, but you needn't be afraid he won't come round. He will—and all the quicker if I'm not there! He don't love me, but he loves you all right and tight!"

She said nothing; and after a moment he held out the banknotes to her again. "Take 'em! No need to mention the mantua-maker's bill to him, unless you choose. You may put the whole on to me: I had three centuries from you, and I've now paid 'em back. I daresay that will surprise him more than if you told him I'd prigged his damned heirloom!"

At these biting words, she flung her arms round his neck, vehemently asserting that no one could ever believe such a thing of him, and again begging him to forgive her.

"Yes, very well, but you needn't think I'm pleased with you, for I'm not!" responded Dysart, disengaging himself from her embrace. "It's not a bit of use hanging round my neck, and playing off your cajolery: *I'm* not Cardross! And mind this! the next time you run into trouble, don't you come to me to drag you out of it!"

"No," Nell said meekly.

"I'll be off now," he announced. "No getting into high fidgets, Nell!"

She shook her head.

"And no turning short about either!" he warned her.

"No, I promise you I mean to tell Cardross as soon as he returns."

"Well, see you do!" he said, relenting sufficiently to bestow a brief hug upon her. "I suppose I ought to stay to bring you up to scratch, but I haven't seen Corny yet, and I must. Besides, it's his birthday, and we mean to make a batch of it."

With that he went off, leaving her to solitude and her melancholy thoughts. She roused herself presently from these to send Sutton to pay Madame Lavalle's bill, and thought, as she gave the bank-notes into her dresser's hand, how happy it would have made her, only four days earlier, to have been able to do this. She could still be thankful that she would not now be obliged to lay the debt before Cardross, but that seemed a very small alleviation of the ills that beset her. The sight of her dresser brought one of these most forcibly to her mind. It would be necessary to tell Sutton that the necklace was not in the hands of Cardross's jeweller, but indeed lost; and how to account for her own prevarication was a problem to which she could discover no answer. Letty might pour out her troubles to her maid; to Nell it was unthinkable that she should admit Sutton into her confidence.

The thought of Letty made her ask Sutton suddenly where she was. The dresser replied that she believed her to have gone with Martha to Owen's in Bond Street, to purchase fresh ribbons for the gown she meant to wear at Almack's that evening. She availed herself of the opportunity to enquire of Nell which gown she herself wished laid out in readiness; but Nell, who had forgotten the engagement, exclaimed: "Almack's! Oh, no! I cannot go there tonight!"

Sutton merely said: "Very well, my lady," and went away. Letty (if she had indeed arranged to meet her lover at the Assembly Rooms) would scarcely be so acquiescent.

As the day drew towards five o'clock Nell began to feel a little sick. Her spirits had been getting steadily lower for some time, and were not improved by the prospect beyond the window. The day had been dull, and the sky had now become so overcast that the drawing-room, which should have been full of sunshine, had put on a mournful twilight air. It even seemed to be a little chilly, but perhaps that was only her fancy.

Cardross came in shortly after five, but when Nell, bracing herself to face the ordeal in store, went downstairs, it was only to learn from the porter that his lordship was engaged with someone who had called to see him on a matter of business. Knowing that Cardross was dining out that evening, and feeling that her courage would be entirely dissipated if she were forced to remain on the rack for many more hours, she said: "It is very vexatious, for I particularly wish to speak with his lordship before he goes out again. Who is it who must come to see him on business at such an hour? Not Mr. Kent, surely?"

"No, my lady. It's a Mr. Catworth. He called this morning, and seeing as he said his business was private, which he wouldn't disclose to Mr. Kent, nor anyone, I told him it was no manner of use for him to wait, because his lordship wasn't expected till five. And back he came, my lady, but I would have put him in the office if I'd known your ladyship was wishful to see my lord. Because my lord give his orders when he come in just now that when Sir John Somerby calls he's to be taken to the library straight, my lady."

"And he may arrive at any moment, I daresay!" Nell exclaimed. "George, if he should do so before this person who is now with his lordship has gone away, show him into the saloon, if you please, and desire him to wait! And—inform his lordship that I wish to see him before he goes to Sir John!"

"Yes, my lady: never fear!" said George, in a reassuring tone that gave her clearly to understand that he had by this time realized that there was something unusual afoot. "I'll tip the— I'll drop a word in Farley's ear, my lady!"

She thanked him, flushing a little, and retreated again to the drawing-room, there to pass another miserable half-hour, wondering how much longer the obtrusive Mr. Catworth meant to linger, and why providence, so falsely called merciful, had not seen fit to remove her from the world when, at the age of five, she had contracted scarlet fever. And yet, when, looking down from the window, she saw a neat individual descending the front steps, and knew that Cardross was at last at liberty, she at once wished that she might be granted just a few more minutes in which to recruit her forces.

But if the dreaded interview were not to be postponed until the morrow there was all too little time left to her; so she went quickly downstairs before a craven panic could wholly master her.

George, his foot on the bottom stair, drew back, saying that he had been on the point of coming to tell her that his lordship was now alone, and ready to receive her. He went before her to hold open the door into the library. He would have liked to have said something encouraging to her, because she looked so young and so scared, and put him in mind of his daughter, but that, of course, was impossible. It was as plain as a pike-staff she was in trouble, poor little thing: it was to be hoped his lordship would let her down easy, but he wasn't looking any too amiable.

He was looking very far from amiable. The instant she had crossed the threshold Nell knew that she had chosen her moment badly. He was standing beside his desk, his countenance very set, and he neither smiled nor moved forward to meet her. She had never before seen so sombre an expression in his eyes; her own eyes dilated a little in sudden alarm; she said involuntarily: "Oh, what is it?"

It was a moment or two before he spoke, and then he said in a very level tone: "I understand you particularly wish to speak to me. I am expecting a visit from Somerby, however, so unless the matter is of immediate importance it would be better, perhaps, if this interview were postponed until the morning."

The cold formality of this speech struck her to the heart; she was only just able to say: "It is of—most immediate importance! I must, I must tell you at once!"

"Very well. What is it?"

It was not encouraging, but she could not draw back. She said: "The necklace—the Cardross necklace! It has gone!"

She thought he stiffened, but he did not speak. Frightened and perplexed, she stammered: "You don't—I think you cannot have understood me!"

"Oh, yes! I understood you!" he said grimly.

"Cardross, pray——! You are very angry—shocked——"

"Both! Too much to discuss it with you now! I will see you in the morning. I may be able to speak to you then with more moderation than is yet at my command!"

"Oh, say what you wish to me, but don't look at me so!" she

begged. "Indeed, indeed I didn't lose it through any carelessness! It has been *stolen*, Cardross!"

"I didn't suppose that you had mislaid it. Are you suggesting that some thief contrived to enter the house without anyone's being aware of it, or do you mean to accuse one of the servants?"

"I don't know, but I am dreadfully afraid it must have been one of the servants!" she said worriedly. "They could have searched for it, but a stranger would not have known where to look, or—surely?—have thought it necessary to make it seem as though no one had been to my rooms, or stolen anything. I—I had no suspicion, you see! It might have been months before I discovered the loss, for it was hidden amongst the clothes Sutton put away in camphor."

"And how does it come about that you have discovered it?" he asked. "That is puzzling me a trifle, you know."

"I didn't—it wasn't I who discovered it! Sutton found the case empty when she went to look over my winter clothes."

"I see. How very disconcerting, to be sure!"

There was a derisive note in his voice, which made her stare at him in bewilderment. "Disconcerting?" she repeated. "Good God, it was far, far more than that, Cardross!"

"I am sure you were excessively shocked. I collect that Sutton did not make this unwelcome discovery until today?"

She did not answer him immediately. She had known that full confession would be difficult, but not that he would make it as difficult as this. She had to overcome an impulse to acquiesce, for it now seemed beyond her power to tell the whole of her tangled tale to this stranger who watched her with such merciless eyes, and spoke to her in so biting a tone. But the inward struggle lasted only for a minute. She drew a shuddering breath, and said faintly: "No. I—I have known—since Tuesday. I must explain to you—try to explain to you—why I haven't told you—until today."

"For God's sake, *no!* At least let me be spared that!"

She was startled, for the words had burst from him with savage violence. Her eyes leaped to his, and she recoiled instinctively from the blaze of anger she saw there. "Cardross——!"

"Be silent!" He flung round towards his desk, and wrenched open one of its drawers. "You need explain nothing to me— as you perceive!"

She stood staring in utter amazement, almost unable to believe her eyes, for what he had taken from the drawer and tossed contemptuously on to the desk was the Cardross necklace.

From a whirl of conjecture nothing coherent emerged; she was so much at a loss that she could only gasp: "*You* have it!"

"Yes, Madam Wife, *I* have it!" he replied.

Relief swept over her. "Oh, how thankful I am!" she cried. "But how—why—I don't understand!"

"Don't you? Then I will tell you!" he said harshly. "It was brought to me not an hour ago by an astute little jeweller whose son—neither as astute, nor, I fancy, as honest as himself! —had bought it, yesterday, for the sum of two thousand pounds! I imagine he must have blessed himself for his good fortune: it cannot be every day that such easy clients present themselves! He would be obliged to cut the necklace up, of course, but even so it is worth a trifle more than two thousand, you know. No, you *don't* know, do you?"

She hardly heard the bitter, jeering note in his voice, or grasped the implication of his words. She was staring at him with knit brows, rather pale, and with her breath coming short and light. "Yesterday," she repeated. *"Yesterday?* Who— Did he tell you—*who*?"

His lips curled disdainfully. "No, he didn't tell me that. His fair client—understandably, one feels!—was heavily veiled." He caught the tiny sigh of relief that escaped her.

"Nor am I quite such a flat as to have wished for further information on that head!" he said, the savagery again rampant in his voice. "A lady—unquestionably a lady! A *young* lady, dressed in the first stare of fashion, who would not disclose her name—how should she, indeed?—or accept a banker's draft in payment! Do you suppose, when I had been told *that,* that I catechised Catworth?"

"Catworth?" she said quickly. "The man who came to see you—came twice to see you—has just been with you?"

"Exactly so! If only you had known!—Is that what you are thinking, my sweet love? How should you have known? It was not he who bought the Cardross necklace for a song! *You* met the son—quite a knowing one, in his way, I should suppose, but by no means as downy as the father! If my new-found acquaintance is to be believed, he had never seen or heard of the Cardross necklace. Well; it may be so! I am much in debt to the father, and should be reluctant to disbelieve him. After all, I have never dealt with a Cranbourn Alley jeweller. Perhaps young Catworth is not fly, but green! It is otherwise with the elder Catworth. *He* recognized the necklace the instant it was shown him, and saw his duty clear before him! I must always regret that I was not just in the humour to enjoy the scene as it deserved to be enjoyed! So discreet, he was! so virtuous! Not an ungentlemanly word spoken throughout! He did not even permit himself to hope for my future patronage, and he accepted without a blink every whisker that I uttered! An admirable man—I must certainly place a little business in his way! How very shabby it would be if I did not!"

He paused, but she did not speak, or move. There was a queer, blank look in her eyes: had he but known it, she was less concerned with the injustice of what he had said than with the realization of what must be the true story.

He picked up the necklace, and put it back in the drawer.

Turning the key in the lock, and removing it, he said sardonically: "You will forgive me, I trust, if henceforward I keep it in my own charge! I am persuaded you must, for you have never admired it, or wished to wear it, have you? You should have discovered its worth, however, before you set out to dispose of it. I cannot have my wife so easily gulled, Lady Cardross!"

At that, she blinked, and half lifted one hand in a beseeching gesture. "Ah, no! Giles, *Giles*!"

It did not move him. "Oh, don't waste your cajolery on me, my pretty one! You will catch cold at that now! I was a bigger flat than you, but, believe me, the game is up! You hoaxed me wonderfully: bowled me out with that sweet face, and those innocent ways! I thought I was up to every move on the board, but when I saw you—when you put your hand in mine, and looked up at me, and smiled——" He broke off, and seemed to make an effort to master the rage that was consuming him. "You must pardon me! I had not meant to open my lips on this subject until I had had time to recover, in some sort, from the chagrin of having every suspicion, forced on me during the few months of our marriage, confirmed! Well! I have come by my deserts! I should have known better than to have been taken in by that lovely face of yours, or to have believed that under your charming manners you had a heart to be won! To be sure, you never gave me reason to think it, did you? How unjust of me to blame you for that! I will engage not to do so again, but must try to fulfill better *my* side of the bargain. It has been brought home to me how lamentably short of expectation I have fallen, but that can be mended, and shall be. Tell me, my sweet life, at what figure do you set your beauty, your dutiful submission, your admirable discretion, and your unfailing politeness?"

She had stood quite still, neither flinching from the ugly shafts aimed at her, nor making any further attempt to speak.

She was very white, but although she heard what was being said to her she hardly attended to it. He was saying such terrible things, but he did not know the truth: he was saying those things to some creature who did not exist, not to her. It hurt her that he could so misjudge her, but she never thought of blaming him. Just so had she misjudged Dysart, and with far less cause.

"Well? Why do you hesitate? Or don't you know what I'm worth?"

She looked at him, and saw a stranger. She couldn't tell him all the truth while this black mood held him, much less disclose to him the shocking suspicion in her own heart. In the end he might have to know that too, but it was not certain yet. But if a worse disaster than he knew threatened him there might still be yet time to avert it. Only she must not waste precious moments in trying to justify herself, or expose Dysart and Letty to the white heat of his anger. Later she would tell him, but not now, when her own part in the affair had suddenly become a matter of very little importance beside what might well prove to be Letty's.

She tried to speak, and found that she had too little command over her voice. He was still watching her with those hard, angry eyes. That hurt her, and made tears spring to her own. She winked them away, and managed to say, with a pathetic attempt at a smile wavering on her lips: "I can't answer you, you s-see. Later, I will. Not now!"

She went rather blindly towards the door. His voice checked her, even startled her a little. "No, come back! I didn't mean it, Nell! *I didn't mean it!*"

He took a quick stride towards her, only to be brought up short by the opening of the door, and the entrance of his butler.

"I beg your lordship's pardon!" Farley said apologetically.

"Well, what is it?" Cardross snapped.

"I thought you would wish to know, my lord, that Sir John

Somerby called to see your lordship ten minutes ago. He is waiting in the saloon."

"Tell him I will be with him presently!"

"No, please go to him now!" Nell said gently, and left the room without again looking at him.

She went swiftly up the stairs, past her own rooms, and up another flight to Letty's. Martha, running up two minutes later, in answer to the summons of a bell clanging so wildly that it was plain its pull had been tugged with peremptory vigour, found her standing in the middle of the room, and quailed under the sternly accusing look in her eyes. "Oh, my lady! I didn't know it was your ladyship!"

"Where is your mistress, Martha?"

With the instinct of her kind to admit nothing, Martha said defensively: "I'm sure I couldn't say, my lady."

"Indeed! Then will you come down, if you please, to his lordship," Nell said calmly, gathering up her half-train and moving towards the door.

That was enough to induce Martha, in a panic, to tell all she knew. It was not very much. She had indeed accompanied Letty to Bond Street that afternoon, where they had met Selina Thorne. Letty had sent her home then, saying that she would go with her cousin to Bryanston Square, and her aunt would convey her home later in her carriage.

"Was Mrs. Thorne with Miss Selina?" Nell demanded.

"Oh yes, my lady!" Martha said, a little too glibly.

"Did you see her?"

Martha hesitated, but the unwavering blue gaze disconcerted her, and she muttered that Miss Selina had said she was in Hookham's.

"I see. At what hour was this?"

"I—I don't know, my lady! Not to say precisely! It was when my Lord Dysart was with your ladyship that we stepped out."

"Lord Dysart left this house before two o'clock. It is now half-past six, but Lady Letitia hasn't returned, and you felt no anxiety?"

"I thought—I thought it was her ladyship that rang for me!" Nell's eyes swept the room. "But you have not laid out her ball-dress?"

"Her ladyship said—perhaps she should not go to the Assembly, my lady! She said—not to get in a pucker if she was late, or to say anything to anyone, except that she was gone to Mrs Thorne's, but she didn't tell me more! On my truth and honour she didn't, my lady!"

"You must have known, however, that she didn't mean to return. No, don't tell me lies, if you please! Lady Letitia does not take her brushes and combs and her toothpowder when she goes shopping."

Martha burst into tears, sobbing that she had not known, that her ladyship had given her a parcel to carry, saying it contained some things she meant to give to Miss Selina. Yes, it was quite a large bundle, but she didn't know what was in it; her ladyship had packed it herself, and never told her; and she would happily lay down her life for her ladyship, particularly when the dear angel was being made so miserable as never was, and not a soul to turn to but one who had served her from the cradle, as it were.

"That will do. I think you have acted this part with the intention of doing your mistress a service, and did not mean to help her to do anything that would bring down the most dreadful consequences on her. But if she has indeed eloped you will have done her the worst turn that lay in your power. I hope she has not—indeed, I believe that Mr. Allandale has a greater regard for her reputation than you have shown. I don't know what I may be obliged to tell his lordship: that must depend on whether I can find her ladyship, and bring her safely home. And also, a little, on your conduct *now*."

The terrified Martha, eyes starting from her head, and teeth chattering, began to gasp out promises of abject obedience, but Nell cut short her protestations, saying: "Stop crying, and listen to me! I am going immediately to Mrs. Thorne's, and if I find your mistress there, or can discover from Miss Selina where she may have gone, perhaps no one need know what has taken place today. So you will not speak of this to anyone. Do you understand me? If you should be asked where I am, you must say that you don't know. Now go downstairs again and desire Sutton to come to my bedchamber, if you please!"

Sutton, entering her room five minutes later, in the expectation of helping her to change her dress, found her clad for the street, in her bonnet and a light pelisse. Before she could give expression to her surprise, Nell said coolly: "Sutton, it is very vexatious, but I am obliged to go out. I don't know how long I may be." She raised her eyes from the gloves she was drawing over her fingers, and said: "Perhaps you may guess my errand. I am persuaded I can rely on your discretion, if that is so."

"Your ladyship may always do so. But if, as I fancy is the case, you are going to find Lady Letitia, I beg you will permit me to accompany you."

"Thank you. It is unnecessary, however. I—have a particular reason for wishing you to remain here. I am very reluctant to let it be known to anyone—if Lady Letitia has done something foolish which—which perhaps I may be able to mend!"

"I understand you perfectly, my lady. My lips shall be sealed, come what may!" announced Sutton, in prim accents, but with the resolute mien of one bound for the torture chamber.

"Well, I don't think anything very dreadful will come of it," said Nell, smiling faintly. "His lordship doesn't dine at home tonight, so perhaps he will not enquire for me. But if he should do so, could you say that you suppose me to have gone out to dinner? He won't ask then where Lady Letitia is, because he will think she must be with me."

"Certainly, my lady. He shall learn nothing from me."

"I am very much obliged to you. One other thing: can you, do you think, contrive to draw George out of the hall so that he doesn't see me leave the house? He would think it odd, and perhaps talk of it, you know."

"Very likely, my lady! I will step downstairs immediately, and desire him to fetch up your ladyship's dressing-case from the boxroom," said Sutton with aplomb.

"But what in the world should I want it for?" Nell objected.

"That, my lady, is none of George's business!" replied Sutton coldly.

Whatever George may have thought, the ruse proved successful. There was no one in the hall to see Nell slip out of the house; and no one within earshot when she softly shut the front-door behind her. She heaved a sigh of relief, and set off quickly in the direction of the nearest hackney-coach stand.

MRS. THORNE'S butler, opening the door to Nell in time to see the hackney which had brought her to Bryanston Square move slowly away, was very much surprised that her ladyship should have deigned to enter such a lowly vehicle, but she had expected that he would be, and told him in the easiest way that her carriage had suffered a slight accident. He seemed satisfied with this explanation, but when she asked for his mistress he was obliged to tell her that Madam had retired to her room to change her dress for dinner.

"Then, if you please, be so good as to ask your mistress if I may go up to her," said Nell, as though it were the most natural thing in the world for a lady of quality to arrive in a common hackney half-an-hour before dinner-time, wearing a morning-dress, and coolly demanding to be taken up to her hostess's bedroom. The butler looked doubtful, but he went to deliver this message, returning almost immediately to beg her ladyship to step upstairs.

Mrs. Thorne was seated before her dressing-table, enveloped in a voluminous wrapper, and with her hair only half-pinned up into the elaborate fashion of her choice. She was a stout, goodnatured looking woman, and when she rose to greet Nell she seemed rather to surge out of her chair. "Oh, my dear Lady Cardross, pray come in, and forgive my receiving you in such a way! But I would not keep you waiting while I scrambled on my clothes, and so I told Thomas to bring you to me straightaway."

"It is very kind of you. I should not be troubling you at such an awkward time," Nell said, shaking hands. "May I talk privately to you for a few minutes?"

"Oh, my dear! Yes, yes, to be sure you may! Go and see if Miss Fanny is dressed yet, Betty! I will ring for you when I want you back again. Set a chair for her ladyship before you go! Do, pray, be seated, Lady Cardross!" She herself sank back into the chair before the dressing-table, saying, almost before her maid was out of the room: "Tell me at once, my dear! When Thomas came to say that you were below, *such* a presentiment shot through me! And I can see by your face I was right!"

"I don't know—I hope not! Mrs. Thorne, has Letty been with you today?"

"Oh, my goodness gracious me!" cried Mrs. Thorne, "If I didn't know it! No, my dear, I haven't seen Letty since she visited us last week. Don't tell me she has gone off with young Allandale! Wait! where are my smelling-salts? Now tell me everything!"

Clutching the vinaigrette, and warding off a series of palpitations by frequently sniffing its aromatic contents, she managed to listen to the story Nell unfolded without succumbing to the various nervous ills which threatened to prostrate her. She was very much shocked, interrupting the tale with groans, and horrified ejaculations, but there was nothing she could do to help Nell, because she knew nothing. She had never encouraged Mr. Allandale: girls liked to flirt, and there was no harm in that; but when she had learnt that Letty considered herself engaged to a young man without a penny to bless himself with, and no prospects worthy to be mentioned, she had never been more upset in her life.

Nell was obliged to break in on her volubility, and to beg that Selina might be sent for. Mrs. Thorne was perfectly agreeable, but she could not think that Selina would be able to throw any light on the mystery of her cousin's whereabouts. When she was told of the meeting that afternoon in Bond Street, she could scarcely be brought to believe that such a thing could have happened. "Selina going off to Bond Street! Oh, you don't mean it, Lady Cardross! I never heard of such a thing!

To be sure, girls aren't kept so strict now as they were when I was young—why, not a step outside the house could I take unless my mother, or the governess was with me! And very irksome it was, I can tell you! I made up my mind I wouldn't use *my* girls so, and nor I have, but as for letting any of them go jauntering about town without one of her sisters, or Betty, to go with her, that would be quite beyond the line! Good gracious, whatever would people say? It doesn't bear thinking of, and if I find Martha was telling you the truth, which, however, it's very likely she wasn't, I declare Selina shall go to Miss Puttenham's seminary, say what she will! It was what Mr. Thorne said she should do, when Miss Woodbridge left us, but she pleaded so hard against it—well, there! But that Martha would say anything! Depend upon it, my dear Lady Cardross, Selina knows no more than the man in the moon where her cousin may be!"

But when Selina presently came into the room it was evident even to her fond parent that she knew very well why she had been sent for. She was in fine feather, and perfectly ready to be martyred in her cousin's cause. Hers had not been the chief rôle in the delightful drama, but she had been able easily to convince herself that without her self-abnegating offices the interested parties would by this time have been obliged to resign themselves to their equally disagreeable fates. Letty (if she did not go into a decline, and expire within the year) would have been ruthlessly forced into marriage with a titled Midas of evil disposition, at whose hands she would have suffered brutal ill-usage; and Mr. Allandale, unaccountably forgotten by his superiors, would have worn out his life in a foreign land, always carrying his lost love's likeness next his heart, and dying (in circumstances of distressing neglect and anguish) with her name on his writhen lips.

Until she found herself confronting Nell, of whom she stood in a good deal of awe, this affecting story had seemed to her so probable as to border on the inevitable. She had several times rehearsed the elevating utterances she would make, if called upon to account for her actions; and in these scenes every effort made by Letty's persecutors to drag from her the secret of her whereabouts failed. Sometimes she remained mute while the storm raged over her devoted head; but in general she was extremely eloquent, expressing herself with such moving sincerity that even such worldly persons as her father and Lord Cardross were often brought to see how false and mercenary were their ideas, and emerged from the encounter with changed hearts, and the highest opinion of her fearlessness, nobility, and good sense.

But in these scenes the other members of the caste spoke the lines laid down for them; in real life they said things so very different as to throw everything quite out of joint. In the event, Selina pronounced only one of her rehearsed speeches. Asked by her mother if she knew what had become of Letty, she clasped her hands at her breast, and declined to answer the question. She then invited the two ladies to threaten her as much as they chose, to do with her what they would; but warned them that they would find it impossible to force her to betray her cousin.

Mrs. Thorne should then have conjured her daughter on her obedience to divulge the truth; instead, and with a lamentable lack of histrionic ability, she begged her irritably not, for goodness sake, to start any of her play-acting; and before Selina could recover from this set-back Nell completed her discomfiture by saying in a tone of grave reproof: "Indeed, Selina, you must not make-believe over this, for I am afraid it is much more serious than you have any idea of."

After that, there could be no recapturing the dramatic flavour of the piece. Selina did say that she wouldn't tell anything, but even in her own ears this sounded very much more sulky than noble; and when Mrs. Thorne, heaving herself out of her chair, declared her intention of hailing her immediately before her papa, who would know how to deal with such impertinence, instead of behaving like a heroine, she collapsed into frightened tears.

It took a little time to drag the whole story out of her and the effect of her revelations on Mrs. Thorne was severe enough to make Nell feel profoundly sorry for the poor lady. She was so much stunned by the discovery that when she had believed Selina to have gone under the escort of her maid to a dancing-class, or a music-lesson, that abandoned damsel had been setting forth by stealth for the most fashionable quarter of the town, alone, and for the purpose of aiding and abetting her cousin in conduct that, if it were to become known, would disgrace them both for ever in the eyes of all persons of ton, that she could do nothing but reproach Selina, and wonder how she came to have a daughter so lost to all sense of propriety. It was left to Nell to question Selina, which she did with a gentle coldness that overawed her far more than did her mother's scoldings.

Letty had sold the necklace to Catworth on the day that she had gone with her cousin to choose a wedding-gift for Fanny. They had dismissed the carriage outside the Pantheon, telling the coachman to call for them at Gunter's, in Berkeley Square, considerably later in the day. After purchasing a couple of thick veils, they had set out in a hack for Cranbourn Alley, having discovered the existence of the firm of Catworth and Son through the simple expedient of asking the jarvey on the box to recommend them a jeweller not patronized by persons of quality. While Letty had transacted her business with the younger Catworth, Selina had remained in the hack, because the jarvey, when instructed to wait outside the shop, apparently suspecting them of trying to give him the slip, had expressed a strong wish of being paid off then and there.

After the sale of the necklace, only one thing was needed for an elopement, and that was the bridegroom, who was then still out of town.

At this point, Mrs. Thorne exclaimed: "Never tell me Allandale was ready to take her with no more than two thousand pounds!"

"My dear ma'am, you cannot suppose that Mr. Allandale was a party to such a thing!" Nell said.

"No, he wasn't," corroborated Selina. "Letty said she would tell him she had it from her godfather, in case he should think she ought not to have taken the necklace."

The two girls had met that afternoon by prearrangement, and as soon as Martha had been got rid of, which was done because Letty wished, with rare consideration, to protect her from blame, they had purchased such necessities as Letty had been unable to pack in her bundle, and brought them to Bryanston Square, to be bestowed in an old cloak-bag belonging to Papa. Finally, Letty had departed in a hackney for Mr. Allandale's lodging in Ryder Street. "But you won't catch them," Selina said, with a last flicker of defiance, "because that was *hours* ago, and you may depend upon it they are many miles away by now!"

This seemed all too probable to Mrs. Thorne, sinking back in her chair with a groan of dismay, but Nell was more hopeful. When Selina had been dismissed to bed, with the promise of bread and water for her supper, an interview with Papa on the morrow, and incarceration for an unspecified length of time in a Bath seminary for young ladies, she rose to her feet, saying that she would go at once to Ryder Street.

"But what is the use, my dear?" wailed Mrs. Thorne. "You heard what that wicked child of mine said! They're off to Gretna Green, depend upon it!"

"I cannot credit it! No doubt that was Letty's plan, but I shall own myself astonished if it was Mr. Allandale's. Oh, he would not do such a thing! I am quite confident he would not!"

"Good gracious, Lady Cardross, where else could they go? They couldn't be married in England, what with Letty's being under age, and special licences, and I don't know what beside! Surely to goodness he wouldn't have let her run away to him if he didn't mean to marry her immediately?"

"I don't believe he knew anything about it," declared Nell. "Only consider, ma'am! He is a respectable man of superior sense, and with extremely nice notions of propriety. I am persuaded he would not entertain for an instant the thought of eloping with a child of Letty's age. Her expectations, too! Oh, no, he couldn't do it! If his own good feeling did not prevent him, the knowledge that he would be thought to have behaved like a most unprincipled fortune-hunter surely would!"

"Ay, there is that," agreed Mrs. Thorne, a little doubtfully. "He would lose his employment, too, I daresay. But, you know, my dear, when a man falls head over ears in love there's no saying what he may do. And you aren't going to tell me Letty ran off to elope with him without him knowing she meant to do it!"

"Yes, I am," Nell said, on a tiny choke of laughter. "It would be exactly like her to do so!"

"Well!" gasped Mrs. Thorne. "Of all the brazen little hussies! A nice surprise it will be for Allandale when he goes home from the Foreign Office, thinking of nothing but his dinner, as I don't doubt he will be, and finds that naughty girl in his lodging, as bold as brass, and expecting him to set out with her for Scotland! Well, I hope it will be a lesson to him, that's all! Only, if that's the way it was, why didn't he bring her back to you long since?"

"I've thought of that," Nell said. "It does seem strange, but if he were kept late at his work——? Then, too, it would take him a little time, you know, to persuade Letty to give up the scheme. In fact, the likeliest chance is that she fell into one of her hysterical fits of crying, and the poor man could not have the least notion how to stop her! Oh, I must go to Ryder Street at once!"

The conviction that she would arrive at Mr. Allandale's lodging to find him endeavouring to soothe his would-be bride grew steadily upon Nell as she was bounced and jolted there in yet another hack, and she began to be quite buoyant again, feeling that if she could only restore his sister to Cardross with her reputation unblemished she would have done much to atone for the follies and extravagances of the past weeks. But when the hackney turned out of St. James's Street into Ryder Street, she suffered a check. The coachman pulled up his aged horse, and clambered down from the box to discover what was the number of the house she wished to visit; and it suddenly occurred to Nell that she did not know it. Nor did the coachman. Asked if he was perhaps familiar with Mr. Allandale, he said he wasn't one to bother his head over the names of the gentlemen who patronized him, and surveyed his fair passenger with unwelcome interest. She was put a little out of countenance by this, and had, indeed, been feeling a trifle uneasy from the moment the hack turned into St. James's Street, and she had seen all the clubs' windows lighted up, and several gentlemen of her acquaintance strolling along the flagway. This quarter of fashionable London, which lay between Pall Mall and Piccadilly, belonged almost exclusively to the Gentlemen, and it was not considered good ton for a lady to be seen within its bounds. Nearly all the clubs were to be found in St. James's Street; and the streets which led from it abounded in bachelor lodgings and gaming-hells. The coachman was plainly wondering whether he had been mistaken in the social status of his fare, and Nell was beginning to feel rather helpless and extremely uncomfortable when she providentially remembered that Mr. Hethersett also lived in Ryder Street, and would no doubt be able to direct her to Mr. Allandale's abode, if she were fortunate enough to find him at home. So she told the coachman to drive her to Number 5. It did not seem probable that Mr. Hethersett would be at home, for it was now past eight o'clock, but fortune favoured her. Just as she was searching in her reticule for her purse the door of No. 5 was opened, and Mr. Hethersett himself came out of the house, very natty in knee-breeches and silk stockings, a waistcoat of watered silk, a swallow-tailed coat, and a snowy cravat arranged by his expert hands in the intricate style known as the Mathematical Tie. Set at a slight angle on his oiled locks was an elegant chapeau bras, and hanging from his shoulders was a silk-lined cloak. He carried a pair of gloves in one hand, and an ebony cane in the other, but perceiving the unusual spectacle of a lady engaged in paying off a hackney-coachman at his very door, he transferred the gloves to his right hand so that he could raise to one eye the quizzing-glass that was slung about his neck. At just this moment, Nell turned to mount the few steps to his door, and uttered a joyful exclamation. "Felix! Oh, how glad I am to have caught you!"

The jarvey, observing that the expression on Mr. Hethersett's face was of profound dismay, clicked his tongue disapprovingly. In his view, Nell—as dimber a mort as he had clapped eyes on in a twelvemonth—was worthy of a warmer greeting than the startled: "Good God!" which broke from Mr. Hethersett.

"What the deuce brings you here?" demanded Mr. Hethersett, alarmed out of his usual address. "Cardross hasn't met with an accident, has he? Or——"

"Oh, no, no! nothing like that!" she assured him. "I shan't keep you above a moment—are you on your way to a party? —but I have most stupidly forgotten the number of the house Mr. Allandale lodges in!"

Disappointed in this conversation, the jarvey adjured his lethargic steed to get up, and drove slowly off.

"Thank the lord he's gone!" said Mr. Hethersett. "You know, cousin, you shouldn't be driving about in a hack, and coming here to ask me for Allandale's direction! I mean— not my business, but it ain't at all the thing! Cardross wouldn't like it. Besides, what do you want with Allandale?"

"Well, that isn't your business either!" Nell pointed out. "And if Cardross knew I was here he would have not the least objection, I assure you, for I am here for a very sufficient purpose. So will you, if you please, tell me the number of Mr. Allandale's lodging, and then you may go to your party, and not trouble your head over me any more?"

"No," said Mr. Hethersett, with unexpected firmness. "I won't! Well, I should be bound to trouble my head over you: stands to reason! Because it seems to me you're up to something dashed smoky, cousin. And as for saying Cardross wouldn't object to your paying calls in a hack at this time of day—well, if that's what you think, you can't know him! What I'm going to do is take you home."

"No, you are not!" said Nell indignantly. "Now, Felix, just because you met me in Clarges Street that day does *not* give you the right to try to bully and hector me over this!"

"Never mind that!—By the by, I hope all's right about that business?"

"Yes, yes, Dysart settled it for me."

"He did, did he?"

"Yes, for he has won a great deal of money on a horse called Cockroach. It was not very handsome of you to have betrayed me to him, however!"

"No, I know it wasn't. Best thing I could think of, though. What we want now is another hack."

"No—though I hope it is what I may want in a very little time. I suppose I shall be obliged to tell you what has happened," she sighed.

"Good God, cousin, do you take me for a flat?" demanded

Mr. Hethersett. "If you're searching all over for Allandale, it means that Letty is up to her tricks. What's she done? Eloped with the fellow?"

"I very much fear it."

"Eh?" he said incredulously. "No, no, not the sort of fellow to do a scaly thing like that! I was only funning!"

But when he had heard all that Nell saw fit to tell him of the day's events he looked a good deal taken aback, and acknowledged that the affair bore all the appearance of an uncommonly rum set-out. "What's more, if Allandale's made off with her—yes, but dash it, cousin, that won't fadge! I mean, it wouldn't be up to the rig, and though I can't say I like him above half there's nothing of the queer nab about him!"

"No, indeed! and that is what makes me very hopeful of finding them still here," she explained. "So pray will you direct me to the house?"

"Yes, but where's Cardross?" he demanded. "He can't have gone out of town again, because I saw him at White's this afternoon! It's his business to find Letty, not yours."

"He—he is dining out tonight, and then, too, he had Sir John Somerby with him, you see."

"What you mean," said Mr. Hethersett severely, "is that you haven't told him."

"No," she confessed. "I—I haven't."

"Well, you ought to have done so. Very unwilling to offend you, cousin, but you've got no right to play the concave suit with Cardross over that chit. Dash it, she's his ward! Daresay you're fond of her, but it won't do to be hoaxing Giles about today's business."

"No," she agreed. "Indeed, I don't mean to, Felix! Only the thing is that—he—he is very much vexed today. Something occurred that put him sadly out of temper, and I particularly don't wish to be obliged to break this news to him when—when perhaps he would be quite dreadfully angry with Letty!"

"Good thing if he was!" said Mr. Hethersett unfeelingly. "If you want to know what I think, it's my belief that the sooner you're rid of that resty girl the better it will be. Unsteady, that's what she is. Maggotty, too: never know where to take her, or what she'll be up to next!" He glanced fleetingly at Nell, but it had grown rather too dark for him to be able to see her face very clearly. However, he had drawn certain conclusions which he was pretty sure were accurate, so he added, in a careless way: "Shouldn't be surprised if it was her starts that had put him out of temper."

Nell said nothing in reply to this. The lamplighter was coming down the street, with his ladder carried between him and the boy who followed at his heels. Nell, who was tired of standing outside Mr. Hethersett's house, pointed this circumstance out to him, saying: "Won't he think it excessively odd that we should be standing here?"

"Yes, but we ain't going to stand here," replied Mr. Hethersett. "It don't look to me as though Allandale's at home, but we may as well enquire for him."

"Do you mean to say that he lives next door to you?" demanded Nell.

"Yes. Well, no reason why he shouldn't!" said Mr. Hethersett, surprised at the indignant note in her voice. "What I mean is, he don't trouble me: hardly ever see him!"

"And you have kept me standing outside all this time! It is a great deal too bad of you!" said Nell, treading up the steps to the door, and grasping the heavy brass knocker.

"I was trying to think what I should do with you while I did the trick here. Trouble is there ain't anywhere for you to go, but you oughtn't to be asking for Allandale, you know! Leave it to me, cousin!"

She was quite ready to do this, but when the door was opened, and Mr. Hethersett asked the proprietor of the establishment if Mr. Allandale was at home, and was told that he was not, he seemed so much inclined to withdraw without pursuing his enquiries any farther that she felt obliged to intervene. Disregarding a horrified murmur of protest from Mr. Hethersett she boldly asked if Mr. Allandale had gone out alone, or accompanied by a lady.

"Would it be Mr. Allandale's sister you was referrring to, ma'am?" asked the man cautiously.

"Yes," said Nell, with great promptness.

"Ah!" said the proprietor, stroking his chin in a ruminative way. "That's what *he* said, I don't deny, but it wasn't what *she* said, which puts me in a fix, in a manner of speaking, because if it was his sister you was wishful to see I couldn't say it was her as was here today, not to take my oath on it, I couldn't. The young party as came here asking for Mr. Allandale told Mrs. Shotwick, which is my good lady, as how she was engaged to be *married* to him. Which is different."

"Well, that is the lady I wish to find," said Nell.

"Ah!" said Mr. Shotwick, still caressing his chin. "*I've* no objection, but the question is, *can* you, ma'am? Because she ain't here. Nor hasn't been, this three hours and more. Which I'm just as glad she hasn't, on account of all the bobbery there was."

"Oh, dear!" Nell said, her heart sinking. "What—what *sort* of bobbery?"

"No, dash it, cousin——!" expostulated Mr. Hethersett, by this time in a state of acute discomfort

At this point Mr. Shotwick was struck by the happy idea of inviting them to step inside so that they might discuss the delicate matter with the mistress of the establishment. Nell readily agreed to this, Mr. Hethersett not so readily, and they were ushered into Mr. Allandale's parlour, on the right of the front door, and left there while Mr. Shotwick went off to summon his wife on to the scene.

"Oh, Felix, what can have happened?" Nell said. "Gone for

more than three hours! When that man said they were not here I thought at first that perhaps Mr. Allandale had taken Letty home, and I should find her there when I return. But three hours! Where can she be, if they have not eloped together?"

"I don't know where she can be," said Mr. Hethersett. "I know where we are, however, and it ain't where I want to be. I'm dashed sure this fellow knows who *I* am, and the next thing we shall find is that he's twigged who *you* are. It'll be all over town before the cat's had time to lick her ear."

"Well, if you don't like to be seen in my company, you may go away!" said Nell, with spirit.

"I *don't*," said Mr. Hethersett frankly. "Particularly in this rig, when you ain't dressed for the evening. Not at all the thing: looks dashed peculiar! We shall have all the quizzes wondering what the deuce we were doing. Can't tell 'em we were looking all over for Letty!"

Anxious as she was, she could not help laughing at this. She said mischievously: "It is very bad, but *your* credit is so good that I am persuaded no one would believe for an instant that you had done anything that was not good ton!"

"Yes, but this is no time for funning, my dear Lady Cardross! Besides, there's no saying what people will believe. The thing is, we're going the quickest way to work to get it set about that that wretched girl has gone clean beyond the line. What's more, Cardross will be as mad as fire with the pair of us for making cakes of ourselves, instead of telling him what had happened."

She felt that this indeed might be true, but before she could reply Mr. Shotwick had come back, with a stout dame in a mob-cap, whom he introduced as his good lady.

From the somewhat involved story that issued from Mrs. Shotwick's lips it became apparent that the eruption of Letty into her hitherto ordered existence had disarranged her mind quite as much as it had shaken her faith in her favourite lodger. "For, not to deceive you, ma'am, what to think I did not know, nor don't!"

Her first impulse, on learning from her spouse that a beautiful young lady, with a cloak-bag, had taken possession of Mr. Allandale's parlour, with the expressed intention of remaining there until he returned to his lodging, had been to eject so bold a hussy immediately; but when she had sailed into the room to accomplish this desirable object she had suffered a check. She beheld Quality, and one did not turn Quality out of one's house, however respectable one might be. But she had been on the watch for Mr. Allandale, and she had waylaid him on his entering the house, and had given him to understand that Goings-on under her roof she would not allow. It had struck her forcibly that upon hearing of his betrothed's presence in his parlour he had looked queer—to put it no higher.

"Queer as Dick's hatband," corroborated Mr. Shotwick.

"I should think he dashed well would look queer!" said Mr. Hethersett, impatient of this circumstantial history.

"Ah!" said Mr. Shotwick. " 'Specially if he was trying to tip her the double, which was what we suspicioned, sir."

"I'll thank you not to use that nasty cant, Shotwick!" said the wife of his bosom sharply. "No such thought crossed *my* mind, not then it didn't!"

"Not till the kick-up started," agreed Mr. Shotwick. "Lor', how she did take on! I thought we should have the neighbours in on us." He shook his head mournfully. "You couldn't help but compassionate her. But what has me fair flummoxed is the way he slumguzzled *us*! Because a quieter, nicer-behaved gentleman you couldn't find, not if you was to look from here to Jericho! But he tipped her the rise, no question!"

"That'll do!" said his wife. She looked significantly at Nell, and said darkly: "Not a word shall pass *my* lips with a gentleman present, but I ask you, ma'am, what is anyone to think when a sweet, pretty young thing carries on like she was desperate, and begs and implores a gentleman—if such you can call him!—to marry her?"

"Crying five loaves a penny, in course," said Mr. Shotwick helpfully.

"Yes, never mind that! What I mean is, no such thing!" intervened Mr. Hethersett, devoutly trusting that this expression was unknown to Nell. Not that there was any chance that she hadn't understood the gist of Mrs. Shotwick's remarks: she was looking aghast, as well she might! "All I want to know is, did they leave this house together, and did you hear where they were bound for?"

"That I cannot say," replied Mrs. Shotwick. "Leave it they did, in a post-chaise and pair."

"A post-chaise!" Nell echoed, in a hollow voice.

"A post-chaise it was, ma'am, as I saw with my own eyes, and which Mr. Allandale stepped out to bespeak his own self," nodded Mrs. Shotwick. "And this I will say: whatever he's done, he means to do right by that poor young thing now, for when I asked him what was to be done he answered me straight out there was only one thing he could do. I don't say he looked like he wanted to, but he was very resolute—oh, very resolute he was! He didn't say anything more to me, but turned sharp about and came back into this very room, where Miss was laid down on that sofa, looking that wore out as never was. But what he said to her I don't know, for he shut the door. All I do know is that whatever it was it had her up off of the sofa in a twinkling, and as happy as a grig! Then he went off to hire a chaise, and Miss called to me to help her pack his valise, and not another tear did she shed!"

"No need to worry about her, then," said Mr. Hethersett, making the best of a bad business. "I'm much obliged to you!" He then requested Mr. Shotwick to step out in search of a

hack, and cast an uneasy glance at Nell. She was looking
quite stricken, but, to his relief, she did not speak until Mrs.
Shotwick had curtseyed herself out of the room. He said curtly:
"Going to take you home. Nothing to be done. Too late.
Very scabby conduct of Allandale's, but I'm bound to say I'm
dashed sorry for him!"

"Oh, could he not have brought her back to her home?"
Nell cried, wringing her hands.

"Not if she was screeching in hysterics," said Mr. Hethersett, with considerable feeling. "What's more, I don't blame
him!"

"I blame myself! If I had told Cardross of my suspicion!
He might have been able then to have overtaken them, but
now——! I was so certain Mr. Allandale would not—I
thought I should be able to set the wretched business to rights,
but I have only helped to ruin Letty!"

"Don't see that at all," he replied. "Plenty of time for
Cardross to catch 'em, if he wants to. Only travelling with a
pair of horses. Wouldn't make much difference if they had
four. Give Cardross his curricle, and four good 'uns, and I'd
back him, over the distance, if they'd had twice as long a start
of him. You ever seen Giles with a four-in-hand? Well, he's
top-of-the-trees, give you my word! Knows how to keep
strange horses together, too."

"Oh, do you think they could still be overtaken?" she said
eagerly.

"Lord, yes! All we have to do—— *Now what is it?*"

She had uttered a chagrined: *"Oh!"* and she now said:
"Cardross is not at home. He was dining out, and I don't
know where!"

"No need to get into a taking over that," replied Mr. Hethersett calmly. "Farley will know."

This made her feel rather more cheerful, and upon Mr.
Shotwick's coming back to announce that a hack was waiting

to take them up she started up, begging Mr. Hethersett to make haste.

There was certainly a hack standing in the street: a large and dilapidated vehicle, whose body, hanging drunkenly between two old-fashioned perches, showed by tarnished silver-work, and an almost obliterated coat of arms, that it had descended a long way in the social scale since the days when, with a powdered coachman on the box, and two Knights of the Rainbow standing up behind, it had been the town chariot of a nobleman. It was not at all the kind of carriage any person of fashion would now choose to ride in, but Nell and Mr. Hethersett, emerging from the house, found that their temporary possession of it was not to be undisputed. Two gentlemen were arguing with the jarvey on their right to claim it, and this worthy man had apparently found it necessary to come down from the box to preserve it from invasion.

Mr. Hethersett, after one glance, tried to obscure the scene from Nell's view, saying tersely: "Better step inside again till I've got rid of 'em!"

"But it's Dysart!" said Nell.

"Yes, I know it is, but we haven't any time to stand talking to him!" said Mr. Hethersett.

"No, of course not, but he is trying to hire our hackney, and he must not!" said Nell, trying to push him out of the way.

"For the lord's sake, cousin, go back into the house!" begged Mr. Hethersett. "He ain't alone!"

"No, but the other is only Mr. Fancot, and I *think*," said Nell knowledgeably, "that they are both of them a trifle foxed. Dysart!"

The Viscount, upon hearing himself addressed, turned. The light from the near-by street-lamp enabled him quite plainly to recognize his sister, but he knew better than to trust his eyes when he was (in his own estimation) a little above par. He called upon his companion for assistance. "Corny, that ain't my sister Cardross, is it?"

"No," said Mr. Fancot obligingly.

"What a horrid creature you are, Dy!" remarked Nell, descending the steps. "You cannot drive off in that coach, because it was brought for me, and I must have it. I am in the greatest haste, so do, pray, stop disputing with that poor man, and go away!"

"By God, it *is* my sister Cardross!" exclaimed the Viscount, thunderstruck.

"Yes," agreed Mr. Fancot, smiling vaguely but with immense affability at Nell.

"Well, there's no need to shout it all down the street!" said Mr. Hethersett tartly.

The Viscount looked intently at him, while he wrestled silently with a problem. "It's you, is it?" he said, a certain kindling in his eyes, and a brooding note in his voice. "You, and my sister!"

Mr. Hethersett, who had foreseen from the start that something like this would happen, said soothingly: "Escorting her ladyship home!"

"Oh, you were, were you?" said the Viscount, showing signs of rising choler. "We'll see that! Because it seems to me— Corny! Where are we?"

"Watier's," said Mr. Fancot, after a moment's thought.

"No, we ain't!" said his lordship, irritated.

"*Going* to Watier's," amended Mr. Fancot.

"*I'll* tell you where we are!" announced the Viscount, in menacing accents. "We're in Ryder Street!"

"That's right, sir: Ryder Street it is," said the jarvey encouragingly. "You don't want no 'ack to take you to Watier's!"

"Ryder Street," said the Viscount. "*Now* I know whose

house you were coming out of! *Now* I know what made you take such an uncommon interest in my sister's affairs! By God, if I don't cut your liver out for this! As for you, my girl——"

"That'll do!" interrupted Mr. Hethersett. "You can cut my liver out in the morning, but for the lord's sake stop making such a damned kick-up in the street!"

"Not liver," said Mr. Fancot positively, his wandering attention recalled by this word. "Duck. That's what we said, Dy. Got a way of cooking it at Watier's I like."

"Well, you take Dysart there!" recommended Mr. Hethersett.

" 'E can *take* him, but 'e won't never get 'im past the porter, guv'nor, not as lushy as what they both are!" observed the jarvey sapiently.

"Yes, I will," said Mr. Fancot. "It's my birthday."

"Get into the hack!" Mr. Hethersett said to Nell. "No, not you!"

Mr. Fancot, hauled off the step of the coach by the jarvey, called upon the Viscount to come and give this individual one in the bread-basket, but the Viscount had more important matters to attend to. Addressing himself to Mr. Hethersett, he commanded that harassed exquisite to name his friends.

Alarmed by his evident intention to force a quarrel on to Mr. Hethersett, Nell laid a hand on his arm, and said: "Dy, *pray* don't be so gooseish! You quite mistake the matter, you know! Indeed, it is abominable of you to think such horrid things, besides being excessively embarrassing!"

"Don't you try to bamboozle me!" replied her brother, shaking off her hand. "Are you going to name your friends, sir, or are you not?"

"You wouldn't remember 'em if I did. What you need is a damper: you're as drunk as a brewer's horse!"

"Oh, no, I'm not! I'll tell you what *you* are! A damned

loose fish! A regular hedge-bird! A man-milliner, by God!
Cowhearted!"

"If you ain't stale-drunk in the morning, come round to my
place, and I'll dashed well show you how cowhearted I am!"
promised Mr. Hethersett, stung by these opprobrious terms.
"It'll be bellows to mend with you, what's more! I've seen
you sport your canvas at Jackson's, and when it comes to
handy-blows you ain't any better than a moulder!"

"Now, by God——!" ejaculated the Viscount, squaring up
to him.

The jarvey called out approvingly: "A mill, a mill!" Nell
flung herself between the two incensed gentlemen; and Mr.
Fancot, who had been standing wrapped in thought, suddenly
announced his intention of driving to Watier's in the hack,
and disappeared round the back of the coach.

"Dysart, how dare you be so uncivil!" Nell said hotly. "Pray
don't heed him, Felix! I was never so mortified! Dysart, if
you say another word to Felix——"

"It don't signify!" interrupted Mr. Hethersett, who had
had time to recollect the impropriety of engaging in fisticuffs
in a lady's presence. "Forgot myself!" He looked at the
Viscount. "If you want to fight, you can tell me so tomorrow!
I'm going to escort her ladyship home now."

"Oh, no, you ain't!" retorted the Viscount. "*I* am going to
take her home! Yes, and I'm dashed well going to tell Cardross
what sort of a May-game you've been playing, my buck!"

"Oh, dear, what are we to do?" said Nell distractedly.
"Felix, there are a couple of men coming towards us!"

"Good God! There's nothing for it: we shall have to take
him along with us. Get into the hack, cousin!"

"Take him with us! But if Cardross sees him in this shocking state——!"

"Lord, Giles knows what he is!" said Mr. Hethersett
impatiently.

"Good heavens!" said Nell rather faintly. "Then that must have been what he meant! How very dreadful!"

"Here, wait a bit!" suddenly said the Viscount. "Where's Corny? Can't leave Corny behind: it's his birthday!"

"Well, thank goodness *he* has gone at least!" said Nell, as Mr. Hethersett handed her up into the coach. "If only we could persuade Dy—— *Oh!*"

"Good God, what's the matter?" demanded Mr. Hethersett, as she recoiled from the vehicle.

"He *hasn't* gone!" said Nell despairingly. "He's inside, and I think he's fallen asleep!"

"Well, I'll be gormed!" exclaimed the jarvey, peering into the coach. " 'E must have crope round when I wasn't a-watching of 'im, and got in by t'other door. Now we'll 'ave to 'aul 'im out again!"

"No, no, pray don't!" begged Nell, hurriedly getting into the coach. "Only let us go away from here!"

"But I can't let you drive about the town with a couple of ensign-bearers!" expostulated Mr. Hethersett. "Oh, my God, if it ain't Bottisham bearing down on us! Well, that settles it: we can't stay here another moment! Here, Dysart, stop looking for Fancot *under* the hack! He's *in* it!" With this, he thrust the Viscount into the coach, gave a hurried direction to the jarvey, climbed into the coach himself, and slammed the door.

IT seemed at first as though the drive to Grosvenor Square was to be enlivened by a brawl, for although the Viscount's mind had been diverted by the loss of his friend, this aberration was but of short duration. No sooner had he satisfied himself that Mr. Fancot was still with them than he discovered that Mr. Hethersett was also with them, and took instant exception to his presence. However, before he could attempt to carry out his promise to throw him out Mr. Fancot, roused by the jolting of the wheels over the cobblestones, woke up, and demanded to know where he was.

"Never mind that!" said the Viscount. "Here's this curst fellow, Hethersett, got in with us! Help me to throw him out, will you?"

"No, no, can't do that!" said Mr. Fancot, who was filled with a large tolerance. "Very good sort of a man! Didn't know I'd invited him, but very glad he came."

"You didn't invite him! Nobody invited him!" said the Viscount.

"Must have," said Mr. Fancot. "Wouldn't have come if I hadn't. Polite to a point! Happy to take a glass of wine with him."

"Well, if ever I saw old Corny so castaway!" exclaimed Dysart. "Dashed if he ain't as drunk as a wheelbarrow!"

"Yes, but at least he is perfectly amiable!" said Nell. "He doesn't say outrageous things, or try to throw people into the street!"

This unfortunate remark reminded the Viscount that his purpose was still unaccomplished, but just at that moment Mr. Fancot began to warble an entirely unintelligible ditty. Since he was apparently afflicted with tone-deafness this musical interlude was a severe trial to the rest of the company, and caused the Viscount to forget Mr. Hethersett again. "Stop it, Corny!" he said indignantly.

"Chip-chip, cherry-chip, fol-di-diddle-di-dee!" sang Mr. Fancot.

"*That's* not right!" said Dysart scornfully. "It don't even make sense!" He then upraised his powerful baritone, and favoured the company with the correct version, which, as far as his sister could discover, differed hardly at all from his friend's. But Mr. Hethersett, unmoved by Mr. Fancot's outburst, was powerfully affected by the Viscount's. No sooner did the refrain of *Chip-chow, cherry-chow, fol-lol-di-riddle-low* break upon his ears than Nell felt him stiffen, and heard him utter an exclamation under his breath.

The Viscount beguiled the rest of the way with song, and was still singing when Cardross's astonished butler admitted the party into the house.

But it did not appear to be Lord Dysart's condition that surprised Farley. It was the sight of his mistress that made his eyes widen. He exclaimed involuntarily: "My lady!"

"Yes, did you not know that I had been obliged to go out?" said Nell, with an attempt to carry the situation off unconcernedly. "Pray show Lord Dysart and Mr. Fancot into the library! They—they have come to take supper with me!"

"My birthday," said Mr. Fancot affably. "Celebrating it! Blackbeetle, too."

"*I* see, sir," responded Farley, gently removing the hat from his grasp.

"Blackbeetle be damned!" said the Viscount. "Cockroach! Where's his lordship?"

"His lordship is not at home, but he will be in directly, my lord," replied Farley, consigning the visitors into the care of the footman who had followed him into the hall.

Mr. Fancot was easily shepherded into the library, but the

Viscount was recalcitrant. "It ain't a bit of use trying to fob me off," he told his sister sternly. "I'm not letting you out of my sight, Nell, so don't think it! Not with that fellow in the house!"

"Dysart, for heaven's sake——!"

"You'd better go with him, cousin," advised Mr. Hethersett. "No sense in starting him off again on his high ropes! Much better leave this to me."

Since Dysart had acquired a firm grip on her arm, there really seemed to be nothing else she could do, so, with a low-voiced entreaty to Mr. Hethersett to lose no time in setting forth in search of Cardross, she retired to the library.

Here she was made welcome by Mr. Fancot, happy in the belief that he was entertaining friends under his own roof. He shook her warmly by the hand, and offered her a glass of wine. She declined this, which distressed him; but Dysart, who had discovered glasses and a decanter set out on a side-table, said: "No use pressing her: only two glasses!"

Mr. Fancot was shocked. "Only two glasses?" he repeated. "That's absurd, Dy! No other word for it: absurd! Stupid fellow of mine misunderstood. Ring for more glasses!"

"We don't need any more glasses," replied Dysart, lavishly pouring wine into the two that stood on the table.

"Yes, we do," insisted Mr. Fancot. "Can't give a party with two glasses: stand to reason!"

"Well, it ain't a party. It ain't your house either."

"It ain't?" Mr. Fancot said incredulously. He subjected his surroundings to a keen, if somewhat owlish scrutiny. "By Jove, Dy, so it ain't! Dashed if I know whose house it is! You know what, dear boy? Come to the wrong house! Better go."

"No, we haven't. Came here to see Cardross," said Dysart, with a darkling look.

Mr. Fancot thought this over profoundly. "No," he pronounced at last. "Not sure why we came here, but we don't want to see Cardross. Nothing against him, mind! Not particularly acquainted with him, but capital fellow! Bang up to the mark. Honoured to meet him, but the thing is, not what we set out to do. Tell me this, Dy! Have we *dined*?"

"To hell with dinner! I'm going to see Cardross!" said Dysart obstinately.

"Oh, Dysart, I wish you will go away!" Nell exclaimed. "You don't want to meet Cardross! you know you don't!"

"That's what I said," nodded Mr. Fancot, gratified. "Not what we set out to do. Besides, he ain't here. Go to Watier's!"

"Not till I've seen Cardross. Got something to say to him. No business to let that fellow dangle after my sister! I'm going to tell him so."

"Which fellow?" enquired Mr. Fancot.

"Hethersett," replied the Viscount, tossing off the wine in his glass. "You know what he is, Corny? A damned Man of the Town! And there's Cardross, letting him make up to my sister, while he goes off like a regular Care-for-Nobody! What I say is, he's got no business to neglect her, and so I shall tell him!"

"He doesn't neglect me!" said Nell hotly. "And if you were not so odiously foxed, Dy, you wouldn't say such detestable things!"

"Yes, I should," he retorted. "In fact, the more I think of it the more I can see he's too high in the instep by half! Took a pet because I held you up. Very well! if he didn't want me to hold you up, why didn't he do it himself? Tell me that! Who brought the dibs in tune for you? *I* did! Who stopped you getting into Jew King's clutches?——"

"Felix Hethersett did!" she intervened crossly, taking off her bonnet, and running her fingers through her flattened curls.

"Yes, by Jove, so he did!" exclaimed the Viscount, his eyes kindling. "Like his damned impudence!"

Fortunately, since his mood was becoming increasingly belligerent, he was diverted by Mr. Fancot, who suddenly offered to set him a main. He turned to find that his amiable friend, losing interest in the conversation, had seated himself by the table in the middle of the room, produced a dice-box from his pocket, and was engaged in throwing right hand against left. Drunk or sober, the Viscount was not the man to refuse a challenge of this nature. He instantly sat down on the other side of the table, and, to Nell's relief, became absorbed in his ruling passion. From this he was momentarily disturbed by the entrance of the footman, who came in bearing two tankards, which he silently set down at either gentleman's elbow. Dysart, staring at them, demanded to know what the devil he thought he was doing, and told him to bring in a bottle of brandy. The footman bowed, and withdrew, saying: "Very good, my lord," but he did not remove the homely tankards. Nor did he return to the library, but as the Viscount immediately struck a run of amazing and most unaccustomed good fortune his failure to bring in the brandy went unnoticed, both gamesters refreshing themselves with draughts of porter, and Dysart, having rapidly relieved Mr. Fancot of his ready money, beginning to amass a number of notes of hand which that well-breeched young gentleman scrawled somewhat illegibly but with the greatest goodwill on leaves torn from his pocket-book.

Meanwhile, Mr. Hethersett, to whose thoughtful offices they owed a beverage well-known for its sobering quality, had suffered a check. Farley was unable to tell him where his master had gone when he had left the house earlier in the evening.

Mr. Hethersett eyed him. "Dashed discreet, ain't you? Did he go off with Sir John Somerby?"

"No, sir, although I had understood that such was his intention. A meeting at the Daffy Club, sir, I fancy. But his lordship cried off."

"Well, there's no need to make a mystery of it!" said Mr. Hethersett, irritated. "Where *did* he go?"

"That, sir, I cannot say, his lordship not having informed me. He had his whisky brought round, but he didn't take his groom with him, nor yet his Tiger, and when I ventured to ask him if he would wish supper to be prepared for him he said that he didn't know when he should be returning. His lordship appeared, sir, to be in quite a fret, if I may say so. Not at all like himself."

The mystery was now plain to Mr. Hethersett. In his experience it was a foolish waste of time to attempt to hoodwink one's servants. He had not for a moment imagined that the supposed secret of Letty's flight was not known to every member of the household, so he had no hesitation in saying bluntly: "Set off after Lady Letitia, did he? Oh, well, if that's so, no need for me to find him!"

"No, sir," replied Farley. "His lordship was not aware that her ladyship had not returned to the house. I was not myself aware of it, until Miss Sutton—my lady's dresser, sir—informed me that Lady Letitia was gone to spend the night with Mrs. Thorne. His lordship did not enquire for Lady Letitia. It was my Lady Cardross which his lordship was anxious to find." He coughed delicately. "No doubt some urgent matter which he wished to discuss with her ladyship," he said, gazing limpidly at Mr. Hethersett. "Being as they were disturbed by Sir John Somerby, and her ladyship, in consequence, leaving the book-room rather hastily, sir."

"Oh!" said Mr. Hethersett, looking at him very hard.

"Yes, sir. So, as soon as he was rid—as soon, I should say, as Sir John left the house, his lordship went upstairs to find her ladyship, which, not being able to do, vexed him a trifle. Quite put out, he was, which was not to be wondered at, because it seems her ladyship forgot to inform him she was obliged to go out quite suddenly. And, of course, his lordship couldn't help but be in a fidget when he found that my lady's carriage had not been sent for. Very understandable, I am sure, sir, that his lordship should have felt anxious, for it was going on towards dinner-time, and naturally he wouldn't like to think of my lady's going out in such a way. Particularly," he added, in a disinterested voice, "if she was going on a journey."

"Is that what he thought she was meaning to do?" demanded Mr. Hethersett.

"Well, sir, that is not for me to say," replied Farley carefully. "But when his lordship questioned George, it came out that her ladyship had sent down to have her dressing-case taken up to her room. Just after she had parted from his lordship, that would have been." He looked Mr. Hethersett firmly in the eye, and said: "What I thought, sir, was that very likely her ladyship had had word brought her that my Lord Pevensey was lying on his deathbed, perhaps—which would account for her going off like she did. Being quite distracted, which no one could wonder at."

"Yes, well, you can stop pitching your gammon!" said Mr. Hethersett indignantly. "Dashed well ought to know better! Must know I ain't such an easy cove as to swallow all that humdudgeon! I know what you thought, and it was a bag of moonshine!"

"Yes, sir," said Farley, bowing. "I am very glad of it. I apprehend that her ladyship went in search of Lady Letitia, but on that subject I shall not presume to open my lips."

"Well, see you don't!" recommended Mr. Hethersett.

He then repaired to the library, where the Viscount, intent upon throwing a difficult chance, did not at first notice him. Nell, seated on the sofa at the end of the room, was a good deal dismayed to see him come walking in, for she had supposed him to have gone in search of Cardross. It was evident, since he had shed his cloak, that he had no immediate intention of leaving the house, and she could not help looking reproachfully at him, as he came towards her.

"No use," he said, in an undervoice. "Floored at all points. Farley don't know where Cardross is. Seems to me he's making a dashed cake of himself. In fact, it wouldn't surprise me if he's gone off to Devonshire."

"Gone off to Devonshire?" she echoed, in amazement. "Nonsense, why should he do such a thing?"

"Chasing after you," he said. "Shouldn't think he'd be such a gudgeon as to set off in a whisky, but he may have hired a chaise. Left the whisky at the posting-house."

Quite bewildered, she said: "But why should he think I had gone to Devonshire? Oh, Felix, are *you* foxed too?"

"No, of course I ain't! Been talking to Farley. No wish to pry into what don't concern me, but collect you had a turn-up with Cardross." He added hastily, as the colour rushed into her cheeks: "Not my business! The thing is, Giles found you wasn't in the house. Couldn't discover where you was gone, and, by what I can make out, was thrown into a rare taking. Silly gape-seed of a porter told him some farradiddle about taking your dressing-case up to your room. Sounds to me as if he was pitching it pretty rum, but can't be surprised it put Cardross in the devil of a pucker."

"Oh, good God!" she exclaimed guiltily. "That was only to draw George out of the hall! How *could* he suppose——?" She stopped, and turned apprehensive eyes towards him. "Did —did the servants think I had run away?"

"Lord, yes! Bound to!" he replied. "However, it don't signify. What I mean is, you hadn't."

"No, indeed! But to have caused such a commotion—set them all gossiping—Oh, do you think he will be very angry with me?"

"No, no! Might be in a miff, I daresay, but he'll come about," he said soothingly. "Must see you meant it for the best. Not your fault you made a mull of it."

This well-meant consolation caused her to spring up, wringing her hands. "Letty!" she uttered. "Felix, it *is* my fault! Oh, if I had but told him! He will never forgive me!"

The Viscount, his attention jerked from the bones by her unguarded movement and raised voice, looked round. "What the deuce—Well, by God, if that fellow Hethersett hasn't come sneaking back!"

"What, are you still castaway?" said Mr. Hethersett disgustedly. "I wish you'd take yourself off!"

"Oh, you do, do you?" countered his lordship. "Well, I'm not going to stir from this house while you're in it, my buck, and that you may depend on!"

Mr. Fancot, with a hazy recollection of earlier events, looked puzzled, and said: "But you don't like him, Dy! You said you was going to throw him out."

"Felix!" said Nell, too lost in agitated reflection to heed this interchange. "There is nothing for it but for me to go after them! It may not be too late!"

"Good God, cousin, you can't do that!" said Mr. Hethersett, shocked.

"If I went in our own chaise, and you were so very obliging as to go with me?" she urged. "It may be hours before Giles returns, and then——"

"Well, upon my soul!" ejaculated the Viscount, rising with such hasty violence as to overset his chair. "If that don't beat all hollow!" He seized his sister by the shoulders, and shook her. "Have you taken leave of your senses?" he demanded. "Go off in a chaise with that fellow? Not while I'm here to stop you!" He rounded suddenly on Mr. Hethersett, an ugly look on his face. "What damned cajolery have you been playing off on her?" he said fiercely.

"For the lord's sake, Dysart, go and dip your head in a bucket!" begged Mr. Hethersett.

"Oh, listen!" Nell said sharply, her face turned towards the door.

A quick stride was heard approaching; the door was flung open, and Cardross stood on the threshold. There was a hard, anxious look on his face, and he had not stayed to put off his long, many-caped driving coat. His eyes swept the room, and found his wife. He went quickly forward, totally ignoring the rest of the company, saying in a shaken voice which she hardly recognized: "Nell! Thank God! Oh, my darling, *forgive* me!"

"Giles! Oh, no! it was all my fault!" she cried, casting herself into his arms. "And it is much, much worse than you know! Letty has gone with Mr Allandale!"

"*Damn* Letty!" he said, folding her close. "You have come back to me, and nothing else is of the smallest consequence!"

Mr. Hethersett, averting his eyes with great delicacy from the passionate embrace being exchanged, began to polish his quizzing-glass; the Viscount stared in thunderstruck silence; and Mr. Fancot, after blinking at the extraordinary spectacle offered him, rose carefully to his feet, and twitched his friend's sleeve. "Think we ought to be taking leave, Dy," he said confidentially. "Not the sort of party I like, dear boy! Go for a toddle to the Mutton-walk!"

"Damned if I will!" replied Dysart. "I want a word with Cardross, and I'm going to have it!"

Recalled to a sense of his surroundings, Cardross looked up. Flushing a little, he let Nell go. "By all means, Dysart: what is it?"

"I'll tell you in private," said the Viscount, in whom the effects of his potations were beginning to wear off.

"Well, I don't know why you should suddenly wish to be private!" said Nell, with unusual asperity. "When you have been saying the most abominable things without the least regard for anyone, even the hackney coachman! Besides trying to call poor Felix out in the most insulting way! Oh, Giles, pray tell him he must not do so!"

"But why in the world should he wish to?" asked Cardross, startled, and considerably amused.

"Silly clunch saw her ladyship coming away from Allandale's lodging with me, and would have it that it was *my* lodging," said Mr. Hethersett tersely, responding to the laughing question in his cousin's eye.

"Oh, that's the tale is it?" said the Viscount. "Well, it won't fadge! Didn't think to tell *me* that, did you? Why not? That's what I want to know! *Why not?*"

"Because you were a dashed sight too ripe to attend to a word anyone said to you!" replied Mr. Hethersett, with brutal frankness.

"And in any event there was no need for you to behave in such an outrageous way, Dy," interpolated Nell severely. "Even if it *had* been Felix's house, which it might as well have been, because I had the intention of calling on him, on account of my not knowing the number of Mr. Allandale's. Only, by good fortune, he chanced to be coming out just as I was paying off the hack."

"Yes, you have that mighty pat, haven't you, my girl?" said Dysart. "And I daresay you think it makes all right! Well, it don't! Pretty conduct in a female of quality to be paying calls on every loose fish on the town, I must say! In a common hack, too! Well, that may suit your notions of propriety, Cardross, but it don't suit mine, and so I'll have you know!"

"Dy, how can you be so absurd?" protested Nell. "No one could possibly think poor Mr. Allandale a *loose fish!*"

"Dash it, cousin!" exclaimed Mr. Hethersett indignantly.

"My dear Dysart, do let me assure you that I honour you for such feelings, and enter into all your ideas on the subject!"

said Cardross. "You may safely leave the matter in my hands."

"That's just what it seems to me I can't do!" retorted Dysart. "Yes, and that puts me in mind of another thing I have to say to you! Why the devil don't you take better care of Nell? Did you get her out of a silly scrape? No, you didn't! *I* did! All you did was to put it into her head you thought she only married you for your fortune, when anyone but a gudgeon must have known she's too big a pea-goose to have enough sense to do anything of the kind. So when she finds herself under the hatches she daren't tell you: *I* have to pull her out of the River Tick! A pretty time I had of it! Why, I even had that fellow Hethersett hinting it was *my* fault she was being dunned for some curst dress or other!"

Mr. Hethersett blushed. "Misapprehension! Told you so at the time!"

"Well, it was my fault!" said Dysart furiously. "I daresay if I hadn't borrowed three centuries from her *you* wouldn't have had to snatch her off Jew King's doorstep, but how was I to know it would put her in the basket? Besides, I've paid it back to her!"

"Nell, my poor child, how *could* you think—Did I frighten you as much as *that*?" Cardross said remorsefully.

"No, no, it was all my folly!" she said quickly. "I thought that shocking bill from Lavalle had been with those others, only it *wasn't,* and when she sent it me again it seemed as though I *couldn't* tell you! Oh, Dysart, *pray* don't say any more!"

"Yes, that's all very well, but I am going to say something more! I've a pretty fair notion of what your opinion of me is, Cardross, but I'll have you know that it was not I who prigged that damned necklace of yours!"

"Eh?" ejaculated Mr. Hethersett, startled.

"You have really no need to tell me that, Dysart," Cardross replied, his colour heightened, and his eyes fixed on Nell's face.

"Well, it's what my own sister thought!" said Dysart bitterly.

"Good God, Giles, you've never lost the necklace?" Mr. Hethersett demanded.

"No," answered Cardross, holding Nell's hand rather tightly. "It isn't lost. If it were, I should not imagine for one instant that you had taken it, Dysart."

"Much obliged to you!"

"I must say, that's the outside of enough," observed Mr. Hethersett. "Whatever made you take a notion like that into your head, cousin?"

"It was very, very foolish of me!"

"Well, I call it a dashed insult!" declared the Viscount.

"Yes, Dysart: so do I!" said Cardross, raising Nell's hand to his lips. "I hope you have begged his forgiveness, Nell—as I beg for yours!"

"Oh, Giles, pray *hush*!"

The Viscount, having frowned over this for a moment, exclaimed: "What, did you think *she* had sold the thing? If that don't give you your own again, Nell!"

"That's all very well," objected Mr. Hethersett, "but you said it *wasn't* lost, Cardross!"

"It was lost, but it has been restored to me. I suppose I now know who stole it—and should have known at the outset! Not your sister, Dysart, but mine! Was that it, Nell?"

"Well, yes, it was," she confessed. "But you mustn't be out of *reason* cross with her, because indeed I believe she would never have thought of doing such a thing, only that Dysart put it into her head!"

"What?" exclaimed Dysart. "No, by God, that's too much! I never did so!"

"Yes, Dy, you did! Oh, I don't mean to say that it was what you intended, but I have been thinking about it, and I am persuaded it was your holding me up that night, with Mr. Fancot —good gracious, where *is* Mr. Fancot?"

"Yes, by Jove! Where is he?" exclaimed Dysart.

"No need to worry about him," said Mr. Hethersett, nodding to where Mr. Fancot was peacefully sleeping in a large wing-chair. "Wouldn't have let you all talk in that dashed improper way if he'd been listening to you!"

"If ever I knew anyone like Corny for dropping asleep the instant he gets a trifle above oar!" remarked the Viscount, eyeing his friend with tolerant affection.

"Don't wake him, I beg of you!" said Cardross. "What, my darling, had that hold-up to do with this affair?"

"Yes, *what*?" demanded Dysart.

"Well, you see, Giles, when I wouldn't sell any of the jewels you gave me—and I *still* think it would have been the most odiously deceiving thing to have done, Dy, however tiresome you may have thought it of me!—Dysart hit upon the notion of pretending to be a highwayman, and taking them from me in that way. Only I recognized him, so it came to nothing. But the thing was that Letty thought it had been a famous notion, and I am very sure that *that* was what put it into her head to sell the Cardross necklace!" She broke off, as a thought occurred to her. "Good heavens, *Letty*! What are we about, wasting time in this way? Cardross, we discovered, Felix and I, that they set out with only a pair of horses! It is true that they have several hours start of you, but Felix seems to think that you might easily overtake them before they can reach the Border!"

"I daresay I might—if I were to make the attempt," he agreed.

"But won't you?" she asked anxiously.

"No. I have had my fill of driving this evening! Allandale is welcome to her!"

"Yes, but to be married in such a way! Giles, only think what the consequences must be! I shouldn't wonder at it if it ruined him as well as her! Indeed, I was never more astonished in my life than when I learned he had yielded to her persuasions! I had not thought it of him! And for you, too, how disagreeable must it be! Oh, do, pray, go after them, and bring her back!"

"Dashed if I would!" remarked the Viscount.

"Giles!"

He laid his hand over the small one insistently tugging at the lapel of his coat. "Hush, my love! This is where we must be guided by the judgment of that arbiter of all matters of taste and ton. Well, Felix?"

Mr. Hethersett, impervious to the quizzical look in his cousin's eye, took snuff in a meditative way, his brow creased. "Don't fancy it will make much difference," he pronounced at last, restoring the box to his pocket, and flicking a few grains of King's Martinique from his sleeve. "Bound to be a deal of gossip whatever you do. Can't suppose it won't leak out, if you go careering off after Letty. Devilish nasty scene, too, if you force her to come home. Seems to have gone into strong hysterics when Allandale tried to get her to do that. Not the sort of thing *I* should care for."

"No, my God!" said Cardross, with feeling.

"Better make the best of it," decided Mr. Hethersett. "Think I'll be going now. Daresay you'll like to be left alone."

Nell held out her hand to him. "I have quite ruined your evening!" she said contritely. "Indeed, I am sorry, and so very much obliged to you!"

"No, no, happy to have been of service!" he replied, bowing with exquisite grace over her hand. "Besides, no such thing! Only on my way to White's, before taking a look-in at the Seftons' ball. Night's young yet!"

"Yes, by Jove, so it is!" said the Viscount. "Here, Corny, wake up!"

Mr. Fancot, urgently shaken, opened his eyes, smiled upon the company, and began to hum softly and unmelodiously to himself.

"Now, for the lord's sake, Corny, you ain't as dead-beat as that!" said the Viscount. "Don't start singing again, because you know dashed well you can't do it!"

"It's my birthday," stated Mr. Fancot.

"Well, that's got nothing to say to anything! Come along! Time we were going!"

"I can sing on my birthday," said Mr. Fancot. "I can sing *Sing old rose, and burn the bellows,* and I can sing your song, and I can——"

"*Chip-chow, cherry-chow?*" interrupted Mr. Hethersett.

"That's the one!" nodded Mr. Fancot, pleased. "You know it too?"

"I've heard it," replied Mr. Hethersett, rather grimly. He met the Viscount's challenging gaze, and held it. "You've called me a few names this night, Dysart! Now I'll take leave to tell you that you're the biggest cod's head *I* ever knew!"

"What the devil do you mean by that?" the Viscount shot at him, flushing.

"You know dashed well what I mean! You learned that song from Cripplegate!"

"What if I did?" demanded Dysart.

"*I'll* tell you that, Dysart," interposed Cardross. He nodded dismissal to his cousin, and looked Dysart over. "Beggars' Club, eh? Well, I thought as much! A Hussar regiment should suit you: it would be a pity to waste your horsemanship. Well?"

"Oh, to hell with you! I've told you I can't!" Dysart said.

"You'll find you can, I promise you."

"By Jove, what wouldn't I give to be out there!" Dysart said impulsively.

"You going to join, Dy?" enquired Mr. Fancot, who had been following this conversation with great interest. "That's a devilish good notion! Let's go and join at once!"

"Well, we can't," said Dysart shortly. "Besides, you don't want to join!"

"Yes, I do," asserted Mr. Fancot. "Can't think why I didn't hit on the notion before! There's nothing left to do here, except walk backwards to Brighton, and I don't fancy that above half."

"Who shall blame you?" agreed Cardross, shepherding him kindly but firmly into the hall.

"That's just it," explained Mr. Fancot. "I may have to. Never refused a challenge in my life, and I've a notion Willy means to try me with that one. You know Willy?"

"No, but I should lose no time in leaving the country."

"You're a sensible man," said Mr. Fancot warmly. "Very happy to have met you!"

"The pleasure has been all mine," said Cardross, putting his hat into his hand, and opening the front door.

"Not at all, not at all!" responded Mr. Fancot, ambling down the steps.

"Lord, if ever I saw him in such prime and plummy order before!" said the Viscount. "Now I shall have him going all over town, trying to find the Horse Guards!" He picked up his own hat, and hesitated, looking at Cardross.

Cardross smiled. "You're a damned fool, Dysart, and a damned nuisance besides—but too good a man to be wasting your talents cutting up cork-brained larks! Don't tease yourself about your mother! I'll make all right in that quarter."

He held out his hand, and the Viscount took it, grinning ruefully. "I wish you might!"

"I will."

"Devilish good of you. Got something else to say to you, and it ain't easy. From what Nell told me, when she found herself in that fix—— Well, the long and the short of it is she didn't know till I told her that you were in love with her. Thought you'd married her as a matter of convenience, and had too much civility to let her see it." He gave a crack of laughter. "Convenience! Lord, what a silly little greenhead!"

"Are you serious?" Cardross demanded. "It isn't possible!"

"Ain't it? You don't know my mother, Cardross!" said Dysart. "Good-night! Must go after Corny!"

He went down the steps, waved, and went striding off. Cardross stood looking after him for a moment, and was just about to go back into the house when a post-chaise swept round the angle of the square, and drew up below him. From this vehicle Mr. Allandale jumped down, and turned to give his supporting hand to his betrothed.

"But what a charming surprise!" said Cardross blandly.

M R. ALLANDALE, having paid off the postilion, took
his love in one hand and Mr. Thorne's cloak-bag in the
other, and trod up the steps to the front-door. Here he paused
and looked Cardross squarely in the face. "I have brought her
home, sir," he said.

"I see you have," replied Cardross. "Most understandable, I
am sure!"

Letty cast a scared, resentful look up at him, but said nothing.

"An explanation is due to you," said Mr. Allandale. "But
first I must beg of you most earnestly that whatever wrath you
may feel—and I do not deny that it is a just wrath!—you will
visit upon my head alone!"

"I fail entirely to see why I should visit my wrath on your
head, but if you suppose me to be contemplating a violent
revenge on Letty do let me hasten to reassure you!"

"You see, love?" said Mr. Allandale tenderly.

"I'm n-not afraid of Cardross!" said Letty, in a small,
resentful voice.

"It would have been very much better for you, and all of
us, if you had been," said Cardross. "Come into the house, but
leave your heroism outside!" He led the way into the hall,
and saw Farley standing in the middle of it with his mouth at
half-cock. "Just so!" he remarked.

"I heard a carriage drive up, my lord!" explained the butler,
staring at Letty.

"Yes, Lady Letty decided after all she would not spend the
night in Bryanston Square," said Cardross ironically. "You
may come into the book-room, both of you." He walked
to the door and held it wide. Across the room Nell's eyes
met his, a startled question in them. "Giles, I thought I
heard——"

261

"You did, my love. Can you conceive of anything more delightful? Dear little Letty is once more in our midst!"

"I *hate* you!" said Letty passionately, and burst into tears.

"Letty! Oh, Letty, thank God you've come back!" cried Nell, hurrying forward.

"I wish I hadn't! I wish I were dead!" sobbed Letty.

"No, no, you mustn't say that!" Nell told her, putting an arm round her, and stretching out her other hand to Mr. Allandale. "Mr. Allandale, how *glad* I am that I wasn't mistaken in you! I couldn't think it possible that you would do such an improper thing as to elope with her!"

He kissed her hand punctiliously, and said: "I wish that I could find the words to express to your ladyship the sense of obligation I feel. But when I consider the circumstances, and what cause you have had (the whole truth not being known to you) to think me infamous, I am rendered tongue-tied."

"Not noticeably," said Cardross dryly.

Nell bit her lip, and drew Letty to the sofa. "Come, love, sit down beside me, and try to compose yourself!" She saw how anxiously Mr. Allandale was watching Letty, and smiled at him reassuringly. "She will be better directly: don't pay any heed to her!"

He looked grateful, but turned with a resolute air to Cardross. "Sir, I have a duty to discharge. I speak on behalf of Lady Letitia, and I shall be brief, merely imploring you to remember that she is young, and in the greatest distress, and has thrown herself upon your mercy. What I have to disclose to you cannot but shock you deeply. You do not yet know the worst, and it is my painful duty to inform you of it."

"Oh, yes, I do!" replied Cardross. "You are about to tell me that Letty stole the Cardross necklace."

Letty raised her head from Nell's shoulder. "It *wasn't* stealing! It *wasn't*!" she declared. "It didn't belong to Nell, and she didn't even like it! It belonged to the *family,* and so it was just as much mine as yours, Giles!"

"My love, you are forgetting that I have several times explained to you that that is not so," said Mr. Allandale gravely.

"Yes, but it *is*! And anyway Giles won't let me have my fortune, so what else could I do?"

Mr. Allandale looked pained, but apparently decided that the moment was not ripe for argument. Drawing a package from his pocket, he laid it on the table before him, and said: "That is the sum the necklace realized, my lord. Had I been able, I would have done my utmost to recover the necklace itself. It was not in my power, however: I have not been at liberty to repair to the jeweller to whom it was sold. I will furnish your lordship with——"

"Let me set your mind at rest!" Cardross interrupted. "The jeweller brought it to me earlier today, and I have already redeemed it."

"Sir, you have removed a weight from my mind!" said Mr. Allandale earnestly.

"Yes, I expect I have," agreed Cardross. "I wish you will satisfy the curiosity in mine! Was it the discovery that your bride had stolen the necklace which made you abandon your flight to Gretna Green? At what stage did you turn back?"

"There was no such flight, my lord."

"No, of course not!" Nell said. "But—where *did* you go to, Mr. Allandale?"

"I was guilty of practising deception," he said heavily. "I need not, I hope, assure you that such a course was of the utmost repugnance to me. To deceive one so dear to me, and one who, moreover, placed the most implicit trust in my integrity, was more painful than I can describe. But when I found that no words of mine could avail to persuade my darling to return to her home, when I saw her in such agony of grief and despair——"

"Yes, I've seen Letty in hysterics," said Cardross. "You have no need to describe the scene to me! I pity you sincerely. What, in fact, did you do?"

"Fearing that if I compelled her to return to this house she might put a period to her existence, I agreed to fly with her to the Border," said Mr. Allandale. "She believed that we were on our way north, but it was not so. I did not carry her to Gretna Green, but to Wimbledon."

There was a moment's astonished silence. "To Wimbledon!" said Cardross, in a voice that shook. "I expect you had an excellent reason for your choice."

"Why, to be sure he had!" exclaimed Nell, bestowing a warm smile upon Mr. Allandale. "You mean you took her to your mother's house! How *very* wise of you!"

He bowed. "It seemed to me, ma'am, the only course open to me. In my mother's judgment I could repose complete confidence, for her understanding is superior, her mind of an elevated order, and her firm yet tender command over my sisters such as encouraged me to hope that over my darling also her influence would prevail."

"And we perceive that it did!" said Cardross. "My dear Allandale, why have I never been privileged to meet your mother?"

"I would like to *kill* you!" choked Letty.

"My mother, sir, seldom goes into society," said Mr. Allandale stiffly.

"But I hope she may be persuaded to receive me, nevertheless."

"I am at a loss to understand your lordship," said Mr. Allandale, more stiffly yet. "I apprehend, however, that you are in funning humour!"

"No, I am not funning," Cardross replied. "Oblige me by telling me, in all frankness, whether or not my sister's want of conduct, her excessive sensibility, and the unscrupulous means she does not hesitate to use to attain her ends have convinced you that she is totally unfitted to be your wife?"

"Giles, *don't*!" begged Nell, as Letty broke into renewed weeping.

"Sir," said Mr. Allandale, very pale, but steadily meeting Cardross's eyes, "I do not attempt to condone her faults, though I can perceive excuses for them, but I love her, and must always do so, whatever she is, or whatever she does."

Letty looked up, her tears arrested, awe in her face. "Jeremy!" she said. "Oh, *Jeremy*!"

Cardross turned his head. "You are not worthy of that, Letty."

"No," she said forlornly. "I know I am not, but—oh, I *wish* I were!"

He smiled wryly. "Well, I daresay there may be hope for you. You had better marry her, Allandale."

It seemed for several moments as though neither of the interested parties could believe that they had heard him correctly. It was Letty who found her voice first. "Giles—do you mean *now*? Before he sails?"

"Yes, that's what I mean."

"Oh, my dearest brother, how kind you are!" cried Letty, flying up off the sofa and casting herself upon his chest. "*Pray* forgive me for saying horrid things to you! I didn't mean them! Oh, how happy I am! Oh, Jeremy, I *promise* I will never do anything you don't like!"

"Sir," said Mr. Allandale, "I do not know how to convey to you my sense of your generosity, my gratitude, the——"

"Then don't try!" said Cardross. "You are a very estimable young man, but I should like you so much more if you would refrain from addressing me in flowing periods! I am going to send you away now, but you may come to see me tomorrow, at noon, if that should be convenient to you, when I will arrange the marriage settlements with you. You may escort him to the front door, Letty, and after you have bidden him good-night, you had better go to bed."

"Bed at ten o'clock!" she said, by no means pleased.

"Yes, bed at ten o'clock. If you are not exhausted after a day of unbridled passion, you should be! Don't argue with me! My patience won't stand it."

"Indeed, you should go, love!" Nell urged her. "You are quite worn out. I will come up to you, and——"

"No, you will not," Cardross interrupted.

Overawed by this display of cool and sweeping authority the young lovers withdrew circumspectly. Nell showed her husband a laughing countenance. "Well, *really*, Giles!" she expostulated.

He caught her up from the sofa, and held her a little away from him, looking down into her face with bright, smiling eyes. "Yes, *really, Giles*!" he retorted. "How much longer did you think I would wait to get you to myself?"

She did not answer him, but blushed a little, meeting his gaze shyly but very openly.

"There's so much to say to you, Nell—and, God forgive me, so much to unsay! My darling, I wish I had cut my tongue out before——"

"No, there is nothing to unsay, because you didn't say those things to me," she intervened. "They hurt me only a very little —not as much as I deserved, perhaps! For I am afraid I have been extravagant, and—and deceitful, and very foolish!"

"And above all very foolish," he agreed, turning her words into a caress. "It seems I have been a great deal too easy with you, Madam Wife! *That* will not happen again! So you thought I offered for you because I wanted a wife, and saw nothing in you to disgust me, did you? Nell, how *could* you be such a goose?"

The blush deepened; she hung her head. "Mama said—that you were disposed to be *fond* of me, and considerate, and she warned me not to hang on you, or—or appear to notice it if—perhaps—you had Another Interest."

"I am obliged to Mama! And did it seem to you that I had Another Interest?"

"No. But I knew," she said simply. "The first time we met Letty said that I was prettier than your mistress."

"She was right. I wish I could think that Allandale would beat her regularly every week, but I fear he won't. The lady with whom I enjoyed an agreeable connection for several years need never have troubled you. We parted without regret or ill-will, and when we meet in company today it is with the indifferent pleasure of old acquaintances. From the moment I saw you, Nell, you have had all my heart. That is the truth."

"Dysart said that. He said that everyone knew it, too."

"I infinitely prefer your brother to my sister. But why, my foolish little love, did you then keep me at an even greater distance?"

She looked up again. "You see, I owed Lavalle more than *three hundred pounds,* so how could I do anything else, until that dreadful debt was paid? With that on my conscience I couldn't tell you that I had been *agonizingly* in love with you from the very beginning; and if you had discovered the debt you would never have believed me. But I was, Giles."

Farley, quietly entering the room at that moment, beheld his mistress locked in a crushing embrace, and with instant presence of mind stepped noiselessly back into the hall. There he remained for some few minutes, after which, with a little fumbling with the door-handle, he entered the book-room for the second time. My lord, before the mirror above the fireplace, was pensively absorbed in some delicate adjustment to the folds of his cravat; my lady, a trifle dishevelled, but otherwise a model of fashionable decorum, was seated in a large armchair. "I don't know how it comes about, my lord," she said, in a light, languid voice, "but we do not increase our covers for guests tonight."

"But why, my love, did you not inform me of this circumstance earlier?" enquired my lord reproachfully. "I should then have used my best endeavours to have persuaded your brother and his amiable friend to have given us the pleasure of their company."

"Yes, indeed! How—how stupid of me!" said my lady, with very creditable command over her voice.

"And Allandale," pursued my lord ruthlessly, "in case the conversation should have flagged."

Pained to see such a want of chivalry in my lord, Farley came to the rescue of his sorely-tried mistress, and, in a few dignified and well-chosen words, put an end to this scene "Supper, my lady, is served!" he announced.

Pistols for Two

Contents

PISTOLS FOR TWO

I

In the end, the quarrel, smouldering for so many weeks, flared up over such a trifle that anyone, Tom reflected, would have laughed to have known the cause. Only they had not really reached pistol-point because Jack had stepped backward in a doorway, and cannoned into him, making him spill his glass of champagne, and treading on his foot. Nor had Jack turned pale and tight-lipped with anger because he had cursed him for being a clumsy oaf. If you had known a fellow from the cradle, had played with him, gone to school with him, shot, fished, and hunted with him, you could curse him with impunity, and either it ended in a bout of fisticuffs or in laughter: not in a meeting in the chill morning, attended by seconds. Even had they not been such close friends that sort of thing was out of date: rubbishing stuff, fit only for the stage! Tom's grandfather, of course, had been out five times, if the family legends were to be believed, on the most trifling provocation. He had once fought Jack's great-uncle George—and very comical they must have looked, Jack and he had often thought, giggling over it, with their shaven polls (for they had worn wigs, both of them), and the absurd ruffles they affected in place of wristbands, and had to tuck up, and their bare feet probably much bruised by the unkind ground. Nowadays, if one fought a duel, one chose pistols, and one didn't make a cake of oneself over the business. But very few people did fight duels, and certainly not because they had been jostled in doorways.

Only it wasn't that. This unthinkable situation had arisen out of something far more serious. Not that one could call Marianne Treen serious: she was the gayest and most light-hearted of all possible causes of dissension.

Strange what changes a few years could wreak in a female! There had been nothing remarkable in little Marianne Treen before she went south to boarding-school: in fact Tom could distinctly recall that he and Jack and Harry Denver had thought her a silly creature, with freckles on her nose, and a tiresome way of intruding where girls were not wanted. Her departure from Yorkshire left their withers unwrung; and since she spent her holidays in London, with her grandmama, they were very soon able to forget her.

But she had come back to Yorkshire. She had enjoyed a brilliant London season, and when most of the *haut ton* had gone to Brighton, Mrs Treen had brought her home to Treen Hall, and the neighbourhood had renewed their acquaintance with her at one of the assemblies at High Harrowgate. A stunning shock that had been to all the young gentlemen for miles around, for who would have supposed that this dazzling beauty was none other than freckled little Marianne, who was used to whine: 'Let me come with you! Oh, pray, let me come too!'

They rarely had let her, and now she had her revenge on them. Only she was too sweet and too gay to care for that, and if she did favour some more than others it was easy to see that she used her best endeavours to be impartial.

Jack and Tom were her favourites, as they were certainly the most assiduous, of her courtiers. Everyone laughed at this, and they were roasted a little for doing everything together, even when it came to falling in love

2

for the first time. That did nothing to soothe exacerbated tempers. It was a strange and a deplorable circumstance that one's relatives were unable to see when one was in earnest, but, on the contrary, laboured under the delusion that if one had not yet come down from Oxford one was too young to think of marriage.

Each knew himself to be an eligible suitor. Perhaps Jack had a little the advantage over Tom, for his father was a baronet. But Tom's father was the Squire, which counted for something, and Tom was his only son, whereas Jack had two younger brothers to be provided for.

At first their courtship had been unattended by any rancour. They were agreed that Marianne was incomparable, and their rivalry had been conducted in the friendliest spirit. Perhaps neither knew when the change had crept into their relationship with one another. Perhaps Jack was jealous of Tom's superior height, and breadth of shoulder (sure to appeal to a female!); perhaps Tom envied Jack his air of elegance, and his handsome profile. Whatever the cause, the rift appeared between them. They had become hostile, each eyeing the other with suspicion, each on the watch for any cause for offence. A dozen times they had come within an ace of indulging in a maul; but never until this disastrous night had they considered the possibility of settling their quarrel at dawn, in Stanhope's Clearing—by tradition an honourable meeting-place.

That Marianne would choose one or other of them before the summer ended neither doubted. The only question was which it would be, and this made it of paramount importance that neither should steal an unfair advantage over the other. After one or two squabbles they had agreed to this—or so Tom had believed, until on this night of the Treens' Dress Party he had beheld with his own eyes the proof of Jack's perfidy. Both had meant to send Marianne a posy of flowers to carry at the ball, with a suitable message attached to the holder: which posy she chose would clearly indicate her heart's preference. Tom had bullied the Squire's head gardener into making up an exquisite bouquet of pink roses and sweet-peas. He had ridden over to Treen Hall himself that morning, to leave the tribute with the Treens' quelling butler, and the most shocking mischance had occurred. The mare had been stung by a horse-fly, and Tom, that bruising rider, lost in some beatific dream, and riding with a loose rein and his head in the clouds, had abruptly parted company with Bess. Alas for the delicate bouquet grasped in his right hand! A shower of petals in the road, a dismal array of broken stalks in the filigree holder: that was all that remained of it.

He had only just caught Bess when, as ill-fortune would have it, Jack came driving along the road from Melbury Court in his smart new tilbury. A bouquet of yellow roses lay on the seat beside him, so that there was no need to enquire his errand.

Three months earlier Jack would have roared with laughter at Tom's mishap; today Jack was politeness itself, and not even the sight of that abject posy did more than make his lip quiver. Jack had had the infernal impudence to behave with magnanimity. He had said that since misfortune had overtaken Tom he should not present his own bouquet. This was precisely what Tom had been about to demand as his due, under the terms of their agreement. He said so, hating Jack for his punctiliousness. So Jack smiled in a slighting way, and had more than hinted that only a cork-brained fellow like Tom would have thought of offering pink roses to a goddess whose hair was a glorious Titian red.

4

Tom had brooded over it all the afternoon, but it was not then that the thought of calling Jack out had even remotely occurred to him. It hadn't really occurred to him when, on arriving at Treen Hall that evening, he had seen Marianne, adorable in a cloud of jonquil gauze over a white satin robe, holding in one gloved hand a posy of yellow roses. If any reasoned thought found room in his brain, it was merely a vague resolve to give Jack a leveller at the first convenient opportunity—if (for Jack was a clever boxer) Jack did not first plant him a heavy facer.

It was a very grand party, with several London swells, who were staying at Treen Hall, much in evidence. At any other time, Tom, aspiring to fashion, would have taken careful note of the folds of the neckcloth worn by the Tulip talking to Mrs Treen, or regarded with envy the cut of the coat moulded across the shoulders of the gentleman from London who was dancing with Marianne. He would not have been jealous of this personage, for all his handsome face, and exquisite bearing, for he was quite old—thirty at least, Tom judged—and probably already the father of a hopeful family.

All his jealousy, all his seething rancour, was reserved for Jack, his closest friend. Mr Treen's excellent champagne did nothing to assuage it. Before an hour had elapsed it must have been a very obtuse person who failed to realize that the two handsome boys from the Manor and Melbury Court were itching to be at one another's throats.

And then Jack, stepping back politely for an elderly gentleman to pass him, trod on Tom's toes, and made him spill his champagne.

Somehow they were confronting one another in the small saloon that led out of the ballroom, and Tom was cursing Jack, and Jack, instead of punching him in the ribs, or meekly apologizing for his clumsiness, was standing straight and stiff, white-faced and close-lipped, his pleasant grey eyes as cold and as hard as the granite of the country. Then Tom had uttered the words from which there could be no retreat. 'I shall send my friends to wait on yours!' he said, in a grand way that was only marred by his shaking voice of fury.

Dear, good Harry Denver, who had seen the encounter, and had followed the injured parties into the saloon, tried to make peace, urging them not to be gudgeons, to remember where they were.

'Harry, will you act for me?' demanded Tom.

Poor Harry stuttered and floundered. 'Now, Tom, you know this is the outside of enough! Jack meant no harm! Jack, for God's sake——!'

'I am perfectly ready to meet Mr Crawley, when and where he pleases!' replied Jack, in a chill, brittle voice.

'Be good enough to name your friends, Mr Frith!' said Tom, not to be outdone in formality.

'Jack, *you're* not three parts foxed!' Harry said urgently. 'Don't be such a damned fool, man!'

Then he saw that they were no longer alone. The gentleman from London, who had been waltzing with Marianne, had come into the saloon, and closed the door behind him. All three young men glared at him, the hostility of the native towards the stranger patent in their eyes.

'You must forgive me!' he said affably. 'An affair of honour, I collect? So much better to shut the door, don't you agree? Can I be of service to either of you?'

They stared at him. Harry, in desperate need of an ally, blurted out the ostensible cause of the quarrel, and besought the gentleman from London to assure the sworn enemies that they were behaving like idiots.

Jack, who had been mentally passing in review his acquaintances in the district, and rejecting them all as being unsuitable candidates for the post of second, said haughtily: 'I am persuaded no man of honour would advise another to refuse a challenge. Of course, if Mr Crawley cares to withdraw his rash words——'

This was a studied insult, as Tom well knew, for Jack was by far the better shot. He snapped out one word: 'No!'

'But they mustn't fight!' Harry protested, distress writ plain on his honest countenance. 'Sir, tell them so!'

The gentleman from London said apologetically: 'But I am in agreement with Mr Frith. A man of honour, sir, cannot refuse such a challenge.'

Jack looked at him with a certain approval, but said stiffly: 'You have the advantage of me, sir.'

'My name is Kilham,' said the gentleman from London. 'May I again offer my services? I shall be happy to act for you, Mr Frith.'

Three pairs of young eyes stared at him. One might live remote from London, but one was not such a Johnny Raw that one had not heard of Sir Gavin Kilham, friend of princes, member of the Bow Window set at White's, amateur of sport, Nonesuch amongst whips, arbiter of fashion. No wonder the folds of his neckcloth baffled the closest scrutiny! no wonder his coat fitted him like a glove!

Jack, bemused at the thought of having such an exalted person for his second, swallowed, and only just managed to achieve a creditable bow; Tom ground his teeth in rage that Jack should yet again have all the luck; and Harry, in relief, supposed that Beau Kilham must know as well as any man what ought now to be done. He ventured to say: 'I—I shall call upon you, sir, at your convenience!'

'That might be a trifle awkward,' said Sir Gavin, to whom the tragic situation seemed to be the merest commonplace. 'I am only a guest in this house, you see. Let us settle it here and now!'

Harry, who had a dim notion that the correct behaviour of a second was to seek a reconciliation between the principals, looked doubtful, but the prospective duellists emphatically applauded the suggestion.

Sir Gavin, drawing out his snuff-box, flicked it open, and took a delicate pinch. 'Since we, sir, have the choice, we shall elect to fight with pistols, at twenty-five yards, tomorrow, at an hour and a place which I shall ask you to suggest.'

Deep trouble was in Harry's face, for the longer range gave all the advantage to the better shot. Before he could speak, Jack said, quite insufferably, Tom considered: 'I prefer to fight Mr Crawley at a range of twelve yards, sir.'

'Well, I won't fight you at twelve yards!' retorted Tom furiously. 'Twenty-five, and be damned to you!'

'Tom, do, for God's sake——! Now, listen, you crazy fools, this is nonsense! The quarrel can be composed in a trice!' exclaimed Harry.

They rounded on him, all their pent-up feelings finding expression in the loathing with which they commanded him to hold his tongue.

8

So there was nothing for poor Harry to do but to appoint the time and the place, both of which Sir Gavin accepted with the utmost amiability.

Then a paralysing thought occurred to all three young gentlemen.

'The—the weapons?' uttered Harry, exchanging an anguished glance with Tom.

For a moment no one said anything. Sir Gavin's lazy eyes were lowered to the contemplation of his charming snuff-box, and if his lips twitched it was so tiny a betrayal that it passed unnoticed. Bitter reflections on the ways of fathers, who kept under lock and key their duelling-pistols (if indeed they owned such things) possessed the minds of Jack and Tom. Anyone would have thought that a prudent parent would have given his son a good pair of Manton pistols instead of a pair of shot-guns, and would have taught him how to conduct himself in such a situation as this. Neither Sir John nor the Squire had made the least push to be of real service to their heirs; and intimate knowledge of both gentlemen could only lead those heirs to face the disagreeable fact that an appeal to them now would end in nothing but the summary end to their quarrel.

Harry, anxious though he might be to stop the affair, was not going to allow the gentleman from London to suppose that his principal owned no duelling-pistols. He said that unfortunately Tom's pistols had been sent back to the maker for a trifling repair. Jack was not going to be outdone by this sort of thing, and since he could not think of any reason that was not grossly plagiaristic for failing to produce a pair of pistols of his own, he said, with an odiously curling lip: 'Strange that I should not have been permitted to see Mr Crawley's weapons!'

9

'You have none either, so be damned to that humbug!' instantly replied Tom.

'In that case,' said Sir Gavin, restoring the snuff-box to his pocket, 'I will be responsible for the weapons. And since the hour of the meeting is not far distant, may I suggest that you should both now retire from this party, and go home to get what sleep you can? Mr Frith, I shall call for you in my curricle at half-past five; Mr Denver, I should like a word with you before we part!'

3

It was easy to talk of sleeping if you were only the second in an encounter, Tom reflected bitterly. He had slipped away from Treen Hall, and had driven himself home by the light of a full moon. The chill air sweeping over the moors cooled his head, and, to a great extent, his rage. By the time he reached the Manor, and had stabled the cob, he was finding it increasingly difficult to look forward with any pleasure to the morrow—no, not the morrow: it was past midnight, he observed, as he entered the Manor, and saw the tall-case clock at the foot of the stairs.

His mother had gone to bed, but as ill-luck would have it, the Squire was still up, and called to him from the library. 'Is that you, Tom?'

He was obliged to go into the room, and there was his father, and not alone either. He was playing chess with Sir John Frith. Tom regarded Sir John in the light of an uncle, and was much attached to him, but there was no one he wanted to see less tonight.

'You are back very early,' remarked the Squire, shooting a look up at him under his bushy brows.

'Yes, sir,' he said, in a careless voice. 'It was such a squeeze—and Harry and I mean to go out early, to fish the Brown Pool.'

'Oh!' said the Squire, his gaze bent again on the board. 'You have me, John, I fancy.'

'I think so,' agreed his guest. 'Jack going with you, Tom?'

Tom knew the tell-tale colour was rising to his cheeks. 'Yes—oh yes!' he stammered, feeling like a Judas—only that it was more likely that it would be he, and not Jack, who would be brought home on a hurdle so few short hours ahead.

'Glad to hear it!' said Sir John. 'Better than dangling after a petticoat at your age, pair of young fools that you are!'

That was the way dotards of forty-five (and very likely even older) talked to one, so senile they had forgotten what it meant to be young, and in love! Tom said stiffly that he would go to bed.

'Yes, you go,' agreed his father. 'Good night, my boy: don't wake the whole household when you get up! The mistake I made, John, was in moving my queen's bishop when I did.'

Tom went away, quite unnoticed by the insensate old men, who were already playing their game all over again. The last thing he wanted was for either of them to suspect the truth, but somehow it made him feel ill-used and resentful that they didn't even notice that something was amiss.

When he got into bed he hoped that Harry would not oversleep. Harry was coming to fetch him in his gig, and it would be a dreadful thing if he were to be late on the ground, perhaps oversleeping himself. The gentleman from London would certainly bring his man punctually to the rendezvous.

He soon found that there was no fear of his oversleeping. He could not sleep at all. He tossed and turned; threw off blankets; pulled them over him again; punched his pillows—all to no avail. He was wide awake, his mind so lively that his thoughts crowded in on it, jostling one another in a restless, worrying way he was not at all accustomed to.

He was not, he thought, afraid—or, at any rate, not more afraid than one was before going out to bat at Eton; but he felt sorry for his father, who would in all probability come down to breakfast to be greeted with the pleasing intelligence that the hope of his house was either a lifeless corpse, or hideously wounded. His mother would never recover from the blow; and what a terrible thing it would be for Sir John and Lady Frith, with their heir obliged to fly the country, and all communication with the Manor severed from that hour! Poor, deluded Uncle John, asking so casually if Jack were going fishing too!

Suddenly, as that thought flitted into his head, it was elbowed out by another: if only it had been true, and he and Jack were going to tramp off through the dewy early morning, sandwiches in their pockets, rods in their hands, creels on their backs, and nothing between them but the comfortable, idle chat of close friendship! No need for Harry on that expedition; in fact, better without Harry, though he might come if he chose, for he was a good sort of a fellow—a very faithful friend, really, though not to compare, of course, with Jack. He was apt to be a little in the way sometimes, as when he had gone with them when—— Tom checked that thought quickly. Fatal to remember all the things he and Jack had done together, and the sport they had had, and the scrapes they had plunged into! That was all over; and even if their encounter did not end in the death of one of them, nothing would ever be the same again between them. But he couldn't help remembering, and it didn't seem to be of any use to dwell on Jack's miserable double-dealing today, because whether Jack gave Marianne flowers behind his best friend's back, or whether he behaved as impeccably as one had been so sure he would, he was still the friend who had shared one's every thought, helped one out of tight corners, called on one for instant aid himself, so that one would as readily have doubted Father's loyalty as his.

And it was all because of freckled little Marianne Treen, who was a shocking flirt, when one came to consider the matter dispassionately, and probably didn't care a rap for either of them! One dance each—and only country dances at that!—had she granted them tonight, but she had waltzed twice with Sir Gavin Kilham, and had engaged herself to another town-buck for the quadrille. When one thought of the time one had wasted, trying to fix her interest—yes, wasted *was* the word! All these summer months, when he and Jack might have been so much better employed, squandered on toadying a chit who had never been anything but a dead bore to either of them!

The more one thought of it the less vivid grew Marianne's present image, the clearer the memory of a tiresome little girl with freckles, spoiling one's sport by insisting on accompanying one, and then falling into the brook, or complaining that she was tired, or dared not cross a field with cows grazing in it. The idea that he and Jack—*Jack*! —should stand up to shoot at one another for the sake of Marianne Treen would have been a grand jest if it had not been so tragic. And just suppose that by some quirk of fortune it was not Jack's bullet that found its mark, but his? Why, if that happened he would blow out his own brains, because there would be nothing left in all the world for Jack's friend to do!

4

When his thoughts had slid into unquiet dreams he did not know, but he must have dozed a little, for he opened his eyes to find that the moonlight was no longer sliding between the chinks of the blinds, but a disagreeable morning-light instead. His watch informed him that it was after five o'clock, so he sprang out of his tumbled bed in a hurry. By the time he heard stealthy footsteps on the gravel-walk below his window, he was dressed, and he leaned out to tell Harry so. Harry had been about to throw a handful of pebbles up, but he dropped them, and made signs indicating that it was time to be off.

Tom stole downstairs, and slipped out of the house by a side door. No one was stirring. He and Harry went in silence down the drive to where Harry had left his gig.

Harry said, unhitching the reins from the gate-post: 'You know, I don't like this above half, old fellow.'

One could not draw back from an encounter, particularly when it was one's first, and one had never had the chance to prove one's mettle. 'Do you imagine I am going to cry off?' demanded Tom.

'Well, I don't know,' said Harry, climbing up beside him into the gig. 'After all, you and Jack——!'

'Don't waste your breath on me!' recommended Tom. 'Try what Jack will say to you! If I know him you'll have a short answer!'

'You couldn't expect Jack to draw back,' said Harry. 'I don't!'

'No, but I mean it wasn't his challenge! You were foxed, Tom—you know you were!'

'No, I was not,' said Tom.

'Dash it, to call a man out only because he jostles you in a doorway, without in the least meaning to——'

'It wasn't that,' answered Tom. 'And it's no use to prose at me: I shan't listen!'

So Harry said no more, and the rest of the drive was accomplished in silence. They came punctually on to the ground, just as a white-winged curricle with a pair of magnificent bays harnessed in the bar bowled up the broad woodland ride. Only two men sat in it, nor was there any sign of a doctor. Tom wondered if his stolid second would point this omission out to Sir Gavin. It was not, he decided, for himself to mention the matter. He stole one look at Jack, alighting from the curricle, and casting off the drab overcoat he wore, and then averted his gaze. Jack was still wearing his flint-face, and his eyes did not warm an atom as fleetingly they met his. Tom looked instead at those match-bays, thinking how much he would like to ask Jack if they were the sweet-goers they looked to be, and whether Sir Gavin had allowed him to handle the ribbons.

Sir Gavin was walking unhurriedly across the clearing to meet Harry. He wore top-boots polished till you might almost see your face in them; and a many-caped benjamin; and he carried an ominous case under one arm. He and Harry conferred together, and inspected the wicked-looking weapons in that case, and paced out the ground. Tom felt queasy, and rather cold, and a leaden weight seemed to have settled in his chest. He wished the seconds

15

would make haste: they were being maddeningly deliber-
ate. Another glance at Jack showed him that Jack was
perfectly cool and collected, only rather pale.

Harry was coming towards him, to conduct him to his
position. Sir Gavin was holding the pistols by their bar-
rels; Jack took one in his right hand, and stood with it
pointing downwards, his body turned sideways from his
adversary.

Sir Gavin gave Harry the second pistol. He saw that it
was cocked, and took it carefully, thankful to see that his
hand was quite steady. He listened to what Sir Gavin was
saying, about dropping his handkerchief, and nodded.
Then Sir Gavin and Harry both stepped back, and he was
looking straight at Jack, across, as it seemed to him, a vast
stretch of greensward.

The handkerchief was fluttering aloft in the light
breeze; it dropped, and Tom deliberately fired high in the
air. His eyes were fixed on Jack, and even before he realized
that his weapon had misfired he saw Jack's hand jerk up,
so that his gun too pointed skywards. Only Jack didn't
even take the trouble to pull the trigger, apparently, for
nothing happened—not even a flash in the pan. Suddenly
Tom was indignant with Jack for behaving in this heroic
style, and he flung down his pistol, and strode forward,
exclaiming: 'What the devil do you mean by that? *Shoot*,
damn you! Deloping—not even pulling the trigger——!'

'I did pull the trigger!' Jack retorted. 'The curst piece
misfired! It was *you* who didn't shoot! You crazy fool, I
might have killed you!'

'You aimed in the air!' said Tom. 'Serve you right if
I had killed *you*! I won't have it! Damn it, it's insulting!'

'So did you fire in the air!' Jack flung at him. 'And you

might as well have aimed at me, because you couldn't hit a barn at twenty-five yards!'

'Oh, couldn't I?' said Tom.

'No—or at twelve!'

'Oh?' said Tom. 'Well, there's one thing I can do, and that's draw your cork!'

'You may try!' said Jack, casting his own pistol from him, and putting up his fists.

They closed with enthusiasm, far too anxious to get to grips to waste time in taking off their coats. It was rather a scrambling fight, because the coats hampered them, and mingled relief and exasperation made them spar wildly, and soon fall into a clinch, each striving to throw the other a cross-buttock. Since Tom was the larger and the stronger of the two the outcome of that was never in doubt.

'Damn you!' panted Jack, picking himself up, and rubbing one elbow.

They looked at one another. Tom's fists sank. 'Jack,' he said uncertainly, 'we—we came to fight a duel!'

Jack's mouth quivered. He bit his underlip, but it was to no avail. If Tom had not begun to grin, like the gudgeon he was, he might have kept his countenance, but Tom was grinning, and the huge bubble of laughter which had been growing within him burst.

5

The same thought occurred to both of them, as the gusts of mirth died, and they wiped their streaming eyes. '*Neither* pistol went off!' Jack said.

'By God, you're right!' Tom said, and swung round to confront the seconds.

Both he and Jack had forgotten the presence of the gentleman from London when they came to fisticuffs. Torn between wrath at his suspected falsity, and dread of his contempt for their schoolboyish behaviour, they glared at him, flushed, and still panting.

Sir Gavin, who was seated negligently on a tree-stump, rose, and strolled forward, saying approvingly: 'Excellent! Rather glaringly abroad sometimes, perhaps, but I should like to see you both stripped. When you come to London you must tell me of your visit, and I'll take you to Jackson's Boxing Saloon.'

This gratifying invitation, from a noted Patron of the Ring, could not but mollify the injured feelings of the late combatants. Decency, however, had to be preserved. 'Sir,' said Jack accusingly, 'neither my friend's gun nor mine was loaded!'

'Do you know, that notion has just crossed my mind?' said Sir Gavin. 'I have such a wretched memory! Really, I must apologize, but I am quite famous for my lapses, and you must forgive me.'

They had a suspicion they were being laughed at, but it was very difficult to pick a quarrel with the gentleman from London. Tom solved the problem by rounding on Harry, and saying sternly: 'You should have inspected the weapons! You're my second!'

'I did!' said Harry, going off into a guffaw.

It might be difficult to know how to deal with the gentleman from London, but there was no difficulty at all in deciding how to deal with Harry—who had had the effrontery to make fools of two persons who, out of sheer compassion, had suffered him to join them occasionally in their chosen pursuits. They eyed him measuringly, and they advanced upon him in a purposeful way.

The gentleman from London seemed to be in the path. He said: 'The blame rests entirely on my shoulders. Er— did you wish to kill one another?'

'No!' said Jack. 'And it was—it was dashed officious of you, sir, to leave out the ball, for we meant all the time to delope!'

'My lack of tact often keeps me awake at night,' apologized Sir Gavin. 'You see, I was requested—by a lady—to intervene in your quarrel, so what else could I do?'

Jack looked at Tom, a little trouble in his face, as he recalled the events of the previous evening. 'Tom, *why*?' he asked.

Tom flushed. 'It don't signify! I dare say all's fair in— in love and war, but it was the roses! I never thought you would use me so!'

'What roses?' Jack demanded.

'Yours. The ones she carried!'

'They were *not* mine!' Jack said, his eyes kindling. 'By Jupiter, Tom, I have a mind to call you out for thinking I would serve you such a backhanded turn! It passes everything, so it does!'

'*Not* yours?' ejaculated Tom.

Sir Gavin coughed deprecatingly. 'If you refer to the roses Miss Treen carried last night, they were mine!' They stared at him. 'I hope you will not both call me out,' he said, 'but the fact is that Miss Treen has done me the honour to become my affianced wife. Our betrothal was announced at supper last night.'

This was shocking news. Each unsuccessful suitor tried to realize that his life was blighted, and failed. Tom said, with dignity: 'You might have told us so last night, sir!'

'I might, of course, but I had the oddest notion that it wouldn't have been of the least avail,' confessed Sir Gavin.

They thought this over. A reluctant grin overset Tom's dignity. 'Well, perhaps not,' he conceded.

Jack executed his best bow. 'We must beg leave to wish you happy, sir,' he said nobly.

'I am very much obliged to you,' responded Sir Gavin, with great civility.

'I suppose,' said Tom, blushing, 'you think we have made great cakes of ourselves, sir?'

'Not at all,' said Sir Gavin. 'You have conducted your-selves with perfect propriety, and I am happy to have assisted in an affair of honour so creditable to both parties. Let us repair to the inn beyond this charming coppice, and partake of breakfast! I bespoke it half an hour ago, and I am sure it will by now be awaiting us. Besides, I do not care to keep my horses standing any longer.'

'I should think not indeed!' Tom exclaimed. 'I say, sir, what a bang-up set-out it is! Real blood-and-bone!'

'I am so glad you like them,' said Sir Gavin. 'Do, pray, try their paces as far as to the Rising Sun! If you will allow me, I will drive the gig.'

It was rather too much to expect two budding whips to nurse their broken hearts when offered the chance of driv-ing a match-pair of thoroughbreds. Briefly but fervently thanking Sir Gavin, Tom and Jack hurried off to the curricle, arguing with some heat on which of them was first to handle the ribbons.

Sir Gavin, devoutly trusting that his confidence in their ability to cope with a high-couraged pair had not been misplaced, took his fellow-second by the arm, and pushed him gently towards the humbler gig.

A CLANDESTINE AFFAIR

Miss Tresilian surveyed the young couple before her with perturbation in her usually humorous grey eyes. Not that there was anything in the picture presented by Mr Rosely and Miss Lucy Tresilian to dismay the most captious of critics, for a better-looking pair would have been hard to find: the lady was a glowing brunette, the gentleman a fair youth with golden locks, classic features, and a graceful figure. He was dressed very correctly for a morning visit in a blue coat, with fawn pantaloons and Hessian boots; and if the folds of his neckcloth did not aspire to dandified heights it was easy to see that he had arranged these to the best of his ability. Mr Rosely, in fact, was doing justice to a momentous occasion: he had come to make an offer for the hand of Miss Tresilian's niece.

He said, with a shy smile: 'It can't, I fancy, come as a surprise to you, ma'am! You have been so kind that I'm persuaded—that is, I have ventured to indulge the hope that you wouldn't be displeased.'

No, it had not come as a surprise to Miss Tresilian. It was nearly a year since Mr Rosely had been introduced to Lucy in the Lower Rooms, at Bath; but although Lucy did not want for admirers, and it was scarcely to be supposed that anyone so handsomely endowed in face and fortune as Mr Rosely had not had a great many caps set at him, neither had swerved in allegiance since that date. Nor could Miss Tresilian deny that she had favoured the match: it had seemed so eminently suitable!

'Of course she's not displeased!' said Lucy. 'You knew from the start how it was, didn't you, Aunt Elinor?'

'Yes,' acknowledged Miss Tresilian. 'But I didn't know until I brought you to London, love, that the connection was disliked by Arthur's family.'

'Oh, no!' he said quickly. 'Only by Iver! My sister likes it excessively!'

'And Lord Iver is only Arthur's cousin,' said Lucy. 'Removed, too! Scarcely a relation at all!'

He demurred at this, saying diffidently: 'Well, it's more than that, for he has been my guardian, you know. I wouldn't for the world displease him, only that in *this* case he fancies we are both of us too young—or some such nonsense! He will come about! Particularly if I am able to tell him *you* don't frown on the marriage, ma'am!'

'No, I don't *frown* upon it,' said Miss Tresilian, 'but I agree with Lord Iver that you are very young. This is Lucy's first season, you know, and——'

'How *can* you, aunt?' protested her niece. 'I may not have been regularly presented until last month, but you know you would have brought me to town a year ago if Aunt Clara hadn't insisted she was too unwell to be left alone! Why, I am nineteen, and have been out in Bath above a twelve-month!'

'Yes, my dear, but I never knew until just the other day how awkwardly Arthur is situated. Or even that he had a guardian, much less——'

'No, no, ma'am!' interrupted Mr Rosely anxiously. 'Iver isn't my guardian now that I am of age, but only my trustee! He has no power to prevent my marriage—no authority over me at all!'

'It appears to me that if he holds your purse-strings

until you are five-and-twenty he has a great deal of power over you,' responded Miss Tresilian dryly.

He looked troubled, but said: 'He wouldn't—I *know* he wouldn't! People think him tyrannical, but he has never been so to me! The kindest of guardians—and he must have wished me at the devil, for I was only eight when my father died, and *he* not much above five-and-twenty. I wonder he didn't leave me to be reared in my own house, for I was used to follow him about like a tanthony-pig!'

Miss Tresilian refrained from comment. It seemed to her unlikely that Mr Rosely had ever offered Lord Iver the least pretext for a display of tyranny, for while she could not but acknowledge the sweetness of his disposition she did not feel that resolution was amongst his many virtues. No hint of a strong will was to be detected in his delicate countenance, none of the determination that characterized Lucy.

'And even if he doesn't consent, we shall come off all right,' said Lucy cheerfully. 'After all, I have quite a genteel fortune of my own, and we can subsist on that, until your stupid Trust comes to an end.'

But at this Miss Tresilian intervened, saying firmly that neither she nor Lucy's papa could countenance an engagement entered into without Lord Iver's sanction. Lucy, always outspoken, said: 'Dearest, you know that's fudge! All Papa would say is that you must settle it as you think best!'

Miss Tresilian laughed, but said: 'Well, I can't settle it, precisely, but I can and must forbid an engagement at this present. I am very sorry for you both, but unless Lord Iver should change his mind I am afraid there is nothing for it but to wait until Arthur's fortune passes into his own hands.'

It was not to be expected that two young persons deep in love could view with anything but dismay the prospect of waiting more than three years before becoming engaged. Mr Rosely took a dejected leave of the ladies, and went away, saying that he was sure he *must* be able to prevail upon Iver to relent; and Lucy at once set about the task of convincing her aunt that her attachment to her Arthur was no girlish fancy to be speedily forgotten.

It was unnecessary. Although she had been virtually in her aunt's charge since her childhood only fifteen years separated them, and the bonds of affection between them were strong. Miss Tresilian knew that her niece was neither volatile nor impressionable. She had been much courted in Bath, but none of her suitors, before the arrival on the scene of Mr Rosely, had done so much as turn her head. But she had fallen in love with Mr Rosely at first sight, and not for the sake of his handsome face. 'Handsome?' said Lucy. 'I suppose he is—oh, yes, of course he is! Everyone says so! But, to own the truth, I don't in general care about fair men, and try as I will I *cannot* admire Grecian profiles!' She added, such a glow in her eyes as Miss Tresilian had never before seen: 'His nature is by far more beautiful than his countenance. He has so much sensibility—such quickness of apprehension! It is as though we had known each other all our lives. Oh, my dearest aunt, I never dreamed I could be so happy!'

No, Lucy was not likely to fall out of love, nor was it possible to suppose her to be infatuated. She seemed to be aware of the flaw in his character, for when her aunt ventured to suggest that his amiability perhaps made him a trifle too persuadable she replied without hesitation: 'Exactly so! I don't mean to say that he could be persuaded to do wrong, for his principles are fixed; but his nature is gentle, and his diffidence leads him to rely more on another's judgment than his own. That is one reason why I can't and won't wait for nearly four years before marrying him!'

'Lucy dear, could you be *happy* with a husband who would allow you to rule the roast?'

'To own the truth,' replied Lucy mischievously, 'I have a strong notion that I couldn't be happy with any other! You know what a detestably managing disposition *I* have!' She added, in a more serious tone: 'Please help me, dear Aunt Elinor! If there were any *reason* for Lord Iver's refusal to give his consent I promise you I would respect it! There is none! But Arthur has been so much in the habit of deferring to him that if all must remain at a stand for nearly four years—Oh, aunt, he is the *horridest* creature, and my enemy besides! I couldn't mistake! I have met him only once, when Mrs Crewe took me to the Walton's ball, and Arthur brought him up to me, but he looked at me in *such* a way! If I had been a shabby-genteel wretch on the catch for a rich husband he couldn't have been more repelling! But he must know I'm nothing of the kind, for Lady Windlesham does—and if Arthur's *sister* likes the match I wish you will tell me what right Lord Iver has——' She checked herself. 'Well! Talking won't pay toll. Think for me, Aunt Elinor! Useless to suppose that Arthur will be able to bring that creature about!'

Even less than her niece did Miss Tresilian believe that Mr Rosely's efforts would meet with success, and much more astonished than Lucy was she when, two days later, Lord Iver came to call at the slim house in Green Street which she had hired for the season. Indeed, the news that he was awaiting her in the drawing-room startled her into exclaiming: 'Oh, no! No, no, I cannot——!' However, she recollected herself almost immediately, sent the servant down again to tell his lordship she would be with him directly, and turned to cast an anxious glance at her reflection in the mirror.

With the buoyancy of youth, Lucy was much inclined to think that Lord Iver had miraculously capitulated, and had come to discuss the marriage settlements. Miss Tresilian, with no such expectation, begged her not to indulge optimism, and trod resolutely downstairs, pledged to support the lovers' cause.

The visitor was standing with his back to the room, looking out of the window, but when he heard the door open he turned, and stared with hard, challenging eyes at his hostess.

She shut the door, but remained by it, meeting that fierce scrutiny resolutely. For a minute neither spoke, but each scanned the other, the lady perceiving a powerfully-built man, harsh-featured and swarthy, whose close-cropped hair, sporting neckcloth, and gleaming top-boots proclaimed the Corinthian; the gentleman gazing at an uncommonly pretty woman. Miss Tresilian was on the shady side of thirty, but although she had lately taken to wearing a cap over her soft brown curls, and bore herself with the assurance of her years, she retained the face and figure of a much younger woman.

It was she who broke the silence, saying, as she moved forward: 'You wished, I think, to see me, sir. May I know why?'

He bowed stiffly. 'I am obliged to you for receiving me, ma'am. As to my *wishes*——! I thought it best to come here in person, that there should be no misunderstanding between us.'

'Pray be seated, sir!' said Miss Tresilian, disposing herself gracefully in a winged armchair.

He did not avail himself of this invitation, but said abruptly: 'I imagine you must know what my errand is. If you are indeed your niece's guardian—but you will permit me to say that I find it incredible that you should be! She has a father, and you are by far too young to be her guardian!'

'Certainly she has a father,' replied Miss Tresilian coldly. 'When he married again, however, it was agreed that his daughter should remain in my charge. Let me remind you that I am no longer a young woman, sir!'

At this point, the conversation, which had been conducted with the appearance at least of formality, underwent a change. 'I know to a day how old you are, so don't talk nonsense to me!' said his lordship impatiently. 'A more ramshackle arrangement——! Is your sister with you?'

'No,' said Miss Tresilian, eyeing him with hostility, 'she is not! The indifferent state of her health——'

He gave a crack of sardonic laughter. 'You needn't tell me! Still suffering spasms and vapours to throw a rub in your way, is she?'

'Pray, did you come here merely to discuss my sister's constitution?' demanded Miss Tresilian.

'You know very well why I am here! This lamentable affair between your niece and my cousin—which you appear to have encouraged!'

'I can assure you, however, that had I known of Mr Rosely's relationship to you, sir, I should have done my utmost to *discourage* an affair which I dislike quite as much as you do!'

'A pretty sort of guardian, not to have made it your business to enquire who were Arthur's relations!' he said scathingly.

'And did you make it your business to acquaint yourself with all Lucy's remote cousins?' she retorted.

'It was unnecessary. I knew her to be your niece, and that was enough! In plain words, I don't wish for the connection, and shall do what I may to put an end to it. Don't under-rate me! you'll find I can do a great deal!'

'Do rid your mind of the notion that the connection is any more welcome to me than it is to you!' begged Miss Tresilian. 'Nothing could be more repugnant to me than an alliance with any member of your family!'

'So I should suppose—since you made it plain enough when you jilted me!'

'If you mean by that that I terminated an unfortunate engagement which you were regretting quite as much as I——'

'I didn't come here to discuss ancient history!' he interrupted roughly.

'Well, if you came merely to inform me that you don't wish your precious cousin to marry Lucy you've wasted your time!' she countered.

'Ah!' instantly responded his lordship. 'So you do support them, do you? I might have known it!'

She was about to repudiate this suggestion when it occurred to her that to do so would scarcely be in accordance with her promise to help her niece. It cost her a severe struggle, but she managed to summon up a smile, and to say with creditable composure: 'Come! It won't serve for us to rip up at each other, Iver. We may regret this business, but a twelve-year-old quarrel between *us* doesn't constitute a bar to these children's marriage.'

'Have you told your niece?'

'No—any more than you, I collect, have told your cousin! Much good would that do! They would say, and rightly, that it was no concern of theirs!'

'Well, I won't have it!' he announced.

'Now, don't fly into a pelter!' she begged. 'Our differences apart, what is there to be said against the match? Nothing, I dare say, could be more suitable!' She hesitated, and then added, with a little difficulty: 'How odiously selfish we should be if we were to let them break their hearts only because we once quarrelled!'

His lips curled disdainfully. 'Hearts are not so easily broken!'

'No one knows that better than I!' she retorted.

'We need not, then, discuss such an absurdity.'

Realizing, too late, the infelicity of her retort, she tried to recover lost ground. 'Neither of us is in a position to judge what may be the sufferings of two people who *truly* love one another! Lucy's character is unlike mine: her affection is not easily won, and is by far more tenacious than mine.'

'It could hardly be less!' he interpolated. 'Spare me any more moving speeches! She is young enough to recover from her disappointment, and will no doubt transfer her affections soon enough to some other, and, I trust, equally eligible suitor!'

Stung, she retaliated: 'She might well do *that*!'

'Oh, play off no airs for my edification!' he said angrily. 'You won't hoax me into believing that you are not well aware that my cousin is one of the biggest prizes in the Matrimonial Mart! A feather in any girl's cap!'

Rising hastily to her feet, she said: 'If I have anything

29

to say to it, he won't be a feather in Lucy's cap, and that, my lord, you may depend on!'

'Thank you!' he replied. 'You have given me the assurance I sought, and I have nothing further to do here than to take my leave of you! Your obedient servant, ma'am!'

'Lucy,' said Miss Tresilian, with determined calm, 'if your pride doesn't revolt at the imputation of having snared a rich matrimonial prize, mine does! I am not asking you to put all thought of Arthur out of your head: I am merely saying that until he is in every respect his own master, and you have come of age, I will neither countenance his visits to this house, nor allow you to go where there is the least likelihood of your meeting him.'

The youngest Miss Tresilian said, with a brave attempt to speak lightly: 'Dearest, do you mean to lock me up? I must meet him at all the ton parties, and at Almack's too!'

'I know it,' said her aunt. 'And *you* know I don't mean to lock you up! I have a much better scheme in mind, and one which I think you must like. Indeed, I know you will, for you have always wished to visit foreign countries, only, of course, while that dreadful Bonaparte was at large it was impossible. *Now*, however——'

'Oh, no, no!' Lucy cried. 'I don't care a straw for anything Lord Iver may think! He has no power to forbid my marriage to Arthur, and if he is so spiteful as to cut off Arthur's allowance we shall contrive to live tolerably comfortably on *my* inheritance. And no one will think ill of Arthur for doing so, because the instant he is five-and-twenty he may pay me back every groat, if he feels he ought! All we need is Papa's consent—which is to say yours, my dear aunt!'

30

'And you won't get it!' said Miss Tresilian, with unusual asperity. 'Dear child, consider! How can you expect me to behave so improperly as to support a marriage which the person most nearly concerned with Arthur's affairs has expressly forbidden?' She saw that her words had struck home, and lost no time in representing to Lucy all the advantages of her scheme. She was listened to in silence, but had the satisfaction, when she had talked herself out of arguments, of being caught into a warm embrace, and tightly hugged.

'You are the best and kindest of aunts!' Lucy declared. 'I do understand what you must feel—indeed, I do! *Never* would I ask you to do what you think wrong! I had not reflected how impossible it must be for you! Forgive me!'

Much heartened, Miss Tresilian recommended her not to be a goose, and wondered how speedily she could put her plans into execution, and what her exacting elder sister would say when she learned that she meant, instead of returning to her home in Camden Place, to embark on an extended foreign tour.

It could not have been said that Lucy entered into any of the arrangements which occupied Miss Tresilian's every moment during the follow week, or evinced the smallest enthusiasm for any of the promised treats in store, but she uttered no protests, and that, in Miss Tresilian's opinion, was as much as could be hoped for in the natural oppression of her spirits. Calculating ways and means, Miss Tresilian paused to consider the likelihood of Mr Rosely's following his inamorata. Probably Lord Iver would scotch any such scheme, but she determined nevertheless to add her prohibition to his.

In the event, she was denied the opportunity of private

speech with Mr Rosely. Returning to Green Street just after eleven one morning, after a protracted appointment in the City, she was met by her personal maid, who did not scruple to read her a scold for having sallied forth alone on what this severe critic apparently believed to have been an expedition fraught with peril. 'And breakfast waiting for you this hour past!' said Miss Baggeridge, relieving her of her shawl and gloves. 'Now, you sit down this instant, Miss Elinor! Traipsing all about the town, and knocking yourself up like you are! What your poor mama would have said I'm sure I don't know!'

Accustomed from her childhood to her henchwoman's strictures, Miss Tresilian only said, as she removed her becoming hat of chip-straw: 'Where's Miss Lucy? I suppose she breakfasted an hour ago.'

'It's what anyone *might* suppose of a young lady of quality,' said Miss Baggeridge grimly. 'Though why they should, with you setting her the example you do, miss——'

'—you are sure you don't know!' supplied Miss Tresilian.

Miss Baggeridge fixed her with a kindling eye. 'Well do I know it's not my place to utter a word, miss, and far be it from me to unclose my lips on the subject, but when it comes to a young lady gallivanting about the town without so much as the page-boy to escort her, and carrying a bandbox on her arm like a common person, I couldn't reconcile it with my conscience not to speak!'

'If she was carrying a bandbox, she has only gone to take back that French cambric half-robe which must be altered,' said Miss Tresilian prosaically.

Miss Baggeridge sniffed, but refrained from further comment. Having seen her mistress supplied with fresh coffee and bread and butter, she produced from her pocket a sealed missive, saying, in a grudging tone: 'There's a letter from Miss Clara. There was a shilling to pay on it, too. I suppose you'd better have it, but if I was you, miss, I wouldn't worrit myself with it till you've eaten your breakfast.'

With these sage words of advice she withdrew; and Miss Tresilian, never one to shirk a disagreeable duty, broke the wafer of her sister's letter, and spread open three crossed pages of complaint.

While she sipped her coffee she perused these. Nothing could have been more discouraging than the eldest Miss Tresilian's account of her health, but as her detailed descriptions of the torment she endured from rheumatism, nervous tic, spasm, and insomnia were interspersed with the latest Bath on-dits, and some animadversions on the wretched cards she had held at the whist-table, Miss Elinor Tresilian's withers remained unwrung. She gathered that Clara was contriving to amuse herself tolerably well; was relieved to read no very serious criticism of the indigent lady engaged to act as companion to the invalid; and got up to place the letter in her writing-bureau. She never did so. No sooner had she raised the lid of the bureau than she found herself staring down at a letter addressed to herself in Lucy's handwriting. Clara's missive dropped to the floor, and Miss Tresilian, with a premonition of disaster, snatched up her niece's letter, and tore off the wafer that sealed it.

Dear, dearest aunt, she read. *This will come as a Shock to you, and I can only implore you to forgive me, and to understand (as I am persuaded you will) the Exigency of my Situation, nothing less than which could have prevailed upon me to act in a maner as Repugnant to me as, alas, it will be to*

33

you. By the time your eyes alight on these lines I shall be many miles distant, and when I Cast myself at your feet to beg your Pardon it will be as the Bride of my Adored Arthur. Oh, my dear aunt, believe that I have not reached this Momentous Decision without an Agonizing Struggle, for to Approach the Altar without your Blessing, or your presence to support me at that Solemn Moment, so sinks my spirits that only my Conviction that your Refusal to sanction my Engagement sprang not from your Heart but from your sense of Propriety gives me courage to pursue a Line of Conduct which must Shock you and all the world. My only Comfort (besides the Bliss of being united to the Best and Noblest of men) is that You cannot be held accountable, even by Lord Iver, for what I must call (though my hand shrinks from penning the Dreadful Syllables) my Elopement. . . .

Stunned by this communication, Miss Tresilian could not for many minutes collect her scattered wits. With every will in the world to spring to instant action she felt as though she had been smitten with paralysis. From this distressing condition she was reclaimed by the sudden opening of the door, and the sound of a harsh, too-well remembered voice saying: 'Thank you, I'll announce myself!'

She raised her head, and stared blankly across the room at Lord Iver.

He was dressed for travel, and had not stayed to put off his long, many-caped driving-coat of white drab. It was plain, from his blazing eyes and close-gripped lips, that he was in a towering rage, but he did not immediately speak. After a searing moment, his gaze dropped to the letter in her hand, and he said: 'Mine is an empty errand, I apprehend! Is that from your niece?'

Hardly knowing what she did, she held it out to him. He rapidly scanned it, and said contemptuously: 'Very affecting!—if you have a taste for the romantic! I have not!' His eyes searched her face; he gave a short laugh. 'Don't look so tragic! You don't imagine, do you, that I shan't stop this crazy project?'

She pressed her fingers to her throbbing temples. '*Can* you do so? Do you know where—Has Arthur written to you?'

'Yes—like the silly widgeon he is!' he replied. 'As for knowing *where*, there was no need to tell me *that*! Or you either, I imagine!'

'But I haven't the least notion!' she said distractedly. 'Where *could* they have gone? She's under age! Even if Arthur has a special licence, no one would marry them! *She* knows that, and surely *he* must?'

'Of course they know it, and also the one place where they may be married, with no questions asked!' He read bewilderment in her face, and strode up to her, and gave her a rough little shake. 'They've set off for the Border, my innocent! This is to be a Gretna Green affair: a charming scheme, isn't it?'

'*Gretna Green?*' she repeated. The colour rushed up into her face; she thrust him away, exclaiming: 'How dare you say such a thing? *Never* would Lucy behave with such impropriety!'

'Then have the goodness to tell me where else she has gone—with a wedding as her acknowledged goal!'

'I don't *know*!' she cried, unconsciously wringing her hands. 'Unless—— Oh, could they have hoaxed some cleric into believing Lucy to be of age?'

'They can hardly have needed a post-chaise-and-four for that fetch! Oh yes, I've ascertained that much already

35

—and also that the chaise has been hired for an unspecified time, and the post-boys for the first two stages. To Welwyn, in fact, and Welwyn, I would remind you, is on the Great North Road!'

'Oh *no*!' she protested. 'I don't believe it!'

'Well, that's of no consequence!' he said unkindly. 'I have discharged *my* duty, at all events, and must now be off. I shall overtake them long before they reach the Border, and will engage myself, to restore your niece to you with as little scandal as may be possible, so don't fall into despair!'

'Wait!' she uttered. 'If this is true—What was it she wrote?—repugnant to her as it must be to me—agonizing struggle—shock the world—Good God, she must be out of her senses! Iver, she left the house before ten o'clock! *Can* you overtake them!'

'Do you care to hazard a bet on the chance that I shan't have done so before nightfall? I shouldn't, if I were you!'

'Then grant me ten minutes, and I'll be ready to go with you!' she said, hurrying to the door.

'Don't be so absurd! I'm not taking you with me on this chase, or anyone! Not even my groom!'

'I should hope you were not taking your groom! But me you are taking, make up your mind to that, Iver! Who is to protect Lucy's reputation if I don't! *You* cannot!—in fact, you would be very much more likely to blast it!'

'Thank you! Let me tell you that I am not travelling in a post-chaise, but in my own curricle!'

'So I should suppose! And let *me* tell you, my lord, that this won't be the first time I've travelled in a curricle —or driven one, if it comes to that!'

'It will *not* come to that!' declared his lordship, flinging these words after her retreating form.

The first few miles of the journey were accomplished in silence, since Miss Tresilian was absorbed in her agitating reflections, and Lord Iver's attention was fully engaged by the task of guiding a spirited team through the noise and bustle of the crowded streets. His curricle was lightly built and well sprung; and since, like every other sporting blood of his day, he had not two but four horses harnessed to it, and was himself a Nonesuch of the first stare, it bowled over the ground, when the streets were left behind, at a speed that allayed one at least of Miss Tresilian's fears. The June day was bright and warm, the road in excellent condition, and these circumstances helped materially to restore her spirits. When my lord swept through Barnet without a check she asked him where he meant to change horses. He replied curtly that his team was good for two stages. Miss Tresilian relapsed into silence, but, after some twenty minutes, said suddenly: 'Try as I will, I can't believe we haven't come on a wild goose chase!'

'Then perhaps you will tell me why you forced yourself upon me?'

'On the chance that you might be right—but the more I consider it the less do I think you can be!'

But at Welwyn, where my lord arranged for the stabling of his own horses, and had a fresh team put-to, her optimism was quenched. One of the waiters at the White Hart had had ample opportunity to observe the handsome young gentleman who had jumped down from a chaise to procure a glass of lemonade for his lady; and he described him in terms which left no room for doubt. Miss Tresilian's rising spirits went into eclipse, and were not improved by his lordship's saying, as he drove out of the yard: 'Satisfied?'

Spurred by this unhandsome taunt, she responded: A very odd notion you must have of me if you suppose I could be *satisfied* by such intelligence! I was never more shocked in my life!'

'I should hope you had not been! If anything had been needed to prove me right in thinking you wholly unfit for the post of guardian your niece has supplied it!'

'Well, if it comes to that, you've made a sad botch of *your* ward, haven't you?' she retorted.

'I have not the smallest doubt that Arthur was cajoled into this escapade by your niece's wiles!'

'To own the truth,' said Miss Tresilian frankly, 'nor have I! Lucy has ten times his spirit! There is a want of resolution in him which I can't but deplore, even though I perfectly understand the cause of it. Poor boy! It must have been hard indeed to have developed strength of character, bullied and browbeaten as he has been almost from infancy!'

'*Bullied and browbeaten?*' echoed his lordship.

'I dare say you never knew you were crushing his spirit,' she offered, in a palliative tone.

'No! Nor he either, let me tell you! You have only to add that fear of me has driven him into this elopement, and you will have gone your length!'

'Well, of course it has!' she said, turning her head, in genuine astonishment, to scan his grim profile.

'God grant me patience!' he ejaculated. 'So you mean to shuffle off the blame on to my shoulders, do you? Well, you won't do it! *You* are to blame, not I!'

'*I?*' she gasped.

'Yes, you! With your henwitted scheme to carry the girl

out of the country! Of all the cork-brained, ill-judged——'

'This,' interrupted Miss Tresilian, 'goes beyond belief! Next you will say that it was I who forbade the marriage!'

'You were the only person with the authority to do so, at all events!'

'Indeed? I collect I merely dreamed that you said you would put an end to the project, and warned me not to under-rate your power?'

'When I said that I gave you credit for having enough sense not to precipitate a crisis which any but a confirmed pea-goose must have foreseen!'

'No, that is too much!' she exclaimed. 'And don't dare to tell me that you are without power, Iver, because I know very well that you hold Arthur's purse-strings, and can withhold every penny of his fortune from him!'

'Don't be so ridiculous!' he said irritably. 'How could I possibly do so? A pretty figure I should cut!'

'You threatened to do it!'

'Very likely I may have, but if he believed I meant it he's a bigger gapeseed than I knew! If he was in earnest, there was nothing I could do to prevent the marriage—eligible enough in the eyes of the world, if not in mine! Had *you* refrained from interfering, I could have handled him: it wasn't any threat of mine which goaded him into this clandestine start, but *your* determination to carry the girl out of his reach!'

'Well, of all the wickedly unjust things you have ever said to me, this is without parallel!' she exclaimed. 'So I *interfered*! And for what other purpose, Iver, did you call in Green Street than to prevail upon me to do so?' She saw a slight flush creep into his lean cheek: a sign of discomfiture which afforded her far more gratification than she was prepared to admit. After a tiny pause, she added severely: 'If there is any virtue in you you'll own yourself at fault, and beg my pardon!'

That drew a disconcerting reply from him. He glanced at her, fire in his eyes. 'Oh no! Not again! *Once* I did so—took on myself the blame for a quarrel which was *not* of my making—begged you to forgive——' He checked himself, and said bitterly: 'Even Arthur isn't as big a gudgeon as I was!'

He reined in, for they had reached a toll-gate. She was never more glad to be spared the necessity of answering. While he bought a ticket to open the pikes on the next stage she had time to recover her countenance, and was able to say, quite calmly, as the curricle moved forward: 'If that man is to be believed, we have certainly gained on them, but they must be a great way ahead still. Where do you expect to overtake them?'

'Not short of Stamford, unless they meet with some accident.'

They were entering Baldock, and neither spoke again until they had proceeded for some way along the road beyond the town. Lord Iver then demanded abruptly: 'Why did you never answer me? Did you think it cost me nothing to write that letter?'

She shook her head, a constriction in her throat making it for a moment impossible for her to speak. She overcame it, and said, keeping her eyes lowered: 'I thought it better not to reply—not to reopen—when it reached me, you see, Mama had suffered the stroke which left her paralysed. You know what our household was at the Manor! My father so dependent on her—Lucy motherless—Clara—well, there can be no need for me to explain why it was useless to suppose that Clara could fill Mama's place!'

He had listened to her in thunderstruck silence, but at

this he said, with suppressed violence: 'And equally use-less for me to tell you that nothing ever ailed Clara but jealousy, and a selfishness I have never seen surpassed! We have quarrelled enough on *that* head!'

She smiled. 'We have indeed! Must I own that you were right? Perhaps you were—though it would be unjust to deny that her constitution was always sickly.'

'I told you years ago that she would spoil your life, if she could do it! I learn now that she spoiled mine as well, thanks to your blind, obstinate refusal to credit me with more wit than you had!'

'Nonsense!' said Miss Tresilian. 'You know very well that no two persons could have been less suited than we were! As for spoiled lives, I hope you don't mean to tell me you've been wearing the willow for the past twelve years, because I know very well you haven't! In fact, if only half the tales I've heard are true you've never lacked consolation!'

'Is that what the Bath quizzes say of me? No, I haven't worn the willow, but one tale you've never heard: that I was hanging out for a wife!'

'Very true, and I think you are wise to remain single. I am persuaded you must have a much more amusing time as a bachelor.'

A muscle quivered at the corner of his mouth. 'You haven't altered! How often have I wanted to wring your neck for just such a remark as that!'

'No doubt! But there is nothing to be gained by discussing what you very rightly called ancient history. We have a more important matter to decide. What's to be done with those abominable children when we do catch them?'

'Wring *their* necks!'

'Quite impractical! *I* have no fancy for Newgate, if you have!'

He laughed, but said: 'You may at least depend upon my giving Arthur the finest trimming of his life!'

'I do, and shall be strongly tempted to do the same to Lucy! But it won't answer, Iver: we shall be obliged to give our consent, and with as good a grace as we may.'

'Oh, why stop at that? Let us escort them to the anvil!'

She regarded him with misgiving. 'Iver, don't, I implore you, get upon your high ropes! You said yourself that you could not stop the marriage if Arthur was in earnest! You can hardly want more proof of that!'

'I can want no more proof that he hasn't outgrown his puppyhood! Good God, only a scoundrel or a paper-skulled schoolboy would do such a thing as this!'

'It's very bad, of course, but——'

'And if he, or your hoydenish niece, think they can force my hand, they will very soon learn to know me better!'

'Yes!' said Miss Tresilian bitterly. 'I might have guessed you'd turn mulish, might I not? You always did make bad worse, and you always will!'

By the time Stamford was reached, Miss Tresilian was herself so weary that she could only suppose her companion to be made of iron. More than eighty miles had been covered, often at a pace which demanded the strictest concentration, and in six hours of fast driving he had allowed himself only two brief respites. During one of these Miss Tresilian had found the time to swallow a mouthful of ham, and a few sips of scalding coffee, and on this meagre fare she had been obliged to subsist, encouraged by a disagreeable reminder from his lordship that he had warned her how it would be if she insisted on accompanying him. She forgave him for that: he sat as erect as at the start of the journey, his hands as steady and his eyes as watchful, but she knew, without the evidence of the crease between his brows, how tired he must be. No conversation had been held during the past hour; Miss Tresilian, in fact, had fallen into an uneasy doze, and woke up in the yard of the George, demanding to know where she was.

'Stamford,' replied Lord Iver, looking down at her. 'Quite done up?'

'A little tired—nothing to signify!'

'I'll say this for you: you were always full of pluck! Our runaways are not here, but there are two other posting-houses in the town, and several smaller inns. They may well be racking up at one of them for the night.'

'But it is still daylight!'

'It will be daylight for some hours yet, but it is nevertheless past six o'clock. If they knew they were being followed no doubt they would go on, but I've no reason to believe that they do. They have been travelling at a fair rate, but with no suggestion of flight. Come, let me help you down! You will have time to dine while I am making enquiries at the other houses.'

She agreed to this, but when he left her installed in a private parlour she discovered herself to be too anxious to be hungry. She ordered some tea, however, which revived her, though it drew a sharp rebuke from his lordship, when he presently returned to the George. 'Don't scold!' she begged. 'It was all I wanted, I promise you. And *you* have eaten nothing!'

'On the contrary, I had a sandwich and some beer at the Swan.' His frown deepened. 'I've been unable to get any news of them: they are certainly not in the town. If they

43

changed horses here, no one recalls having seen them—
though that's not wonderful: the ostlers are kept too busy
to take particular note of all the travellers who pass
through the place.'

Her heart sank, but she said: 'There's nothing for it but
to go on, then.'

He said roughly: 'You've come far enough! I'll have
that portmanteau of yours carried up to a bed-chamber,
and you may remain here. You needn't be afraid I shan't
catch that pair: I shall, and will bring Lucy to you at once,
so don't argue with me, if you please!'

'I don't mean to,' said Miss Tresilian, tying the strings
of her bonnet. 'Nor do I mean to be abandoned in this very
noisy inn!'

'Now, listen to me, my girl!' said his lordship, in menacing accents.

'Go and order the horses to be put-to!' said Miss
Tresilian, unimpressed.

No reliable news was to be gained at either of the two
first pikes north of Stamford, but at Greetham, where they
stopped for a change, an ostler clearly remembered the
young lady and gentleman, for he had helped to fig out
four lively 'uns for them, and not so many minutes ago
neither. He'd suspicioned all along that there was something havey-cavey about them. Argufying, they were, the
young gentleman being wishful to put up for the night,
and Miss being that set on going on she was ready to nap
her bib. Nothing would do for her but to get to Grantham,
so off they'd gone.

'Having made it plain that they were an eloping couple!'
said Miss Tresilian, as they drove away. 'How Lucy could
be so dead to shame——!'

Lord Iver returned no answer, and she sat staring with unseeing eyes at the fading landscape, lost in the gloomiest reflections. From these she was presently recalled by his lordship's voice, ejaculating: 'At last!'

The curricle had swept round a bend, and brought into view a post-chaise and four, bowling ahead at a spanking pace. 'Hand me the yard of tin!' commanded his lordship grimly.

'You look after your horses!' returned Miss Tresilian, already in possession of the long horn. 'I can sound this quite as well as you can!'

In proof of this statement, she raised the horn to her lips and produced an ear-splitting blast.

'That should startle them!' observed his lordship. 'Oh, my God, of all the infernal *cawkers*——!'

This outburst of exasperation was provoked by the sudden widening of the gap between the two vehicles: the post-boys, instead of making way for the curricle to pass, were springing their horses. 'Hold on tightly!' snapped his lordship, following suit.

'Iver, for heaven's sake——!' she uttered, as the curricle swayed and bounded alarmingly.

He paid no heed; and one glance at his face showed her that to suggest that he might just as well, and far more safely, drive behind the chaise until the fugitives realized the folly of trying to escape from him would be a waste of breath. This foolish gesture of defiance had thoroughly enraged him: he was going to pass the chaise at the first opportunity that offered.

Feeling sick with apprehension, Miss Tresilian fixed her eyes on the road, and tried not to speculate on what would happen if some vehicle were to come round one of the bends towards them. My lord had swung out to the

45

right, not yet attempting to pass, but obviously ready to open out his leaders. The road was narrow, and the chaise held obstinately to the centre. They rocked round another bend, and Miss Tresilian saw a straight stretch ahead. It was a little broader, but not broad enough yet, she decided. Then she saw his lordship drop his hands, and shut her eyes, realizing that her last hour had come. Rigid with fright, she awaited the inevitable crash.

'Good girl!' said his lordship approvingly.

Her eyes flew open. 'You don't mean to say you've *done* it?' she gasped.

'Of course I've done it! What, were you afraid I should lock the wheels? Absurd creature!' He glanced over his shoulder, saw that the post-boys had reined in their horses to a trot, and checked his own team. In another minute he had brought them to a halt, swinging them across the road to form a barrier. He gave the reins into Miss Tresilian's hands, and, as the chaise drew up, sprang down, and strode towards it.

The post-boys eyed him in some trepidation, but he paid no attention to them. He lifted a hand to wrench open the door of the chaise, but before he could grasp the handle the door was thrust open from within, and a fresh-faced youth, not waiting to let down the steps, jumped out, saying, in an impetuous, rueful voice: 'I beg your pardon, sir! I didn't mean—at least, I—oh, by Jupiter, sir, *how* you did give us the go-by! It was the most bang-up thing I ever saw in my life! But I'm afraid you're very vexed!' he added, gazing up in dismay at Lord Iver's countenance.

His lordship was, in fact, thunderstruck, but his expression was certainly alarming. The unknown youth said contritely: 'We shouldn't have done so—*indeed*, I am very sorry! We were only funning—that's to say—well, I dare

46

say you know how it is, sir, when one is in spirits, and—
and——' His voice petered out unhappily, for he perceived no understanding at all in the eyes that stared so fiercely at him.

At this point, there was an intervention. A damsel, clad in the demure raiment suitable for a school-room miss, peeped out of the chaise, and said, with an engaging mixture of mischief and penitence: 'It was all my fault! Because I wouldn't put up at Stamford, and so we came on, because it is a whole year since I was at home, and I couldn't have slept a wink, and it's not so *very* much farther! Only when we changed horses at Greetham Jack said the light had begun to go, and Papa would say we shouldn't have come on, but *I* said we might easily reach Grantham if we drove fast, and give them all *such* a surprise, for they don't expect to see us until tomorrow. So Jack said: *"Oh, very well!"* but we should have everyone thinking we were eloping to Gretna Green, which sent us both into whoops, of course! And *that* was what put the notion into our heads!'

'I should explain, sir, that she's my sister,' interpolated the youth, anxious to throw light upon dark places. 'She has been at school, you see.'

'Yes, but Mama let me come away before any of the others, so that Jack could bring me home. Isn't it *famous*?' rapturously exclaimed his sister. 'Because Jack, you know, is *my* particular brother, just as Ned is Cecy's!'

His lordship, stunned as much by all these whirling words as by the shock of finding that he had waylaid two complete strangers, could think of nothing to say but: 'Oh!' and that in a blank voice which made it necessary for Miss Tresilian, deeply appreciative of the scene, to take her underlip firmly between her teeth.

Frowning down his sister's irrelevance, the young gentleman embarked manfully on an explanation of his conduct. 'The thing was, sir, that I always *meant* to spring the horses, if the road was clear, because we have still more than twenty miles to go before we reach home, and my father—— Oh, I should have told you that Father is Sir John Holloway, and we live near Grantham! Well—well, we were joking each other about being a runaway couple when you blew up to pass us, and I shouted to the post-boys to put 'em along—just cutting a lark, you know! But, of course, I shouldn't have done so!' he added hastily. 'And I didn't mean to keep it up. Only—well, when you gave chase it was so exciting—and when I saw you were going to make the attempt—well, I *do* beg your pardon, sir, but I wouldn't have missed it for anything! You drove to an inch!'

'I see,' said his lordship. 'Well, when next you try your hand at racing on the road, don't do it in a post-chaise, and don't take your sister with you! Tell me, have you come from London?'

'Oh no! From Oxford, sir. One of the old tabbies at Bella's school brought her up from Bath—— Oh, I should have told you that I'm at Magdalen!'

'Are you? Well, if you are to reach home before dark you'd best lose no more time. Up with you!'

'*Thank you!*' said Mr Holloway, greatly relieved. 'I'm excessively obliged to you for not—— Oh, you go first, sir!'

'No, I should only hold you up: I'm not going to drive at your hell-for-leather pace!'

Laughing heartily at this, Mr Holloway, after fervently shaking hands with his lordship, hoisted himself into the chaise, and it moved forward, Miss Tresilian having by this time drawn the curricle to the side of the road. His lordship, heavily frowning, walked back to it. He observed that Miss Tresilian had succumbed to her emotions, and regarded her balefully.

'Oh, don't look at me like that, Iver!' she begged, wiping her streaming eyes. 'If you could but have seen your own face——!'

'Much help *you* were!' he said, with a reluctant grin. 'Yes, it's all very well for you to laugh yourself into stitches, my girl, but where the devil *are* those pernicious brats?'

'I *said* we had come on a wild goose chase! Have we all the time been pursuing that enchanting couple?'

'Certainly not! Didn't you hear the boy say they had come from Oxford? They can never have been on our road until they entered Stamford. I have not the smallest doubt that when *we* entered Stamford we were hard on the heels of our own pair.'

That sobered her. She said, in dismay: 'Do you mean that they are ahead of us still?'

'No, I don't,' he said decidedly. 'They haven't passed any of the pikes. From Stamford we have been following the Holloways.'

She was disturbed, but could not resist quizzing him. 'Flying from a scent, Iver? *You?*'

He smiled, but absently, and remained for some moments in frowning silence. He said suddenly: 'If the line was crossed in Stamford—Good God, why didn't I think of that before? He has taken the girl to Grantley, of course!' He saw that Miss Tresilian was bewildered, and added impatiently: 'Windlesham's place, beyond Market Deeping! You've met Arthur's sister, haven't you?'

'Lady Windlesham! Yes, but what could he hope to achieve by that?'

'Depend upon it, he has a special licence in his pocket, and means to be married under Caroline's ægis.'

'But *she* has no authority to sanction Lucy's marriage!'

'Much she would care for that! Arthur can bring her round his thumb any time he chooses to do it: she dotes on him! She's of a romantic disposition, what's more, and to judge by the impassioned entreaties she addressed to me on this subject has confused that precious pair with Romeo and Juliet.'

'Iver, she *could* not be so unprincipled as to——'

'Nothing of the sort!' he interrupted. 'She knows that Arthur is his own master, and if she doesn't know already that you liked the connection well enough until you discovered that I was Arthur's guardian, it wouldn't, I assure you, take Arthur more than five minutes to convince her that if only the knot could be tied without your knowledge you would be more likely to fall on her neck than to try to overset the marriage!'

He climbed into his seat again as he spoke, and took the reins from her. She relinquished them unheedingly. 'If that is indeed so, I can't deny that it is a great deal better than a flight to the Border, but a marriage performed in such circumstances *must* give rise to the most odious gossip! I *cannot* allow it!'

'There's no need to fly into high fidgets,' said his lordship, possibly to soothe alarm, but with a sad lack of sensibility. 'Caroline is a pretty ninnyhammer, but Windlesham is a man of excellent good sense, and can be depended on to put his foot down on such a scheme.'

'Yes, but——'

'Oh, for God's sake——!' he exclaimed. 'Can't you

think of anything but that addle-brained pair? For my part, they may go to the devil! I'm sick and tired of both, and have been thinking them a dead bore for the last three hours!'

Jerked by this sudden violence from her preoccupation, she realized that the horses had been set in motion. 'Pray, where are we off to?' she demanded. 'If Arthur has taken Lucy to his sister's house we have no need to proceed farther north! How can you be so idiotish, Iver?'

'I'm not idiotish,' he replied, with an odd laugh. 'We set out for Gretna Green, and to Gretna Green we'll go! Our immediate destination, however, is Coltersworth. We shall spend the night at the Angel, and tomorrow, unless you should very much dislike it, we will resume our journey to the Border.'

'I should dislike it excessively,' said Miss Tresilian, after a little pause.

He halted his team and turned, laying his hand on one of hers, and strongly grasping it. 'Nell!' he said, in quite another voice. 'So many years wasted—so much bitterness——! Nell, my dear love, don't say it's too late! You *must* marry me—you *shall*!'

Her fingers clung to his, and there was the sparkle of tears in her smiling eyes, but she replied with great dignity: 'I have every intention of marrying you, but *not*, I promise you, in such a clandestine fashion as that! Iver, for heaven's sake——! There's an Accommodation coach coming towards us—*George*!'

But as his lordship, with his usual top-lofty disregard of appearances, paid no heed whatsoever to this warning, and Miss Tresilian was powerless (even had she made the attempt) to free herself from his embrace, the roof pas-

51

sengers on the coach were afforded a shocking example of the decay of modern manners, one moralist going so far as to express his desire to see such shameless persons set in the stocks. 'Kissing and hugging on the public highway!' he said, craning his neck to obtain the last possible glimpse of the disgusting spectacle. 'Calling themselves Quality, too!'

But in this he was wrong. With her cheek against his lordship's, Miss Tresilian said, on a choke of laughter: 'What a *vulgar* couple we are, love!'

'Well, who cares a rush for that?' he demanded. 'Oh, my darling, what *fools* we have been!'

BATH MISS

I

'PAPA,' said Miss Massingham, 'is persuaded you would have not the least objection, or you may be sure I should not have ventured to ask you, dear Charles, for perhaps you might not quite wish to oblige him in this way.'

She paused, and glanced doubtfully up at dear Charles. It could not have been said that his handsome countenance bore the expression of one delighted to oblige his Mama's old friend, but he bowed politely. Miss Massingham reminded herself that this elegant gentleman, with his great shoulders setting off a coat of blue superfine, and his shapely leg encased in a skin-tight pantaloon and a Hessian boot of dazzling gloss, was the bouncing baby on whom, thirty years before, she had bestowed a coral rattle. She said archly: 'You are grown so grand that I declare I stand quite in awe of you!'

The expression of boredom on Sir Charles Wainfleet's countenance became more pronounced.

'I am sure, a most notable dandy!' said Miss Massingham, hopeful of giving pleasure.

'Believe me, ma'am, you flatter me!' said Sir Charles.

The third person present here came, as her duty was, to his rescue. 'No, Louisa!' she said. '*Not* a dandy! *They* only care for their clothes, and Charles cares for a great deal besides, such as prize-fighting, and cocking, and all the *horridest* things! He is a Corinthian!'

'Thank you, Mama, but shall we leave this subject, and

53

discover instead just what it is that the General feels I shall have not the least objection to doing?'

Encouraged by this speech, Miss Massingham plunged into a tangle of words. 'It is so very obliging of you! The notion came into Papa's head when I mentioned the circumstance of your Mama's going to Bath next week, and that you mean to escort her! "Well, then," he said, "if that is so, Charles may bring Anne home!" I instantly demurred, but, "Balderdash!" exclaimed Papa—you know his soldierly way!—"If he fancies himself to have become too great a man to escort my granddaughter home from school, let him come and tell me so!" Which, however, I do beg you will not do, Charles, for Papa's gout has been very troublesome lately!'

'Have no fear, ma'am! I should not dare!' said Sir Charles, his weary boredom suddenly dissipated by a smile of singular charm.

'Oh, Charles, you are so very——! The thing is, you see, that ever since the Mail was held up in that shocking way at Hounslow last month we have not known how to bring Nan home in safety! You must know that she has been a parlour boarder this year past at the Misses Titterstone's seminary in Queen's Square, and we have promised that she shall come home at Christmas. But for the circumstance of Papa's illness last winter, we had intended —but it was not to be! And now we find ourselves at a stand, and how we may entrust my poor brother's only child, left to our care when he was killed in that dreadful Peninsula—how we may entrust her, as I say, to the perils of the road, without some gentleman to escort her, we know not! And I am confident,' added Miss Massingham earnestly, 'that she would not tease you, Charles, for we shall send her old nurse down to Bath, and you need do no more than drive your curricle within sight of the chaise, and so we may be easy!'

If Sir Charles wondered why General Sir James Massingham should consider that his presence, within sight of his granddaughter's chaise, would afford a better protection against highwaymen than an armed escort, he did not betray this. Nor did he betray the reluctance of a Nonpareil to assume charge of a Bath miss. It was Lady Wainfleet who raised an objection. 'Oh, but I depend on having Charles with me for Christmas!' she said. 'Dearest Almeria has been to visit me today, expressly to tell me that she will be in Bath herself for several weeks. She is to stay with her aunt, in Camden Place, and her brother, Stourbridge, is to bring her to town only a few days after we ourselves shall have left.'

Miss Massingham's face fell. The notice that Sir Charles Wainfleet, wealthiest of baronets, had at last fulfilled the expectations of the impoverished Earl of Alford, by offering for the hand of the Lady Almeria Spalding, eldest daughter of this improvident peer, had appeared some weeks previously in the *Gazette*, and she recognized that Lady Almeria's claims must take precedence of her niece's.

It was at this point that Sir Charles shook off his air of detachment. 'Almeria is going to Bath?' he said.

'Yes, is it not a happy chance? I was about to tell you of it when Louisa was announced.'

'On the contrary!' he returned. 'It is unfortunate that I should not have been apprized of this circumstance earlier. It so happens that I have engagements in town which I must not break. It will not be in my power, ma'am, to remain in Bath above a couple of nights.'

'You cannot mean to do such an uncivil thing as to

55

leave Bath before Almeria arrives!' cried his mother. 'Good God, you would very likely meet her on the road!'

'Were I to delay my departure until after her arrival,' said Sir Charles glibly, 'I dare say I should find it impossible to tear myself away. I could not reconcile it with my conscience to disoblige so old a friend as the General. I shall be happy, Miss Massingham, to afford your niece all the protection of which I am capable.'

It was impossible for Lady Wainfleet to say more. Miss Massingham was already overwhelming Sir Charles with her gratitude. She said that she could not thank him enough, and she was still thanking him when he escorted her out to her carriage. But when he strolled back to the drawing-room, Lady Wainfleet begged him to consider before deciding to leave Bath so soon. 'Now that Almeria is to go there——'

'That circumstance, Mama, *did* decide me,' interrupted Sir Charles. 'Within a few months I shall be obliged to spend the rest of my life in Almeria's company. Allow me to enjoy what is left to me of my liberty!'

'Charles!' she faltered. 'Oh, dear! if I had thought that you would dislike it so much I would never—— Not that I have the least power to force you into a marriage you don't like, only it has been an understood thing for so many years, and it is not as though you had ever a *tendre* for another eligible lady, and you are past thirty now, so that——'

'Oh yes, yes, ma'am!' he said impatiently. 'It is high time that I settled down! I have no doubt that Almeria will do me great credit. We were clearly made for one another—but I shall not spend Christmas in Bath!'

56

Eight days later, having sustained an interview with two
genteel spinsters in mittens and mob-caps, who were much
flustered to find their parlour invaded by a large and disturbingly handsome gentleman, wearing a drab driving-
coat with no fewer than sixteen shoulder-capes, Sir
Charles made the acquaintance of his youthful charge. He
beheld a demure schoolgirl, attired in a plain pelisse, and
with a close bonnet almost entirely concealing her braided
locks. She stood in meek silence while Miss Titterstone
assured Sir Charles that dear Anne would be no trouble to
him. Miss Maria, endorsing this statement, added, with
rather odd anxiety, that she knew Anne would behave
just as she ought. Both ladies seemed to derive consolation from the presence of Mrs Fitton, who all the
while stood beaming fondly upon her nurseling.

Sir Charles, amused, wondered whether the good ladies
suspected him of cherishing improper designs towards a
chit of a schoolgirl in the most unbecoming hat and pelisse
he had ever seen. Their evident uneasiness seemed to him
absurd.

Farewells having been spoken, the travellers went out
into the Square, where two vehicles stood waiting. One
was a post-chaise and pair; the other a sporting curricle.
Miss Massingham's large grey eyes took due note of this
equipage, but she made no remark. Only, as Sir Charles
handed her up into the chaise, she said: 'If you please,
sir, would you be so *very* obliging as to permit me to
stop for a few minutes at Madame Lucille's, in Milsom
Street?'

'Certainly. I will direct your post-boy to drive there,' he replied.

Upon arrival in Milsom Street, one glance at Madame Lucille's establishment was enough to inform Sir Charles that Miss Massingham proposed to visit a mantua-maker. Assuring him that she would not keep him waiting for very long, she disappeared into the shop, followed by Mrs Fitton, whose smile, Sir Charles noticed, had given place to a look of decided anxiety.

Time passed. Sir Charles drew out his watch, and frowned. Speenhamland, where rooms for the night had been bespoken, was fully fifty-five miles distant, and the start of the journey had already been delayed by the chattiness of the Misses Titterstone. The horses were on the fret. Sir Charles walked them to the top of the street, and back again. When he had repeated this exercise some half a dozen times, there was a sparkle in his eye which made his groom thankful that it was the young lady and not himself who was keeping Sir Charles waiting.

At the end of another twenty minutes there erupted from the shop a vision in whom Sir Charles with difficulty recognized Miss Anne Massingham. Not only was she now arrayed in a crimson velvet pelisse, but she had set upon her head an all-too dashing hat, whose huge, upstanding poke-front was lined with gathered silk, and whose high crown was embellished with a plume of curled ostrich feathers. This confection was secured by broad satin ribbons, tied in a jaunty bow under one ear; and it displayed to advantage Miss Massingham's dark curls, now released from bondage, and rioting frivolously. A tippet and muff completed this modish toilet; and she carried, with its forepaws drooping over the muff, a curly-tailed puppy of mixed parentage. This circumstance did not immediately strike Sir Charles, for his gaze was riveted to that preposterous hat.

'Good God!' he ejaculated. 'My good child, you are not, I trust, proposing to travel to London in that bonnet?'

'Yes, I am,' asserted Miss Massingham. 'It is the high kick of fashion!'

'It is quite unsuited to a journey, and still more so to your years,' said Sir Charles crushingly.

'Fiddle!' said Miss Massingham. 'I am not a schoolgirl now, and if it had not been for Grandpapa's illness I should have ceased to be one a year ago! I am nineteen, you know, and I have been saving all my money for months to buy just such a hat as this! You could not be so unkind as to forbid me to wear it!'

Sir Charles looked down into the pleading, upturned face; Sir Charles's groom stared woodenly ahead. 'What,' demanded Sir Charles, turning upon the unhappy Mrs Fitton, 'possessed you to let your mistress buy such a hat?'

'Oh, don't scold poor Fitton!' begged Miss Massingham. 'Indeed, she implored me not to!'

Sir Charles found himself quite unable to withstand the look of entreaty in those big eyes. A whimper from the creature in Miss Massingham's arms provided him with a diversion. 'How did you come by that animal?' he asked sternly.

'Is he not the dearest little dog? He came running into the shop, and Madame Lucille told me that her pug has had six puppies just like him! She let me buy this one very cheaply, because she is very desirous of disposing of them all.'

'I imagine she might be,' said Sir Charles, viewing the pup with disfavour. 'However, it is no concern of mine, and we have wasted too much time already. If we are to reach

Speenhamland in time for dinner we must make haste.'

'Oh, yes!' said Miss Massingham blithely. 'And may I ride with you in your curricle, Sir Charles?' She read prohibition in his eye, and added coaxingly: 'Just for a *little* way, may I? For your groom, you know, may easily go with Fitton in the chaise.'

Again Sir Charles found it impossible to withstand the entreaty in those eyes. 'Very well,' he said. 'If you think you won't be cold, you may jump up beside me.'

3

By the time the curricle had reached Bath Easton, Miss Massingham had begged Sir Charles to call her Nan, because, she said, everyone did so; and Sir Charles had reprimanded her for saying that her friends in Queen's Square had greatly envied her her good fortune in being escorted to London by one who was well-known to be a buck of the first head.

'A *what*?' said Sir Charles.

'Well, it is what Priscilla Gretton's brother said, when she rallied him on the way he tied his neckcloth,' explained Nan. 'He said it was just how you tie yours, and that you were a buck of the first head.'

'I am obliged to Mr Gretton for his approval,' said Sir Charles, and I dare say that when he has learnt to refrain alike from trying to copy my way with a neckcloth and from teaching cant phrases to schoolgirls he may do tolerably well.'

'I can see that it is an expression I should not have used,' said Nan knowledgeably. 'Must I not call you a Nonpareil either, sir?'

He laughed. 'If you wish! But why should you talk about me at all? Tell me about yourself!'

She was doubtful whether so limited a subject could interest him, but since she was of a confiding nature it was not long before she was chatting happily to him. When the horses were changed, there was very little about Miss Massingham that he did not know; and since he found her curious mixture of innocence and worldly wisdom something quite out of the common way he was not sorry that she spurned a suggestion that she should continue the journey in the chaise. She was not, she said, at all chilly; she had been wondering, on the contrary, whether she might perhaps be allowed to take the ribbons.

'Certainly not!' said Sir Charles.

'You are such a famous whip yourself, sir, that you could very easily teach me to drive,' argued Miss Massingham, in persuasive accents.

'No doubt I could, but I shall not. I dislike being driven.'

'Oh!' said Miss Massingham, damped. 'I don't mean to tease you, only it would be *such* a thing to boast of!'

He could not help laughing. 'Absurd brat! Well—for half an hour, then, but no longer!'

'*Thank* you!' said Miss Massingham, her air of gentle melancholy vanishing.

When she was at last induced to give the reins back to her instructor, the Beckhampton Inn had been passed, and the chaise had long been out of sight. Sir Charles put his pair along at a spanking pace, and would no doubt have overtaken the chaise had his companion not announced suddenly that she was hungry. A glance at his watch showed him that it was past one o'clock. He said ruefully: 'I should have stopped to give you a nuncheon rather than have let you take the ribbons.'

'We could stop now, could we not, sir?' said Miss Massingham hopefully.

'If we do it must only be for a few minutes,' he warned her.

She agreed readily to this; and as they were approaching Marlborough he drove to the Castle Inn, and commanded the waiter to bring some cold meat and fruit as speedily as possible. Miss Massingham and her puppy, whom she had christened Duke, in doubtful compliment to his Grace of Wellington, both made hearty meals, after which Miss Massingham, while Sir Charles settled the reckoning, took her pet for a run on the end of a blind-cord, which she abstracted from the coffee-room, and for which Sir Charles was called upon to pay. She said that she would walk along the broad village street, and that he might pick her up in the curricle. Ten minutes later he ran her to earth outside a bird-fancier's shop, the centre of a small crowd of partisans and critics. Upon demand, he learned that Miss Massingham, discovering a number of song-birds cooped inside small wicker-cages, which were piled up outside the shop, had not only released the wretched prisoners, but had hotly harangued the fancier on the cruelty of his trade. It cost Sir Charles a sum grossly in excess of the birds' worth, and the exercise of his prestige as an obvious member of the Quality, to extricate his charge from this imbroglio, and she was not in the least grateful to him for having done it. She censured his conduct in having given the man money instead of knocking him down. 'Which I am persuaded you might have done, because Priscilla's brother told us that you are a Pink of the Fancy,' she said severely.

'I shall be obliged to you,' said Sir Charles, with asperity, 'if you will refrain from repeating the extremely improper remarks made to you by Priscilla's cub of a brother!'

'Now you are vexed with me!' said Nan.

'Yes, for your conduct is disgraceful!' said Sir Charles sternly.

'I did not mean to do what you would not like,' said Miss Massingham, in a small voice.

Sir Charles preserved an unbending silence for several minutes. It was then borne in upon him that Nan, having apparently lost her handkerchief, was wiping away large teardrops with a gloved finger. The result was not happy. Sir Charles, pulling up, produced his own handkerchief, took Nan's chin in one hand, and with the other removed the disfiguring smudges. 'There! Don't cry, my child! Come, smile at me!'

She managed to obey this behest. He knew an impulse to kiss the face he had upturned, but he repressed it, released her chin, and drove on. By the time Froxfield was reached, he had succeeded in diverting her mind, and the rest of the way to Speenhamland might have been accomplished without incident had not Duke, who had been sleeping off his meal, awakened, and signified, in no uncertain manner, his wish to leave the curricle.

4

Pulling up beside a spinney, Sir Charles set down his passengers, adjuring Miss Massingham not to allow her disreputable pet to stray. Unfortunately, she had neglected to tie the cord round his neck again, and no sooner did he find himself on the ground than he dashed into the spinney, yapping joyfully. She ran after him, and was

63

soon lost to sight. Sir Charles was left to study the sky, which was developing a leaden look which he did not like. When a quarter of an hour had passed, he alighted, patience at an end, led his horses into the spinney, tied the reins round a sapling, and strode off in search of the truants.

For several moments there was no response to his irate shouts, but suddenly he was checked by a hail. It came from quite near at hand, but it was disturbingly faint. Alarmed, he followed the direction of the cry, rounded a thicket, and came upon Miss Massingham, trying to raise herself from the ground. Beside her sat Duke, with his tongue lolling out.

'*Now* what have you done?' said Sir Charles, exasperated. Then he saw that Miss Massingham's face was paper-white, and he went quickly up to her, and dropped on to one knee, saying in quite another voice: 'My child! Are you hurt?'

Miss Massingham, leaning thankfully against his supporting arm, said: 'I am so very sorry, sir! I didn't perceive the rabbit-hole, and I tripped, and I think I must have d-done something to my ankle, because when I tried to stand up it hurt me so much that I f-fainted. Indeed, I did not mean to be troublesome again!'

'No, of course you did not!' he said soothingly. 'Put your arm round my neck! I am going to carry you to the curricle, and then we'll see what can be done.'

But although, when he had set her gently in her place, one glance at her ankle was enough to inform him that the first thing to be done was to remove her boot, a second glance, at her face, equally certainly informed him that to subject her to this added pain would cause her to faint again. He untethered the horses, and led them back on to

64

the road, telling Nan curtly that he was going to drive her
to Hungerford.

'Duke!' she uttered imploringly.

Sir Charles looked round impatiently, found Duke at his
feet, and, grasping him by the scruff of his neck, handed
him up to his mistress.

The short distance that separated them from Hungerford was covered in record time. Miss Massingham endured the anguish of the journey with a fortitude that
touched her protector, even contriving to utter a small,
gallant jest. Sir Charles, lifting her down, and carrying
her into the Bear Inn, said: 'There, my poor child! You
will soon be easier, I promise! You are a good, brave girl!'

He then bore her in to the empty coffee-room, laid her
on a settle, and, while the waiter hurried to summon the
landlady, removed the boot from a fast-swelling foot. As he
had feared, Nan fainted. By the time she had recovered
from this swoon, she had been established in a private parlour. She came round to find herself lying on a sofa, with a
stout woman holding burnt feathers under her nose, and
two chambermaids applying wet cloths to her ankle.

'Ah!' said Sir Charles bracingly. 'That's better! Come
now, my child!'

Miss Massingham then felt herself raised, was commanded to open her mouth, and underwent the unpleasant
experience of having a measure of neat brandy tilted down
her throat. She choked, and burst into tears.

'There, there!' said Sir Charles, patting her in a comforting way. 'Don't cry! You will soon feel very much
more the thing!'

Miss Massingham, a resilient girl, began to revive. The
visit of the local surgeon, fetched by one of the ostlers after
prolonged search, tried her endurance high, but as he pro-

nounced that, although she had badly sprained her ankle, she had broken no bones, she soon took a more hopeful view of her situation, and was even able to think that she might very well be driven on to Speenhamland.

But this was now impossible. Not only was she in no state to be conveyed thirteen miles in an open curricle, but the short winter's day had ended, and the snow had begun to fall. Sir Charles was obliged to disclose to his charge that she must remain at the Bear until the following morning.

'To own the truth,' confided Nan, 'I am excessively glad of it. I am a great deal better, I assure you, but I would as lief not drive any farther for a little while.'

'Just so,' agreed Sir Charles, with a wry smile. 'But as I can place not the slightest dependence upon Mrs Fitton's feeling alarm until it will be too late for her to return in quest of you, I have thought it advisable to inform them here that you are my young sister.'

'Now, that,' said Miss Massingham, betraying at once her innocence and her sophistication, 'is a truly splendid thing, sir, for it shows that *at last* I am a grown-up lady!'

'Let me tell you,' said Sir Charles severely, 'that if you had refrained from buying that outrageous hat I should have had no need to employ this subterfuge! Never in my life have I encountered such an abominably behaved brat as you are, Nan!'

'I have been very troublesome to you, sir,' said Nan penitently. 'Are you *very* much vexed with me?'

He laughed. 'No. But you will ruin all if you call me "sir" in this inn! Remember that I am your brother, and say "Charles"!'

66

A night's rest did much to restore Miss Massingham to the enjoyment of her usual spirits. She partook of an excellent breakfast; hoped that Duke, in whose company Sir Charles had endured a disturbed night, had not discommoded her protector; and demonstrated the ease with which she could, with the aid of a stick, hop about on one foot. Sir Charles, who had been relieved to find, on pulling back his blinds, that only a light powdering of snow lay upon the road, recommended her to sit quietly on the sofa, and went out to see a pair of horses put-to. It was upon his return to the inn that, entering from a door at the back of the house, he was halted in his tracks by the sight of a handsome young woman, who had just come in through the front door.

This lady, catching sight of him, exclaimed: 'Charles! You here?'

'Almeria!' returned her betrothed, in hollow accents.

'But how comes this about?' demanded her ladyship, advancing towards him with her hand held out. 'Is it possible you can have come to meet me? We spent the night at the Pelican, you know. A broken trace has made this halt necessary, or we must have missed you. There was not the least occasion for you have to come all this way, my dear Charles!'

'I am ashamed to say,' replied Sir Charles, dutifully kissing the hand extended to him, 'that such was not my intention. I am bound for London, to keep an engagement I must not break!'

She did not look to be very well pleased with this response, but just as she was about to demand the nature of his engagement, the landlady came down the stairs, with a large bolster in her arm. 'This will be just the thing, sir!' she announced. 'It has been laying in the loft these years past, and I'm sure Miss is welcome to take it, the sweet, pretty young lady that she is! I'll carry it out directly, and see if it can't be arranged so as to make her comfortable!'

With this kindly speech, she disappeared through the door opening on to the stable-yard. Sir Charles, closing his eyes for an anguished moment, opened them again to find that his betrothed was regarding him through unpleasantly narrowed eyes.

'Miss?' said the Lady Almeria icily.

'Why, yes!' he returned. 'I am escorting the granddaughter of an old friend home from her school in Bath.'

'Indeed?' said Lady Almeria, her brows rising.

'Oh, good God, Almeria!' he said impatiently. 'There is no occasion for you to assume the air of a Siddons! It's only a child!'

'A new come-out for you, Charles, to be taking care of children! May I know why a bolster is necessarry to her comfort? An infant in arms, I collect?'

'Nothing but a romp of a schoolgirl, who had the misfortune to sprain her ankle yesterday!'

It was at this inopportune moment that Nan, dressed for the road, hopped out of the parlour, Duke frisking beside her, and announced brightly that she was ready to set forward on the journey. Duke, perceiving that the door to a larger freedom stood open, made a dash for it.

'Charles! Stop him!' shrieked Nan.

The voice in which Sir Charles commanded Duke to come to heel startled that animal into cowering instinctively. Before he could recover his assurance, he had been picked up, and tucked under Sir Charles's arm.

'You frightened him!' said Nan reproachfully. She

found that she was being surveyed from head to foot by a lady with an arctic eye and contemptuously smiling lips, and glanced enquiringly at Sir Charles.

'So this,' said Lady Almeria, 'is your schoolgirl!'

Sir Charles, only too well aware of the impression likely to be created by Miss Massingham's hat, sighed, and prepared to embark on what was (as he ruefully admitted to himself) an improbable explanation of his circumstances.

'Sir Charles is my brother, ma'am!' said Miss Massingham, coming helpfully to the rescue.

Lady Almeria's lip curled. 'My good girl, I am well acquainted with Sir Charles's sister, and I imagine I need be in no doubt of the relationship which exists between you and him!'

'Be silent!' Sir Charles snapped. He put Duke into Nan's free arm. 'Go back into the parlour, Nan! I will be with you directly,' he said, smiling reassuringly down at her.

He closed the parlour door upon her, and turned to confront his betrothed. That he was very angry could be seen by the glint in his eyes, but he spoke with studied amiability. 'Do you know, Almeria, I never knew until today how very vulgar you can be?' he said.

The Lady Almeria then lost her temper. In the middle of the scene which followed, her brother walked into the inn and stood goggling. His intellect was not quick, and it was several minutes before he could understand anything beyond the appalling fact that his sister, whose uncertain temper had chased away many a promising suitor, was engaged in whistling down the wind a bridegroom rich beyond the dreams of avarice. He looked utterly aghast, and seemed not to know what to say. Sir Charles, who had been refreshing himself with a pinch of snuff, shut his box, and said: 'The lady in question, Stourbridge, as I have already informed Almeria, is a schoolgirl, whom I am escorting to London.'

'Well, then, Almeria——!' said his lordship, relieved.

'Don't be a fool!' said Almeria. '*I* have seen the creature!'

'I should be loth to offer you violence, Almeria,' said Sir Charles, 'but if you again refer to that child in such terms I shall soundly box your ears!'

'You forget, I think, that I am not unprotected!'

'Stourbridge?' said Sir Charles. 'Oh, no, I don't forget him! If he cares to call me to book I shall be happy to answer him!'

At this point, Lord Stourbridge, who wished to come to fisticuffs with Sir Charles as little as he wished to expose his portly person to that gentleman's deadly accuracy with a pistol, attempted to remonstrate with his sister. A glance silenced him; she said furiously: 'Understand, Sir Charles, that our engagement is at an end! I shall be obliged to you if you will send the necessary notice to the *Gazette*!'

He bowed. 'It is always a happiness to me to obey you, Almeria!' he said outrageously.

6

Rejoining Miss Massingham in the parlour, he found her conscience-stricken. 'Who was that lady, sir?' she asked anxiously. 'Why was she so very angry?'

'That, my child, was the Lady Almeria Spalding. If you are ready to go——'

'Lady Almeria! Are—are you not engaged to her?'

'I *was* engaged to her!'

'Oh!' she cried. 'What have I done? Did she cry off because of me?'

'She did, but as we are not at all suited to one another I shall not reproach you for that. Foisting a repellant mongrel on me, however, which whined the better part of the night, is another matter; while as for your conduct in Marlborough——'

'But—but don't you care that your engagement is broken?' she interrupted.

'Not a bit!'

'Perhaps she will think better of it, and forgive you,' suggested Nan, in a somewhat wistful tone.

'I am obliged to you for the warning, and shall insert into the *Gazette* the notice that my marriage will not take place the instant I reach London,' he said cheerfully.

'It is very dreadful, but, do you know, sir, I find I *cannot* be sorry for it!'

'I am glad of that,' he said, smiling.

'She did not seem to me the kind of female you would *like* to be married to.'

'I can imagine none more unlike *that* female!'

She looked enquiringly up at him, but he only laughed, and said: 'Come, we must finish this journey of yours, if your grandfather is not to think that we have perished by the wayside!'

'Do you think he will be angry when he hears all that has happened?' she asked uneasily.

'I fear that his anger will fall upon *my* head. He will say and with truth!—that I have made a poor hand at looking after you. However, I trust that when he has heard the full tale of your atrocious conduct he will realize that it was experience, and not goodwill, that was lacking in me, and give me leave to study how to do better in future.'

'I know you are quizzing me,' said Nan, 'but I don't precisely understand what you mean, sir!'

'I will tell you one day,' promised Sir Charles. 'But now we are going to drive to London! Come along!'

She went obediently with him to where the curricle waited, but when he lifted her into it, and disposed her injured foot upon the folded bolster, she sighed, and said shyly: 'Shall I ever see you again, once I am fixed in Brook Street?'

'Frequently!' said Sir Charles, mounting into the curricle, and feeling his horses' mouths.

Miss Massingham heaved a relieved sigh. 'I am so glad!' she said simply. 'For I don't feel that I could ever like anyone half as well!'

'That,' said Sir Charles, flicking a coin to the expectant ostler, 'is what I mean to make very sure of, my dear and abominable brat!'

PINK DOMINO

I

IT WAS a silken domino, of a shade of rose-pink admirably becoming to a brunette. One of the footmen had carried up the bandbox to the Blue Saloon in the great house in Grosvenor Square, where Miss Wrexham was engaged in solving a complimentary charade, sent to her by one of her admirers. This was abandoned; Miss Wrexham pounced on the bandbox, and lifted the lid. The domino was packed in sheet upon sheet of tissue-paper, and as Miss Wrexham lifted it from the box these fluttered to the ground, and lay there in drifts. Miss Wrexham gave a coo of delight, and held the cloak up against herself, looking in one of the long mirrors to see how it became her. It became her very well indeed: trust the most expensive modiste in London for that! Somewhere, on the floor, there was a rather staggering bill, but Miss Wrexham cared nothing for that. Bills were of no consequence to a Wrexham of Lyonshall. Being under age, one existed upon an allowance, and frequently outran the constable. But that was of no consequence either, since there was always Mama to come to one's rescue, or even, at a pinch, Giles. But only at a pinch. A brother who was eight years one's senior, and one's legal guardian into the bargain, could not be thought an ideal banker. He had never yet refused to pay one's debts, but there had been several distressing scenes, and one in particular, when she had lost a considerable sum of money playing loo for high stakes, which she preferred not to remember. For several quaking hours she had expected to be banished to Lyonshall, in charge of her old governess; and Mama, who seemed to have incurred more blame even than herself, had had one of her worst spasms. She had been forgiven, but she still thought it astonishingly mean of Giles to grudge her a few paltry hundreds out of his thirty thousand pounds a year.

All this, however, was forgotten, for she had a new and absorbing interest to distract her. Still holding up the pink domino, she wondered how the new interest would like it; and came to the conclusion that he must be hard indeed to please if he did not.

She was so lost in these agreeable speculations that she did not hear the door open behind her, and had no notion that she was not alone until a dry voice, which made her jump nearly out of her skin, said: 'Charming!'

She spun about, instinctively bundling the domino into a heap. 'Oh! I thought you was gone out!' she gasped.

Mr Wrexham shut the door, and walked forward. He was a tall man, with raven-black hair, and uncomfortably penetrating grey eyes. His air of distinction owed nothing to his dress, for this was careless. Stultz certainly made his coats, but he was never permitted to give his genius full rein. Mr Wrexham preferred to enter his coats without the assistance of his valet; and was so indifferent to the exigencies of the mode that when every Pink of the Ton was to be seen abroad in pantaloons and Hessians it was the Bank of England to a Charley's shelter that he would emerge from Jackson's Boxing Saloon attired in riding-breeches and top-boots, and with a Belcher handkerchief negligently knotted about his neck. In a lesser man such conduct would have occasioned severe censure; but, as his mama pointed out to his sister, if you were Wrexham of

Lyonshall there was nothing you might not do with the approval of Society.

'It—it is a gown I chose yesterday!' said Letty.

'Do you take me for a flat?' replied her brother. 'It is a domino.' He picked up from the floor Madame Celestine's bill, and his brows rose. 'Quite an expensive domino, in fact!'

'I am sure there is no reason why I should not buy expensive things!' said Letty, trying to turn the issue.

'None at all, but this seems an extortionate price to pay for something you will not wear.'

Colour rushed up into her exquisite little face. 'I shall! I *shall* wear it!' she declared.

'I have already told you, my dear sister, that I will not permit you to go to a Pantheon masquerade, least of all in the company of a military fortune-hunter!'

Her eyes blazed with wrath. 'How dare you say such a thing? You have never so much as set eyes on Edwin!'

'He would appear to have taken good care of that,' said Mr Wrexham, with a curl of his lip.

'It is untrue! He would have been very glad to have met you! It was *I* who forbade it, because I knew how horrid you would be!'

At this moment, the door opened, and a faded lady came in, saying in a voice that matched her ethereal mien: 'Oh, here you are, my love! If we are to visit the Exhibition— Oh, is that you, Giles?'

'As you see, Mama. Pray postpone your visit to the Exhibition, and look at this!' He twitched the domino out of Letty's hands as he spoke, and shook it out before his mother's eyes.

Lady Albinia Wrexham, realizing that a scene highly prejudicial to her enfeebled constitution was about to take place, sank into a chair, and groped in her reticule for her vinaigrette. 'Oh, dear!' she sighed. 'Dearest child, if your brother dislikes it so very much, don't you think——?'

'No!' said Letty. 'Giles dislikes everything I wish to do, and—and *every* gentleman who admires me!'

'With reason!' said Giles. 'You have now been on the town for less than a year, my girl, and I have been obliged to repulse no fewer than eight gazetted fortune-hunters!'

'Edwin is not a fortune-hunter!'

'Indeed, Giles, I think him an unexceptionable young man!' interpolated Lady Albinia.

'Let me remind you, ma'am, that you said the same of Winforton!'

'To be sure, I could wish that he were not serving in a Line regiment,' said her ladyship feebly. 'But his birth is perfectly respectable! I own, I should wish dear Letty to make a far more brilliant match, but——'

'Not I! I am going to marry Edwin, and follow the drum!' announced Letty.

Her brother threw her a glance half of amusement, half of exasperation. 'I should be sorry for any penniless lieutenant of Foot who was saddled with you for a wife, my dear!'

'But if he married Letty,' pointed out her ladyship, not entirely felicitously, 'he would not be penniless, Giles!'

'Exactly so!' he said sardonically.

'You are unjust!' Letty cried. 'All you care for is that I should make a splendid marriage, and nothing for my happiness!'

'At present,' he returned, 'I am not anxious to see you make any marriage at all. When you have ceased to imagine yourself to be in love with every man who dangles after you—why, yes! I should wish you to make a good match!'

'Then I wonder you don't make one yourself!' she flashed. 'I dare say there must be a score of eligible females casting out lures to you!'

'You flatter me,' he replied, unmoved.

'Oh, no, it is very true, Giles!' his mother assured him. 'And I wish very much that I could see you creditably established! There is Rothwell's daughter, or——'

'Oh, no, Mama!' Letty struck in, with an angry little titter. 'Giles does not make Earls' daughters the objects of his gallantry! When he marries, he will choose a dab of a girl in an outmoded bonnet, and a black pelisse!'

2

A tinge of colour stole into her brother's lean cheeks, but he said nothing. Lady Albinia, looking very much shocked, exclaimed: 'Dear child, I do not know what you can possibly mean!'

'It is wickedly unjust!' Letty declared, a sob in her throat. 'Giles will have nothing to say to my dearest Edwin because he has neither title nor fortune, but I know very well that if he could but have discovered where she lived *he* would have offered for a Nobody that was never at Almack's or—or anywhere one would look for a lady of quality!'

'Your imagination is as unbridled as your tongue,' Mr Wrexham said curtly.

'But what is this?' demanded Lady Albinia, greatly bewildered.

'You may well ask!' he replied. 'I hope you mean to enlighten us, Letty: who is the Nobody your fancy has marked down as my bride?'

'You know very well that I mean the girl who was knocked down in Bond Street, that day you and I were going to Hookham's Library! You may try to hoax me, but *I* know why you have been so obliging as to escort me to Almack's three times this month, and why you have taken to driving your phaeton in the Park every afternoon! You are trying to find her, because you were so much struck by the *sweetest face you ever beheld* that you lost your wits, and never even discovered what was her name!'

Lady Albinia turned astonished eyes towards her son. He uttered a short laugh. 'One of Letty's high flights, ma'am! The truth is merely that some girl had the misfortune to be knocked down by a curricle and pair, and I rendered her such assistance as lay within my power. Had she come by her deserts, she must have suffered serious injury. Happily, she was merely stunned for a minute. I trust that the incident has served to convince her of the folly of stepping into the road before ascertaining that no vehicle is at that moment approaching.'

Letty, who had listened to this speech with growing indignation, exclaimed: 'How can you, Giles? When you carried her into the Library, and sent me running to a chemist's shop, and told the man in the curricle, in the *rudest* way, that he was unfit even to drive a donkey! Yes, and if the girl would have permitted it you would have conveyed her to her home, and abandoned me in the middle of Bond Street!'

'Had the girl not been accompanied by a servant, I dare say I should have done so,' he replied coolly. 'I collect that this rodomontade is designed to divert my attention from your evident purpose. Understand me, Letty, I will not permit you to go to a Pantheon masquerade under any circumstances whatsoever, least of all in the company of an unknown officer of Foot!' He glanced down at his parent, and added: 'I must say, ma'am, I am amazed that you could sanction so improper a scheme!'

Lady Albinia had recourse to her vinaigrette. 'But, indeed, Giles, you do not perfectly understand how it was to be! The thing is that Mr Ledbury's married sister was to have escorted Letty. She was so civil as to write a letter to me, just as she ought, assuring me that she would take every care of her. There is to be a little party, and Letty is invited to dine at this Mrs Crewe's house before going to the Pantheon. But, of course, if you do not quite like it, I am persuaded she will give up the project!'

'No! No!' said Letty hotly.

'If you have a grain of common-sense, you will!' said her brother. 'Recollect that for two years to come you are in my wardship! Banish this new swain of yours from your thoughts, for if you do not I give you fair warning I shall find the means to compel you!' He paused, looking rather grimly at the stormy countenance upraised to his. After a moment, his own face softened, and he said: 'Come, Letty, don't be a goosecap! Indeed, these masquerades are not at all the thing! Be a good girl, and I will take you instead to the play!'

3

Mr Wrexham, withdrawing, left his sister mutinous, and his mother in a flutter of apprehension. To Letty's diatribe she could find nothing better to say than: 'Yes, indeed, my love, but you know how it is with Giles! I told you how it would be! He will never suffer you to marry a Nobody!'

'I will not be browbeaten by Giles!' said Letty. 'I know

very well he means me to marry to oblige him—Rothbury, I daresay!—but I won't do it! I *know* that I shall never love anyone but Edwin!'

Lady Albinia uttered distressful sounds. 'My love, do not say so! He will never let you throw yourself away like that! And I must say I think it was most imprudent of you, Letty, to set up his back with that nonsensical story!'

'Mama, I vow to you that he was so much struck by the girl that I scarce knew him for my own brother! And he *did* say that she had the sweetest face he ever beheld!'

'Very likely, my love, but you must know that such fancies are common amongst gentlemen, and they do not lead to marriage! If you imagine *that* was in his head, you are a great goose! He has more pride even than his sainted papa, and he, you know—— Well, never mind that! But the Wrexhams *always* make good marriages. It has grown to be quite a habit with them!'

Letty said no more, but went away, carrying the domino over her arm.

Mr Wrexham, meanwhile, had left the house. He did not return to it until shortly before seven o'clock, when he was greeted by the staggering tidings that Miss Letty, so far from being in her dressing-room, had driven away in a hackney a few minutes earlier.

'To what address?' asked Mr Wrexham, in a voice of dangerous calm.

Never had the butler been more thankful to be able to disclaim all responsibility for his young mistress's actions. None of the servants had been employed to summon the hackney; and but for the accident of one of the abigails looking out of a window just as Miss Letty was stepping up into the vehicle, no one would have known that she had gone out.

80

Mr Wrexham went up to Lady Albinia's dressing-room two steps at a time. He found her resting upon a sofa, and, with a total disregard for her nerves, demanded to be told whether she was aware that her daughter had left the house in a manner which he did not scruple to call clandestine.

Her face of shocked dismay was answer enough. Curbing a strong inclination to animadvert severely upon the negligence that had made it possible for Letty to steal from the house, Mr Wrexham curtly requested his parent to furnish him with Mrs Crewe's direction.

'Giles!' protested her ladyship. 'You cannot wrest your sister away from a dinner-party!'

'Oh, yes, I can!' retorted Mr Wrexham.

Lady Albinia, perceiving that he was in a towering rage, sank back against her cushions, and said in a dying voice: 'I can feel a spasm coming on!'

'Furnish me with Mrs Crewe's direction, ma'am, and I will leave you to enjoy it in private!'

'But I don't know it!' wailed her ladyship, almost beyond human aid. 'I never kept her letter, for why should I? And I don't recall the direction, though I am sure it was perfectly respectable, for if it had not been I must have noticed it!'

Controlling himself with a visible effort, Mr Wrexham strode from the room.

He dined alone, the butler informing him that her ladyship had bespoken a bowl of broth in her dressing-room. Since this was his mother's invariable custom, whenever she was confronted by a disagreeable situation, Mr Wrexham was neither surprised nor alarmed. He ate his dinner in frowning silence, and then went upstairs to his room, and rang for his valet. Less than an hour later, clad in the satin knee-breeches and black coat that betokened a gentleman of fashion on his way to an evening party, he left the house, a half-mask in his pocket, and an old black domino, unearthed from the recesses of his wardrobe, over his arm.

4

The Pantheon, which was on the south side of Oxford Street, was a magnificent structure, decorated in a style which rendered it obnoxious to the eye of the fastidious. It comprised a large suite of saloons, and a ballroom, which was a huge rectangular hall, with a painted ceiling, a raised platform for the musicians, and numerous boxes and alcoves. Crystal chandeliers hung from the ceiling, and from every Gothic arch which lined the room; all was gilding and glitter. Originally, it had been patronized by members of the *haut ton*, but when the first building was burnt to the ground, and a new structure erected, the company became so far from select that Mr Wrexham had every excuse for forbidding his sister to be seen there.

Although the hour was early when he arrived there, the ballroom was already full of a motley crowd of persons, some in dominoes, some in historical costume, all masked, and many behaving with the license encouraged by the wearing of disguises. After watching a quadrille for a few minutes, Mr Wrexham decided that his sister had not yet arrived, for although he could see two ladies in pink dominoes one was by far too tall, and the other had pushed back the hood of her domino to show a head of yellow curls. He began to stroll through the saloons, successfully resisting the efforts of two ladies of Covent Garden notoriety to beguile him into dalliance.

It was nearly an hour later, when the revelry was becoming a trifle indecorous, that he suddenly saw Letty. She had her hood drawn over her head, but he caught a glimpse of dusky curls, and recognized her little trim figure. She was waltzing with a large man in a purple domino, and the only circumstance which afforded her brother some slight degree of satisfaction was her obvious lack of pleasure in the exercise. Leaning his broad shoulders against one of the decorated pillars, and folding his arms across his chest, he watched her circle round the room, and very soon realized that her partner (whom he suspected of being slightly foxed) was subjecting her to a form of gallantry which was extremely unwelcome. He thought it would be a salutary lesson to her, and had almost made up his mind not to intervene for a little while, when she suddenly broke away from her partner, and hurried off the floor, hotly pursued. Mr Wrexham, shouldering his way through the loungers at the side of the hall, reached her just as Purple Domino caught her round the waist, saying with a laugh: 'You shan't escape me thus, pretty prude!'

Mr Wrexham, setting a hand on his shoulder, swung him aside. A glance at his sister showed him that she was shaking like a leaf; he was afraid that she might be going to faint, and pushed her into the alcove behind her, saying briefly: 'Sit down!'

At the sound of his voice she jumped under his hand, and gave a gasp.

'Yes, my girl, it is I!' said Mr Wrexham very dryly indeed, and turned to confront Purple Domino.

In a voice which bore out Mr Wrexham's previous

estimate of his condition, Purple Domino demanded to know what the devil he meant by it.

'I mean,' said Mr Wrexham, 'that unless you remove yourself within one minute, my fine buck, I shall have the greatest pleasure in supplying you with a little of the home-brewed!'

Purple Domino recoiled instinctively, but recovered, and said in a blustering tone: 'Damme, what right have you to spoil sport?'

'Let me inform you,' said Mr Wrexham, 'that I am this lady's brother!'

'*B-brother?*' echoed Purple Domino, in a dazed voice. 'But I didn't—— Curse you, how was I to know?'

He stood staring through the slits of his mask for a moment, in an undecided way, and then, muttering something indistinguishable, took himself off.

Mr Wrexham felt a hand touch his sleeve. He drew it through his arm. It was trembling so much that instead of uttering the blistering words hovering on his tongue, he merely said: 'You see, Letty, I am not quite so gothic as you think me. Come, I am going to take you home now, and we will forget this military suitor of yours!'

She did not answer, but went meekly with him to the entrance-hall. It was deserted, save for the porter. Mr Wrexham said: 'I sent the carriage home, so I must procure a hack. Go and put on your cloak! There is no need to be in a quake: I am not an ogre!'

5

'No,' said the Pink Domino, in a shaken voice. 'But I— I am not your sister, sir!'

He had turned away, but at this he wheeled about, startled, staring at her. With an impatient movement he ripped off his mask, and it was to be seen that he was suddenly very pale, his eyes fiercely intent upon her face. 'Take off your mask!' he commanded imperatively. 'I know your voice! *Surely* I know your voice?'

She put up her hands to untie the strings of her mask. 'I knew yours,' she said simply. 'You—you are always rescuing me from the consequences of my folly, sir!'

He found himself gazing into the sweetest face he had ever beheld. It was heart-shaped, possessed of a pair of smiling grey eyes, which met his shyly yet frankly, and of a tender, generous mouth. Oblivious of the porter's bored presence, he grasped her hands, ejaculating: '*You*! Oh, my little love, where have you been hiding yourself? I have searched everywhere for you! Such a zany as I was never to have discovered even your name!'

She blushed, and her gaze fell. 'I don't know yours either, sir,' she said, trying to speak lightly.

'I am Giles Wrexham. And you?'

It meant nothing to her; she replied: 'Ruth Welborne. I have not been in hiding, only, when I met you before I was still in mourning for my father, and so, you see, I have not till now gone into society. Did you indeed look for me?'

'Everywhere!' he declared, still grasping her hands. 'I had abandoned hope! Where do you live? Let me not lose you again!'

She gave a little laugh. 'How absurd you are! In Harley Street, with my uncle, who was kind enough to take me into his family when my father died.'

He had never encountered a Welborne; from the direction it seemed probable that her uncle might be a banker, or a merchant, or an Indian nabob. His brain fleetingly acknowledged the possibility, and discarded it as a matter of no consequence. 'But what, in God's name, are you doing at a Pantheon masquerade?' he demanded. 'In *such* company, too! Do you tell me that your uncle brought you here?'

'Oh, no, no!' she said quickly. 'Indeed, I do not think that he or my aunt knew just how it would be, for they do not go into society much.'

'Then how comes it about that you are here?'

She did not seem to resent the question, but it was a moment before she answered it. She said then, with a little difficulty: 'It was a party of Sir Godfrey Claines's contriving. He is the man in the purple domino. A cousin of his, a Mrs Worksop, invited me, and my aunt wished me not to refuse. You see, sir, I—I have not the advantage of fortune, and my aunt has three daughters of her own, the eldest of whom she will bring out next year. It would not be reasonable to suppose that she would desire to be saddled with me under such circumstances.'

'I understand you!' he said, tightly holding her hands.

She had lowered her eyes, but she raised them at that, and said: 'Ah, you are not to be thinking that I have met with unkindness! It is not so! I was bred in the country, and perhaps I am missish in not liking—— But I was never more thankful in my life, sir, than when you came to my rescue just now!'

He released her hands at last. 'Go and put on your cloak!' he said, smiling down at her. 'I will take you back to your uncle's house.'

'Mrs Worksop!' she faltered. 'Ought I not——'

'No. She did not take such care of you that you owe her a particle of civility.'

'Your sister! I collect that she too is present. I must not——'

86

'It is of no consequence,' he interrupted. 'If she is here, it is not under my protection! Come, do as I bid you! Do you think I mean to let you slip through my fingers again?'

<h2 style="text-align:center">6</h2>

'Surely I must be dreaming!' Ruth said, as the hack drew to a standstill. 'I thought I should never see you again, and now——! But how can it be? You do not know me!'

'I am very sure that I do. As for my own mind, I knew that the instant you opened your dear eyes, that day in Bond Street, and looked up into my face.'

'It was so with you too!' she said wonderingly.

He kissed her hand, and let it go. 'It was so. Come, we must get out of this musty coach, and brave your uncle and aunt!'

'Good heavens, you will not tell them——? They must think you mad! Pray do not——!'

'No, not tonight,' he said reassuringly, assisting her to alight.

'I fear my aunt may be much displeased with me,' she said. 'Should you perhaps leave me now?'

'No. Nor, I fancy, will your aunt be displeased,' he replied.

The master of the house, they were informed by the servant who admitted them, was still at his club, but Mrs Welborne was at home, and in the drawing-room

They found her deep in the pages of the newest marble-backed novel from the Circulating Library. Taken unawares, she looked up in surprise, and exclaimed: 'Good God, Ruth, what in the world brings you home so soon? I declare, you are the most vexatious——' She stopped short, her gaze travelling past Ruth to Mr Wrexham. One instant she sat with her jaw dropping, then she cast aside her novel and sprang up, a look compound of amazement and delight transfiguring her sharp countenance. 'Oh——! Surely I cannot be mistaken? Is it not—*Mr Wrexham*?'

He bowed. 'Yes, I am Wrexham, ma'am,' he said. 'I made the acquaintance of Miss Welborne a month and more ago, in Bond Street, as she may have told you.'

Her face was a study. 'In Bond Street! *You* were the gentleman who——? Good God, Ruth, why did you not inform me? I am sure, sir, that had we but known my husband would have called on you to convey the sense of his obligation!'

Mr Wrexham, inured to flattery, and never famed for his social graces, cut her short, saying in his incisive way: 'It is of no consequence, ma'am. What *is* of consequence is that I have brought Miss Welborne home this evening because I found her where no young lady of quality should be, and being subjected to such embarrassment as, I am persuaded, you would not wish her to be obliged to endure.'

'No, indeed! I am sure, if I had had the least notion——'

'Just so, ma'am. *I* am sure that I need not enlarge upon this topic. May I beg that you will give me leave to call tomorrow to see how Miss Welborne does?'

She was wreathed in smiles. 'We shall be *most* happy, sir!'

'Thank you. I shall hope to have the felicity of finding Mr Welborne at home, for there is something I wish to say to him.'

'He *shall* be at home!' declared Mrs Welborne.

He bowed again, and turned from her to Ruth, who had

been listening in bewilderment to her aunt's affability. He held out his hand, and she put hers into it, as though compelled. He raised it to his lips. 'Have I *your* permission to visit you tomorrow?' he asked, smiling into her wondering eyes.

The smile was reflected in them. 'If you please, sir!' Ruth said, blushing adorably.

Mrs Welborne, much affected, rang for the servant to show Mr Wrexham out of the house. When he had gone, Ruth, looking doubtfully at her aunt, said in her soft voice: 'I hope you are not vexed with me, ma'am? Indeed, I——'

'*Vexed* with you?' cried Mrs Welborne, embracing her with unaccustomed fervour. 'Dearest Ruth, what nonsensical notions you do take into your head! Dear, dear child, I know that when you are rich and fashionable you will not forget your cousins! They say he has never yet attached himself to any female, and you may imagine the caps that have been set at him! Ruth, is it possible——? Why, you innocent puss, that was *Wrexham of Lyonshall*!'

7

Mr Wrexham, returning to Grosvenor Square just before midnight, learned, with vague surprise, that he was awaited by her ladyship in the drawing-room. He found, in fact, that he was awaited not only by her ladyship, but by his sister, and a well set-up young man in scarlet regimentals, who had a crop of fair, curly hair, a pair of serious blue eyes, set in an open countenance, and a general air of one about to engage in a Forlorn Hope. Both he and Letty rose at Mr Wrexham's entrance. The gentleman eased his black cravat, and was seen to draw a deep breath; the lady burst into tempestuous speech.

'Good heavens, Giles, where can you have been this age? We have been waiting for you these two hours! Giles, this is Edwin!'

'How do you do?' said Mr Wrexham, holding out his hand.

Mr Ledbury's orbs showed a tendency to start from their sockets. He coloured richly, and grasped the out-stretched hand. 'How—how do you do?' he stammered. 'I have long been wishful of meeting you, sir!'

'Have you?' said Mr Wrexham abstractedly. He opened his snuff-box, and offered it to his guest. His eyes took in the facings to that scarlet jacket. 'In the 40th are you?'

Mr Ledbury acknowledged it. Almost stunned by the honour done him in being invited to help himself to snuff from Mr Wrexham's own box, he took too large a pinch, and fell into a fit of sneezing. This left the field open to Letty, and she at once said: 'You must know, Giles, that but for my entreaties this visit would have been paid you more than a month ago! No sooner did I divulge to Edwin what had passed between you and me this morning than he declared his unshakeable resolve to wait upon you immediately! We stayed only to dine with his sister.'

'Did you?' said Mr Wrexham. 'I can only offer my apologies for having been absent from home. What do you want with me?'

Letty stared at him. 'Giles, are you quite well?' she gasped.

'I was thinking of something else,' he apologized, a tinge of colour mounting to his cheek. 'Did you say you had been awaiting me for two hours? Were you not at the masquerade, then?'

Mr Ledbury, mastering his paroxysm, said: 'Sir, it is on that head that I was resolved to have speech with you this very night! When I learned that you had taken the scheme in such aversion, nothing, believe me, would have prevailed with me to continue with it! In this determination my sister was steadfast in upholding me. It was only in response to my earnest representations that she was induced, at the outset, to take part in the scheme.'

'These masquerades are not at all the thing, you know,' said Mr Wrexham.

Mr Ledbury blushed more vividly still. 'Sir, from the circumstance of my having been employed since the age of fifteen, first in the Peninsula, and later in America, returning thence only just in time to take part in the late conflict at Waterloo, I have never been on the town, as the saying is. Had I suspected that any impropriety would attach to my escorting Miss Wrexham to such a function, I must have been resolute in refusing to lend myself to the project.'

'Letty's notion, was it?' said Mr Wrexham, with what none of his listeners could feel to be more than tepid interest.

His mother and sister gazed at him in uneasy astonishment. Mr Ledbury, emboldened by his mild aspect, plunged into a recital of his ambitions, his present circumstances, and his future expectations. Mr Wrexham, lost in dreams of his own, caught such phrases as 'eldest son',— 'my father's estate in Somerset', and soon interrupted the flow, saying: 'I wish you will not talk so much! It is time you had your company: you had a great deal better exchange into another regiment, but I cannot discuss that with you at this hour!'

Mr Ledbury, transported to find his Letty's brother so

much less formidable than he had been led to expect, delivered himself of a rehearsed peroration. In the maximum number of words he conveyed to Mr Wrexham the intelligence that, if it were possible, he would prefer Letty to renounce all claim to her inheritance. This noble speech at last jerked Mr Wrexham out of his abstraction, and caused him to retort with considerable acerbity: 'Happily, it is not possible! I wish you will go away, for I am in no mood for these heroics! Come and talk to me tomorrow morning! You wish to marry my sister: very well, but you must transfer! She will make you the devil of a wife, but that, I thank God, is no concern of mine!'

With these words of encouragement, he inexorably ushered his guest off the premises, barely allowing him time to take a punctilious leave of Lady Albinia, and a fond one of Letty. When he returned to the drawing-room, he found his mother and sister with their heads together, but whatever they were so earnestly discussing remained undisclosed. 'Giles,' said Letty anxiously, 'did you perfectly understand? Edwin has offered for me!'

'I dare say an estimable young man, but he uses too many words,' commented Mr Wrexham. 'Do you think he would like to transfer into a cavalry regiment?'

Alarmed, she laid her hand on his arm. 'Giles, are you sure you are well?'

'Perfectly!' he said, lifting her hand, and gripping it. 'I was never better!'

She cried sharply: 'Giles! You have *found* her!'

'I have found her! The sweetest face I ever beheld, Letty! Mama, I hope you do not mean to succumb to the vapours, for I wish you to make a call of ceremony in Harley Street tomorrow!'

A HUSBAND FOR FANNY

I

'His attentions,' said the widow, fixing a pair of large, rather anxious brown eyes on her cousin's face, 'are becoming most marked, I assure you, Honoria!'

'Fiddle!' said Lady Pednor.

The widow, who had just raised a delicate cup to her lips, started, and spilled some of the morning chocolate into the saucer. A drop fell on her dress. She set the cup and saucer down, and began to rub the mark with her handkerchief, saying despairingly: 'There! Only see what you have made me do! I dare say it will never come out!'

'Very likely it will not,' agreed her hostess, in no way repentant. 'You will be obliged to buy a new dress, and that, let me tell you, Clarissa, will be an excellent thing!'

'I cannot afford a new dress!' said the widow indignantly. 'All very well for you, as rich as you are, to talk in that unfeeling way, but you know——'

'I am not rich,' said Lady Pednor composedly, 'but I can afford a new dress, because I do not squander every penny I possess upon my daughter.'

Mrs Wingham blushed, but replied with spirit: 'You have no daughter!'

'What is more,' continued her ladyship, unheeding, 'I will accompany you to buy the dress, or I dare say you will choose just such another dowdy colour!'

'Purple-bloom, and very suitable!' said Mrs Wingham defiantly.

'Extremely so—for dowagers!'

'I am a dowager.'

'You are a goose,' replied her cousin calmly. 'It would be interesting to know what you spent on that spangled gauze gown Fanny wore at Almack's last night!' She paused, but Mrs Wingham only looked guilty. 'Pray, what is to be the end of all this extravagance, Clarissa? You will be ruined!'

'No, no! I have saved every penny I could spare ever since Fanny was a baby, just for this one season! If only I can see her creditably established, it will have been worth it! And although you may say "fiddle!" if you choose to be so uncivil, it is true about Harleston! From the moment of your bringing him up to me at Almack's that night, I could see that he was instantly struck by my darling's beauty. And never can I be sufficiently obliged to you, Honoria!'

'If I had thought that you would be so foolish, my dear, I never would have presented him,' said Lady Pednor. 'Harleston and Fanny! Good God, he must be forty if he is a day! How old is she? Seventeen? You are out of your senses!'

The widow shook her head. 'I don't wish her to be poor, and——' She broke off, and looked away from her cousin. 'Or to marry a very young man. It doesn't endure, the sort of attachment one forms when one is young, and young men don't make comfortable husbands, Honoria. With such a man as Lord Harleston—in every way so exactly what one would desire for one's child!—she would be very happy and never know care, and—and the disagreeable effects of poverty!'

'My love,' said Lady Pednor, because your mama made a bad bargain for you when she married you to Tom Wingham, is not to say that every young man must prove to be a monster of selfishness!'

'I was in love with Tom: it was not all Mama's doing!'

'I dare say. An excessively handsome creature, and he could be perfectly amiable, if events fell out according to his wishes.'

'I have sometimes thought,' said Mrs Wingham wistfully, 'that if only his Uncle Horsham had not married again and had a son, after all those years, and poor Tom had succeeded to the title, as he always expected to do, he would have been quite different!'

'Well, he would have had more money to fling away,' said Lady Pednor dryly. 'That might, of course, have made him more amiable.'

'But that is exactly what I have been saying,' said the widow eagerly. 'It was the poverty that made him often so cross and so disobliging! Heaven knows I do not wish to say unkind things of Tom, but can you wonder at me for— yes, for *scheming,* like the most odious match-maker alive, to provide my Fanny with everything that will make her life all that mine was not?'

'I wish you will stop talking as though you were in your dotage!' said her ladyship irascibly. 'Let me remind you that you are not yet thirty-seven years old! If you would not drape yourself in purple you might well pass for Fanny's sister! As for these precious schemes of yours, Fanny should rather be falling in love with an ineligible young man. In fact, I thought that that was what she had done. Didn't you tell me of some boy in the –th Foot?'

'No, no!' cried the widow. 'At least, I did, but it was only a childish fancy. He has no expectations, and I am persuaded that it was nothing more than the circumstance of his being a neighbour of ours in Buckinghamshire. Why, he cannot afford even to buy his promotion! And since I have brought Fanny to town, and she has met so many gentlemen of *far* greater address than Richard Kenton, I am persuaded she has forgotten all about him. Fanny marry into a Line regiment, pinching and scraping, living in garrison towns, and—— No, a thousand times, no!'

'I dare say she would enjoy it very much,' said Lady Pednor.

'I won't have it!' declared the widow. 'Call me worldly, if you will, but only consider! What comparison can there be between Richard Kenton and the Marquis of Harleston? Mind, if Harleston were not the man he is, I would not for one moment countenance his suit. But have you ever, Honoria—tell me candidly—have you ever, I say, met any gentleman more likely to make a female happy? Setting aside his position and his wealth, where will you find such delightful manners, such engaging solicitude, and, oh, such smiling eyes? What could Fanny find in Richard to rival these attributes?'

'His youth,' replied Lady Pednor, with a wry smile. 'Indeed, I hope she may find a dozen things, for I tell you, Clarissa, if she is setting her cap at Harleston——'

'Never! I have not uttered a word to her on this subject, and to suppose that she could do anything so vulgar——'

'So much the better! Not, however, that she would be the first to do so, my love. No man has been more pursued than Harleston; no man has more frequently confounded expectation. They say that he suffered a severe disappointment in youth: be that as it may, it is certain that he has now no thought of marriage. If you had not buried yourself in the country these fifteen years, Clara, you would know that not even such a hardened match-maker as Augusta Daventry would waste one moment's speculation on Harleston.'

The widow began to pull on her gloves. 'Very likely she

might not. She has a bevy of daughters, but I fancy there is not one amongst them who would not be cast into the shade by my Fanny.'

'That, I own, is true,' said Lady Pednor fairly. 'Fanny casts them all into the shade.'

Mrs Wingham turned quite pink. Her brown eyes sparkled through a sudden mist of tears. She said, in her pretty, imploring way: 'Oh, Honoria, she *is* beautiful, is she not?'

'She is beautiful; her manners are engaging—and to suppose that you will catch Harleston for her is the greatest piece of nonsense ever I heard,' said her ladyship.

2

Since Lady Pednor's mansion was in Berkeley Square, and the furnished house, hired by Mrs Wingham for the season at shocking cost, in Albemarle Street, the widow had not far to go to reach her own door when she parted from her cousin. Disregarding the solicitations of several chairmen, she stepped out briskly, one hand holding up her demi-train, the other plunged into a feather muff. Her face, framed by the brim of a bonnet with a high crown and three curled ostrich plumes, still wore its faintly anxious expression, for her cousin's words had a little ruffled her spirits. Lady Pednor spoke with all the authority of one who moved habitually in the circle Mrs Wingham had re-entered only at the start of the season; and although her kind offices, as much as the Wingham connection (headed by the youthful Lord Horsham, whose birth had put an end to Tom Wingham's expectations), had thrust an almost forgotten widow and her lovely daughter into

97

the heart of the *ton*, there could be no doubt that she was in a better position to pronounce on the Marquis of Harleston's probable intentions than one who had met him for the first time barely two months previously.

This reflection deepened the frown between Mrs Wingham's brows. She had for some time been conscious of a depression on her spirits, which might, she thought, be due to fatigue, or to the prospect of losing the companionship of her child. Her morning visit had done nothing to lift the cloud. Not content with trying to damp her hopes of a brilliant marriage for Fanny, Lady Pednor had, most unnecessarily, recalled Richard Kenton to her mind.

Not that the thought of Richard disturbed her very much. There had certainly been some boy-and-girl nonsense between him and Fanny, but both had behaved very well. Indeed, Richard seemed to realize that he could not support a wife on a lieutenant's pay; and he had manfully agreed with Mrs Wingham that it would be wrong to permit Fanny to enter upon an engagement until she had seen rather more of the world. Nor had Fanny raised more than a faint demur at her mama's plans for a London season. She had always been a biddable daughter, and if she had a will of her own it did not find expression in tantrums or odd humours. Launched into society, she behaved just as she ought, neither losing her head at so much unaccustomed gaiety, nor grieving her mama by appearing not to enjoy herself. She had many admirers, but not quite as many suitors, her want of fortune making her an ineligible choice for those who looked for more than birth and beauty in a bride. Mrs Wingham had foreseen that this would be so. She had been hopeful of achieving a good match for her; not until Lord Harleston had shown how strongly he was attracted towards Albemarle Street had she dreamed of a brilliant one. But his lordship, upon first setting eyes on Fanny, had requested Lady Pednor to present him to Fanny's mama, and, during that evening, at Almack's Assembly Rooms, when he had civilly devoted himself to Mrs Wingham, conversing with her while Fanny went down a country dance with young Mr Bute, she had known that he was the very man who could be depended on to make Fanny happy. When Fanny had joined them, he had solicited her to dance; later, he had called in Albemarle Street, and had begged Mrs Wingham to bring her daughter to a party of his contriving at Vauxhall Gardens. Since that day they had seemed always to be in his company; and if Mrs Wingham had at first doubted the serious nature of his intentions, such doubts were banished by a morning visit from his sister, a gentle lady who certainly called at her brother's desire, and who not only treated the widow with distinguishing kindness, but complimented her on Fanny's beauty, saying, with a smile: 'My brother has told me, ma'am, that you have a very lovely daughter.'

Lady Pednor had not known *that* when she tried to depress her cousin's hopes, reflected Mrs Wingham, mounting the steps to her own front door.

Fanny was going on a picnic expedition to Richmond Park, but her hostess's carriage had not yet arrived in Albemarle Street. Mrs Wingham found her trying to decide whether to wear a green spencer over her muslin dress, or a shawl of Norwich silk. Mrs Wingham thought that the spencer would be the more suitable wear, and enquired who was to be of the party. Fanny, tying a straw bonnet over her dark curls, replied: 'I don't know, Mama, but there are to be two carriages, besides Mr Whitby's curricle, and Eliza said that most of the other gentlemen would ride, so that it must be quite a large party. I think it was very obliging of Mrs Stratton to have invited me, don't you?'

Mrs Wingham agreed to it, but added: 'I hope you will be home in good time, dearest, for I should like you to rest before our own party. And I think you should wear the figured lace. I will lend you my pearls.'

'And *I* think you will wear the pearls yourself, and on no account that horrid turban, which makes you look like some dreadful dowager, and not in the least like my own, pretty Mama!' retorted Fanny, bestowing a butterfly's kiss on the widow's cheek. She then turned away and began to hunt for a pair of gloves. 'We sent out a great many cards, didn't we?' she said. 'I quite forget how many guests are coming!'

'About fifty,' said Mrs Wingham, with a touch of pride.

'Gracious, it will be a regular squeeze! I suppose all our particular friends? The Shanklins, and the Yeovils, and Lord Harleston?'

This was airily said. Mrs Wingham, unable to see her daughter's face, replied calmly: 'Oh yes!'

'Of course!' Fanny said, considering the rival claims of one pair of silk mittens and one pair of French kid gloves. 'Mama?'

'My love!'

'Mama, do you—do you like Lord Harleston?' Fanny asked shyly.

Whatever ambitious schemes Mrs Wingham had in mind, she would have relinquished them all rather than have encouraged her unspoiled daughter to share them. She replied, therefore, in a cool tone: 'Why, yes, very much! Do you?'

A glowing face was turned towards her. 'Oh, Mama, *indeed* I do! I think him quite the nicest person we have met in London. One could tell him almost anything, and be sure that he would understand just how it was,' Fanny said impulsively. She bestowed a brief hug upon the widow. 'Dearest Mama, I am so *glad* you like him!'

Mrs Wingham, returning the embrace, felt tears—thankful tears—sting her eyelids, but was spared the necessity of answering by a scratch on the door, which heralded the entrance of the page-boy, come to inform Miss Wingham that Mrs Stratton's barouche awaited her.

3

Fanny did not return from her picnic in time to indulge in rest, but she was in her best looks that evening. Several persons commented on her radiance; and Lord Harleston, obliging his hostess to recruit her energies with a glass of champagne, said, with his attractive smile: 'You are to be congratulated, ma'am! I do not know when I have seen so engaging a creature as your daughter. Such a bloom of health! Such frank, open manners! I think, too, that she has a disposition that matches her face.'

'Indeed, my lord, she is the dearest girl!' Mrs Wingham said, blushing with gratification and raising her eyes to his. 'I do think—but I might be partial—that she is very pretty. She favours her papa, you know.'

'Does she?' said his lordship, seating himself beside her on the sofa. 'I own that it is her mama I perceive in her countenance.'

'Oh no!' the widow assured him earnestly. 'My husband was an excessively handsome man.'

He bowed. 'Indeed? I think I had not the pleasure of the late Mr Wingham's acquaintance. He would certainly be proud of his daughter, were he alive today.' His eyes had been resting on Fanny, as she chatted, not many paces distant, to a gentleman with very high points to his shirt-collar, but he brought them back to Mrs Wingham's face, adding: 'And also of her mama. It is seldom that one discovers a well-informed mind behind a lovely face, ma'am; and Fanny has told me that she owes her education to you.'

'Why, yes!' admitted Mrs Wingham frankly. 'It has not been within my power to provide Fanny with the governesses and the professors I should have desired for her. If you do not find her deficient in attainments, I think myself complimented indeed!'

'May I say that I believe no governess or professor could have achieved so admirable a result?'

'You are too flattering, my lord!' was all she could find to say, and that in faltering accents.

'No, I never flatter,' he responded, taking the empty glass from her hand. 'I perceive that we are about to be interrupted by Lady Luton. I have something of a very particular nature to say to you, but this is neither the time nor the occasion for it. May I beg of you to indulge me with the favour of a private interview with you, at whatever time may be most agreeable to you?'

Such a tumult of emotion swelled in the widow's breast that she could scarcely find voice enough to utter the words: 'Whenever you wish, my lord! I shall be happy to receive you!'

He rose, as Lady Luton surged down upon them. 'Then, shall we say, at three o'clock tomorrow?'

She inclined her head; he bowed and moved away; and a moment later she had the felicity of seeing his tall, well-knit frame beside Fanny. Fanny was looking up at him, with her sweet smile, and putting out her hand, which he took in his and held for an instant, while he addressed some quizzing remark to her that made her laugh and blush. A queer little pang shot through the widow, seeing them on such comfortable terms. She reflected that her absorption in Fanny had made her stupidly jealous, and resolutely turned her attention to Lady Luton.

4

Having ascertained that her daughter had no engagement on the following afternoon, Mrs Wingham was surprised, when she returned from a shopping expedition in Bond Street, to find that only one cover had been laid for a luncheon of cold meat and fruit. She enquired of the butler, hired, like the house, for the season, whether Miss Fanny had gone out with her maid.

'No, madam, with a military gentleman.'

These fell words caused the widow to feel so strong a presentiment of disaster that she turned pale, and repeated numbly: 'A military gentleman!'

'A Mr Kenton, madam. Miss Fanny appeared to be well acquainted with him. *Extremely* well acquainted with him, if I may say so, madam!'

Making a creditable effort to maintain her composure, Mrs Wingham said: 'Oh, Mr Kenton is an old friend! I had no notion he was in town. He and Miss Fanny went out together, I think you said?'

'Yes, madam, in a hackney carriage. I understand, to the City, Mr Kenton desiring the coachman to set them down at the Temple.'

This very respectable address did nothing to soothe Mrs Wingham's agitated nerves. The whole locality, from

103

Temple Bar to St Paul's Cathedral, appeared to her to be sinister in the extreme. Amongst the thoughts which jostled one another in her head, the most prominent were Fleet Marriages, Doctors' Commons and Special Licences. She was obliged to sit down, for her knees were trembling. Her butler then proffered a tray on which lay a note, twisted into a little cocked hat.

It was scribbled in pencil, and it was brief:

> *Dearest Mama,—Forgive me, but I have gone with Richard. You shall know it all, but I have no time now. Pray do not be vexed with me! I am so happy I am sure you cannot be.*

Mrs Wingham became aware that she was being asked if she would partake of luncheon or wait for Miss Fanny, and heard her own voice replying with surprising calm: 'I don't think Miss Fanny will be home to luncheon.'

She then drew her chair to the table and managed to swallow a few mouthfuls of chicken, and to sip a glass of wine. A period of quiet reflection, if it did not lighten her heart, at least assuaged the worst of her fears. She could not believe that either Fanny or Richard would for a moment contemplate the impropriety of a clandestine marriage. But that the sight of Richard had revived all Fanny's tenderness for him she could not, in the face of Fanny's note, doubt. What to do she could not think, and in a state of wretched indecision presently went up to her bedroom. After removing her hat, setting a becoming lace cap on her head and tying it under her chin, there seemed to be nothing to do but to await further news of the truants, so she went to sit in the drawing-room, and tried to occupy herself with her needle.

Fortunately, she had not long to wait. Shortly after two o'clock an impetuous step on the stair smote her listening ears, and Fanny herself came into the room, out of breath, her cheeks in a glow, and her eyes sparkling. 'Mama? Oh, Mama, Mama, it is *true*, and you *will* give your consent now, won't you?'

She came running across the room as she spoke and cast herself at her mother's feet, flinging her arms round her, and seeming not to know whether to laugh or cry. Behind her Mr Kenton, very smart in his regimentals, shut the door and remained at a little distance, as though doubtful of his reception. He was a well-set-up young man, with a pleasant countenance and an air of considerable resolution. At the moment, however, he was looking a trifle anxious, and he seemed to find his neckcloth rather too tight.

'Fanny, my dear, pray———!' remonstrated Mrs Wingham. 'I don't know what you are talking about! How do you do, Richard? I am very pleased to see you. Are you on furlough?'

'Mama, we have such news for you! Richard's god-mother has died!' interrupted Fanny ecstatically. 'And she has left Richard a great deal of money so that he *can* support a wife after all! He came to tell me at once, and I went with him to the lawyer, and it is *true*!'

Mrs Wingham turned her bewildered eyes towards Mr Kenton. He said bluntly: 'No, it is not a great deal of money, ma'am, but it will enable me to buy my exchange, for you must know that I have been offered the chance of a company in the —th, only I never thought I should be able———. However, I can *now* afford the purchase money, and once I am in the—th, I hope I shan't be obliged to wait upon the chance of Boney's escaping a second time, and starting another kick-up, for my promotion. And I thought, if you would give your consent to our marriage, I would settle what will be left of the legacy on Fanny. It won't be a fortune, but—but it will be *something*!'

'Mama, you will consent?' Fanny said imploringly. 'You said I must see something of the world before I made up my mind, but I have now seen a great deal of the world, and I haven't met anyone I like better than Richard, and I know I never shall. And although it is very amusing to lead a fashionable life, and, *indeed*, I have enjoyed all the parties, I would much prefer to follow the drum with Richard! You *will* consent?'

Mrs Wingham stared down into the radiant face upturned to hers. A dozen objections died on her lips. She said, with a wavering smile:

'Yes, Fanny. If you are quite, quite sure, I suppose I must consent!'

Her daughter's lips were pressed to her cheek, Mr Kenton's to her hand. Seated amongst the ruins of her ambition, with that weight of depression upon her heart, she said: 'And Lord Harleston is coming to visit me at three o'clock!'

'Lord Harleston!' exclaimed Fanny. 'Oh, will you tell him, Mama, that I am going to marry Richard? I should have wished to have told him myself, but the thing is that Richard has leave of absence only for one day, and he must rejoin the regiment immediately. Mama, if I take Maria with me, may I go with him to the coach office? Pray, Mama!'

'Yes—oh yes!' said Mrs Wingham. 'I will tell Lord Harleston.'

Thus it was that when one of the biggest but most un-
obtainable prizes of the Matrimonial Mart was ushered into Mrs Wingham's drawing-room, he found the widow
alone and sunk in melancholy. The depression, of which
she had been conscious for so many weeks, threatened now
to overcome her, and was in no way alleviated by her
inability to decide which of the various evils confronting
her was at the root of her strong desire to indulge in a
hearty bout of tears. The years of economy had been wasted; yet she could not regret the weeks spent in London.
Her maternal ambition was utterly dashed; but when she
saw the happiness in Fanny's face she could not be sorry.
She must soon lose the daughter on whom her every
thought had been centred for years; but if by the lifting of
a finger she could have kept Fanny, she would have held
her hands tightly folded in her lap, as they were when the
Marquis walked into the room.

He paused upon the threshold. The one glance she
permitted herself to cast at his face showed her that
there was an arrested expression in his eyes, a look of
swift concern. The pain she was about to inflict on him
most poignantly affected her; for a startling moment she
found herself blaming Fanny for having wounded one
of whom she was all unworthy. She was unable to sustain
his steady regard; her eyes fell to the contemplation of
the little gold tassels on his Hessian boots. They moved,
swinging jauntily as he came towards her. 'Mrs Wingham!
Something has occurred to distress you. May I

know what it is? If there is anything I may do——'

He was bending solicitously over her, one shapely hand lifting one of hers, and holding it in a sustaining clasp. She said disjointedly: 'Yes—no! It is nothing, my lord! I beg you will not——! Indeed, it is nothing!'

She drew her hand away as she spoke. He said: 'Shall I leave you? I have come, I believe, at an unfortunate time. Tell me what you wish! I would not for the world add to your distress!'

'Oh no! Do not go! This interview ought not to be—must not be—postponed!'

He looked intently at her, as much anxiety in his eyes as there was in hers. 'I came—I believe you must know for what purpose.'

She bowed her head. 'I do know. I wish—oh, how deeply I wish that you had not come!'

'You wish that I had not come!'

'Because it is useless!' said the widow tragically. 'I can give you no hope, my lord!'

There was a moment's silence. He was looking at once astonished and chagrined, but, after a pause, he said quietly: 'Forgive me! But when I spoke to you last night I was encouraged to think that you would not be averse from hearing me! You have said that you guessed the object of my visit—am I a coxcomb to imagine that my suit was not then disagreeable to you?'

'Oh no, no, no!' she uttered, raising her swimming eyes to his face. 'I should have been most happy—I may say that I most sincerely desired it! But all is now changed! I can only beg of you to say no more!'

'You desired it! In heaven's name, what can possibly have occurred to alter this?' he exclaimed. Trying for a lighter note, he said: 'Has someone traduced my character to you? Or is it that——'

'Oh no, how could anyone——? My lord, I must tell you that there is Another Man! When I agreed last night to receive you today, I did not know—that is, I thought—' Her voice became suspended; she was obliged to wipe teardrops from her face.

He had stiffened. Another silence fell, broken only by the widow's unhappy sniffs into her handkerchief. At last he said, in a constrained tone: 'I collect—a prior attachment, ma'am?'

She nodded; a sob shook her. He said gently: 'I will say no more. Pray do not cry, ma'am! You have been very frank, and I thank you for it. Will you accept my best wishes for your future happiness, and believe that——'

'Happiness!' she interrupted. 'I am sure I am the wretchedest creature alive! You are all kindness, my lord: no one could be more sensible than I am of the exquisite forbearance you have shown me! You have every right to blame me for having encouraged you to suppose that your suit might be successful.' Again her voice failed.

'I have no blame for you at all, ma'am. Let us say no more! I will take my leave of you, but before I go will you permit me to discharge an obligation? I may not have the opportunity of speaking to you alone again. It concerns Fanny.'

'Fanny?' she repeated. 'An *obligation*?'

He smiled with a slight effort. 'Why, yes, ma'am! I had hoped to have won the right to speak to you on this subject. Well—I have not won that right, and you may deem it an impertinence that I should still venture, but since Fanny has honoured me with her confidence, and I promised her that I would do what I might, perhaps you will forgive me, and hear me with patience?'

She looked wonderingly at him. 'Of course! That is——
What can you possibly mean, my lord?'

'She is, I collect, deeply attached to a young man whom
she has known since her childhood. She has told me that
you are opposed to the match, ma'am. Perhaps there exists
some reason beyond his want of fortune to render his suit
ineligible, but if it is not so—if your dislike of it arises only
from a very natural desire that Fanny should contract some
more brilliant alliance—may I beg of you, with all the
earnestness at my command, not to stand between her and
what may be her future happiness? Believe me, I do not
speak without experience! In my youth I was the victim of
such an ambition. I shall not say that one does not recover
from an early disappointment—indeed, you know that I at
least have done so!—but I am most sincerely fond of
Fanny, and I would do much to save her from what I
suffered. I have some little influence: I should be glad to
exert it in this young man's favour.'

The damp handkerchief had dropped from the widow's
clutch to the floor; she sat gazing up at his lordship with so
odd an expression in her face that he added quickly: 'You
find it strange that Fanny should have confided in me. Do
not be hurt by it! I believe it is often the case that a girl will
more easily give her confidence to her father than to a most
beloved mother. When she spoke, it was in the belief that I
might become—— But I will say no more on *that* head!'

The widow found her voice at last. 'My lord,' she said,
'do I—do I understand that you are desirous of becoming
Fanny's *father*?'

'That is not quite as I should phrase it, perhaps,' he
said, with a wry smile.

'Not,' asked the widow anxiously, '*not*—you are quite
sure?—Fanny's *husband*?'

He looked thunderstruck. '*Fanny's* husband?' he echoed. '*I*? Good God, no! Why—is it possible that you can have supposed——?'

'I have never fainted in all my life,' stated Mrs Wingham, in an uncertain voice. 'I very much fear, however——'

'No, no, this is no time for swoons!' he said, seizing her hands. 'You cannot have thought that it was Fanny I loved! Yes, yes, I know what Fanny has been to you, but you cannot have been so absurd!'

'Yes, I was,' averred the widow. 'I could even be so absurd as not to have the remotest guess why I have felt so low ever since I met you, and thought you wished to marry her!'

He knelt beside her chair, still clasping her hands. 'What a fool I was! But I thought my only hope of being in any way acceptable to you was to praise Fanny to you! And, indeed, she is a delightful girl! But all you have said to me today—you were not speaking of *yourself*?'

'Oh no, no! Of Fanny! You see, she and Richard——'

'Never mind Fanny and Richard!' he interrupted. 'Is it still useless for me to persist in my errand to you?'

'Quite ridiculous!' she said, clinging to his hands. 'You have not the least need to *persist* in it! That is, if you do indeed wish to marry such a blind goose as I have been!'

His lordship disengaged his hands, but only that he might take her in his arms. 'I wish it more than for anything else on this earth!' he assured her.

TO HAVE THE HONOUR

I

YOUNG Lord Allerton, a little pale under his tan, glanced from his mother to his man of business. 'But—good God, why was I never told in what case I stood?'

Mr Thimbleby did not attempt to answer this home question. He perceived that young Lord Allerton's facial resemblance to his deceased father was misleading. There was nothing the late Viscount had desired less than to be told in what case he stood. Three years of campaigning in the Peninsula had apparently engendered in the Fifth Viscount a sense of responsibility which, however welcome it might be in the future to his man of business, seemed at the moment likely to lead to unpleasantness. Mr Thimbleby directed an appealing look towards the widow.

She did not fail him. Regarding her handsome eldest born with an eye of fond pride, she said: 'But when poor Papa died, you had been wounded, dearest! I would not for the world have distressed you!'

The Viscount said impatiently: 'A scratch! I was back in the saddle within a week! Mama, how *could* you keep me in ignorance of our circumstances? Had I had the least notion of the truth I must have returned to England immediately!'

'Exactly so!' nodded his parent. 'And that, dearest Alan, I was determined you should not be obliged to do! Everyone said the war would so soon be over, and I knew how mortified you would be to be forced to sell out before the glorious end! To be sure, I did hope that directly after Toulouse you might have been released, but it was not to be, and it is of no consequence, except that here we are, with all the foreign notables upon us, and I have the greatest dread that your tailor may not have your evening dress ready for you to wear at my ball next week!'

'That, Mama, believe me, is the least of our problems!'

'Very true, my love,' agreed her ladyship. 'Trix has been in despair, but "Depend upon it", I have said from the outset, "even though your brother may patronize Scott, instead of Weston, who always did so well by poor Papa, you may be confident that *no* tailor would fail at such a juncture!"' Her gaze dwelled appreciatively upon his lordship's new coat of olive-green, upon the pantaloons of delicate yellow which clung to his shapely legs, upon the Hessian boots which shone so bravely, and upon the neckcloth which was tied with such nicety, and she heaved a satisfied sigh.

The Viscount turned in desperation to his man of business. 'Thimbleby!' he uttered. 'Be so good as to explain to me why *you* did not think it proper to inform me that my father had left me encumbered with debt.'

Mr Thimbleby cast another imploring glance at the widow. 'Her ladyship having done me the honour to admit me into her confidence, my lord, it seemed to me—that is, I was encouraged to hope . . .'

'To hope what?'

'My dear son, you must not blame our good Thimbleby!' intervened Lady Allerton. 'Indeed, no one is to be blamed, for if you will but consider you will perceive that our case is not desperate!'

'Desperate! I trust not! But that there is the most urgent need of the strictest economy—even, I fear, of measures as repugnant to me as they must be to you, ma'am, I cannot doubt! I dare not think what my own charges upon the estate have been during these months, when I should have been doing what lies within my power to repair what I do not scruple to call a shockingly wasted fortune!'

'No, no, it is not as bad as *that*!' she assured him. 'My dear Alan, there is *one* circumstance you are forgetting!'

He stared at her with knitted brows. 'Pray, what am I forgetting, ma'am?'

'Hetty!' she said, opening her eyes at him.

'I certainly do not forget my cousin, Mama, but in what way my embarrassments can be thought to concern her I have not the remotest conjecture!' said his lordship. A dreadful thought flashed into his mind; he said quickly: 'You are not trying to tell me, ma'am, that my cousin's fortune has been used to—— No, no, impossible! She is still under age, and cannot have been allowed—— There was another trustee besides my father, after all! Old Ossett could never have countenanced such a thing!'

'Nothing of the sort!' said her ladyship. 'And I must say, Alan, that I wonder at your supposing that I would entertain such a notion, except, of course, under such circumstances as must render it entirely proper! My own niece! I might almost say my *daughter*, for I am sure she is as dear to me as Trix!'

Mr Thimbleby, who had been unobtrusively engaged in putting up his papers, now judged it to be time to withdraw from a discussion which was not progressing according to hopeful expectation. The Viscount, beyond reminding him rather sharply that he should require his attendance

114

upon the morrow, made no objection to his bowing himself out of the room, but began to pace about the floor, his brow furrowed, and his lips compressed as though to force back unwise speech.

His parent said sympathetically: 'I was afraid you would be a trifle shocked, dearest. It was hazard, of course. I knew no good would come of it when poor Papa forsook faro, at which he had always been so fortunate!'

The Viscount halted, and said with careful self-control: 'Mama, have you realized that to win free from this mountain of debt I must sell some—perhaps all!—of the unentailed property? When I learned that my father had left everything to me, making not the least provision for Timothy or for Trix, I own I was astonished! I see now why he did so, but how I am to provide for them I know not! Ma'am, you have been talking ever since my arrival of the ball you are giving in honour of this Grandduchess of yours, of the drawing-room at which you mean to present my sister, but have you realized that there is no money to pay for these things?'

'Good gracious, Alan, you should realize that if I do not?' exclaimed her ladyship. 'I declare I can scarcely recall when I was last able to pay a bill, and the tiresome thing is that there are now so many of them in that drawer in my desk that I can't open it!'

'For God's sake, Mama, how have you contrived to continue living in this style?' demanded the Viscount.

'Oh, well, my love, upon credit! Everyone has been most obliging!'

'Merciful heavens!' muttered the Viscount. '*What* credit, ma'am?'

'But, Alan, they all guess that you are going to marry dear Hetty, and they know *her* fortune to be immense!'

'O my God!' said the Viscount, and strode over to the window. 'So that's it, is it?'

Lady Allerton regarded his straight back in some dismay. 'It has always been an understood thing!' she faltered.

'Nonsense!'

'But it was my dear brother's wish!'

'It can scarcely have been his wish that his daughter should be married to an impoverished—fortune-hunter!' said the Viscount bitterly. 'And it must be very far from Sir John Ossett's wish!'

'Now there you are out!' said her ladyship triumphantly. 'Sir John will raise not the smallest objection to the match, for he has told me so! He knows it is what my brother intended, and, what is more, he has a great regard for you, my love!'

'I am obliged to him!'

'Alan!' ejaculated her ladyship. 'You—you have not formed an attachment for another?'

'No!'

'No, I was persuaded—— Dearest, I thought—— Of course, she was very young when you went away, but it did seem to me——'

'Mama,' he interrupted, 'whatever my sentiments, you cannot have supposed it possible that I would offer for my cousin in my present circumstances!'

'But it seems just the moment!' protested his mother. 'Besides, she expects it!'

He wheeled about. '*Expects* it?'

'Yes, I assure you she does! Dearest Hetty! If she could have done it, she would have bestowed her entire fortune on me! I never knew a better-hearted girl, never!'

'Oh, good God, then that is why she is now so shy of

me!' said the Viscount. 'My poor little cousin! How *could* you let her think it was her duty to marry me, Mama? It is infamous! Have you kept her shut away from the world in case she should meet a more eligible suitor than ever I can be?'

'No, I have not!' replied Lady Allerton, affronted. 'I brought her out two years ago, and she has had a great many suitors, and has refused them all! She is a very well-behaved girl, and would never dream of marrying to disoblige me!'

'She has been shamefully used!' he said.

2

The object of the Viscount's pity, Miss Henrietta Clitheroe, was at the moment seated in a small saloon at the back of the house, studying, with her young cousin, the latest issue of *La Belle Assemblée*, and endeavouring to convince Miss Allerton that a dress of gauze worn over a damped and transparent petticoat was a toilette scarcely designed to advance her in the good graces of those august members of the *ton* who were pledged to appear at her mama's party given in honour of the Grandduchess Catherine of Oldenburg. This was not a circumstance which weighed with Miss Allerton, who, at seventeen, was thought by the censorious to have been born for the express purpose of driving her mother into her grave by the outrageous nature of her pranks; but she knew that she would never be permitted to wear such a dress, and so allowed herself to be distracted by the picture of a damsel arrayed in white satin embellished with rose-buds and love-knots.

She was just saying, though disconsolately, that she supposed it was quite a pretty dress, when the Viscount came into the room, and, still holding the door, said: 'The latest fashions? Am I very much in the way, or may I have a word with you, cousin?'

The colour flooded Henrietta's cheeks; she stammered: 'Oh no! I mean, to be sure you may, Alan!'

Miss Allerton, unwontedly meek, obeyed the command contained in the jerk of his lordship's head, and tripped out of the room. The Viscount shut the door, and turned to look across the saloon at his cousin. Her colour rose higher still, and she pretended to search for something in the litter of objects on the table.

'Henry . . .' the Viscount said.

She looked up at that, a little shy smile on her lips. 'Oh, Alan, no one has called me that since you went away! How nice it sounds!'

He returned the smile, although with an effort. 'Does it? You will always be Henry to me, you know.' He paused; and then said with a good deal of constraint: 'I have been with my mother and with Thimbleby for the past hour. What I have learnt from them has made me feel that I must speak to you immediately.'

'Oh—oh, yes?' said Henrietta.

'Yes. I think I was never more shocked in my life than when I realized——' He broke off, conscious of the awkwardness of his situation. His own colour rose; he said with a rueful laugh: 'The devil! I'm as tongue-tied as a schoolboy! Henry, I only wanted to say—I'm not going to offer for you!'

The flush in Henrietta's cheeks began to ebb. 'Oh!' she said. '*N-not* going to offer for me?'

He came towards her, and took her hands, giving them a

reassuring squeeze. 'Of course I am not! How could you think I would do so, you foolish Henry? You have been made to believe that you were in some way promised to me, haven't you? Some absurd talk of what your father desired—of what you owed to my family. Well, you owe us nothing, my dearest cousin! It is rather we who owe you a great debt. You have been our—most beloved sister —ever since you came to live with us. I am ashamed that it should ever have been suggested to you that it is your duty to marry me: it is no such thing! You are free to marry whom you please.'

This did not, at the moment, appear likely to the heiress. She disengaged her hands. 'Am—am I?'

'Indeed you are!' With an attempt at lightness, he added: 'Unless you choose someone quite ineligible! I warn you, I should do what I could to prevent *that*, Henry!'

She managed to smile. 'I should be obliged to elope, then, should I not? I—I am glad you have been so frank with me. Now we can be comfortable again!'

'My poor girl!' he said quickly. 'If only you had told me what was in the wind——! There was never a hint in any of your letters. I would have set your mind at rest months ago! No: you could not, of course!'

She turned away, and began to tidy the litter on the table. She said, in a voice that did not sound to her ears quite like her own: 'I own, I had as lief not be married for my fortune!' He returned no answer; after a pause, she added: 'Are your affairs in very bad case, Alan?'

'Not so bad that I shall not be able, with time and good management, to set them to rights, I hope,' he replied. 'I could wish that my mother had not chosen, at this moment, to entertain upon so lavish a scale. I suppose nothing can be done about this party for the Russian woman, but for the rest—the White's Ball, Trix's presentation——'

'Good God, do not tell my aunt she must postpone *that*!' exclaimed Henrietta. 'If she is obliged to wait another year, Trix will very likely run off with a handsome Ensign!' She saw the startled look on his face, and added: 'You don't yet know her, Alan!'

'My dear Henry, at seventeen she can hardly be thinking of marriage, surely!'

'The last man she fell in love with was young Stillington,' said Henrietta thoughtfully. 'To be sure, he was better than that actor she saw in Cheltenham, but still quite ineligible of course. Fortunately, her mind was diverted by the plans for her first season.'

'It is time Trix was broke to bridle!' said his lordship roundly. He then favoured his cousin with a few animadversions upon the conduct of his lively young sister, and left her to her reflections.

These were not for many moments concerned with the almost inevitable clash between brother and sister. They led Henrietta to the mirror, and caused her to stare long at her own image.

It should have comforted her. Dark ringlets framed a charming countenance in which two speaking eyes of blue became gradually filled with tears that obscured her vision of a short, straight nose, a provocative upper lip, and an elusive dimple. These attributes had apparently failed to captivate the Viscount. The heiress uttered a strangled sob, and dabbed resolutely at her eyes, realizing that she would shortly be obliged to confront Miss Allerton, agog to know whether the date of her wedding had been fixed.

Nor was she mistaken. In a very few minutes, Trix

peeped into the room, and, finding her cousin alone, at once demanded to be told what Alan had said to her.

Henrietta replied in the most cheerful of accents: 'I am so much relieved! He does not wish to marry me at all!'

Trix, shocked by these tidings, could only stare at her.

'You may imagine how happy he has made me!' continued Henrietta glibly. 'Had he desired it, I must have thought it my duty to marry him, but he has set my mind at rest on this head, and now I can be easy again!'

'But you have loved him for years!' Trix blurted out.

'Indeed I have!' said Henrietta cordially. 'I am sure I always shall!'

'*Hetty!* When you have been writing to him for ever!'

'Pray, what has that to say to anything? To me, he is the elder brother I never had.'

'Hetty, what a hum! He is *my* brother, and I never wrote to him above twice in my life!'

Before Henrietta could reply suitably to this, they were joined by a willowy young gentleman in whom only the very stupid could have failed to recognize a Pink of the Ton. From the tip of his pomaded head to the soles of his dazzling Hessians, the Honourable Timothy Allerton was beautiful to behold. He was generally supposed to care for nothing but the fashion of his neckcloth, but he showed unmistakable signs of caring for the news which his sister broke to him. '*Not* going to offer for Hetty?' he repeated, aghast. 'Well, upon my soul! Well, what I mean is, might think what's due to the rest of us! Mind, I don't say I'm surprised he don't like it above half, but the thing is he's the head of the family, and he dashed well ought to do it! What's more,' he said, his amiable countenance darkening, 'if he thinks he can make *me* offer for her he'll find he's devilish mistaken! It ain't that I don't like you,

Hetty,' he added kindly, 'because I do, but that's coming it a trifle too strong!'

3

If the Viscount had harboured doubts of his mother's veracity, these were speedily dispelled. His cousin, far from having been kept in seclusion, seemed to him to be acquainted with all the eligible bachelors upon the town, and with far too many of those whom he did not hesitate to stigmatize as gazetted fortune-hunters. She dispensed her favours impartially amongst these gentlemen, whirled about town under the chaperonage of various not wholly disinterested matrons, and in general conducted herself with such frivolity that her perturbed aunt said that she had never known her to be in such a flow of spirits. She raised hopes in a dozen breasts, but the only suitor for whom she betrayed the smallest partiality was Sir Matthew Kirkham; and it was absurd to suppose (as Lady Allerton assured Alan) that a girl with as much good sense as Hetty would for an instant entertain the pretensions of a penniless roué, past his first youth, and with at least two unsavoury scandals attached to his name.

Alan could place no such dependence on his cousin's good sense. It was rarely that he took a dislike to anyone, but he took a quite violent dislike to Sir Matthew, and warned Henrietta to give the fellow no encouragement: an exercise of cousinly privilege which had no other effect than to cause her to wear Sir Matthew's flowers at the Opera House that very evening.

He was brought to realize that however obnoxious Kirkham might appear in the eyes of his fellow-men he possessed considerable charm for the ladies: Trix told him so. Trix listened with interest to his trenchantly expressed opinion of Sir Matthew, and then disgusted him by talking of the fellow's polished manners, and of the distinguishing attentions he had for so long bestowed upon Hetty.

Sir Matthew was not one of the two hundred guests invited to have the honour of being presented to the Tsar's sister. This lady had arrived in England some time before the various Kings, Princes, Generals, and Diplomats who were coming to take part in the grand Peace celebrations, and was putting up at the Pulteney Hotel. She was neither beautiful nor particularly amiable, but she was being much courted, and had already created a mild sensation by being rude to the Prince Regent, and by parading the town in enormous coal-scuttle bonnets, which instantly became the rage. Trix, giggling over the story of her having abruptly left the party at Carlton House just as soon as the expensive orchestra provided for her entertainment had struck up, because (she said) music made her want to vomit, prophesied that her departure from Lady Allerton's ball would be equally speedy; but Lady Allerton, well-acquainted with the Grandduchess, said, No: she only behaved like that when she wished to be disagreeable.

Trix was not to appear at the ball either. The Viscount had told her that with all the will in the world to do so he was unable at present to find the funds which would enable his mama to launch her into society; and Lady Allerton's sense of propriety was too nice to allow of her consenting to let her daughter attend a ball of such importance before she was out.

Trix bore her disappointment surprisingly well, neither arguing with Alan nor reproaching him. Touched by her restraint, he promised her a magnificent début the following spring, if he had to sell every available acre to achieve it. She thanked him, and said that she had made up her mind to help him in his difficulties.

Such unprecedented docility ought to have alarmed Henrietta, but Henrietta was too much occupied with her own affairs to notice it. It was not until the very evening of the ball, when Trix helped her, in the most selfless way, to array herself in all the elegance of primrose satin and pale green gauze, that it occurred to her that this saintly conduct was as suspicious as it was unusual. But Trix, looking the picture of hurt innocence, assured her that she had no intention of perpetrating some shocking practical joke, and she was obliged to be satisfied. Trix embraced her with great fondness, and she went away to join Lady Allerton feeling that she had misjudged her wayward cousin.

In this belief she continued until midnight, when she suffered a rude disillusionment.

4

Mr Allerton, seizing a respite from his conscientious labours on the floor, stood in the doorway of the ballroom, and delicately wiped his brow. The May night was very warm, and although the long windows stood open scarcely a breath of wind stirred the curtains which masked them, and the heat from the hundreds of wax candles burning in the wall-sconces and in the huge crystal chandelier which hung from the ceiling was making not only the flowers wilt, but every gentleman's starched shirt-points as well. But this was a small matter. Mr Allerton, a captious critic, was well-satisfied with the success of the ball. Every domestic detail had been perfectly arranged; his mother did him the greatest credit in a robe of sapphire satin lavishly trimmed with broad lace; his cousin was in quite her best looks; and even his brother, although dressed by a military tailor, did not disgrace him. The Grandduchess was in high good humour; besides the flower of the ton, two of the Royal Dukes were lending lustre to the evening; and, to set the final *cachet* upon a brilliant function, the great Mr Brummell himself was present.

These agreeable reflections were interrupted. A hand grasped Mr Allerton's wrist, and his cousin's voice said urgently in his ear: 'Timothy, come quickly to my aunt's dressing-room! I must speak to you alone!'

A horrible premonition that the champagne had run out and the ice melted away seized Mr Allerton. But the news which Henrietta had to impart to him had nothing to do with domestic arrangements. She was clutching in one hand a sheet of writing-paper, with part of the wafer that had sealed it still sticking to its edge, and this she dumbly proffered. Mr Allerton took it, and mechanically lifted his quizzing-glass to his eye. 'What the deuce——?' he demanded. 'Lord, I can't read this scrawl! What is it?'

'Trix!' she uttered, in a strangled voice.

'Well, that settles it,' he said, giving the letter back to her. 'Never been able to make head or tail of her writing! You'd better tell me what it is.'

'Timothy, it is the most terrible thing! She has eloped with Jack Boynton!'

'What?' gasped Timothy. 'No, hang it, Hetty! Must be bamming you!'

'No, no, it is the truth! She is not in the house, and she left this note for me. Dawson has this instant given it to me!'

'Well, I'm dashed!' said Timothy. '*Jack Boynton?* Y'know, Hetty, I wouldn't have thought it of him!'

Too well accustomed to Mr Allerton's mental processes to be exasperated, Henrietta replied: 'No, indeed! She must have persuaded him to do it: he is so very young! I never dreamed—Good God, I thought that affair had ended months ago! How could she have been so sly? But I might have guessed how it would be! If I had not been so selfishly taken up with my own troub—— I mean, *pleasures!*—it could never have happened! Timothy, I must act immediately, and you must help me!'

He blinked at her. 'Dash it, can't do anything in the middle of m'mother's party!'

'We can, and we must! They have fled to Gretna Green, and they must be overtaken!'

'Gretna Green?' echoed Mr Allerton, revolted. 'No, really, Hetty! Can't have!'

'She makes no secret of it. Besides, where else could they be married, two children under age? She supposed, of course, that I should not receive her letter until too late, but Dawson, good, faithful soul, thought it right to give it to me as soon as she might, and it is not too late! You and I may slip away, and it can't signify to anyone if our absence is noticed. I have thought it all out, and I have the greatest hope of overtaking them before morning! I am persuaded that boy cannot have scraped together enough money to pay for the hire of more than a pair of horses. You and I may hire four, and change them at every stage. The moon is at the full; we shall come up with them before they have gone thirty miles beyond London! Then we may bring Trix home, and no one need know what happened, not even my poor aunt, for I can trust Dawson to keep the secret, and ten to one my aunt won't leave her room until noon tomorrow!'

'Seems to me we'd do better to tell Alan,' objected Timothy.

'Upon no consideration! The Grandduchess is still here, and Sussex too! He at least cannot leave the house! Besides, Trix trusts me not to betray her to him, and however dreadfully she may have behaved I *could* not do so! He would be so angry! Oh, dear, it is all his fault for having postponed her coming-out! I warned him how it would be! Timothy, *you* must know where we can hire a post-chaise and four good horses!'

He admitted it, but entered a caveat. 'Thing is, dare say you're right about Boynton, but I ain't got the ready to pay for a chaise and four either!'

'No, but I have! I drew quite a large sum only yesterday, and I will give it to you,' said Henrietta. 'I will fetch my cloak, and instruct Dawson in what she must say if she should be questioned, and then we may be off. Do not tell Helmsley to call up a hackney! We will creep out by the door into the yard, and find one for ourselves directly!'

'But, Hetty!' protested Mr Allerton. 'Can't go driving about the countryside in evening-dress! Must change!'

But long acquaintance with her cousin had made Henrietta too familiar with the exigencies of his toilet to allow him this indulgence. Assuring him that his swallow-tailed coat and satin knee-breeches would be hidden by a driving-cloak, she so admonished and hustled him that within a very few minutes he found himself being smuggled out of the house by way of the back stairs and a door leading from the nether regions into the stable-yard.

'No,' said Mr Allerton, some five hours later. 'I won't tell 'em to drive on to the Norman Cross inn! And it ain't a bit of use arguing with me, Hetty, because I'm not going to go another mile on a dashed wild-goose chase, and so I tell you! If you want to go on jolting over a devilish bad road, asking questions at every pike of a set of gapeseeds who wouldn't be able to tell you whether Cinderella had driven by in a dashed great pumpkin, let alone Trix in a chaise, you do it! We've come a cool seventy miles, and never had so much as a whiff of Trix, and I want my breakfast! What's more, when I've had it I'm going back to town! She's hoaxing you; told you so at the outset!'

Miss Clitheroe, who had been ushered by an astonished waiter into one of the private parlours of the Talbot Inn, in Stilton, untied the strings of her cloak and pushed back its hood from her dishevelled curls. Pressing her hands to her tired eyes, she said wretchedly: 'She would not do such a thing! I know she plays shocking pranks, but she would never do this, only for mischief!'

'If I know Trix,' said Timothy, 'very likely told you she was off to Gretna Green to set you on a false scent!'

Henrietta stared at him in dismay. 'You mean she may have fled in quite another direction? Timothy, that would be worse than anything! It may be days before we can discover her whereabouts, and where, in heaven's name, will they find a clergyman to marry them?'

'Exactly so!' said Timothy. He added ghoulishly: 'Won't be a case of taking her home. Have to get 'em married in a hurry to save scandal.'

'No, no, I will not believe it!' cried Henrietta. 'They are ahead of us still! We must go on!'

Mr Allerton's reply was brief and unequivocal, but when he perceived the real distress in his cousin's face he relented sufficiently to promise that when he had eaten breakfast he would make enquiries at each of the other three posting-houses in the town. With this Henrietta was obliged to be content. The waiter set breakfast before them, listened with polite incredulity to the story, hastily manufactured by Timothy, to account for their appearance in Stilton at eight o'clock in the morning in full dress, of the moribund relative to whose bedside they had been summoned, and withdrew, shaking his head over the reprehensible habits of the Quality.

Mr Allerton then applied himself to a substantial repast. Henrietta, unable to do more than drink a cup of coffee, and nibble a slice of bread and butter, eyed him in growing impatience, but knew better than to expostulate. He finished at last, and, with a kindly recommendation to her not to expect any good outcome, went off to call at the Bell, the Angel, and the Woolpack.

She was left to await his return with what patience she could muster. The time lagged unbearably; when half an hour had passed she could no longer sit still, but got up, and began to pace about the room, trying to think what were best to be done if he failed to obtain news of the fugitives in Stilton.

The sound of a vehicle approaching at a smart pace, and pulling up outside the inn, made her run to the window. The sight that met her eyes was so unexpected and so unwelcome that she caught her breath on a gasp of dismay. Leaning from his own sporting curricle to interrogate one of the ostlers was her cousin Alan, and one glance at his face was enough to inform her that he was quite as angry as she had known he must be, if ever his sister's escapade came to his ears. As she stared out at him, he sprang down from the curricle, and came striding to the door into the inn.

She retreated from the window, wondering how much Dawson had disclosed to him, and what she should say to mollify him. She could almost wish now that the eloping couple had fled beyond recall, for it seemed to her that young Mr Boynton would be fortunate to escape with his bare life if the Viscount caught him.

The Viscount came in, and cast a swift, searching look round the room. Unlike his brother, he had found time to change his ball-dress for a riding-habit, over which he wore a caped greatcoat with large buttons of mother-of-pearl. He was looking extremely handsome, and singularly unyielding. After that one glance round the parlour, his attention became fixed on his cousin, his pleasant gray eyes so full of wrath that she took an involuntary step backward. Stripping off his gloves, he said furiously: 'How *dared* you do this, Henry? How *could* you?'

It had not occurred to her that any part of his anger would be directed against her. She said pleadingly: 'I suppose it was improper, but it seemed to be the only thing I could do!'

'*Improper?*' he exclaimed. 'So that's what you call it, is it? The most damnable escapade!'

'Alan! No, no! Imprudent I may have been, but what other course was open to me? I would not for the world tell my aunt, and I dared not say a word of it to you, because—'

'That at least I believe!' he interrupted. 'You knew well I would never permit it! You were right, my girl, very right! Where is the fellow?'

'I don't know. Oh, Alan, pray don't be so out of reason cross with me! Indeed I meant it for the best! *Alan!*'

The Viscount, who had most ungently grasped her shoulders, shook her. 'Don't lie to me! Where is he?'

'I tell you I don't know! And if I did I would not tell you while you are in such a rage!' said Henrietta, with spirit.

'We'll see that! said the Viscount grimly. 'I'll settle with him when I've settled with you! Had you chosen an honest man I would have stood aside, whatever it cost me, but this fellow——! No, by God! If you are determined to marry a fortune-hunter, Henry, let him be me! At least I *love* you!'

Shock bereft her of the power of speech; she could only gaze up into his face. He dragged her into his arms, and kissed her with such savagery that she uttered an inarticulate protest. To this he paid no heed at all, but demanded sternly: 'Do you understand me, Henry? Give you up to Kirkham I will not!'

'Oh, Alan, don't give me up to anyone!' begged Henrietta, laughing and crying together. 'Oh, dear, how *odious* you are! Of all the infamous notions to—— Alan, let me go! Someone is coming!'

The door opened. 'Told you no good would come of it,' said Mr Allerton, with gloomy satisfaction. 'Not a trace of 'em to be——' He broke off, staring at his brother. 'Well, upon my word!' he said, mildly surprised.

'What the devil are *you* doing here?' exclaimed the Viscount.

'Came with Hetty,' explained Timothy. 'Said it was a stupid thing to do, but she would have it we should overtake 'em.'

'Came with Hetty? Overtake——?' repeated the Viscount. 'In heaven's name, what are you talking about?'

Mr Allerton raised his quizzing-glass. 'You been in the sun, old fellow?' he asked solicitously.

'Timothy, he doesn't know!' Henrietta said. '*That* is not what brought him here! Alan, a dreadful thing has happened. Trix has eloped! I can't think what made you suppose that *I* had! Timothy and I came in pursuit, and oh, I was so hopeful of catching them, but we can discover no trace of them!'

'Quite true,' corroborated Timothy, observing that the tidings had apparently stunned his brother. 'Eloped with Jack Boynton. At least, that's what she said.'

'Are you mad?' demanded the Viscount. 'Trix is at home!'

'Alas, Alan, she is not!' said Henrietta. 'She slipped out in the middle of the party, leaving a letter, which her maid gave me at midnight. She wrote that she had gone with Boynton to Gretna Green, but I very much fear that she was deceiving me, and that is not her destination.'

The Viscount, who had listened to this with an arrested expression on his face, drew an audible breath. 'Most certainly she was deceiving you!' he said, in an odd tone. 'I see! The—little—cunning—*devil*!'

'He *is* cut, Hetty!' said Timothy.

A rueful smile was quivering at the corners of the Viscount's mouth. He paid no heed to this brotherly remark, but said: 'Let me tell you, my love, that an hour after you had left Grosvenor Square, I also received a billet from Trix!'

'You?' said Henrietta incredulously.

'Yes, I! It summoned me with the utmost urgency to join her in Mama's dressing-room. There she disclosed to me that *you* had slipped out of the house, to elope to the Border with Kirkham. She said that you had bound her to secrecy, but that her conscience misgave her, and she felt it to be her duty to betray you to me.'

'*Oh!*' gasped Henrietta. 'The little *wretch*! She—she deserves to be *flogged*!'

'Well, yes, I suppose she does,' admitted the Viscount. 'You cannot, however, expect *me* to flog her, for she has put me deep in her debt! Besides, you must own her strategy has been masterly!'

'Abominable!' scolded Henrietta, trying not to laugh.

'Told you she was hoaxing you,' said Timothy. 'Good notion, as it chances. What I mean is, if you *are* going to marry Hetty, Alan, we shall be all right and tight. The thing that's worrying me is that you must have left home before the ball was over. Dashed improper, y'know! That dishfaced Grandduchess! Half the *ton* invited to have the honour of meeting her, and you walk off in the middle of the party!'

'Well,' said the Viscount impenitently, 'they *had* the honour of meeting her, and *I* have the honour of asking Henry to be my wife, and so we may all be satisfied!' He held out his hands as he spoke, and Henrietta put hers into them.

'Yes, I dare say,' said Mr Allerton, 'but it ain't the thing. What's more,' he added severely, 'it ain't the thing to kiss Hetty in a dashed inn parlour, and with me watching you, either!'

NIGHT AT THE INN

I

THERE WERE only three persons partaking of dinner at the inn, for it was neither a posting-house, nor a hostelry much patronized by stage-coaches. The man in the moleskin waistcoat, who sat on one of the settles flanking the fireplace in the coffee-room, gave no information about himself; the young lady and gentleman on the other side were more forthcoming.

The lady had been set down at the Pelican after dusk by a cross-country coach. Her baggage was as modest as her appearance, the one consisting of a bandbox and a corded trunk; the other of brown curls smoothed neatly under a bonnet, a round cashmere gown made high to the neck and boasting neither frills nor lace, serviceable half-boots, and tan gloves, and a drab pelisse. Only two things belied the air of primness she seemed so carefully to cultivate: the jaunty bow which tied her bonnet under one ear, and the twinkle in her eye, which was as sudden as it was refreshing.

The gentleman was her senior by several years: an open-faced, pleasant young man whose habit proclaimed the man of business. He wore a decent suit of clothes, with a waistcoat that betrayed slight sartorial ambition; his linen was well-laundered, and the points of his shirt-collar starched; but he had tied his neckcloth with more regard for propriety than fashion, and he displayed none of the trinkets that proclaimed the dandy. However, the watch he consulted was a handsome gold repeater, and he wore upon one finger a signet-ring, with his monogram engraved, so that it was reasonable to suppose him to be a man of some substance.

He was fresh from Lisbon, he told the landlord, as he set down his two valises in the tap-room, and had landed at Portsmouth that very day. Tomorrow he was going to board a coach which would carry him within walking-distance of his paternal home: a rare surprise for his parents that would be, for they had not the least expectation of seeing him! He had been out of England for three years: it seemed like a dream to be back again.

The landlord, a burly, rubicund man with a smiling countenance, entered into the exile's excitement with indulgent good humour. Young master was no doubt come home on leave from the Peninsula? Not wounded, he did hope? No, oh, no! Young master had not the good fortune to be a soldier. He was employed in a counting-house, and had no expectation of getting his transfer from Lisbon for years. But—with offhand pride—he had suddenly been informed that there was a place for him at headquarters in the City, and had jumped aboard the first packet. No time to warn his parents: he would take them by surprise, and wouldn't they gape and bless themselves at the sight of him, by Jupiter! He had meant to have put up at the Swan, in the centre of the town, but such a press of custom had they that they had been obliged to turn him away. The same at the George: he hoped he was going to be more fortunate at the Pelican?

The landlord, gently edging him into the coffee-room, reassured him: he should have a good bedchamber, and the sheets well aired, a hot brick placed in the bed, and a fire lit in the grate. The gentleman from Lisbon said:

'Thank the Lord for that! I have had my fill of tramping from inn to inn, I can tell you! What's more, I'm devilish sharp-set! What's for dinner?'

He was promised a dish of mutton and haricot beans, with soup to go before it, and a dish of broccoli to accompany it. He rubbed his hands together, saying boyishly: 'Mutton! Real English mutton! That's the dandy! That's what I've been longing for any time these three years! Bustle about, man!—I could eat the whole carcase!'

By this time he had been coaxed into the coffee-room, a low-pitched apartment, with shuttered windows, one long table, and an old-fashioned hearth flanked by high-backed settles. On one of these, toasting her feet, sat the young lady; on the other, his countenance obscured by the journal he was perusing, was the man in the moleskin waistcoat. He paid no heed to the newcomer; but the lady tucked her toes under the settle, and assumed an attitude of stiff propriety.

The gentleman from Lisbon trod over to the fire, and stood before it, warming his hands. After a slight pause he observed with a shy smile that these November evenings were chilly.

The lady agreed to it, but volunteered no further remark. The gentleman, anxious that all the world should have a share in his joy, said that he was quite a stranger to England. He added hopefully that his name was John Cranbrook.

The lady subjected him to a speculative, if slightly surreptitious, scrutiny. Apparently she was satisfied, for she relaxed her decorous pose, and said that hers was Mary Gateshead.

He seemed much gratified by this confidence, and bowed politely, and said how do you do? This civility encouraged Miss Gateshead to invite him to sit down, which he instantly did, noticing as he did so that a pair of narrow eyes had appeared above the sheets of the journal on the opposite settle, and were fixed upon him. But as soon as his own encountered them they disappeared again, and all he could see, in fat black print, was an advertisement for Pears' Soap, and another adjuring him to consider the benefits to be derived from using Russia Oil regularly on the hair.

Searching his mind for something with which to inaugurate a conversation, Mr Cranbrook asked Miss Gateshead whether she too had found the Swan and the George full.

She replied simply: 'Oh, no! I could not afford the prices they charge at the big inns! I am a governess.'

'Are you?' said Mr Cranbrook, with equal simplicity. 'I am a clerk in Nathan Spennymore's Counting-house. In the ordinary way I can't afford 'em either, but I'm very plump in the pocket just now!' He patted his breast as he spoke, and laughed, his eyes dancing with such pride and pleasure that Miss Gateshead warmed to him, and invited him to tell her how this delightful state of affairs had come about.

He was nothing loth, and while the man in the moleskin waistcoat read his paper, and the landlord laid the covers on the table, he told her how he had been sent out to Lisbon three years ago, and what it was like there—very well in its way, but a man would rather choose to be at home!—and how an unexpected stroke of good fortune had befallen him, and he was to occupy a superior place in the London house. He didn't know why he should have been chosen, but Miss Gateshead might imagine how he had jumped at the chance!

Miss Gateshead suggested that the promotion might be a reward for good service, which made Mr Cranbrook blush vividly, and say that he was sure it was no such thing. In haste to change the subject, he enquired after her prospects and destination. Miss Gateshead was the eldest daughter of a curate with a numerous progeny, and she was bound for her first situation. Very eligible, she assured him! A large house, not ten miles from this place; and Mrs Stockton, her employer, had graciously promised to send the gig to the Pelican to fetch her in the morning.

'I should have thought she might have sent a closed carriage in this weather,' said John bluntly.

'Oh, no! Not for the governess!' Miss Gateshead said, shocked.

'It may rain!' he pointed out.

She laughed. 'Pooh, I shan't melt in a shower of rain!'

'You might take a chill,' insisted John severely. 'I don't think Mrs Stockton can be at all an amiable person!'

'Oh, do not say so! I am in such a quake already, in case I do not give satisfaction!' said Miss Gateshead. 'And there are nine children—only fancy!—so that I might be employed there for years!'

She seemed to regard this prospect with satisfaction, but Mr Cranbrook had no hesitation in favouring her with his own quite contrary views on such a fate.

The landlord came in, bearing the leg of mutton, which he set down on a massive sideboard. His wife, a decent-looking, stout woman in a mob-cap, arranged various removes on the table, bobbed a curtsy to Miss Gateshead, and asked if she would care for a glass of porter, or some tea.

Miss Gateshead accepted the offer of tea, and, after a moment's hesitation, untied the strings of her bonnet, and

138

laid this demure creation down on the settle. Her curls, unconfined, showed a tendency to become a trifle wayward, but, rather to John's disappointment, she rigorously smoothed them into decorum.

The man in the moleskin waistcoat folded his journal, and bore it to the table, propping it up against a tarnished cruet, and continuing laboriously to peruse it. His attitude indicated that he preferred his own company, so his fellow-guests abandoned any ideas they might have had of including him in their chat, and took their places at the other end of the board. The landlady dumped a pot of tea at Miss Gateshead's elbow, flanking it with a chipped jug of milk, and a cup and saucer; and John bespoke a pint of ale, informing Miss Gateshead, with his ingenuous grin, that home-brewed was one of the things he had chiefly missed in Portugal.

'And what for you, sir?' asked Mrs Fyton, addressing herself to the man at the bottom of the table.

'Mr Waggleswick'll take a heavy-wet as usual,' said her spouse, sharpening the carving-knife.

It was at this point that John, suppressing an involuntary chuckle, discovered the twinkle in Miss Gateshead's eye. They exchanged looks brimful of merriment, each perfectly understanding that the other found the name of Waggleswick exquisitely humorous.

The soup, ladled from a large tureen, was nameless and savourless, but Miss Gateshead and Mr Cranbrook, busily engaged in disclosing to one another their circumstances, family histories, tastes, dislikes, and aspirations, drank it without complaint. Mr Waggleswick seemed even to like it, for he called for a second helping. The mutton which followed the soup was underdone and tough, and the side-dish of broccoli would have been improved by straining.

Mr Cranbrook grimaced at Miss Gateshead, and remarked during one of the landlord's absences from the room that the quality of the dinner made him fearful of the condition of the bedchambers.

'I don't think they can enjoy much custom here,' said Miss Gateshead wisely. 'It is the most rambling old place, but no one seems to be staying here but ourselves, and you can *lose* yourself in the passages! In fact, I did,' she added, sawing her way through the meat on her plate. 'I have not dared to look at the sheets, but I have the most old-fashioned bed, and I asked them not to make up the fire again because it was smoking so dreadfully. And what is more I haven't seen a chambermaid, and you can see there is no waiter, so I am sure they don't expect guests.'

'Well, I don't think you should be putting up at a place little better than a hedge-tavern!' said John.

'Mrs Stockton wrote that it was cheap, and the landlady would take care of me,' she explained. 'Indeed, both she and the landlord have been most obliging, and if only the sheets are clean I am sure I shall have nothing to regret.'

Some cheese succeeded the mutton, but as it looked more than a little fly-blown the two young persons left Mr Waggleswick to the sole enjoyment of it, and retired again to the settle by the fire. The room being indifferently lit by a single lamp suspended above the table Mr Waggleswick elected to remain in his place with his absorbing journal. When he had finished his repast he noisily picked his teeth for some time, but at last pushed back his chair, and took himself off.

Miss Gateshead, who had been covertly observing him, whispered: 'What a strange-looking man! I don't like him above half, do you?'

'Well, he is not precisely handsome, I own!' John replied, grinning.

'His nose is crooked!'

'Broken. I dare say he is a pugilist.'

'How horrid! I am glad I am not alone with him here!'

That made him laugh. 'Why, we can't accuse him of forcing his attentions on us, I am sure!'

'Oh, no! But there is something about him which I cannot like. Did you notice how he watched you?'

'Watched me? He barely raised his eyes above the newspaper!'

'He did when he thought you were not looking at him. I know he was listening to every word we said, too. I have the oddest feeling that he may even be listening now!'

'I would wager a large sum he is consuming another of his heavy-wets in the tap rather!' replied John.

The door opened as he spoke, and Miss Gateshead's nervous start was infectious enough to make him look round sharply. But it was only the landlady who came into the room, with a tray, on which she began to pile the plates and cutlery. She remarked that it was a foggy night, so that she had tightly closed the shutters in the bedrooms.

'Get a lot of fog hereabouts, we do,' she said, wiping a spoon on her apron, and casting it into a drawer in the sideboard. 'Like a blanket it'll be before morning, but it'll clear off. I come from Norfolk myself, but a body gets used to anything. It's the clay.'

'Who is our fellow-guest?' asked John.

'Mr Waggleswick? He's an agent of some sort: I don't rightly know. Travels all over, by what he tells me. We've had him here two-three times before. He's not much to look at, but he don't give no trouble. I'll bring your candles in presently. Your room is at the end of the passage, sir: turn to the right at the top of the stairs, and you'll come to it. Fyton took your bags up.'

Waggleswick did not return to the coffee-room, and as no other visitors, other than the local inhabitants, who crowded into the tap-room across the passage, came to the Pelican, Miss Gateshead and Mr Cranbrook were left to sit on either side of the fire, chatting cosily together. Miss Gateshead was most interested to hear about Portugal, and as John, like so many young travellers, had filled a fat sketch-book with his impressions of an unknown countryside, it was not long before she had persuaded him to fetch down from his room this treasure.

The landlord was busy in the tap, and Mrs Fyton was nowhere to be seen, so John went upstairs unescorted, trusting to the landlady's directions.

Another of the hanging oil-lamps lit the staircase, and rather feebly cast a certain amount of light a little way along the passage above, but beyond its radius all was in darkness. For a moment John hesitated, half-inclined to go back for a candle, but as his eyes grew more accustomed to the murk he thought that he could probably grope his way along the corridor to the room at the end of it. He did this, not entirely without mishap, since he tripped down one irrelevant step in the passage, and up two others, slightly ricking his ankle in the process, and uttering an exasperated oath. However, he reached the end of the passage, and found that there was a door confronting him. He opened it, and peeped in, and saw, by the light of a fire burning in the high barred grate, his two valises, standing in the centre of the room. As he knelt before them, tugging at the strap round the larger of them, he glanced cursorily round the apartment. It was of a respectable size, and boasted a very large bed, hung with ancient curtains, and bearing upon it a quilt so thick as to present more the appearance of a feather-mattress than of a coverlet. The rest of the furniture was commonplace and old-fashioned, and comprised several chairs, a dressing-table, a wash-stand, a huge mahogany wardrobe, a table by the bed, and a wall-cupboard on the same side of the room as the fire-place. A pair of dingy blinds imperfectly concealed the warped shutters bolted across the window. Some attempt to embellish the room had been made, for a singularly hideous china group stood in the middle of the mantel-piece, and a religious engraving hung above it. Mr Cranbrook hoped that Miss Gateshead's room might be less gloomy: for himself he cared little for his surroundings, but he could imagine that a lady might find such an apartment comfortless, and even rather daunting.

The sketch-book was easily found, and he went off with it, shutting the door of the room behind him. He remembered the treacherous steps in the corridor, and went more carefully, putting out a hand to feel his way by touching the wall. It encountered not the wall, but something warm and furry.

He snatched it back, his eyes straining in the darkness, his heart suddenly hammering. Whatever he had touched was living and silent, and quite motionless. 'Who's that?' he said quickly, an absurd, nameless dread knocking in his chest.

There was a slight pause, as though of hesitation, and then a voice said in a grumbling tone: 'Why can't you take care where you're a-going, young master?'

Mr Cranbrook recognized the voice, which he had heard speaking to the landlord, and knew that what he had touched was a moleskin waistcoat. 'What are you doing here?' he demanded, relieved, yet suspicious.

'What's that to you?' retorted Waggleswick. 'I suppose a cove can go to his room without axing *your* leave!'

'I didn't mean—— But why were you spying on me?'

'Spying on you? That's a loud one! What would I want to do that for?' said Waggleswick scornfully.

John could think of no reason, and was silent. He heard a movement, and guessed that Waggleswick was walking away from him. A moment later a door opened farther down the passage, and the glow of firelight within the room silhouetted Waggleswick's figure for a brief instant before he went in, and shut the door behind him.

John hesitated, on the brink of retracing his steps to lock his own door. Then he recollected that he carried his money on his person, and had packed nothing of value in his valises, and he shrugged, and proceeded on his way.

Miss Gateshead was seated where he had left her. She greeted him with a smile that held some relief, and confided to him that she hated foggy nights.

'There's not much fog in the house,' he replied reassuringly.

'No, but it muffles all the noises, and makes one think the world outside dead!' she said. She perceived that he did not quite appreciate this, and coloured. 'It is only a foolish fancy, of course! I don't think I like this house. A rat has been gnawing in the wainscoting in that corner, and a few minutes ago I heard the stairs creak, and quite thought it must be you. Do you believe in ghosts?'

'No, certainly not,' said John firmly, resolving to make no mention of his encounter with Mr Waggleswick.

'Well, I didn't think I did,' confessed Miss Gateshead,

144

'but I have the horridest feeling all the time that there is someone just behind me!'

Mr Cranbrook did not feel quite comfortable about the Pelican himself, but since it was plainly his part to comfort Miss Gateshead he adopted a bracing tone, saying that she was perhaps tired after her journey, and was suffering from an irritation of the nerves. She accepted this explanation meekly, and came to sit at the table, so that she could more clearly see Mr Cranbrook's Peninsular sketches.

Shortly after ten o'clock the landlady came in with two tallow candles, stuck into pewter holders. She offered to escort Miss Gateshead up to bed, and since John thought he might as well go to bed too as sit on a settle beside a dying fire, he said that he would also go upstairs. He and Miss Gateshead had reached an excellent understanding by this time, and although nothing so blunt had passed between them as a declaration on Mr Cranbrook's part that he meant to follow up this chance acquaintanceship with a view to extending it rather considerably, his intention was as patent as it was unavowed. Nor did Miss Gateshead make any attempt to discourage him in his resolve. She was even much inclined to think there was a good deal to be said for his vehemently expressed opinion that the life of a governess would not at all suit her.

They took up their candles, and followed Mrs Fyton upstairs. The noise had died down in the tap; Mrs Fyton said that they kept early hours in these parts, besides that folks were anxious to get home before the fog came down really thick. The light of the candle she carried threw wavering, grotesque shadows on the walls, and disclosed, upstairs, two other passages, leading off at right-angles from the one which ran the length of the house.

'You know your way, sir,' said Mrs Fyton, nodding a

chaperon's dismissal to John. 'Come along, miss!'

John knew an impulse to accompany Miss Gateshead at least to her door. He thought she was looking scared, and guessed that this was probably the first time she had ever been alone in a strange inn. However, Mrs Fyton seemed a motherly woman, who might be trusted to look after a young lady, so he said good night, and contented himself with lingering at the head of the stairs until he had seen which door it was that led into Miss Gateshead's room. It lay at the far end of the house to his, with Waggleswick's between them; an arrangement John did not much like—though what evil intentions a middle-aged man of business putting up at an unfrequented inn could harbour in his breast he was unable to imagine. He went on to his own room, leaving the door ajar behind him. His valises were just as he had left them, and until he heard the landlady go down the stairs again he occupied himself in unpacking such articles as he would require for the night. When Mrs Fyton's footsteps had died away, he picked up his candle, and went softly along the passage, and scratched on Miss Gateshead's door.

'Who is it?'

Her voice sounded frightened; he said reassuringly: 'Only me—Cranbrook! I wanted to be sure you are quite comfortable: I won't come in.'

Apparently Miss Gateshead had no dread of this new acquaintance at least. There was a step within the room, the door was opened, and she stood on the threshold, whispering: 'I am so glad you have come! I have discovered that there is no key in this lock, and I know I shan't sleep a wink! Did you see that dreadful creature as we came up the stairs?'

'Waggleswick?' he said sharply, looking down the passage. 'No! Where was he?'

'In the corridor that leads to the back stairs. I caught a glimpse of him, but he stepped out of sight on the instant. I *told* you he was spying on us!'

'It's impossible! Why should he?' Mr Cranbrook said, in a lowered tone. 'Shall I go down and ask Mrs Fyton for a key to your door?'

'I am persuaded it would not be the least avail. I dare say it has been lost for years, for this is the most ramshackle, neglected place I ever was in! The dust under my bed——! Oh, I do wish Mrs Stockton would have fetched me tonight!'

'So do I—at least, no, I don't, for if she had I should not have met you,' said John honestly. 'But it is very uncomfortable for you, and I don't like *that*! Mind, I don't believe that fellow Waggleswick means any harm: ten to one it is all curiosity! but put a chair under your door-handle, if you are afraid.'

This suggestion found favour. Miss Gateshead wondered that she should not have thought of it for herself, thanked him, and once more bade him good night.

He went back to his own room, pausing at the entrance to the corridor that led to the back stairs, and peering down it. He could see no one, nor did any sound, other than those issuing from the tap downstairs, come to his ears.

3

He had a book packed in his valise, which he had meant to read in the chair by his fire, but this was reduced to glowing embers, and when he would have put more coal on it he found that there was no scuttle in the room. It hardly seemed worth while to ring for it, so he undressed, and got into bed, setting the candle on the table beside him, and thrusting his watch and his pocket-book under the pillow. The bed was a feather one, and though rather smothering, not uncomfortable. He opened his book, and began to read, occasionally raising his head to listen intently. His room was situated too far from the tap for him to be able to hear the murmur of voices there. He heard nothing at all, not even the stir of a mouse.

This dense stillness began presently to make him feel uneasy. It was not very late, and it would have been natural had some sounds broken the silence. In any inn one expected to hear noises: the voices of other guests; footsteps; the slam of a door; the clatter of crockery; or the rumble of wheels in the courtyard. The Pelican, of course, had no courtyard, and obviously did not enjoy much custom; but it did seem odd that he had seen no servant in the house other than the tapster. One would have thought that there would have been at least a waiter, and a chambermaid. He wondered who would clean the boots he had put outside his door, and whether anyone would bring him any shaving-water in the morning.

The silence was so profound that when a coal dropped in the grate it made him start. He was neither a nervous nor an imaginative young man, and the realization that Miss Gateshead had communicated to him some of her alarm vexed him. More than once he found himself lowering his book to glance round the room; and the creak of the chair in which he had sat to pull off his boots actually made him sit up in bed to make sure that he was alone.

When the candle was burnt down to a stub he began to be sleepy; and after finding that the printed words before his eyes were running one into the other, he closed the book, and snuffed the candle. A faint glow showed that the fire still lived. He turned on his side, the feather-bed billowing about him, and in less than ten minutes was asleep.

He awoke he knew not how much later, but so suddenly and with such a certainty that something had roused him that he was alert on the instant, and listening intently. His first thought was that Miss Gateshead must have called to him, but not a sound reached his ears. The glow from the hearth had disappeared; the room was in darkness.

He raised himself on his elbow. As he crouched thus, his ears straining, his eyes trying unavailingly to pierce the night, the conviction that he was not alone took such strong possession of his mind that the sweat broke out on his body. He stretched out his hand, and groped cautiously on the table for the tinder-box. It brushed against the candlestick, which made a tiny sound as it was shifted on the table, and in that moment it seemed to John that something moved in the room. He said breathlessly: 'Who's there?'

As he spoke, his fingers closed over the tinder-box. He sat up with a jerk, felt the bed move as something cannoned into it, and, even as he flung up his hands to grapple his unknown visitant, was thrust roughly down again on to his pillows, a hand clamped over his mouth, and another gripping his throat in a strangling hold. He struggled madly, trying to wrench away the clutch on his windpipe. His hands brushed against something warm and furry; a voice breathed in his ear: 'Dub your mummer!'

He tore at the unyielding hands, writhing, and trying to kick his feet free of the bedclothes, the bed creaking under his frenzied efforts. The grip on his throat tightened till the blood roared in his ears, and he felt his senses slipping from him. 'Still! *Still!*' hissed Waggleswick. 'One squeak out of you, and I'll land you a facer as'll put you to sleep for a se'ennight! Bow Street, clodpole!—*Bow Street!*'

He stopped struggling, partly from surprise at these last words, partly because the breath was choked out of him. The hand on his throat slightly relaxed its grip. He drew a sobbing breath, and distinctly heard the creak of boards under a stealthy footfall. It seemed to come from the direction of the wall-cupboard beside the fireplace.

'For God's sake, lay you still!' Mr Waggleswick's breath was hot in his ear.

He was free, and heard the stir of the bed-curtains, as though Waggleswick had shrunk behind them. He lay perfectly still, rigid and sweating. If Waggleswick were indeed a Bow Street Runner, he ought undoubtedly to obey his instructions; if he were not, it did not seem as though he would have much compunction in silencing those who defied him in a manner highly unpleasant to them. The darkness seemed to press on his eyeballs; he had difficulty still in breathing, but his senses were quite acute, and he caught the sound of a key softly, slowly turning in a lock. This unquestionably came from the direction of the cupboard; a faint lightening of the gloom gradually appeared as the door of the cupboard opened, as though a very dim light had been concealed there. It was obscured by a monstrous shadow, and then dwindled, as the door was pushed to again.

A loose floor-board cracked; John's fists clenched unconsciously, but a warning hand coming from out of the curtains and pressing his shoulder kept him otherwise motionless.

Someone was coming inch by inch towards the bed: someone who knew the disposition of the furniture so exactly that he made no blunder. The heavy coverlet stirred over John's limbs, and, as his hands came up instinctively, smothering folds were over his face, pressed down and down over nose and mouth. He grabbed at this new assailant's wrists, but before his fingers could close on them the pressure abruptly left his face, and he heard a sudden scuffle, a strangled, startled oath, and the quick shifting of stockinged feet on the floor.

He flung the quilt off, groping for the tinder-box, which he had dropped on the bed.

'The glim! light the glim!' panted Waggleswick.

A chair went over with a crash; something was knocked flying from the dressing-table, as the two men swayed and struggled about the room. John's desperate fingers found the tinder-box, and as with trembling fingers he contrived to strike a light from it, a heavy thud shook the room.

The tiny flame flared up; the landlord and Waggleswick were writhing and heaving together on the floor, silent but murderous.

John lit the candle, and tumbled out of bed, hurrying to Waggleswick's aid. The treatment he had suffered during the last few minutes had considerably shaken him, and he felt rather dizzy, nor did a wild kick from one of Fyton's plunging legs do anything to improve his condition. The landlord was immensely strong, and for several minutes he made it impossible for the two other men to overpower him. He and Waggleswick rolled on the floor, locked together, but at last John managed to grab one of his arms, as he was attempting to gouge out Waggleswick's eye, and to twist it with all his might. Waggleswick, who happened at that moment to be uppermost, was thus enabled to drive home a shattering blow to the jaw. This half stunned the landlord, and before he could recover Waggleswick had vigorously banged his head on the floor. This deprived him of his wits for several minutes, and by the time he was at all able to continue the struggle a pair of handcuffs had been locked round his wrists.

'Bide, and watch him!' commanded Waggleswick, out of breath, much abraded, but still surprisingly active. 'Take my barker and don't stand no gammon!' With that, he thrust a pistol into Mr Cranbrook's hand, and dived into the cupboard, adding over his shoulder: 'Hit him over the head with the butt, if he don't stay still! I don't want him shot: he's one for the Nubbing Cheat, he is!'

John found that his knees were shaking. He sat down, and curtly bade the landlord, who seemed to be trying to get up, to stay where he was. He had only just recovered his breath when a glimmer of light shone through the cupboard door, growing brighter as footsteps approached. Mr Waggleswick came back into the room with a lamp.

'All's bowman!' he announced, taking his gun away from John. 'Caught both the bites red-handed. *She's* as bad as he is, and worse! Get up, hang-gallows!'

He endorsed this command with a kick, and the landlord heaved himself to his feet. A settled, dogged expression had descended on to his face; he did not speak, but when John met his eyes he saw that there was so malevolent a look in them that it was almost impossible to believe he could be the same man as the comfortable, smiling host of a few hours earlier.

John shuddered, and turned away to pick up his breeches. When he had pulled these on over his nightshirt, and had thrust his feet into a pair of shoes, Waggleswick invited him to come down and see what had awaited him in the wash-house below his room.

'Jem and me'll lock the cull and his moll in the cellar till morning,' he said. 'Taken me a rare time to snabble you, my buck, ain't it? You'll pay for it! Get down them dancers, and don't you go for to forget that this little pop o' mine is mighty liable to go off! *Mighty* liable it is!'

He motioned the landlord to go before him into the cupboard, grinning at John's face of horror. 'Didn't suspicion what there was behind these here doors, did you?' he said.

'I never tried to open them. Good God, *a stairway?*'

'Down to the wash-house. Took me three visits to get a sight of them, too! Ah, and you'd have gone down 'em feet first if I hadn't have been here, master, like a good few other young chubs! To think I been here four times, and never a blow come worth the biting until you walked in tonight, with your pocket-book full o' flimseys, and your talk of no one suspicioning you was in England! Axing your pardon, you was a regular noddy, wasn't you, sir?'

Mr Cranbrook agreed to it humbly, and brought up the rear of the little procession that wound its way down a steep, twisting stair to a stone-flagged wash-house, where a huge copper was steaming in one corner, and the tapster was standing over Mrs Fyton, loudly protesting her innocence of evil intent in a chair in the middle of the room.

'My assistant—junior, o' course, but a fly cove!' said Waggleswick, jerking a thumb at the tapster. 'All right, Jem: we'll stow 'em away under hatches now!'

John, whose revolted gaze had alighted on a chopper, lying on a stout, scrubbed table, was looking a little pale. He was left to his own reflections while the prisoners were driven down to the cellar; and his half-incredulous and wholly nauseated inspection of the wash-house made it unnecessary for Waggleswick to inform him, as he did upon his return with Jem, that it had been the Fytons' practice to chop up the bodies of their victims, and to boil down the remains in the copper. 'Though I don't rightly know what they done with the heads,' added Mr Waggles-wick thoughtfully.

John had heard tales reminiscent of this gruesome disclosure, but he had imagined that they belonged to an age long past.

'Lor' no, sir!' said Waggleswick indulgently. 'There's plenty of willains alive today! We've had this ken in our eye I dunno how long, but that Fyton he was a cunning one!'

'Ah!' nodded Jem, signifying portentous assent.

'You might have told me!' John said hotly.

'Well,' said Waggleswick, scratching his chin, 'I might, o' course, but you was in the nature of a honey-fall, sir, and I wasn't so werry sure as you'd be agreeable to laying in your bed awaiting for Fyton to come an' murder you unbeknownst if I was to tell you what my lay was.'

A horrible thought crossed John's mind. 'Miss Gates-head!'

'*She's* all right and tight! She was knowed to be putting up here, and Fyton never ran no silly risks.'

''Adn't got no 'addock stuffed with beans neither,' interpolated Jem, somewhat incomprehensibly.

Waggleswick said severely: 'Don't talk that cant to flash coves as don't understand it, sap-head! What he means, sir, is she hadn't no full purse, like you told us all *you* had!'

'Not but what Fyton might ha' done a bit in the body-snatching line,' suggested Jem.

Mr Cranbrook shuddered.

'Well, he ain't snatched *her* body,' pointed out Mr Waggleswick.

John looked at him. 'She must not know of this! It is ghastly!'

Waggleswick scratched his chin again. 'I dunno as she

154

need. She won't be wanted as a witness—like you will, sir!'

'Yes, of course: I know that! I am very willing. Has that monster disposed of many travellers in this frightful way?'

'There's no saying,' replied Waggleswick. 'Not above two or three since we got wind of it in Bow Street.'

'And before? It is horrible to think of!'

'Ah!' agreed Jem. 'Dear knows *'ow* many went into that there copper afore us Runners come down 'ere!'

On this macabre thought, Mr Cranbrook retired again to his interrupted repose, if not to enjoy much slumber, at least to employ his time profitably in thinking out what plausible tale he would concoct for Miss Gateshead's benefit in the morning.

4

They met in the coffee-room, still shuttered and un-aired. Miss Gateshead was unbarring the shutters when John came into the room, and her comments on the lack of orderly management in the inn were pungent and to the point.

'I tugged and tugged at the bell, and who do you think brought me a can of hot water at last?' she said. 'The tapster!'

'It is too bad! But the thing is that they were cast into a pucker by the landlady's being taken ill in the night,' explained John glibly. 'Should you mind putting on your bonnet, and stepping out with me to partake of breakfast at one of the other inns?'

'Not at all!' replied Miss Gateshead promptly. 'I am very sorry for the landlady, but she almost deserves to be taken ill for keeping her house in such a shocking state! I will fetch my bonnet and pelisse directly.' She paused, coloured slightly, and said in a shamefaced voice: 'I am afraid you must have thought me very foolish last night! Indeed, I cannot imagine what can have possessed me to be so nonsensical! I never slept better in my life! Is it not odd what absurd fancies one can take into one's head when one is a little tired?'

'Most odd!' agreed Mr Cranbrook, barely repressing a shiver.

THE DUEL

I

IT AMUSED HIM, entering his house so unexpectedly early in the evening, to know that he had disconcerted Criddon, his porter. He suspected Criddon of having slipped out to dally with a serving-maid at the top of some area steps. The rogue was out of breath, as though, having perceived his master sauntering up the flag-way in the light of the oil street lamps, he had scurried back into the house more swiftly than befitted a man of his bulk. As he took the silk-lined cloak, the curly-brimmer beaver, and the tall cane, he wore a faint air of injury. No doubt he felt ill-used because his master, leaving the ball hours before his carriage had been ordered to call for him, had chosen to walk home, instead of looking in at Watier's, according to his more usual custom.

He told Criddon he might go to bed, and strolled to the side table, where a letter, delivered during the evening, awaited him. As he broke the wafer and spread open the sheet, his butler came up from the nether regions, but he waved him away, as irritated by his presence as he would have been angered by his absence. He threw the letter aside and opened the door into the dining-room. The room was in darkness, a circumstance which almost caused him to summon back the butler. It was his pleasure that lights should burn in every room which he might conceivably wish to enter in his great house, and well did his servants know it. But he did not call to Radstock, for his nostrils had caught the acrid smell of candles newly blown out, and he was indefinably aware that he was not alone in the room. Some of the boredom left his face: a turn-up with a house-breaker might relieve the monotony of his existence, and would certainly surprise the housebreaker, who would no doubt consider a seeming dandy in satin knee-breeches and a long-tailed coat easy game. He stepped back into the hall, and picked up the heavy chandelier from the side table there. Carrying this into the dining-room, he stood for a moment on the threshold, looking keenly round. The flames of half a dozen candles flickered, and showed him only the furniture, and the wavering shadows it threw. He glanced towards the windows and it seemed to him that one of the brocade curtains bulged slightly. He set the chandelier down, trod silently to the window, and flung the curtains back.

As he did so, he sprang out of range, and brought his hands up in two purposeful fists. They dropped to his sides. No housebreaker met his astonished gaze, but a girl, shrinking back against the window, the hood of her cloak fallen away from a tangle of silken curls, her frightened face, in which two dark eyes dilated, upturned to his.

For a moment he wondered if Criddon had hidden his doxy in the dining-room; then his critical glance informed him that the girl's cloak was of velvet, and her gown of sprigged muslin the demure but expensive raiment of the débutante. His astonishment grew. He was so eligible a bachelor that he was accustomed to being pursued, and could recognize and evade every snare set in his path. But this seemed to go beyond all bounds. Anger came into his eyes; he thought he must have been mistaken in his assessment of the girl's quality, and that a fair Cyprian had invaded his house.

Then she spoke, and her words confirmed him in his first impression. 'Oh, I *beg* your pardon! P-pray forgive me, sir!' she said, in a pretty, conscience-stricken voice.

Anger gave way to amusement. 'What, ma'am, may I ask, are you doing in my house?' he demanded.

She hung her head. 'Indeed, you must think it most odd in me!'

'I do.'

'The door was open, so—so I ran in,' she explained. 'You see, there—there was a man following me!'

'If you must walk through the streets of London at this hour, I should hope your footman was following you!'

'Oh no! No one knows I am not in my bed! My mission is most secret! And I never meant to walk, but the hackney carried me to the wrong house—at least, I fear I gave the coachman the wrong direction, and he had driven away before I was made aware of my mistake. The servant told me that it was only a step, so I thought I might walk, only there was an *odious* man——! I ran as fast as I could into this street, and—and your door stood open. Indeed, I meant only to hide in the hall until that creature was gone, but then your porter came in, and I was obliged to run into this room, because how could I explain? When I told that other servant where I wished to go, he—he——' She broke off, lifting her hand to a burning cheek. 'And then you came in, so I slipped behind the curtain.'

It occurred to him, while she offered this explanation of her presence in his house, that although she was agitated she was not at all shy, and seemed not to be much afraid of him. He said: 'You intrigue me greatly. Where, in fact, *do* you wish to go?'

'I wish—I have a particular desire—to go to Lord Rotherfield's house,' she replied.

The amusement left his face. He looked frowningly at her, a hint of contempt in his rather hard eyes. He said in a dry tone: 'No doubt to call upon his lordship?'

She put up her chin. 'If you will be so obliging as to direct me to Lord Rotherfield's house, which I believe to be in this street, sir, I need no longer trespass upon your hospitality!'

'It is the last house in London to which I would direct you. I will rather escort you back to your own house, wherever that may be.'

'No, no, I must see Lord Rotherfield!' she cried.

'He is not a proper person for you to visit, my good girl. Moreover, it is unlikely that you would find him at home at this hour.'

'Then I must wait for him,' she declared. 'I am persuaded he will not be so very late tonight, for he is going to fight a duel in the morning!'

He stared at her, his eyes narrowed. 'Indeed?'

'Yes!—with my brother!' she said, a catch in her voice. 'I must—I *must* prevent him!'

'Is it possible,' he demanded, 'that you imagine you can persuade Rotherfield to draw back from an engagement? You do not know him! Who sent you on this fantastic errand? Who can have exposed you to such a risk?'

'Oh, no one, no one! I discovered what Charlie meant to do by the luckiest accident, and surely Lord Rotherfield cannot be so *very* bad? I know he is said to be heartless and excessively dangerous, but he cannot be such a monster as to shoot poor Charlie when I have explained to him how young Charlie is, and how it would utterly prostrate Mama, who is an invalid, and suffers from the most shocking palpitations!'

He moved away from the window, and pulled a chair out from the table. 'Come and sit down!' he said curtly.

'But, sir——'

'Do as I bid you!'

She came reluctantly to the chair and sat down on the edge of it, looking up at him in a little trepidation.

He drew his snuff-box from his pocket and flicked it open. 'You, I apprehend, are Miss Saltwood,' he stated.

'Well, I am Dorothea Saltwood,' she amended. 'My sister Augusta is Miss Saltwood, because no one has offered for her yet. And that is why I am not yet out, though I am turned nineteen! But how did you know my name is Saltwood?'

He raised a pinch of snuff to one nostril. 'I was present, ma'am, when your brother insulted Rotherfield.'

She seemed grieved. 'At that horrid gaming-hell?'

'On the contrary! At an exclusive club, to which few of us, I fancy, know how Lord Saltwood gained admission.'

She flushed. 'He prevailed upon that stupid creature, Torryburn, to take him there. I dare say he should not have done so, but Lord Rotherfield need not have give him *such* a set-down! You will own it was the unkindest thing!'

'Certainly,' he said. 'Pray do not think that I have the smallest desire to defend Rotherfield! But in justice to his lordship I must tell you that your brother offered him an insupportable insult. His lordship has many faults— indeed, I sometimes think I dislike him more than any-one of my acquaintance!—but I assure you that in all matters of play he is scrupulous. Forgive me if I venture to suggest, ma'am, that your brother will be the better for a sharp lesson, to teach him, in future, not to accuse a gentleman of using loaded dice!'

'Indeed, I know it was very bad, but if he meets Lord Rotherfield he won't have a future!'

'This is high Cheltenham tragedy with a vengeance!' he replied, amused. 'Rotherfield will scarcely proceed to such extremes as you dread, my dear child!'

'They say he never misses!' she uttered, her cheeks blanched.

'Then he will hit Saltwood precisely where he means to.'

'They must not, and they *shall* not meet!' she said earnestly. 'I am persuaded that if I can only tell Lord Rotherfield how it is with Charlie, he cannot be so cruel as to persist in this affair!'

'You would be better advised to prevail upon your brother to apologize for his conduct.'

'Yes,' she agreed mournfully. 'That is what Bernard said, but the thing is that Lord Rotherfield is so deadly a shot that Charlie would never, never do that, because everyone would think he was afraid to meet him!'

'And who, may I ask, is Bernard?'

'Mr Wadworth. We have known him for ever, and he is one of Charlie's seconds. It was he who told me about it. I made him do so. I promised I would not disclose to Charlie that he had breathed a word to me, so what can I do but throw myself upon Lord Rotherfield's mercy?'

'Lord Rotherfield, as you are aware, has no mercy. You would, moreover, be doing Mr Wadworth a vast disservice if you were to betray to anyone the impropriety of his conduct in speaking one word to you on this subject.'

'Oh, dear, I would not injure him for the world, poor Bernard! But I have told *you* already, sir!'

'Your confidence is quite safe in my keeping.'

She smiled engagingly up at him. 'Indeed, I know it

must be! You are so very kind! But I am determined to see Lord Rotherfield.'

'And I am determined that you shall return to your home. Rotherfield's is no house for you to visit in this style. Good God, if it should become known that you had done so——!'

She got up, clasping her hands. 'Yes, but it is *desperate*! If anything were to happen to Charlie, it would kill Mama! I assure you, it is of no consequence what becomes of me! Augusta says I am bound to ruin myself, because I have no notion how I should go on, so I might as well ruin myself now as later, don't you think?'

'I do not!' he replied, laughing. 'Oh, don't look so much distressed, you absurd child! Will you trust me to see that no harm comes to your tiresome brother?'

She stared at him, sudden hope in her eyes. 'You, sir? Oh, will *you* see Lord Rotherfield, and explain to him that it was only that poor Charlie has been so sadly indulged, because my father died when he was a little boy, and Mama would not let him go to school, or permit anyone to cross him, and he has only just come to town, and he does not know how to guard his temper, or——'

He interrupted this tumbled speech, possessing himself of one agitated little hand, and kissing it lightly. 'Rest assured I will not allow Lord Rotherfield to hurt poor Charlie at all!'

'Will he listen to you?' she asked doubtfully. 'Augusta's particular friend, Miss Stanstead, says he is a very proud, disagreeable man, and cares nothing for anyone's opinion.'

'Very true, but I have it in my power to compel him to do what I wish. You may safely trust in me.'

She heaved a relieved sigh, and again the enchanting smile trembled on her lips. 'Oh yes! I do, sir! It is the oddest thing, for, to own the truth, I was a little afraid when you pulled back the curtain. You looked at me in *such* a way! But that was quite my own fault, and I saw in a trice that there was not the smallest need for me to be afraid. You are so very kind! I don't know how I may thank you.'

'Forget that I looked at you in *such* a way, and I shall be satisfied. I am going to take you home now. I think you said that no one knew you had left the house. Have you the means to enter it again without being seen by the servants?' She nodded, a gleam of mischief in her big eyes. The amusement in his deepened. 'Abominable girl! Lady Saltwood has my sincere sympathy!'

'I know I have behaved shockingly,' she said contritely. 'But what was I to do? And you must own that it has come about for the best, sir! For I *have* saved Charlie, and I know you will never tell anyone what a scrape I have been in. I hope—I hope you don't truthfully think me abominable?'

'If I were to tell you what I truthfully think, *I* should be abominable. Come! I must convey you home, my little one.'

2

Never did a young gentleman embarking on his first affair of honour receive less encouragement from his seconds than Lord Saltwood received from Sir Francis Upchurch and Mr Wadworth. Sir Francis, being inarticulate, did little more than shake his head, but Mr Wadworth, presuming upon an acquaintance with his principal which dated from the cradle, did not hesitate to speak his mind. 'Made a dashed cake of yourself!' he said.

'Worse!' said Sir Francis, contributing his mite.

'Much worse!' corroborated Mr Wadworth. 'Devilish bad ton, Charlie! You were foxed, of course.'

'I wasn't. At least, not very much.'

'Drunk as a wheelbarrow. I don't say you showed it, but you must have been!'

'Stands to reason!' said Sir Francis.

'No right to bully Torryburn into taking you to the Corinthian Club in the first place. Above your touch, my boy! Told you so, when you asked me to take you. No right to have stayed there after Rotherfield gave you that set-down.'

Lord Saltwood ground his teeth. 'He need not have said *that*!'

'No, I dare say he need not. Got a nasty tongue. But that don't signify. You'd no right to accuse him of using Fulhams!'

Sir Francis shuddered, and closed his eyes for an anguished moment.

'Ought to have begged his pardon then and there,' pursued Mr Wadworth relentlessly. 'Instead of that, dashed well forced a quarrel on him!'

'If he hadn't told a waiter—a *waiter*!—to show me out——!'

'Ought to have called for the porter,' agreed Sir Francis. He then perceived that this amiable response had failed to please his fiery young friend, and begged pardon. A powerful thought assailed him. He turned his eyes towards Mr Wadworth, and said suddenly: 'You know what, Bernie? He shouldn't have accepted Charlie's challenge. Must know he ain't been on the town above six months!'

'The point is he *did* accept it,' said Mr Wadworth. 'But it ain't too late. Charlie dashed well ought to apologize.'

'I *will* not!' said Lord Saltwood tensely.

'You were in the wrong,' insisted Mr Wadworth.

'I know it, and I mean to fire in the air. That will show that I acknowledge my fault, but was not afraid to meet Rotherfield!'

This noble utterance caused Sir Francis to drop with a clatter the cane whose amber knob he had been meditatively sucking, and Mr Wadworth to stare at his principal as though he feared for his reason. 'Delope?' he gasped. 'Against Rotherfield? You must be queer in your attic! Why, man, you'd be cold meat! Now, you listen to me, Charlie! If you won't beg the fellow's pardon, you'll come up the instant you see the handkerchief drop, and shoot to kill, or I'm dashed if I'll have anything more to do with it!'

'Awkward business, if he killed him,' objected Sir Francis. 'Might have to leave the country.'

'He won't kill him,' said Mr Wadworth shortly.

He said no more, but it was plain to Saltwood that his seconds thought poorly of his chances of being able to hit his opponent at a range of twenty-five yards. He was by no means a contemptible shot, but he suspected that it might be easier to hit a small wafer at Manton's Galleries than a large man at Paddington Green.

Mr Wadworth called for him in a tilbury very early in the morning. He did not find it necessary to throw stones up at his lordship's window, for his lordship had not slept well, and was already dressed. He stole downstairs, and let himself out of the house, bidding Mr Wadworth good morning with very creditable composure. Mr Wadworth nodded, and cast a knowledgeable eye over him. 'No bright buttons on your coat?' he asked.

The question did nothing to allay the slightly sick feeling at the pit of Saltwood's stomach. Mr Wadworth followed it up with a reminder to him to turn up his collar, and to be careful to present the narrowest possible target to his adversary. Lord Saltwood, climbing into the tilbury, answered with spurious cheerfulness: 'I must suppose it can make little difference to such a shot as they say Rotherfield is.'

'Oh, well——! No sense in taking needless risks,' said Mr Wadworth awkwardly.

After that, conversation became desultory. They were the first to arrive on the ground, but they were soon joined by Sir Francis, and a man in a sober-hued coat, who chatted about the weather. Saltwood realized that this insensate person must be the doctor, gritted his teeth, and hoped that Rotherfield would not be late. It seemed to him that he had strayed into nightmare. He felt cold, sick, and ashamed; and it said much for the underlying steel in his spoilt and wayward nature that it did not enter his head that he might even now escape from a terrifying encounter by apologizing to Rotherfield for conduct which he knew to have been disgraceful.

Rotherfield arrived even as the church clocks were striking the hour. He was driving himself in his sporting curricle, one of his friends seated beside him, the other following him in a high-perch phaeton. He appeared to be quite nonchalant, and it was obvious that he had dressed with all his usual care. The points of his shirt stood up stiffly above an intricate neckcloth; his dark locks were arranged with casual nicety; there was not a speck upon the gleaming black leather of his Hessian boots. He sprang down from the curricle and cast his drab driving-coat into it. The seconds met, and conferred, and presently led their principals to their positions, and gave into their hands the long-barrelled duelling-pistols, primed and cocked.

Across what seemed to be an immeasureable stretch of turf, Saltwood stared at Rotherfield. That cold, handsome face might have been carved in stone; it looked merciless, faintly mocking.

The doctor turned his back; Saltwood drew in his breath, and grasped his pistol firmly. One of Rotherfield's seconds was holding the handkerchief high in the air. It fell, and Saltwood jerked up his arm and fired.

He had been so sure that Rotherfield would hit him that it seemed to him that he must have been hit. He recalled having been told that the bullet had a numbing effect, and cast an instinctive glance down his person. But there did not seem to be any blood, and he was certainly still standing on his feet. Then he heard someone ejaculate: 'Good God! *Rotherfield!*' and, looking in bewilderment across the grass, he saw that Mr Mayfield was beside Rotherfield, an arm flung round him, and that the doctor was hurrying towards them. Then Mr Wadworth removed his own pistol from his hand, and said in a stupefied voice: 'He *missed*!'

Young Lord Saltwood, realizing that he had hit the finest pistol-shot in town and was himself untouched, was for a moment in danger of collapsing in a swoon. Recovering, he pushed Mr Wadworth away, and strode impetuously up to the group gathered round Rotherfield. He reached it in time to hear that detested voice say: 'The cub shoots better than I bargained for! Oh, go to the devil, Ned! It's nothing—a graze!'

'My lord!' uttered Saltwood. 'I wish to offer you my apology for——'

'Not now, not now!' interrupted the doctor testily.

Saltwood found himself waved aside. He tried once more to present Rotherfield with an apology, and was then led firmly away by his seconds.

'Most extraordinary thing I ever saw!' Mr Wadworth told Dorothea, when dragged by her into the small saloon, and bidden disclose the whole to her. 'Mind, now! Not a word to Charlie! Rotherfield missed!'

Her eyes widened. 'Fired in the air?'

'No, no! Couldn't expect him to do that! Dash it, Dolly, when a man does that he's owning he was at fault! Don't mind telling you I felt as sick as a horse. He was looking devilish grim. Queer smile on his face, too. I didn't like it above half. I'll swear he took careful aim. Fired a good second before Charlie did. Couldn't have missed him by more than a hair's breadth! Charlie got him in the shoulder: don't think it's serious. Thing is, shouldn't be surprised if it's done Charlie good. Tried to beg Rotherfield's pardon on the ground, and he's called once in Mount Street since then. Not admitted: butler said his lordship was not receiving visitors. Given Charlie a fright: he'll be more the thing now. But don't you breathe a word, Dolly!'

She assured him she would not mention the matter. An attempt to discover from him who, besides Lord Rotherfield, resided in Mount Street could not have been said to have advanced the object she had in mind. Mr Wadworth was able to recite the names of several persons living in that street; but when asked to identify a gentleman who apparently resembled a demi-god rather than an ordinary mortal, he said without hesitation that he had never beheld anyone remotely corresponding to Miss Saltwood's description. He began then to show signs of suspicion, so Dorothea was obliged to abandon her enquiries and to cast round in her mind for some other means of discovering the name of her brother's unknown preserver. None presented itself; nor, when she walked down Mount Street with her maid, was she able to recognize the house in which she had taken refuge. A wistful fancy that the unknown gentleman might perhaps write to tell her that he had kept his word was never very strong, and by the end of the week had vanished entirely. She could only hope that she would one day meet him, and be able to thank him for his kind offices. In the meantime, she found herself to be sadly out of spirits, and behaved with such listless propriety that even Augusta, who had frequently expressed the wish that something should occur to tame her sister's wildness, asked her if she were feeling well. Lady Saltwood feared that she was going into a decline, and herself succumbed immediately to a severe nervous spasm.

Before any such extreme measures for the restoration to health of the younger Miss Saltwood as bringing her out that very season had been more than fleetingly contemplated by her mama and angrily vetoed by her sister, her disorder was happily arrested. Eight days after Saltwood's duel, on an afternoon in June, the butler sought out Dorothea, who was reading aloud to her afflicted parent, and contrived to get her out of the drawing-room without arousing any suspicion in Lady Saltwood's mind that she was wanted by anyone more dangerous than the dressmaker. But once outside the drawing-room Porlock placed a sealed billet in Dorothea's hand, saying with the air of a conspirator that the gentleman was in the Red Saloon.

The billet was quite short, and it was written in the third person. *'One who had the pleasure of rendering a trifling service to Miss Dorothea Saltwood begs the honour of a few words with her.'*

'Oh!' gasped Dorothea, all her listlessness vanished. 'Porlock, pray do not tell Mama or my sister! *Pray* do not!'

'Certainly not, miss!' he responded, with a readiness not wholly due to the very handsome sum already bestowed upon him downstairs. He watched his young mistress speed down the stairs, and thought with pleasure that when Miss Augusta discovered what kind of an out-and-outer was courting her sister she would very likely go off in an apoplexy. The gentleman in the Red Saloon, to his experienced eye, was a bang-up Corinthian, a Nonpareil, a very Tulip of Fashion.

Dorothea, coming impetuously into the saloon, exclaimed on the threshold: 'Oh, I am so very glad to see you, sir! I have wished so much to thank you, and I have not known how to do so, for I never asked you your name! I don't know how I came to be such a goose!'

He came towards her, and took her outstretched hand in his left one, bowing over it. She perceived that he was quite as handsome as she had remembered, and that his right arm lay in a sling. She said in quick concern: 'How comes this about? Have you broke your arm, sir?'

'No, no!' he replied, retaining her hand. 'A slight accident to my shoulder merely! It is of no consequence. I trust that all went well that evening, and that your absence had not been discovered?'

'No, and I have not mentioned it to anyone!' she assured him. 'I am so very much obliged to you! I cannot imagine how you contrived to prevail upon that man not to hit Charlie! Bernard told me that Charlie hit *him*, and I must say I am sorry, because it was quite my fault, and although he is so odious I did not wish him to be hurt precisely!'

'To own the truth, he had little expectation of being hurt,' he said, with a smile. He released her hand, and

171

seemed to hesitate. 'Lord Rotherfield,' Miss Saltwood, does not wish to appear odious in your eyes, believe me!'

'Is he a friend of yours?' she asked. 'Pray forgive me! I am sure he cannot be so very bad if that is so!'

'I fear he has been quite my worst friend,' he said ruefully. 'Forgive me, my child! *I* am Lord Rotherfield!'

She stood quite still, staring at him, at first pale, and then with a flush in her cheeks and tears sparkling in her eyes. '*You* are Lord Rotherfield?' she repeated. 'And I said *such* things about you, and you let me, and were so very kind, and allowed yourself to be wounded——Oh, I am sure you must be the best person in the world!'

'I am certainly not that, though I hope I am not the worst. Will you forgive me for having deceived you?'

She put out her hand, and again he took it, and held it. 'How can you talk so? I am quite ashamed! I wonder you did not turn me out of doors! How *good* you are! How truly noble!'

'Ah, how can *you* talk so?' he said quickly. 'Do not! I do not think I had ever, before that evening, wished to please anyone but myself. You came to me—enchanting and abominable child that you are!—and I wanted more than anything in life to please you. I am neither good nor noble —though I am not as black as I was painted to you. I assure you, I had never the least intention of wounding your brother mortally.'

'Oh *no*! Had I known it was you I should never have thought that!'

He raised her hand to his lips. The slight fingers seemed to tremble, and then to clasp his. He looked up, but before he could speak Lord Saltwood walked into the room.

Lord Saltwood stopped dead on the threshold, his eyes starting from their sockets. He stared in a dazed way, opened his mouth, shut it again, and swallowed convulsively.

'How do you do?' said Rotherfield, with cool civility. 'You must forgive me for having been unable to receive you when you called at my house the other day.'

'I came—I wished—I wrote you a letter!' stammered Saltwood, acutely uncomfortable.

'Certainly you did, and I have come to acknowledge it. I am much obliged to you, and beg you will think no more of the incident.'

'C-came to see *me*?' gasped Saltwood.

'Yes, for I understand you to be the head of your family, and I have a request to make of you. I trust that our late unfortunate contretemps may not have made the granting of it wholly repugnant to you.'

'No, no! I mean—anything in my power, of course! I shall be very happy——! If you would care to step into the book-room, my lord——?'

'Thank you.' Rotherfield turned, and smiled down into Dorothea's anxious eyes. 'I must take my leave of you now, but I trust Lady Saltwood will permit me to call on her to-morrow.'

'Yes, indeed, I am persuaded—that is, I do hope she will!' said Dorothea naïvely.

There was a laugh in his eye, but he bowed formally and went out with Saltwood, leaving her beset by a great many agitating emotions, foremost amongst which was a dread that Lady Saltwood would, in the failing state of her health, feel herself to be unequal to the strain of receiving his lordship. When, presently, Saltwood went up to the drawing-room, looking as though he had sustained a severe shock, Dorothea was seized by a conviction that her escapade had been disclosed to him, and she fled to the sanctuary of her bedchamber, and indulged in a hearty bout of tears. From this abyss of woe she was jerked by the unmistakable sounds of Augusta in strong hysterics. Hastily drying her cheeks, she ran down the stairs to render whatever assistance might be needed, and to support her parent through this ordeal. To her amazement, she found Lady Saltwood, whom she had left languishing on the sofa, not only upon her feet, but looking remarkably well. To her still greater amazement, the invalid folded her in the fondest of embraces, and said: 'Dearest, dearest child! I declare I don't know if I am on my head or my heels! *Rotherfield!* A countess! You sly little puss, never to have told me that you had met him! And not even out yet! You must be presented at once: *that* I am determined upon! He is coming to visit me tomorrow. Thank heaven you are just Augusta's size! You must wear the pomona silk dress Celestine has just made for her: I knew how it would be, the instant I brought you out! I was never so happy in my life!'

Quite bewildered, Dorothea said: 'Presented? Wear Augusta's new dress? Mama, *why*?'

'My innocent treasure!' exclaimed Lady Saltwood. 'Tell me, my love, for you must know I am scarcely acquainted with him, do you—do you *like* Lord Rotherfield?'

'Oh, Mama!' said Dorothea impulsively. 'He is exactly like Sir Charles Grandison, and Lord Orville, only far, far better!'

'Dearest Dorothea!' sighed her ladyship ecstatically. 'Charlie, do not stand there staring! Go and throw a jug of water over Augusta this instant! This is *not* the moment for hysterics!'

HAZARD

THE GIRL stood under the light of the guttering candles, still as a statue, her hands clasped in front of her, and no colour in her cheeks. She was dressed in a simple muslin gown with blue ribbons, and wore no ornament save the fillet threaded through her gold hair. She did not look at her half-brother, nor at any one of the five other men who were gathered round the table in the centre of the over-heated room. But she knew who was present; she had seen them all in the one swift glance she had cast at them under her lashes as she had entered the room. There was Lord Amberfield, sprawling over the table with his head pillowed on his arm; Mr Marmaduke Shapley, not so drunk as Amberfield, leaning on his chair and giggling; Sir Thomas Fort, a little blear-eyed, very purple in the face; Mr Lionel Winter, idiotically smiling; and Carlington Carlington with his black curls in disorder, and his exquisite cravat crumpled, his lean cheeks hectically flushed, and a reckless look in his bright eyes.

And there was Half-brother Ralph, in answer to whose peremptory summons she had got up out of her bed, and dressed herself, and come down to this stuffy room in the chill small hours. He was lounging back in his chair, still grasping the dice-box in one hand, while the other sought to refill his empty glass. Some of the wine slopped over on to the baize cloth that covered the table; Sir Ralph cursed it, and thrust the bottle on towards his left-hand neigh-

175

bour. 'Fill up, Lionel! Fill up!' he said, hiccuping. 'Now, my lord—now Carlington! You want to play on, hey? But I'm done-up, d'ye see? Only one thing left to stake, and that's m'sister!' A fit of insane laughter shook him; he made a gesture towards the girl, who stood motionless still, her gaze fixed on a point above Carlington's handsome head. 'I'll set her for my last stake, gen'lemen. Who'll cover?'

Mr Winter said: 'Tha's—tha's Miss Helen,' and nodded wisely.

'Damme, Morland, this—this is not right!' said Sir Thomas, getting on to his feet. 'Miss Morland—very obedient servant, ma'am! Amberfield—my lord! ladies present!'

He lurched towards the sleeping Viscount, and shook him by one shoulder. Lord Amberfield moaned, and muttered: 'Pockets to let: all my vowels in—in Carlington's hands.'

'Freddy, my boy, I'm saying it's not right. Can't stake a lady.'

Lord Amberfield said: 'Can't stake anything. Nothing to stake. Going to sleep.'

Mr Marmaduke Shapley clasped his head in his hands, as though to steady it, and said rather indistinctly: 'It's the wine. Confound you, Ralph, you're drunk!'

Sir Ralph gave a boisterous laugh, and rattled the dice in the box. 'Who'll cover?' he demanded. 'What d'ye say, Lionel? Will you have my jade of a sister to wife?'

Mr Winter rose to his feet, and stood precariously balancing on his heels. 'Sir,' he said, looking owlishly at his host, 'shall take leave to tell you—no one will cover prepost'rous stake!'

Sir Ralph's wicked eyes went past him to where Carlington sat, gazing at the girl under frowning, night-black brows. By the Marquis' left arm, stretched negligently before him on the table, scraps of paper were littered, vowels for the money he had won. There were rouleaus of guineas at his elbow, and more guineas spilled under his hand. Through Sir Ralph's blurred mind drifted a thought that he had never seen the young Marquis in so wild a humour before. He leaned forward, and said mockingly: 'Will you cover, my lord, or do you refuse the bet?'

Carlington's eyes turned slowly towards him. They were not glazed but unnaturally bright. 'I—refuse?' he said.

'There's the true elbow-shaker!' crowed Sir Ralph. 'Cover, Carlington! What's the jade worth?'

Mr Winter laid hold of his chair-back, and with difficulty enunciated four words: 'My lord, you're d-drunk!'

'Drunk or sober, no man shall set me a stake I won't cover,' Carlington answered. His long fingers closed over the heap of vowels, crushing them into a ball. He thrust them forward, and his rouleaus with them.

'Good God, Charles!' cried Sir Thomas, catching at his wrist. 'There's a matter of twenty thousand pounds there! Have sense, man, have sense!'

Carlington shook him off. 'A main, Morland, call a main!' he said.

'Seven!' Sir Ralph responded, and cast the dice on to the table.

Carlington laughed, and dived a hand into his pocket for his snuff-box, and flicked it open.

'Five to seven!' announced Mr Shapley, peering at the dice.

The girl's fixed gaze had wavered as the dice rattled in the box, and she had shot a swift glance downwards at the chance, as it lay on the table. Her brother gathered up the dice, shook them together and again threw them.

They rolled across the table, and settled into five and ace.

'Cinque-ace!' called Mr Shapley, constituting himself groom-porter. 'Any bets, gentlemen? any bets?'

No one answered; the Marquis took snuff.

The dice were shaken a third time, and cast. 'Quatre-trey!' called out Mr Shapley. 'Carlington, you've—you've the d-devil's own luck!'

The girl's eyes remained fixed for a moment on the four and the three lying on the green cloth; then she raised them, and looked across the table at Carlington.

The Marquis leaped up, and achieved a bow. 'Ma'am, I have won your hand in fair play!' he said, and stretched out his own imperatively.

Sir Ralph was staring at the dice, his lower lip pouting, and some of the high colour fading from his cheeks. Without a glance at him Miss Morland walked round the table, and curtsied, and laid her hand in Carlington's.

His fingers closed on it; he swung it gently to and fro, and said recklessly: 'It's time we were going. Will you come, my golden girl?'

Miss Morland spoke for the first time, in a composed, matter-of-fact voice. 'Certainly I will come, sir,' she said.

Carlington's eyes danced. 'I'm drunk, you know,' he offered.

'Yes,' she said.

He shook with laughter. 'By God, I like your spirit! Come, then!'

Sir Thomas started forward, lurched heavily against the table, and caught at it to steady himself. 'Damme, you're mad! Ralph, this won't do—bet's off—joke's a joke—gone far enough!'

'Play or pay!' the Marquis retorted, a smile not quite pleasant curling his lips.

Sir Ralph raised his eyes, and looked sullenly towards his sister. She returned his gaze thoughtfully, dispassionately, and transferred her attention to Carlington. 'I think,' she said tranquilly, 'I had better go and fetch a cloak if we are leaving now, sir.'

The Marquis escorted her to the door, and opened it, and set a shout ringing for his carriage. Miss Morland passed out of the hot room into the hall, and went across it to the stairs.

When she came down again some minutes later, cloaked, and with a chip hat on her head, and a bandbox in her hand, her brother had joined the Marquis in the hall, and was standing leaning against the lintel of the front door, scowling. The Marquis had put on a high-waisted driving-coat of drab cloth with row upon row of capes, and buttons of mother-of-pearl as large as crown-pieces. He had a curly-brimmed beaver, and a pair of York tan gloves in one hand, and his ebony cane in the other, and he flourished another bow at Miss Morland as she trod unhurriedly across the hall towards him.

'If you go, by God, you shan't return!' Sir Ralph said.

Miss Morland laid her hand on Carlington's proffered arm. 'I shall never return,' she said.

'I mean it!' Sir Ralph threatened.

'And I,' she replied. 'I have been in your ward three years. Do you think I would not sooner die than return to this house?'

He flushed, and addressed the Marquis. 'You're crazy to take her!'

'Crazy or drunk, what odds?' said Carlington, and opened the front door.

Sir Ralph caught at his coat. 'Where are you going?' he asked.

Carlington's wild laugh broke from him. 'Gretna!' he answered, and flung his arm about Miss Morland's waist, and swept her out of the house into the misty dawn.

His post-chaise and four was waiting, drawn up by the steps of the house, with the postilions shivering in their saddles, and one of Sir Ralph's servants holding the chaise door open.

The sharp morning air had an inevitable effect on the Marquis. He reeled, and had to catch at the footman's shoulder to steady himself. He was able, however, to flourish another bow in Miss Morland's direction, and to hand her up into the chaise.

Sir Ralph's house being situated at Hadley Green, and the Marquis having driven out from London to attend his card-party, the postilions had faced the chaise southwards. Upon receiving their master's order to drive to Gretna Green they were at first a great deal too astonished to do more than blink at him, but as, assisted by the footman, he began to climb up into the chaise, the boy astride one of the leaders ventured to point out that Gretna Green was some three hundred miles off, and his lordship totally unprepared for a long journey. The Marquis, however, merely reiterated: 'Gretna!' and entered the chaise, and sank down on to the seat beside Miss Morland.

The postilions were quite aware that their master was extremely drunk, but they knew him well enough to be sure that however much he might, in the morning, regret having ordered them to drive north he would blame them less for obeying him than for disregarding his instructions, and carrying him safely home. No sooner were the steps folded up than they wheeled the chaise, and set off in the direction of the Great North Road.

The Marquis let his hat slide on to the floor, and rested

his handsome head back against the blue velvet squabs. Turning it a little he smiled sweetly upon his companion, and said, still with a surprising clarity of diction: 'I've a notion I shall regret this, but I'm badly foxed, my dear— badly foxed.'

'Yes,' said Miss Morland. 'I know. It doesn't signify. I am quite accustomed to it.'

That was the sum of their discourse. The Marquis closed his eyes, and went to sleep. Miss Morland sat quite still beside him, only occasionally clasping and unclasping her hands in her lap.

Potter's Bar, Bell Bar, Hatfield were all passed. Miss Morland paid for the tickets at the turnpikes with some loose coins found in the sleeping Viscount's pockets. A little more than two miles out of Hatfield the chaise passed through the hamlet of Stanborough, and began the long rise of Digswell Hill. At the Brickwall pike the postilion mounted on one of the wheelers informed Miss Morland that if his lordship desired to press on horses must be changed at Welwyn. An attempt to rouse the Marquis was unavailing; he only groaned, and seemed to sink deeper into slumber. Miss Morland, who had had time to reflect upon the rashness of this flight, to which sheer anger had prompted her, hesitated for a moment, and then desired the postilions to drive to a respectable posting-house in Welwyn, where they might put up for what was left of the night.

In a little while the chaise had drawn up at the White Hart; the landlord had been awakened, and a couple of drowsy ostlers, still in their nightcaps, had lifted the Marquis out of the coach, and carried him up to a bed-chamber on the first floor.

No one seemed to feel very much surprise at this strange

arrival in the small hours of the morning. The Marquis, who was well-known to the landlord, was obviously drunk, and this circumstance provided a perfectly reasonable explanation for both his and Miss Morland's presence. 'Though I must say,' remarked the landlord, as he once more rejoined his sleepy wife, 'I didn't know he was one of them hard topers—not Carlington. Wild, of course, very wild.'

The Marquis did not wake until past nine o'clock. His first sensations were those of supreme discomfort. His head ached, and his mouth was parched. He lay for some time with closed eyes, but presently, as fuller consciousness returned to him, he became aware of being almost completely clad. He opened his eyes, stared filmily upon his strange surroundings, and with a groan sat up in bed, clasping his temples between his hands. He found that with the exception of his neckcloth and his shining Hessians he was indeed fully clad, the kind hands that had relieved him of boots and cravat having failed in their endeavour to extricate him from the perfectly fitting coat of Mr Weston's cutting.

After another dazed look round the room, the Marquis reached for the bell-pull, and tugged at it vigorously.

The summons was answered by the landlord in person. Carlington, still clasping his aching head, looked at him with acute misgiving and pronounced: 'I've seen your rascally face before. Where am I?'

The landlord smiled ingratiatingly, and replied: 'To be sure, my lord, your lordship is in the very best room at the White Hart.'

'Which White Hart?' demanded the Marquis irritably. 'I know of fifty at least!'

'Why, at Welwyn, my lord!'

'Welwyn!' ejaculated Carlington, letting his hands fall. 'What the devil am I doing in Welwyn?'

This question the landlord, who had had an illuminating conversation with the two postilions, thought it prudent to leave unanswered. He coughed, and said vaguely that he was sure he couldn't say. He waited for his noble client's memory to assert itself, but the Marquis, with another groan, merely sank back upon his pillows, and closed his eyes again. The landlord gave another cough, and said: 'The lady has ordered breakfast in a private parlour, my lord.'

The Marquis' eyes opened at that. 'Lady? What lady?' he said sharply.

'The—the lady who accompanies your lordship,' replied the landlord.

'My God!' said the Marquis, and clasped his head in his hands again. There was a pause. 'Oh, my God, what have I done?' said the Marquis. 'Where is she?'

'The lady, my lord, spent the night in the bedchamber adjacent to this, and awaits your lordship in the parlour. Your lordship—er—does not appear to have any trunk or cloak-bag.'

'I know that, curse you!' said the Marquis, casting off the coverlet, and setting his stockinged feet to the ground. 'Damnation take this head of mine! Help me out of this coat, fool!'

The landlord extricated him from it, not without difficulty, and suggested that his lordship might like to be shaved. 'For I have a very reliable lad, my lord, and should be honoured to lend your lordship my own razors.'

The Marquis had poured a jugful of hot water into the washbasin. 'Send him up, man, send him up!' he said. He dipped his head into the basin, but raised it again to say:

'My compliments to the lady, and I shall do myself the honour of joining her in half an hour.'

Downstairs in the private parlour Miss Morland had ordered breakfast for half-past nine. When the Marquis at last appeared she was drinking a cup of coffee, and looking as neat and as fresh as though she had had her maid with her, and several trunks of clothes.

The Marquis had been shaved, had had the creases pressed out of his coat, and had contrived to arrange his starched but crumpled cravat in decent folds, but he did not look very fresh. He was pale, and the reckless look had gone from his face, leaving it worried, and rather stern. He came into the parlour, and shut the door behind him, and paused with his hand still on the knob, looking across at Miss Morland with a mixture of remorse and bewilderment in his fine eyes.

Miss Morland's colour rose, but she said calmly: 'Good morning, sir. A very fine day, is it not?'

'I have not noticed whether it is fine or not,' replied Carlington. 'I have to beg your pardon, ma'am. I have no very clear recollection of what occurred last night. I was drunk.'

'Yes,' said Miss Morland, a slice of bread and butter halfway to her mouth. 'You explained that at the time. May I give you some coffee?'

He came to the table, and stood looking down at her in even greater bewilderment. 'Miss Morland, drunk I may have been, but was I so drunk that I forced you to accompany me to this place?'

'I came with you quite willingly,' she assured him.

He grasped the back of the chair before him. 'In God's name, what induced you to commit so imprudent an action?'

'You won me,' she explained. 'I was the stake set by my brother.'

'I remember,' he said. 'I must have been mad, and he——' He broke off. 'Good heavens, ma'am, that you should have been subjected to such an indignity!'

'It was not very pleasant,' she agreed. 'It seemed to me preferable to go away with you than to remain under that roof another hour.' She paused, and raised her eyes to his face. 'You have always treated me with a courtesy my brother does not accord me. Besides,' she added, 'you assured me that your intentions were honourable.'

'My intentions!' he exclaimed.

'Certainly, sir,' said Miss Morland, casting down her eyes to hide the gleam of mischief in them. 'You informed my brother that you would take me to Gretna Green. We are on our way there now.'

The Marquis pulled the chair out from the table, and sank down into it. 'Gretna Green!' he said. 'My dear girl, you don't know—— This is appalling!'

Miss Morland winced a little, but said in a considering voice: 'A little irregular, perhaps. But if I do not mind that I am sure you need not. You have a reputation for doing odd things, after all.'

He brought his open hand down on the table. 'If I have, the more reason for you to have refused to come with me on this insane journey! Were you mad, Miss Morland?'

'Oh, by no means!' she replied, cutting her bread and butter into thin strips. 'Of course, it is not precisely what I should have chosen, but you offered me a way of escape from a house in which I was determined not to spend another night.'

'You must have relatives—someone to whom——'

'Unfortunately I have no one,' said Miss Morland composedly.

The Marquis leaned his head in his hand, and said: 'My poor girl, you do not appear to realize the scandal this escapade will give rise to! I must get you to some place where you will be safe from it.'

Miss Morland bit into one of her strips of bread and butter. 'As your wife, sir, I shall expect you to protect me from slanderous tongues,' she said blandly.

The Marquis raised his head, and said with a groan: 'Helen, the notice of my engagement is in today's *Gazette*!'

There was just a moment's silence. The faintest tremor shook Miss Morland's hand, and she grew rather white. But when she spoke it was in a voice of mild interest. 'Dear me, then what can have possessed you to accept my brother's stake?'

He looked at her with a queer hungriness in his eyes, and answered: 'I have told you that I was drunk. Drunk, I only knew what I wanted, not what I must not do.' He got up, and began to walk about the room. 'No use talking of that. We are in the devil of a fix, my girl.'

'May I ask,' enquired Miss Morland, 'who is the lady to whom you are so lately become engaged?'

'Miss Fanny Wyse,' he answered. 'It is a long-standing arrangement. I can't, with honour, draw back from it. That accursed notice in the *Gazette*—It is impossible for me to repudiate it.'

She regarded him rather inscrutably. 'Are you attached to Miss Wyse, sir?'

'It is not that!' he said impatiently. 'Our parents made this match for us when we were in our cradles. It has been an understood thing. Yesterday I made a formal offer for Miss Wyse's hand, and she accepted me.'

'I suppose,' remarked Miss Morland thoughtfully, 'that your excesses last night were in the nature of a celebration?'

He gave an ugly little laugh. 'My excesses, ma'am, were an all too brief escape from reality!'

Miss Morland looked meditatively at the coffee-pot. 'If you do not care for Miss Wyse, my lord, why did you offer for her?'

'You don't understand!' he said. 'She has been brought up to think herself destined to become my wife! I could do no less than offer for her.'

'Oh!' said Miss Morland. 'Is she very fond of you?'

He flushed slightly. 'It is not for me to say. I believe—— I think she wishes to marry me.' A somewhat sardonic smile crossed his lips; he added: 'And God help both of us if ever this adventure should come to her ears!'

Miss Morland poured herself out some more coffee. 'Do you mean to abandon me, sir?' she asked.

'Certainly not,' replied his lordship. 'I shall put you in charge of a respectable female, and compel your brother to make provision for you.'

She raised her brows. 'But you told my brother you would marry me,' she pointed out.

He paused in his striding to and fro, and said: 'I can't marry you! God knows I would, but I can't elope with you the very day my engagement to Fanny is published!'

She smiled at that, but not very mirthfully, and got up from the table. 'Calm yourself, my lord. I have only been — punishing you a little. I came away with you because I was a great deal too angry to consider what I was about. What I really wish you to do is to convey me to London where I shall take refuge with my old governess.' She picked up her hat, and added: 'I think—I am sure—that she will be very willing to engage me to teach music and perhaps painting in her school.'

He strode over to the window, and with his back to her said: 'A Queen's Square boarding-school! Helen, Helen——' He broke off, biting his lips, and staring with unseeing eyes at a chaise that had just drawn up outside the inn. The chaise door opened, a young lady looked out, and the Marquis recoiled from the window with a startled oath.

Miss Morland was tying the strings of her cloak, and merely looked an enquiry.

'Fanny!' the Marquis ejaculated. 'Good God, what's to be done?'

Miss Morland blinked at him. 'Surely you must be mistaken!'

'Mistaken! Do you think I don't know my promised wife?' demanded his lordship savagely. 'I tell you it is she! Someone must have sent her word—that meddling fool, Fort, I dare say!'

'But surely Miss Wyse would not pursue you?' said Miss Morland, rather aghast.

'Wouldn't she?' said Carlington grimly. 'You don't know her! If she does not have hysterical spasms we may count ourselves fortunate!' He looked round the room, saw a door at the opposite end of it, and hurried across to open it. A roomy cupboard was disclosed. 'Go in there, my dear,' commanded Carlington. 'I must get hold of that landlord, and warn him to keep his mouth shut.' With which he thrust Miss Morland into the cupboard, closed the door on her, and went quickly towards the other leading into the coffee-room.

He was not, however, in time to warn the landlord. As he stepped out of the parlour that worthy was escorting Miss Wyse into the coffee-room.

Carlington, realizing that it would be useless now to deny his extraordinary elopement, greeted his betrothed with biting civility. 'Good morning, Fanny,' he said. 'An unexpected pleasure!'

Miss Wyse was a plump little lady, just nineteen years old, with huge, soulful brown eyes, and a riot of dark curls. When she saw Carlington she let fall a very pretty muff of taffeta, and clasped her hands to her bosom. 'You!' she gasped, with a strong suggestion of loathing in her voice. 'Carlington!'

The Marquis grasped her wrist in a somewhat cavalier fashion, and said angrily: 'Let me have no vapours, if you please! Come into the parlour!'

Miss Wyse uttered a throbbing moan. 'How *could* you, Granville? Oh, I wish I were dead!'

The Marquis fairly dragged her into the parlour, and shut the door upon the landlord's scarcely-veiled curiosity. 'You do not waste much time, Fanny,' he said. 'Is this a sample of what I am to expect in the future? The very day our engagement is announced!'

'Do not speak to me!' shuddered Miss Wyse, who seemed to have a leaning towards the dramatic. 'I am so mortified, so——'

'I know, I know!' he interrupted. 'But you would have done better to have stayed at home.'

Miss Wyse, who had tottered to the nearest chair, sprang up again at this, and said: 'No! Never! Do you hear me, Carlington? Never!'

'I hear you,' he replied. 'So, I imagine, can everyone else in the place. There is a great deal I must say to you, but this is not the moment. My whole object now is to avert a scandal. Explanations—oh yes, they will be hard enough to make!—can come later.'

'I don't care a fig for scandal!' declared Miss Wyse stormily. 'People may say what they please: it is nothing to me! But that I should find you here—that you should have —— Oh, it is cruel of you, Carlington!'

'I'm sorry, Fanny,' he said. 'You'll find the truth hard to believe, but I promise you you shall hear the truth from me. I beg of you, be calm! I will myself escort you back to town——'

'Do not touch me!' said Miss Wyse, retreating. 'You shan't take me back! I won't go with you!'

'Don't be such a little fool!' said the Marquis, exasperated. 'I warn you, this is no moment to play-act to me! I shall take you home, and there shall be no scandal, but help you to create a scene I will not!'

Miss Wyse burst into tears. 'I dare say you're very angry with me,' she sobbed, 'and I know I have behaved badly, but indeed, indeed I couldn't help it! I meant to be sensible —really, I did Carlington!—but I couldn't bear it! Oh, you don't understand! You've no s-sensibility at all!'

Rather pale, he answered: 'Don't distress yourself, Fanny. Upon my soul, there is no need! This escapade means nothing: I will engage to give you no cause for complaint when we are married.'

'I can't!' said Miss Wyse desperately. 'You shan't escort me home!'

He regarded her with a kind of weary patience. 'Then perhaps you will tell me what you do mean to do?' he said.

Miss Wyse lowered her handkerchief and looked boldly across at him. 'I'm going to Gretna Green!' she announced. 'And nothing you can say will stop me!'

'Have you taken leave of your senses?' he demanded. 'There's no question of going to Gretna! And if there were what in the name of heaven could possess you to go there?'

'I'm going to be married there!' said Miss Wyse in a rapt voice.

'Oh no, you are not!' replied the Marquis forcibly. 'Though it is just like you to do your best to turn everything to dramatic account! If you go to Gretna, you'll go alone!'

Miss Wyse gave a shriek at this. 'Good God, what do you mean to do?' she cried, running forward, and clasping her hands about his arm. 'Granville, I implore you, have mercy!'

The Marquis disengaged himself, looking down at her in the liveliest astonishment. Even supposing her to be on the verge of a fit of strong hysterics her behaviour seemed to him inexplicable. He was just about to inquire the reason for her last outburst when the door into the coffee-room was thrust open, and a young man in a bottle-green coat strode into the parlour, and checked on the threshold, staring in a challenging way at Carlington.

His bearing, though not his dress, proclaimed the soldier. He was about five-and-twenty years old, with a fresh, pleasant countenance, and a curly crop of brown hair brushed into the Brutus style made fashionable by Mr Brummell.

Carlington, turning his head to observe the newcomer, said somewhat irascibly: 'This, my good sir, is a private room!'

Miss Wyse released Carlington's arm, and sped towards the intruder, upon whose manly bosom she seemed more than half inclined to swoon. 'Henry!' she cried. 'This is Carlington himself!'

Henry said in a grave, rather conscious voice: 'I apprehended that it could be none other. I beg of you, however, not to be alarmed. My lord, I must request the favour of a few words with you alone.'

'Oh no, he will kill you!' quavered Miss Wyse, grasping the lapels of his coat.

The Marquis put a hand to his brow. 'Who the devil are you?' he demanded.

'I do not expect my name to be known to your lordship, but it is Dobell—Henry Dobell, Captain in the—the Foot, and at present on furlough from the Peninsula. I am aware that my action must appear to you desperate; of the impropriety of it I am, alas, miserably aware. Yet, my lord, I believe that when it is explained any man of sensibility must inevitably——'

The Marquis checked this flow of eloquence with an upflung hand. 'Captain Dobell, have you ever been badly foxed?' he said sternly.

'Foxed, sir?' repeated the Captain, quite taken aback.

'Yes, foxed!' snapped the Marquis.

The Captain gave a cough, and replied: 'Well, sir, well——! I must suppose that every man at some time or another——'

'*Have* you?' interrupted the Marquis.

'Yes, sir, I have!'

'Then you must know what it is to have a head like mine this morning, and I beg you'll spare me any more long-winded speeches, and tell me in plain words what you're doing here!' said Carlington.

Miss Wyse, finding herself out of the picture, thought it proper at this moment to interject: 'I love him!'

'You need not hang upon his neck if you do,' replied the Marquis unsympathetically. 'Is he a relative of yours whom you have dragged into this affair?'

'Relative! No!' said Miss Wyse, affronted. 'He is the man I love!'

'The man you——?' The Marquis stopped short. 'Good God, is this an elopement?' he demanded.

'But—but you know it is!' stammered Miss Wyse.

The Marquis, who had almost reeled under the shock, recovered himself, and came towards them. 'No, no, I'd not the least idea of it!' he said. 'I thought—— well, it's no matter what I thought. You must allow me to offer you my most sincere felicitations! Are you on your way to Gretna Green? Let me advise you to lose no time! In fact, I think you should set forward again at once. You may be pursued, you know.'

'But did *you* not come in pursuit of us, sir?' asked the astonished Captain.

'No, no, nothing of the sort!' replied the Marquis, grasping his hand, and wringing it fervently. 'You have nothing in the world to fear from me, my dear fellow. I wish you every imaginable happiness!'

'Every imaginable happiness?' cried Miss Wyse indignantly. 'Have you forgot that I am engaged to you, Carlington?'

'You will be much happier with Henry,' the Marquis assured her.

'The advertisement will be in today's *Gazette*!'

'Don't let that weigh with you! Is a mere advertisement to stand in the path of true love?' said the Marquis. 'I'll repudiate it immediately. Leave everything to me!'

'Don't you *want* to marry me?' gasped Miss Wyse.

'Not in the—— Not when your heart is given to another!' said his lordship, with aplomb.

'But Mama said—and your Mama too—and everybody—that I must accept you because you were desperately in love with me, and it had been understood for so many years! Only when I had done it I knew all at once

I couldn't bear it, and I sent for Henry, and——'

'Very right and proper,' approved his lordship. 'I could wish, of course, that you had sent for Henry before I wrote the advertisement for the *Gazette*, but never mind that now. The thing is for you to waste no time upon this journey.'

The Captain, who had been gazing upon his lordship in a bemused way, said in a much-moved voice: 'Sir, your generosity does you honour! An explanation of conduct which you must deem treacherous indeed is due to you.'

'No, no, pray don't explain anything to me!' begged the Marquis. 'My head is none too clear, you know. Let me take you out to your chaise!'

The Captain, finding himself propelled towards the door, hung back, and said: 'We stopped here to partake of breakfast, sir!'

'Not to be thought of!' said Carlington firmly. 'At any moment you may be overtaken, and Fanny wrested from your arms. You must make all possible speed to Gretna.'

The mere thought of being wrested from the Captain's arms caused Miss Wyse to add her entreaties to his lordship's. Captain Dobell, still faintly protesting, was swept out of the inn, informed that this was no time to be thinking of food and drink, and pushed up into his chaise. He made a second attempt to explain his elopement to Carlington, but at a sign from the Marquis the post-boys whipped up their horses, and the chaise bowled off down the street, with the Captain hanging out of the window and shouting a final message to the Marquis, the only words of which to reach him were 'everlasting gratitude' and 'eternally obliged'.

The Marquis turned back into the inn, and strode across the coffee-room to the parlour. Miss Morland had emerged from the cupboard, and was standing by the table, trying hard not to laugh. The Marquis said: 'Did you hear, Helen?'

She nodded. 'Yes. I couldn't help hearing,' she answered, a slight quaver in her otherwise solemn voice.

'We must go back to London at once,' said the Marquis.

'Yes,' agreed Miss Morland.

'For one thing,' said the Marquis, 'I want a change of clothes and for another this Gretna scheme was a piece of nonsense. I am not going to be married in company with that pair. We must have a special licence.'

'But we are not going to be married,' said Miss Morland. 'It was all a jest. I was mad—I never meant to come with you!'

'You had to come with me,' retorted the Marquis. 'I won you and you're mine.'

Miss Morland was trembling a little. 'But——'

'I have been in love with you for months, and you know it!' said the Marquis.

'Oh!' said Miss Morland on the oddest little sob. 'I did think sometimes that you were not—not indifferent to me, but indeed, indeed this is impossible!'

'Is it?' said the Marquis grimly. 'We'll see!'

It seemed to Miss Morland that he swooped on her. Certainly she had no time to escape. She was nipped into a crushing embrace, and kissed so hard and so often that she had no breath left to expostulate. The Marquis did at last stop kissing her, but he showed not the least inclination to let her go, but looked down into her eyes, and said in an awe-inspiring voice: 'Well? Are you going to marry me?'

Miss Morland, quite cowed by such treatment, meekly nodded her head.

SNOWDRIFT

A THIN COVERING of snow already lay on the ground when the Bath and Bristol Light Post Coach set out from Holborn at two o'clock in the afternoon of a bleak December day. Only two hardy gentlemen ventured to ride on the roof; and the inside passengers consisted only of a pessimistic man in a muffler, a stout lady with several bandboxes, a thickset young man with small eyes, and a jowl, a scarlet-coated young lady and a raw-boned countrywoman, who appeared to be her maid.

The scarlet-coated lady and the young man sat opposite each other, and occasionally exchanged glances of acute dislike. Upon their initial encounter in the yard of the White Horse Inn, the gentleman had uttered: '*You* going to Bath? Much good may it do you!' and the lady had retorted: '*You* travelling upon the stage, Joseph? I had thought you would have gone post!'

'I am not one to waste my substance,' had pronounced the gentleman heavily.

Since then they had indulged in no conversation.

The coach was making bad time. At Maidenhead Thicket the snowflakes were swirling dizzily, and the temperature had dropped to an uncomfortably low degree. The young man wrapped himself in a rug; the young lady hummed a defiant tune: she had not provided herself with a rug.

Slower and slower went the coach. At Reading the fat

woman got down, and her place was taken by a farmer, who said that he disremembered when there had been such another hard winter, and prophesied that the roads would be six foot under snow by Christmas. The pessimist said that he had known at the outset that they would never reach their destination.

The coach laboured on, but past Theale actually picked up its pace a little, and for perhaps ten minutes encouraged the passengers to suppose that the weather was clearing. Then the snow began to fall more thickly still, the coachman lost his bearings, and the whole equipage lurched off the road into a deep drift.

It was thrown on to its side with some violence. The two outside passengers were hurled over the hedge into a field, and those inside landed in a heap on the near-side door.

The thickset young man was first to extricate himself, and to force open the off-side door. He scrambled through it, rudely thrusting the pessimist out of the way, floundered into deep snow, and fell upon his face, a circumstance which afforded the pessimist a sour pleasure.

The farmer and the young lady were too much occupied with the abigail, who had fallen awkwardly, to notice this interlude. The abigail said in a faint voice: 'I've broke my leg, Miss Sophy.'

'Oh, Sarah, do not say so!' besought her mistress.

'Well, it's just what she has done,' said the farmer frankly. 'We'll have to get her out of this, missie.' He hauled himself up to look out through the open door, and shouted: 'Hi, you! Come and lend a hand with the poor wench here! Lively, now!'

Thus adjured, the thickset young man came back to the coach, asking rather ungraciously what was wanted. He seemed disinclined to lend his aid, and the scarlet-coated young lady, who had been trying unavailingly to move her henchwoman into an easier position, raised a flushed face in which two large gray eyes sparkled with wrath, and uttered: 'You are the most odious wretch alive, Joseph! Help to lift Sarah out this instant, or I shall tell my grandfather how disobliging you have been!'

'You may tell him what you choose—*if* you reach Bath, which you are not now very likely to do, my dear cousin!' retorted Joseph.

'You hold your gab, and do what I tell you!' interposed the farmer. 'Jump out first, missie: you'll only be in my way here!'

Miss Trent, pausing only to pick up her cousin's abandoned rug, allowed herself to be hoisted through the door. Joseph received her from the farmer, and lost no time in setting her down. Her feet sank above the ankles in the snow, but the pessimistic man helped her to reach the road. By the time she had spread the rug out on the snow Sarah had been extricated from the coach, and the coachman was helping the guard to unharness one of the leaders.

Sarah was laid on the rug; Miss Trent, her bonnet fast whitening under the gathering flakes, knelt beside her; and the coachman informed the assembled company that there was no need for anyone to worry, since the guard would ride on at once to Woolhampton, and get some kind of a vehicle to fetch them all in.

This speech greatly incensed the pessimistic man, who demanded to be told when the next coach to Bath was due. The coachman said: 'Lor' bless you, sir, we'll be snowbound a week, I dessay! Nothing won't get beyond Reading, not if this weather holds!'

There was a general outcry at this; Miss Trent exclaimed: 'Snowbound a week! But I *must* reach Bath tomorrow!'

'Can one hire a chaise in Woolhampton?' asked Joseph suddenly.

'Well, you *might* be able to,' acknowledged the coachman.

'I'll ride in with the guard!' Joseph decided.

Miss Trent started. Stretching up a hand, she grasped a fold of his coat, saying sharply: 'Joseph, if you mean to go on by chaise you'll take me with you?'

'No, by God!' he retorted. '*I* didn't ask you to come to Bath, and *I* shan't help you to get there! You may hire a chaise for yourself!'

'You know I haven't enough money!' she said, in a low, trembling voice.

'Well, it's no concern of mine,' he said sulkily. 'A pretty fool I should be to take you along with me! Besides, you can't go without your woman.'

Miss Trent's eyes were bright with tears, but she would not let them fall. She said passionately: 'I'll get to Bath if I have to *trudge* there, Joseph—and then we shall see!'

He responded to this merely with a jeering laugh, and moved away to confer with the guard. Miss Trent made no further attempt to detain him, and in a very few minutes he had ridden off with the guard in the direction of Woolhampton.

With the departure of the guard a new and more fearful mood descended upon the coachman. He became obsessed by the idea that highwaymen would descend upon the wrecked coach, grasped his blunderbuss nervously, started at shadows, and ended by firing the weapon at the mere sound of muffled hoofbeats.

The sound of horses plunging and snorting was almost immediately followed by the appearance round the bend in the road of a curricle and pair, which drew up alongside the coach. A wrathful voice demanded: 'What in hell's name do you mean by firing at me you fat-witted, cow-handed ensign-bearer?'

The coachman, reassured by this form of address, lowered his weapon, and said that he was sure he begged pardon. The gentleman in the curricle, having by this time taken in the group by the wayside, briefly commanded the groom beside him to go to the horses' heads, and himself jumped down from the curricle, and approached Miss Trent, still kneeling beside her stricken attendant. 'Can I be of assistance, ma'am?' he asked. 'How is she hurt?'

'I very much fear that she has broken her leg,' Miss Trent replied worriedly. 'She is my maid, and I am a wretch to have brought her!'

The gentleman, whose momentary outburst of wrath had swiftly given place to an air of languor which seemed habitual, said calmly: 'Then I had better take you both up, and convey you to the nearest town.'

Miss Trent said impulsively: 'Would you do that, sir? I should be so very grateful! Not only on poor Sarah's account, but on my own! I *must* reach the next town quickly!'

'In that case,' responded the gentleman, rather amused, 'let us waste not a moment. I'll drive you into Newbury.'

The farmer and the pessimistic man, both applauding this scheme, at once volunteered to extricate Miss Trent's baggage from the boot, and to strap it on to the back of the curricle; Sarah was soon lifted up into the carriage, and made as comfortable as possible; and the groom, resigning himself to a most uneasy drive, perched on the baggage behind.

Miss Trent, squeezed between Sarah and her very tall and broad-shouldered rescuer, bade farewell to her old travelling companions, and looked buoyantly towards the future.

This seemed, at the moment, to consist only of snow-flakes. The light, moreover, was beginning to fail, so that she would not have been surprised had the curricle, like the coach, plunged off the road into a drift. But its driver seemed to be very sure of his ability to keep the track, and drove his pair along at a steady pace, his eyes, between narrowed lids, fixed on the road ahead.

'How well you drive!' remarked Miss Trent, with a sort of impulsive candour, as engaging as it was naïve.

A slight smile touched his lips. 'Thank you!'

'I do trust we shall reach Newbury,' confided Miss Trent. 'For one thing, I must have poor Sarah attended to, and for another, I *must* get to Bath!'

'I collect that it is of importance to you to reach Bath immediately?'

'Of vital importance!' asserted Miss Trent.

'You might be able to hire a chaise,' he suggested. 'I fear there will be no stage-coaches running for some days.'

'That,' said Miss Trent bitterly, 'is what my cousin means to do! *He* can afford it, and he knows very well I cannot, and he won't take me along with him. He is an odious man!'

'He sounds quite abominable,' agreed the gentleman gravely. 'Is he one of the unfortunates we were obliged to leave by the wayside?'

'Oh, no! He rode off with the guard to Woolhampton. Trying to steal a march on me, of course!' She added, on an explanatory note: 'He has eyes like a pig's, and his name is Joseph.'

'How shocking! One scarcely knows whether to feel pity or disgust.'

Miss Trent knew no such uncertainty. 'He is a hateful wretch!' she declared.

'In that case it is unthinkable that he should be permitted to steal a march on you. May I know your name? Mine is Arden.'

'Yes, of course! I should have told you before,' she said. 'I am Sophia Trent. Do you live near here? I have come all the way from Norfolk!'

Never before had Sir Julian Arden announced his identity with so little effect! Indeed, it was seldom that he was put to the trouble of announcing it at all. Not only was he the acknowledged leader of Fashion, a crack shot, and a nonpareil amongst whips: he was quite the most eligible bachelor in Society as well. He had been toadied all his life; every eccentricity was forgiven him; every door flew open at his approach. Mothers of likely daughters had laid siege to him for the past ten years; while the efforts of damsels of marriageable age to engage his interest were as ingenious as they were unavailing. He was so bored that nothing kept his interest alive for more than a fleeting moment. Very little, indeed, had the power to rouse his interest at all. But Miss Trent had achieved this feat quite unconsciously. His name meant nothing to her.

He permitted himself one swift glance down at her before resuming his steady scrutiny of the road ahead. There was not a shadow of guile in the big eyes, which met his in a friendly smile. Miss Trent was merely awaiting an answer. He said: 'No I live for the most part in London.'

'But you did not come from London today, in this weather!'

'You see,' he said apologetically, 'someone laid me odds I would not venture on it.'

'And you set out, in an open carriage, for such a reason as that! I beg your pardon, but it seems quite nonsensical!'

He appeared to be much struck by this view of the matter. 'Do you know, ma'am, I believe you are right?'

'I *think*,' said Miss Trent severely, 'that you are quizzing me. Is your destination Newbury?'

'My present destination, yes. We shall forget my original one. I daresay I should have been very much bored there.'

'But your friends will wonder what has become of you!'

'It need not concern us, however.'

This indifferent answer made her blink, but she forbore to press the matter, and chatted away on a number of unexceptionable topics. She held Sarah in one arm, and appeared to be more concerned for the maid's comfort than her own, assuring Sir Julian that she thought the whole episode a famous adventure.

'You see, my home is quite in the country,' she explained, and nothing exciting ever seems to happen, except when Bertram broke his leg, and Ned was thrown over the donkey's head into the horse-pond. Thieves did once steal three of my stepfather's best hens, but we knew nothing about it until the next day, so it was not precisely exciting.'

Entranced by this artless confidence, Sir Julian at once enquired into the identities of Bertram and Ned. He discovered that they were two of Miss Trent's three half-brothers, and that her stepfather was the incumbent of a parish in Norfolk. She had two young half-sisters as well, and very little prompting was needed to induce her to expatiate on their many engaging qualities. In this way the journey to Newbury was largely beguiled, and when Sir Julian turned his horses in under the archway of the great

Pelican Inn, a mile short of the town, Miss Trent exclaimed that she had not thought it possible they could have arrived so soon.

A number of ostlers and waiters came hurrying to serve the newcomer, and in a very short while Sarah had been carried up to a bedchamber, a groom sent off to summon the nearest surgeon to her aid, and a private parlour bespoken for Miss Trent.

She came down to it presently, and found her protector warming himself before a leaping fire. He had shed his hat, and his many-caped greatcoat, and Miss Trent, who had already formed a very good opinion of his person, now perceived that he was decidedly handsome. He was dressed in a coat of blue superfine, which more experienced eyes than Miss Trent's would have recognized as coming from the hands of a master; his buckskins were of impeccable cut; and his cravat was tied in the intricate style that had long baffled all imitators.

Sir Julian was also pleased with what he saw. Now that she had removed her bonnet, and he beheld her in the full candlelight, he perceived that Miss Trent's hair grew in profuse ringlets, and that her eyes were even bigger than he had supposed them to be. He liked the frank way they lifted to his, and found it refreshing, to say the least of it, to encounter a lady who was neither arch nor simpering, and who had obviously not the smallest notion of enslaving him.

She let him lead her to a chair by the fire, and said: 'I have made up my mind to it that the most important thing is for me to reach Bath, sir. I did think at first that I ought not to spend the money I have put by for my fare back to Norwich, but I now feel this would be foolish. So I shall hire a chaise to take me on. Do you think I shall be able to go tonight? I know the coaches travel by night, and the mails too.'

'Nothing travels at night in such weather as this, ma'am. It has been snowing here, I discover, for three days. However, local opinion seems to be that a change is coming, so we must hope that the snow may have ceased to fall by tomorrow.'

'Oh!' said Miss Trent, dashed. She hesitated, and then asked shyly: 'How much will it cost me, do you think, sir, to stay here tonight?'

'As to that,' he replied, 'I have informed the landlord that you are a young relative of mine, travelling in my charge. I think he will expect me to pay your shot, don't you?'

'No!' said Miss Trent, with decision.

'I meant, I need hardly say, a loan!' explained Sir Julian.

Miss Trent, her mind relieved, thanked him, and adjured him to keep a strict account of any sums he might incur on her behalf. He promised most gravely to do so, and an understanding being thus reached Miss Trent was able to relax, and to sip the Madeira he had given her. 'Then all that remains to be done,' she said, 'is to hire a chaise in the morning, for the landlady says she will take care of Sarah for me, so I may be easy on that head.'

'You may be easy on both heads,' Sir Julian said. 'I propose to escort you to Bath tomorrow myself, whatever the weather.'

Miss Trent was too unsophisticated to conceal her pleasure at this prospect. 'Will you indeed?' she cried, warm gratitude in her eyes. 'I do think you are the kindest person I have ever met, sir! But ought you not rather to join your friends?'

'Certainly not,' he replied. 'A very dull set of people! My whole desire is to revisit Bath.'

At this moment the waiter came in to announce the arrival of a surgeon, and Miss Trent went off to lead this practitioner up to the sufferer. When she returned to the parlour, the table had been laid, and dinner awaited her. She made an excellent repast. She said that Sarah must not travel for a few days, but that she was much easier now the limb had been set. 'So there is nothing for it but to leave her here, poor thing!' she said. 'She says she will do very well, but I feel the veriest *brute*! But if my cousin were to get to Bath before me there is no saying what might happen! He would serve me a back-handed turn if he could!'

'But what has engendered this violent antipathy between you, ma'am?' asked Sir Julian, a good deal amused.

'We both want the same thing,' said Miss Trent darkly, 'and he is afraid that I shall get it! But I have detested him all my life.'

She did not stay in the parlour for long after the covers had been removed, but retired early to bed, leaving her protector still ignorant of what her business in Bath could be.

Local prophecy turned out to be exact. It stopped snowing during the night, and although the landscape was thickly shrouded next morning, the sky had lost its leaden hue, and the sun showed some faint signs of breaking through the clouds. Miss Trent came down to breakfast in a mood of high hope. 'I believe it will turn out to be a beautiful day, sir!' she announced. 'And if you will really be so obliging as to escort me to Bath, we may go in your curricle!'

'It would be far too cold for you,' he said.

'No, indeed, I should like it of all things,' she insisted. 'And only think what a deal of expense you may save!'

Sir Julian, who had never in his life considered such a sordid matter, agreed to it meekly, and went out into the yard after breakfast to give orders to his groom.

It was while he was engaged in the stables that Mr Joseph Selsey arrived at the Pelican, having plodded all the way on foot from Woolhampton, carrying his valise. It was perhaps not surprising that he should be in an evil humour, but the head groom made no allowance for this circumstance. Peremptory persons looking suspiciously like provincial merchants would get no extraordinary attention from the Pelican's supercilious servants. No post-chaise, stated the groom, would leave the inn that day. It was not until Mr Selsey had dragged the landlord into the dispute that he was able to hire, not a chaise, but a saddle-horse.

He was obliged to be satisfied, and to trust that he might be able to exchange the horse for a chaise in Hungerford. He then called for hot coffee to be brought him whilst the horse was being saddled, and in crossing the hall of the inn came upon Miss Trent, issuing from the parlour.

He stopped short, staring at her. 'So this is where I find you?' he ejaculated. 'Fine doings, miss! Very pretty behaviour, upon my word!'

'Why, what is wrong?' she demanded.

'Of course *you* would not know!' he said, with one of his jeering laughs. 'But it is of all of a piece! By anything I ever heard, your mother was just such another, always ready to run off with any man who offered!'

'How *dare* you?' cried Miss Trent, her eyes blazing.

Sir Julian, who had come in from the yard in time to overhear this passage of arms, here interposed, saying in his languid way: 'Ah, so this is your cousin Joseph, is it? Dear me, yes! Come with me, sir!'

'Why should I?' demanded Mr Selsey, taken aback.

'That you shall see,' said Sir Julian, leading the way out into the yard.

Mr Selsey followed him in some bewilderment, and Miss Trent, running back into the parlour to peep above the blind, had the felicity of seeing her objectionable relative dropped sprawling in the snow by a blow from Sir Julian's famous right.

Mr Selsey picked himself up and bored in furiously. Sir Julian side-stepped neatly and dropped him again. This time Mr Selsey remained on the ground, nursing his jaw.

'And let that be a lesson to you not, in future, to insult a lady!' said Sir Julian calmly.

Mr Selsey, uneasily measuring the size and style of his opponent, said sulkily: 'I didn't mean—that is, I didn't know——'

'You know now,' said Sir Julian, and turned, and went back into the inn.

He was met by Miss Trent, her face aglow with admiration. '*Thank you!*' she said. 'I have been wanting to do that all my life!'

'What, did you see it, then?' he asked, startled.

'Yes, through the window. I clapped my hands! I wonder you did not hear me!'

He flung back his head and laughed. 'You incorrigible child, you should be in a swoon, or indulging in a fit of the vapours!'

'Pooh, as though I had not seen Bertram and Ned at fisticuffs a score of times! When do we set forward?'

'In about half an hour, if you can be ready then.'

'Should we not go at once? I am sure Joseph will be off now without waiting for his coffee!'

'Very likely, but you have no need to be uneasy: we shall overtake him soon enough.'

They overtook him even sooner than Sir Julian had expected. Only fifteen miles from Newbury, where the road passed between the great trees of Savernake Forest, a solitary figure came into view, leading a very lame nag.

'It's Joseph!' exclaimed Miss Trent. '*Poor* Joseph!' she added piously.

'Humbug!' retorted Sir Julian, a note in his voice no other lady had as yet been privileged to hear.

She laughed. Mr Selsey, upon hearing the muffled beat of horses' hooves, wheeled about, and, although he must have perceived who was driving the curricle, placed himself in its way, and waved his arms. Sir Julian drew up, and sat looking down at him with a sardonic lift to his brows.

'Sir,' said Mr Selsey in a voice of deep chagrin, 'I find myself forced to request you to take me up as far as to the next town!'

'But you cannot leave the poor horse!' said Miss Trent. 'Besides, it belongs to the Pelican!'

'No, it does not!' said her cousin angrily. 'It belongs to a rascally thief! He took my horse and my purse, and left me with this jade!'

'A highwayman? Oh, what an adventure!' cried Miss Trent.

Mr Selsey ground his teeth.

'You have only three or four miles to walk before you reach Marlborough,' said Sir Julian helpfully. 'Stand away from my horses' heads!'

'But I have no money!' shouted Mr Selsey.

Sir Julian's pair began to move forward. Miss Trent

said quickly: 'No, no, we can't leave him in such a case! It would be too shabby!'

Sir Julian glanced curiously down at her earnest little face. 'Do you wish him to reach Bath?'

'Yes!' said Miss Trent resolutely.

'Very well. I will leave word with the landlord of the Castle Inn, sir, and he will provide you with a conveyance,' said Sir Julian, and drove on.

Mr Selsey, by no means content, bawled after the curricle: 'And you stole my rug, you hussy!'

'Oh, dear!' said Miss Trent, dismayed. 'It is quite true, I did! We ought to have taken him up, perhaps!'

'Nonsense! A walk will do him good.'

'Yes, but if his purse has been taken he won't be able to hire a chaise, even if you do bespeak one!' objected Miss Trent.

'Have no fear! I will arrange the whole, since you wish it.'

'I think you have the most extravagant notions!' said Miss Trent severely. 'And, pray, how am I ever to repay you?'

'Very easily.'

'No, how?'

'By satisfying my curiosity and telling me why we are racing Joseph to Bath!'

'Did I not do so?' she cried, astonished. 'I quite thought I had explained it to you! I have the greatest hope that I may win a fortune!'

'Then in that case you will be able to pay your debts, and you have nothing to worry about,' said Sir Julian, only the merest quiver in his voice betraying him.

'Yes, but I shan't win it quite immediately,' she said. 'Not until my grandfather dies, and although he seems to think that will be soon, there is no telling, after all!'

'Very true. Are we going to call upon your grandfather?'

'Yes, and I fear he will prove to be very disagreeable.'

'Are *all* your relatives disagreeable persons, Miss Trent?' he enquired.

'Certainly not! Mama, and my stepfather, and the children are the dearest creatures!' she replied. 'In fact, it is for them that I am going to Bath. If only my grandfather likes me better than Joseph, the boys may go to Eton, and Clara have lessons upon the pianoforte, and Mama another servant, and Papa—— But this cannot interest you, sir!'

'On the contrary. And is Joseph also bent on winning this fortune?'

'Yes, and he does not need it in the least! You see, the case is that my grandfather quarrelled with both his daughters—my mama, and Joseph's mama—because they married men he did not like. Mama says he was determined they should make splendid matches, and they did not. Mama ran away with my papa to Gretna Green— only fancy! He died when I was a baby, and I believe that he was not a very *steady* person. He was related to Lord Cleveland, and in the 1st Foot, only his family cast him off. So, I think, did the 1st Foot,' she added reflectively. 'Mama says he was very wild.'

'Most of that family are,' interpolated Sir Julian.

'Oh, are they? I have never known them. Papa left poor Mama in sad straits, and if it had not been for my step-father I don't know what would have become of her. He married her, you see, and they are most happy! But Papa has a very small stipend, and there are five children, besides me, so that when my grandfather suddenly wrote to say that he felt his end to be approaching, and since he must leave his fortune to someone, I might go to spend

Christmas with him, and perhaps he would leave it to me, it seemed as though it was my duty to go! And then I found that he must have sent for Joseph too, but I do think that he may like me better than Joseph, don't you, sir?'

'Miss Trent,' said Sir Julian, 'unless your grandfather is mad, you need have no doubts on that head!'

'Yes, but *I* think he is!' said Miss Trent candidly.

'Who is he? What is his name?'

'Kennet, and he lives in Laura Place.'

'Good God, not the Miser of Bath?'

'Oh, are you acquainted with him, sir?'

'Only by reputation! Bath used to be full of tales of his oddities. I fear it is you who will not like him!'

'No, but in such a cause one must stifle one's feelings!' said Miss Trent.

He agreed to it with becoming gravity, and for some miles entered in the fullest manner into all her plans for the advancement of her family.

The journey was a long one, and the weather inclement enough to have daunted most females, but Miss Trent remained cheerful throughout. Sir Julian, who had been sure, twenty-four hours earlier, that he had run through every emotion life could hold for him, realized by the time the outskirts of Bath were reached that he had fallen in love for the first time since his salad days.

It was dark when the curricle drew up before a house in Laura Place, and the street lamps had been lit. 'Tired?' Sir Julian said gently.

'A very little,' owned Miss Trent. 'But you must be quite dead with fatigue, sir!'

'I have never enjoyed a day more.'

Miss Trent said shyly: 'I—I have not either!'

'In that case,' said Sir Julian, 'let us go in and beard your grandfather!'

'You too, sir?' she asked doubtfully.

'Certainly. I must ask his permission to pay my addresses to you.'

'To—to——? Oh!' said Miss Trent in a faint voice.

'Yes, may I do so?'

Miss Trent swallowed. 'I have the most lowering feeling that I ought to say it is too sudden, or—or something of that nature,' she confided.

'Say what is in your heart! Would it displease you to receive my addresses?'

'Well, no, it—it wouldn't *displease* me—precisely!' confessed Miss Trent, blushing in the darkness.

'Then let us instantly seek out your grandfather!' he said gaily.

They were admitted into the house by an aged retainer who reluctantly showed them into a bleak parlour on the ground floor. He left them with a single candle. Miss Trent said: 'It is not very—very welcoming, do you think?'

'Most quelling!' said Sir Julian.

In a few minutes the door opened again to admit a buxom lady of uncertain years and improbable golden ringlets. She said without preamble: 'Are you Mr Kennet's Sophia? He's that forgetful he must have forgotten to write! However, if you want to see him you may! Step upstairs with me, dearie! Don't tell me this is Joseph you have brought with you!'

'Who—who are you? gasped Miss Trent, utterly taken aback.

The lady bridled. 'The name's Flint,' she said. 'But I'm changing it. I *was* your grandpa's housekeeper.'

'Oh!' said Miss Trent. 'Then will you have the

goodness to take me to my grandfather, if you please?'

Mrs Flint sniffed, but turned to lead the way up one pair of stairs. She opened a door giving on to a large parlour, and said: 'Here's your granddaughter, Mr K!'

From a winged arm-chair by the fire a desiccated old gentleman peered at Miss Trent. 'Well, it's no use her coming here, because I've altered my mind,' he said. 'Maria's girl, hey? Damme if you don't look like her!'

Mrs Flint, who had taken up a position beside his chair, said with a simper: 'Me and Mr K. is going to be married.'

'It'll be cheaper,' explained Mr Kennet simply.

Miss Trent sank nervelessly into the nearest chair. Mr Kennet was meanwhile subjecting Sir Julian to a severe scrutiny. 'A fine buck you've turned out to be!' he pronounced. 'What's your name? Joseph?'

'No,' said Sir Julian. 'My name is Julian Arden.'

Both Mr Kennet and his prospective bride stared very hard at him. 'Mr K., if it isn't Beau Arden himself!' palpitated the lady.

'Are you the son of Percy Arden, who was up at Oxford with me? demanded Mr Kennet. 'Sir Julian Arden?'

'I am,' said Sir Julian.

'What do you want?' asked the old gentleman suspiciously.

'To marry your granddaughter,' replied Sir Julian coolly.

This intelligence produced an instant change in Mr Kennet's attitude. He rubbed his dry hands together and ejaculated: 'That's good! That's the girl! Come and give me a kiss, Sophy! I'm proud of you, and I'm sorry I said you was like your mother! Damme if I don't do something handsome by you!'

Miss Trent, submitting unwilling to his embrace, was feeling too dazed by the shocks of the past few minutes to speak, but at this her eyes lit with a faint hope.

'I will!' said Mr Kennet, with the air of one reaching a painful decision. 'You shall have your grandmother's pearls!'

'When we're dead and gone, Mr K.,' interpolated the future Mrs Kennet firmly.

'Yes,' agreed Mr Kennet, perceiving the wisdom of this. 'And I'll give her my poor Charlotte's garnet brooch for a bride gift, what's more! I can't lay my hand on it at the moment, but I'll send it. Where are you putting up, my dear?'

Sir Julian, perceiving that Miss Trent was quite stunned, took her hand in a comforting hold, and said: 'She will be staying at the Christopher, sir. And now I think we must take our leave of you.'

Mr Kennet brightened still more at finding that he was not expected to entertain his grandchild and her betrothed to dinner, and said that if she liked she might come to visit him again before she left Bath. 'But I won't have your cousin Joseph coming to batten on me!' he added, suddenly querulous.

'Which leads one to wonder,' remarked Sir Julian, when he had extricated Miss Trent from the house, 'what is to become of Joseph!'

'What is to become of *me*?' said Miss Trent, wringing her hands.

'You are going to marry me.'

'Yes—I mean—— But poor Mama! Bertram! Dear Ned! I have no *right* to be so happy when I have failed so miserably!'

He lifted her up into the curricle. 'My little love, you

have not so far given my circumstances a thought, but I must inform you that I am accounted to be extremely wealthy. Bertram, and Ned, and Tom shall go to Eton, and Oxford, and anywhere else you may choose; and Clara shall have her lessons on the pianoforte; and your mama shall have a dozen maids; and——'

'Good God, you cannot be as rich as that!' cried Miss Trent, quite frightened.

'Much richer!' he averred, mounting on to the box beside her.

'But you must not marry *me*!' she said, in great distress. 'There must be dozens of *eligible* females whom you should rather marry!'

'I am not the Grand Turk!' he protested.

'No, no, but you know I have no expectations!'

'I know nothing of the sort,' he said, possessing himself of her hand, and kissing it. 'You are to inherit your grandmother's pearls! But if I were you,' he added, gathering up the reins, 'I would not build too much upon that garnet brooch, my love!'

FULL MOON

Lord Stavely prepared to descend from his chaise.

'We will stop here,' he announced.

It was certainly a charming inn. It stood at the end of the broad village street, with two great elms behind it and roses rambling over its old red brick frontage. It was not, of course, a posting house, which did not incline the two postilions in its favour. One of them said: 'If we was to drive on for another mile or two, we'd likely find a decent house for your honour to bait at.'

'My dear good fellow,' replied his lordship, 'you have no more notion of where we are than I have. Here we will stop. I like the place.'

The village seemed asleep in the moonlight, not a soul stirring. But the sound of carriage wheels brought the landlord out of the inn, all anxiety to oblige. Lord Stavely, alighting from the chaise, said: 'Arcadia, I presume. Tell me, what is the time?'

The landlord, slightly taken aback, said that it lacked but ten minutes to the hour.

'But what hour?' asked his lordship.

'Why, nine o'clock, sir!'

'How shocking! Am I anywhere in the neighbourhood of Melbury Place?'

'Melbury Place?' repeated the landlord. 'Yes, that you are, sir; it lies only a matter of ten miles from here, though the road's tricky, as you might say.'

'After the experiences of today, I should probably use a more forceful epithet. I imagine it will take me nearly an hour to reach the place. Obviously it behoves me to dine here. Or am I too late for dinner?'

The landlord was not one to turn away distinguished custom from his door. This gentleman, with his high crowned beaver hat, his driving coat of many capes, worn negligently open over a neat blue coat, a cut Venetian waistcoat, and the palest of fawn pantaloons, was plainly a member of the Quality. He assured Lord Stavely that, if he would step into the coffee-room, dinner should be served him in a very few minutes. A qualm then attacked him, and he faltered: 'I'm sorry I can't show your honour to a private parlour, but there's only Mr Tom in the coffee-room, after all.'

'Then if Mr Tom does not take exception to me, I shall do very well,' said his lordship. 'I wonder if I should remain here for the night? Shall I endear myself on my host by presenting myself at past eleven o'clock at night?'

'They do keep very early hours up at the Place, by what I hear, sir,' offered the landlord hopefully. 'Was the Squire expecting of you, sir?'

'He was, and I trust still is. Your manner leads me to fear that he will not be pleased by my tardy arrival?'

'Well, sir, begging your pardon, Squire is that pernickety in his ways, and—in a manner of speaking—a testy gentleman—not meaning any disrespect, I'm sure!'

'In fact, I shall *not* endear myself to him by arriving famished on his doorstep at dead of night. Very well. I'll put up here, then.'

The landlord, mentally resolving to have the best sheets instantly put on the bed in the larger of his two guest chambers, ushered his lordship into the coffee-room.

It had only one occupant, a young gentleman who sat in the window embrasure, with a bottle of brandy on the ledge beside him, and a glass in his hand. The landlord, casting a rather worried glance at the bottle, murmured that Mr Tom would not object to a gentleman's dining in the coffee-room. Mr Tom blinked at Lord Stavely, and inclined his head with dignity. He then resumed his scrutiny of the moon-washed street.

His lordship returned the civility by a slight bow, and a smile hovering about his mouth, but made no attempt to lure Mr Tom into conversation. It was apparent to him that care sat upon the young gentleman's brow. It would have been apparent to someone far less acute than Lord Stavely that Mr Tom was, very properly, drowning his troubles in brandy. He might have been any age between nineteen and twenty-five; he was certainly not older. Leanings towards dandyism were betrayed by the intricate but not entirely successful arrangement of his cravat, and by the inordinate height of his shirt collar, whose starched points reached almost to his cheek-bones. But there was little of the dandy in his sturdy figure and fresh-complexioned countenance. He looked like the son of a country gentleman, which, indeed, he was, and as though he would be very much at home in the hunting-field, or with a gun over his shoulder.

In a short time the landlord laid a simple but very tolerable meal before his new guest, and himself waited upon him. Lord Stavely pronounced the fare to be excellent, commended the burgundy, and tactfully declined the only port offered him on the score that he did not wish to encourage a tendency to the gout. He did not look as though he suffered from gout, or any other ailment; in fact, he looked as healthy as any other man of thirty-five;

but the landlord did not question his words. He merely swept away the covers and set a bottle of old cognac before him.

For some minutes past Lord Stavely had been aware that the young gentleman in the window was subjecting him to an intent scrutiny. He knew well what was engaging this fixed attention, and when the landlord had withdrawn, he said gently: 'I call it the Nonchalent. It is not very difficult, once you acquire the knack of it.'

'Eh?' said the young gentleman, starting.

'My cravat,' explained Lord Stavely, smiling.

The young gentleman coloured and stammered that he begged pardon.

'Not at all,' said his lordship. 'I'll show you how to tie it, if you like.'

'Will you?' exclaimed the young gentleman eagerly. 'I tie mine in an Osbaldeston, but I don't like it above half.'

Lord Stavely waved one hand invitingly towards a chair at the table. 'Won't you join me?'

'Well—thank you!' The young gentleman got up and crossed the floor circumspectly. He brought his glass and the bottle with him, and set both down on the table. 'My name,' he announced carefully, 'is Hatherleigh.'

'Mine is Stavely,' returned his lordship.

They exchanged bows. Only a purist would have said that Mr Hatherleigh was drunk. He could, by taking only reasonable pains, walk and speak with dignity, and if his potations had had the effect of divorcing his brain a little from the normal, at least it was perfectly clear on all important matters. When Lord Stavely, for instance, touching lightly on the country through which he had driven, said that he should suppose it to be good hunting country, young Hatherleigh was able to expatiate on the subject with enthusiasm and really remarkable coherence. The cloud lifted from his brow, his eyes brightened, and he became quite animated. Then the cloud descended again abruptly, and he fetched a sigh, and said gloomily: 'But that is all at an end! I dare say I may think myself lucky if ever I get a leg across a good hunter again.'

'As bad as that?' said his lordship sympathetically.

Mr Hatherleigh nodded, and poured himself out some more brandy. 'I'm eloping with an heiress,' he announced dejectedly.

If Lord Stavely was startled by this intelligence, he managed to conceal his emotions most creditably. His lip did quiver a little, but he said in the politest way: 'Indeed?'

'Yes,' said Mr Hatherleigh, fortifying himself with a deep drink. 'Gretna Green,' he added.

'Forgive me,' said his lordship, 'but do you feel this to be a wise step to take?'

'No, of course I don't!' said Mr Hatherleigh. 'But what is a fellow to do? I can't draw back now! You must see that!'

'I expect it would be very difficult,' agreed Lord Stavely. 'When one has persuaded an heiress to elope with one——'

'No such thing!' interrupted Mr Hatherleigh. 'I dare say I may have said it would be rare sport to do it, if only to kick up a dust, but I never thought Annabella would think I really meant it! But that is Annabella all over. In fact, I think she's devilish like her father! Let her but once take a notion into her head, and there's no persuading her to listen to reason! Mind, though,' he added, bending a sudden, minatory scowl upon his auditor, 'you are not to be thinking that I wish to back out! I have loved Annabella for years. In fact, I swore a blood-oath to marry her when we were children. But that isn't to say that I want to drive off to the Border with her—and just now, too!'

'The moment is not quite convenient?'

Mr Hatherleigh shook his head. 'My uncle has invited me to Yorkshire for the grouse shooting!' he said bitterly. 'Only think what a splendid time I could have had! I have never tried my hand at grouse, you know, but I am accounted a pretty fair shot.'

'You could not, I suppose, postpone the elopement until after the shooting season?' suggested his lordship.

'No, because if we waited there would be no sense in eloping at all, because very likely Annabella will be tied up to the old fogy her father means her to marry. Besides, the moon's at the full now.'

'I see. And who is this old fogy? Is he *very* old?'

'I don't know, but I should think he must be, wouldn't you, if he's a friend of Sir Walter?'

His lordship paused in the act of raising his glass to his lips. 'Sir Walter?'

'Sir Walter Abingdon. He is Annabella's father.'

'Oh!' said his lordship, sipping his brandy. 'I collect that he does not look with favour on your suit?'

'No, and my father does not either. He says we are too young, and should not suit. So very likely I shall be cut off with a shilling, and be obliged to enter a counting-house, or some such thing, for Sir Walter will certainly cut Annabella off. But of course females never consider anything of that nature! They have not the least common sense, beside thinking that it is perfectly easy to hire a chaise for midnight without making anyone suspicious! And it is *not!*' said Mr Hatherleigh, a strong sense of grievance overcoming him. 'Let alone the expense of it— and that, let me tell you, has pretty well made my pockets to let! I have had to go twenty miles to do it, because a rare flutter I should have set up if I'd bespoke a chaise to go to Scotland at the George, or the Sun! Why, my father would have had wind of it within the hour!

'And then I had to rack my brains to think how best to meet it, because it would never do to have it driving up to my home to pick me up, you know. Luckily old Thetford here is very much attached to our interests, so I told the post-boys in the end to come to this inn at half-past ten tonight. Annabella thinks everyone will be asleep by half-past eleven, or twelve at latest, and she is to meet me in the shrubbery. Shrubbery at midnight!' he repeated scornfully. 'I can tell you, it makes me feel like a great cake! Such flummery!'

He picked up the bottle again as he spoke, and poured some more brandy into his glass. Some of the liquor spilled on to the table. Mr Hatherleigh glared at it, and set the bottle down with precision.

'Do you know,' said Lord Stavely conversationally, 'if I were going to elope at midnight I believe I would not drink too much brandy at ten o'clock?'

Mr Hatherleigh eyed him austerely. 'If you think I'm foxed,' he enunciated, 'you're wrong! I have a very hard head.'

'I'm sure you have,' said his lordship. 'But if Miss Annabella were to detect the fumes on your breath she might not be quite pleased.'

'Well, she shouldn't have insisted on eloping with me!' retorted Mr Hatherleigh.

'She must be very much attached to you?'

'Of course she is. Why, she's known me all her life! All the same, she never would have taken this silly notion into her head if that peppery old fool hadn't asked this fellow to stay, and told her she was to marry him. I must say, I was shocked when Annabella told me of it. I dare say he must be fifty at least, and a dead bore! Besides, she has never clapped eyes on him! I quite saw that as a gentleman I must rescue her, though I never thought *then* that my uncle would invite me to stay with him in Yorkshire!'

'But surely even the most peppery of parents cannot in these days marry his daughter out of hand? Must you really elope?' said Lord Stavely.

'Annabella says so, and of course I am bound in honour to oblige her,' replied Mr Hatherleigh grandly. 'I dare say I shan't dislike being married so very much, once I get used to it.'

'I feel very strongly that you are making a mistake,' said his lordship, gently moving the bottle out of reach. 'Perhaps the dead bore will not wish to marry Annabella!'

'Then why is he coming to stay with the Abingdons?' demanded Mr Hatherleigh. 'I expect Sir Walter has it all arranged, in his famous style! My father says he is the most meddlesome, managing old fool in the county.' He drained his glass defiantly. ' 'T all events,' he pronounced, 'it'll be something to overset his precious plans!'

Half an hour later, the landlord, coming in to inform Mr Tom that his chaise was at the door, found that young gentleman stertorously asleep, with his head on the table.

'I don't think,' said Lord Stavely, 'that Mr Tom is in a fit case for travel.'

'There, now, I knew how it would be!' exclaimed Thetford, looking down at Tom in some concern. 'Whatever can be the matter with him? When I see him this evening, I thought to myself: You're up to mischief, Mr Tom, or I don't know the signs! And here's a chaise and four come all the way from Whitworth to take him up! What's to be done?'

'You had better inform the postilions that Mr Tom is indisposed, and send them back to Whitworth,' said his lordship. 'And while you are about it, will you be so good as to inform my own postilions that I have changed my mind, and mean to go to Melbury Place tonight after all? Desire them to put the horses to at once, if you please.'

'Your lordship won't be staying here?' the landlord said, his face falling 'And the bed made up, and a hot brick in it to air the sheets!'

'Carry Mr Tom up to it!' recommended Lord Stavely, with a smile. 'When he wakes——' He glanced down at Mr Tom's unconscious form. 'No, perhaps I had better leave a note for him.' He drew out his pocket-book, and after a moment's hesitation scribbled several lines in it in pencil, tore out the leaf, twisted it into a screw, and gave it to the landlord. 'When he wakes, give him that,' he said.

A quarter of an hour later, Thetford having furnished the post-boys with precise instructions. Lord Stavely was bowling along narrow country lanes to Melbury Place. When the gates came into sight, the post-boys would have turned in, but his lordship checked them, and said that he would get down.

They had long since decided that he was an eccentric, but this quite staggered them. 'It's Melbury Place right enough, my lord!' one assured him.

'I am aware. I have a fancy to stroll through the gardens in this exquisite moonlight. Wait here!'

He left them goggling after him. 'He must be as drunk as a wheelbarrow!' said one.

'Not him!' returned his fellow. 'Queer in his attic! I suspicioned it at the start.'

His lordship, meanwhile, was walking up the drive. He very soon left the gravel for the grass bordering it, so that no sound should betray his presence to anyone in the house. The air was heavy with the scent of roses, and the full moon, riding high overhead, cast ink-black shadows on the ground. It showed the house, outlined against a sky of deepest sapphire, and made it an easy matter for his lordship, traversing the flower gardens, to find the shrubbery. Here, neat walks meandered between high hedges, and several rustic seats were set at convenient spots. No one was present, and no light shone from the long, low house in the background. His lordship sat down to await events.

He had not long to wait. After perhaps twenty minutes, he heard the hush of skirts, and rose just as a cloaked figure came swiftly round a bend in the walk, carrying two band-boxes. He stepped forward, but before he could speak the newcomer exclaimed in a muted voice: 'I thought my aunt would never blow out her candle! But she is snoring now! Did you procure a chaise, Tom?'

Lord Stavely took off his hat, and the moonlight showed the lady the face of a complete stranger. She recoiled with a smothered shriek.

'Don't be afraid!' said his lordship reassuringly. 'I am Mr Hatherleigh's deputy. Let me take those boxes!'

'His *deputy*?' echoed Miss Abingdon, nervelessly relinquishing her baggage into his hands.

'Yes,' said Lord Stavely, setting the bandboxes down beside the seat. 'Shall we sit here while I explain it to you?'

'But who are you, and where is Tom?' demanded Miss Abingdon.

'Tom,' said his lordship diplomatically, 'is indisposed. He was good enough to confide his plans to me, and to— er—charge me with his deepest regrets.'

The lady's fright succumbed to a strong feeling of ill-usage. 'Well!' she said, her bosom swelling. 'If that is not the poorest spirited thing I ever heard! I suppose he was afraid?'

'Not at all!' said his lordship, gently propelling her to-wards the seat. 'He was overcome by a sudden illness.'

Miss Abingdon sat down, perforce, but peered suspici-ously at him. 'It sounds to me like a fudge!' she said, not mincing matters. 'He was perfectly well yesterday!'

'His disorder attacked him unawares,' said Lord Stavely.

Miss Abingdon, who seemed to labour under few illusions, demanded forthrightly: 'Was he *foxed*?'

Lord Stavely did not answer for a moment. He looked at the lady, trying to see her face clearly in the moonlight. The hood had slipped back from her head. The uncertain light made it hard for him to decide whether her hair was dark or fair, but he was sure that it curled riotously, and that her eyes were both large and sparkling. He said: 'Foxed? Certainly not!'

'I don't believe you!' said Miss Abingdon. 'How could he be such a simpleton, on this of all nights?'

Lord Stavely returned no answer to this, and after pondering in silence for a few minutes, Miss Abingdon said: 'I did wonder if he quite liked the scheme. But why could he not have told me that he wanted to draw back from it?'

'That,' said Lord Stavely, 'is the last thing he meant to

227

do. He informed me that you had plighted your troth many years ago.'

'Yes,' agreed Miss Abingdon. 'He cut my wrist with his knife, and we mixed our blood. He said I was chicken-hearted because I squeaked.'

'How very unfeeling of him!' said his lordship gravely. 'May I venture to ask if you love him very dearly?'

Miss Abingdon considered the matter. 'Well, I have always been prodigiously fond of him,' she answered at last. 'I dare say I might not have married him, in spite of the oath, had things not been so desperate, but what else could I do when my papa is behaving so abominably, and I am in such despair? I did hope that Papa would hire a house in London for the Season, for I am nearly twenty years old, and I have never been out of Shropshire, except to go to Bath, which I detest. And instead of that he means to marry me to a horrid old man I have never seen!'

'Yes, so Tom told me,' said his lordship. 'But—forgive me—it seems scarcely possible that he could do such a thing!'

'You don't know my papa!' said Miss Abingdon bitterly. 'He makes the most fantastic schemes, and forces everyone to fall in with them! And he says I must be civil to his odious friend, and if I am not he will pack me off to Bath to stay with my Aunt Charlotte! Sir, what could I do? Aunt Maria—who is Papa's other sister, and has lived with us since my mama died—will do nothing but say that I know what Papa is—and I *do*, and I dare say he would have not the least compunction in sending me to a stuffy house in Queen Square, with Aunt's pug wheezing at me, and Aunt scarcely stirring out of the house, but wishing me to play backgammon with her! *Backgammon!*' she reiterated, with loathing.

'That, certainly, is not to be thought of,' agreed his lordship. 'Yet I cannot help wondering if you are quite wise to elope to Gretna Green.'

'You don't think so?' Miss Abingdon said doubtfully.

'These Border marriages are not quite the thing, you know,' explained his lordship apologetically. 'Then, too, unless you are very much in love with Tom, you might not be perfectly happy with him.'

'No,' agreed Miss Abingdon, 'but how shocking it would be if I were to be an old maid!'

'If you will not think me very saucy for saying so,' said his lordship, a laugh in his voice, 'I cannot think that a very likely fate for you!'

'Yes, but it is!' she said earnestly. 'I have been kept cooped up here all my life, and Papa has not the least notion of taking me to London! He has made up his mind to it that his odious friend will be a very eligible match for me. He and this Lady Tenbury laid their heads together, I dare say——'

'So that was it!' interrupted his lordship. 'I should have guessed it, of course.'

Miss Abingdon was surprised. 'Are you acquainted with Lady Tenbury, sir?' she asked.

'My elder sister,' explained his lordship.

'Your—w-what?' gasped Miss Abingdon, recoiling.

'Don't be alarmed!' he begged. 'Though I shrink from owning to it, I think I must be your papa's odious friend. But I assure you, Miss Abingdon, his and my meddling sister's schemes come as a complete surprise to me!'

Miss Abingdon swallowed convulsively. 'D-do you m-mean to tell me, sir, that you are Lord Stavely?'

'Yes,' confessed his lordship. He added: 'But though I may be a dead bore, I am not really so very old!'

'You should have told me!' said Miss Abingdon, deeply mortified.

'I know I should, but I could not help nourishing the hope that I might not, after all, be the odious old man you and Tom have described in such daunting terms.'

She turned her face away, saying in a stifled tone: 'I would never . . . Oh, how could you let me run on so?'

'Don't mind it!' he said, taking one of her hands in a comforting clasp. 'Only pray don't elope to Gretna just to escape from my attentions!'

'No, no, but——' She lifted her head and looked at him under brows which he guessed rather than saw to be knit. 'But how *can* you be a friend of my papa?' she asked.

'To tell you the truth, I didn't know that I had the right to call myself so,' he replied. 'He and my family have been upon terms any time these twenty years, I suppose, and I know that he is a close friend of my sister and her husband.'

Miss Abingdon still appeared to be dissatisfied. 'Then how did you come to visit me?'

'If I must answer truthfully,' said his lordship, 'I found it impossible to refuse your parent's repeated invitations with the least degree of civility!'

She seemed to find this understandable. She nodded, and said: 'And you haven't come to—I mean, you didn't know——'

'Until this evening, ma'am,' said his lordship, 'I did not know that you existed! My sister, you see, though quite as meddlesome as your father, has by far more tact.'

'It is the most infamous thing!' declared Miss Abingdon. 'He made me think it had all been arranged, and I had nothing to do but encourage your advances! So naturally I made up my mind to marry Tom rather!' She gave a little spurt of involuntary laughter. 'Was ever anything so nonsensical? I thought you had been fifty at least, and very likely fat!'

'I am thirty-five, and I do not *think* I am fat,' said his lordship meekly.

She was still more amused. 'No, I can see you are not! I am afraid I must seem the veriest goose to you! But Papa once thought for a whole month that he would like me to marry Sir Jasper Selkirk, and he is a widower, and has the gout besides! So there is never any telling what absurdity he may have taken into his head, you see.' A thought occurred to her; she turned more fully towards his lordship, and said: 'But how comes it that you are acquainted with Tom, and why are you so late? We were expecting you would arrive to dine, and Papa was in such a fume! And Aunt made them keep dinner back until the chickens were quite spoilt!'

'I cannot sufficiently apologize,' said Lord Stavely. 'A series of unfortunate accidents delayed me shockingly, and when I did at last reach Shropshire I found that your Papa's directions were not quite as helpful as I had supposed they would be. In fact, I lost my way.'

'It is a difficult country,' agreed Miss Abingdon. 'And of course Papa can never direct anyone properly. But how came you to meet Tom?'

'He was awaiting a chaise at the Green Dragon, where, being then so late, I stopped to dine. We fell into conversation, as one does, you know, and he was good enough to confide his intentions to me.'

'He *must* have been drunk!' interpolated Miss Abingdon.

'Let us say, rather, that he was a trifle worried over the

propriety of eloping with you. I did what I could to persuade him against taking so ill-advised a step; he—er—succumbed to the disorder from which he was suffering, and I came here in his stead.'

'It was excessively kind of you, but I don't at all know why you should have taken so much trouble for me!'

He smiled. 'But I could not let you kick your heels in this shrubbery, could I? Besides, I had the liveliest curiosity to meet you, Miss Abingdon!'

She tried to see his face. 'Are you quizzing me?' she demanded.

'Not at all. You will allow that one's curiosity must be aroused when one learns that a lady is prepared to elope to escape from advances one had had not the least intention of making!'

'It is quite dreadful!' she said, blushing. 'I wonder it did not give you the most shocking disgust of me! But indeed I did not think it would be improper to elope with Tom, because he is almost like a brother, you know—and it would have been such an adventure!'

She ended on a distinctly wistful note. Lord Stavely responded promptly: 'If your heart is set on the adventure, my chaise is waiting in the lane: you have only to command me!'

Another of her gurgling laughs escaped her. 'How can you be so absurd? As though I would elope with a stranger!'

'Well, I do feel it might be better if you gave up the notion,' he said. 'I fear I can hardly draw back now from Sir Walter's invitation, but if I give you my word not to press an unwanted suit upon you perhaps you may not find my visit insupportably distasteful.'

'No, no!' she assured him. 'But I very much fear that

Papa may—may cause you a great deal of embarrassment, sir!'

'Quite impossible!' he said, smiling. 'Have no fear on that head!'

'You are the most truly amiable man I ever met!' she exclaimed warmly. 'Indeed, I am very much obliged to you, and quite ashamed to think I should have misjudged you so! You—you won't tell Papa?'

'Miss Abingdon, *that* is the unkindest thing you have yet said to me!'

'No. I know you would not!' she said quickly. She rose and held out her hand. 'I must go back to the house. But you?'

'In about twenty minutes' time,' said Lord Stavely, 'I shall drive up to the front door, with profuse apologies and excuses!'

'Oh, shall you indeed do that?' giggled Miss Abingdon. 'It must be close on midnight! Papa will be so cross!'

'Well, I must brave his wrath,' he said, raising her hand to his lips.

Her hand clung to his; Miss Abingdon jerked up her head and stood listening. In another instant Lord Stavely had also heard what had startled her: footsteps which tried to be stealthy, and a voice whose owner seemed to imagine himself to be speaking under his breath: 'Do you go that way, Mullins, and I'll go this, and mind, no noise!'

'Papa!' breathed Miss Abingdon, in a panic. 'He must have heard me: I tripped on the gravel! Depend upon it, he thinks we are thieves: Sir Jasper was robbed last month! What am I to do?'

'Can you reach the house without being observed if I draw them off?' asked his lordship softly.

'Yes, yes, but you? Papa will very likely have his fowling-piece!'

'Be sure I shall declare myself before he fires at me!' He picked up the bandboxes and gave them to her.

She clutched them and fled. Lord Stavely, having watched her disappear round a corner of the shrubbery, set his hat on his head and sauntered in the opposite direction, taking care to advertise his presence.

He emerged from the shrubbery into the rose garden, and was almost immediately challenged by an elderly gentleman who did indeed level a fowling-piece at him.

'Stand! I have you covered, rogue!' shouted Sir Walter. 'Mullins, you fool, here!'

Lord Stavely stood still, waiting for his host to approach him. This Sir Walter did not do until he had been reinforced by his butler, similarly armed, and sketchily attired in a nightshirt, a pair of breeches, and a greatcoat thrown over all. He then came forward, keeping his lordship covered, and said with gleeful satisfaction: 'Caught you, my lad!'

'How do you do, sir?' said Lord Stavely, holding out his hand. 'I must beg your pardon for presenting myself at this unconscionable hour, but I have been dogged by ill fortune all day. A broken lynch-pin and a lame horse must stand as my excuses.'

Sir Walter nearly dropped his piece. '*Stavely?*' he ejaculated, peering at his lordship in amazement.

Lord Stavely bowed.

'But what the devil are you doing in my garden?' Sir Walter demanded.

Lord Stavely waved an airy hand. 'Communing with Nature, sir, communing with Nature!'

'*Communing with Nature?*' echoed Sir Walter, his eyes fairly starting from his head.

'Roses bathed in moonlight!' said his lordship lyrically. 'Ah—must Mullins continue to point his piece at me?'

'Put it down, you fool!' commanded Sir Walter testily. 'Stavely, my dear fellow, are you feeling quite the thing?'

'Never better!' replied his lordship. 'Oh, you are thinking that I should have driven straight up to the house? Very true, sir, but I was lured out of my chaise by this exquisite scene. I am passionately fond of moonlight, and really, you know, your gardens present so charming a picture that I could not but yield to temptation, and explore them. I am sorry to have disturbed you!'

Sir Walter was staring at him with his jaw dropping almost as prodigiously as the butler's. 'Explore my gardens at midnight!' he uttered, in stupefied accents.

'Is it so late?' said his lordship. 'Yet I dare say one might see to read a book in this clear light!'

Sir Walter swallowed twice before venturing on a response. 'But where's your carriage?' he demanded.

'I told the post-boys to wait in the lane,' replied his lordship vaguely. 'I believe—yes, I believe I can detect the scent of jasmine!'

'Stavely,' said Sir Walter, laying an almost timid hand on his arm, 'do but come up to the house, and to bed! Everything is prepared, and this night air is most unwholesome!'

'On the contrary, I find that it awakens poetry in my soul,' said Lord Stavely. 'I am inspired to write a sonnet on roses drenched with moonshine.'

'Mullins, go and find his lordship's chaise, and direct the postilions to drive up to the house!' ordered Sir Walter, in an urgent under-voice. 'Sonnets, eh, Stavely?

Yes, yes, I have been a rhymester in my time, too, but just come with me, my dear fellow, and you will soon feel better, I dare say! You have had a long and a tedious journey, that's what it is!'

He took his guest by the arm and firmly drew him towards the house. His lordship went with him unresisting, but maintained a slow pace, and frequently paused to admire some effect of trees against the night sky, or the sheen of moonlight on the lily-pond. Sir Walter, curbing his impatience, replied soothingly to these flights, and succeeded at last in coaxing him into the house, and upstairs to the chamber prepared for him. A suspicion that his noble guest had been imbibing too freely gave place to a far worse fear. Not until he was assured by the sound of my lord's deep breathing that he was sleeping soundly did Sir Walter retire from his post outside his guest's door and seek his own couch.

Lord Stavely and Miss Abingdon met officially at a late breakfast table. Sir Walter performed the introduction, eyeing his guest narrowly as he did so.

Lord Stavely, bowing first to Miss Maria Abingdon, apologized gracefully for having knocked the household up at such a late hour, and then turned to confront the heiress. For her part, she had been covertly studying him while he exchanged civilities with her aunt. She was very favourably impressed by what she saw. Lord Stavely was generally held to be a personable man. Miss Abingdon found no reason to quarrel with popular opinion. He had a pair of smiling grey eyes, a humorous mouth and an excellent figure. Both air and address were polished, and his raiment, without being dandified, was extremely elegant. He wore pantaloons and Hessians, which set off his legs to advantage; and Miss Abingdon noticed that his snow-white cravat was arranged in precise and intricate folds.

Miss Abingdon had surprised her aunt by choosing to wear quite her most becoming sprigged muslin gown. Miss Maria, who had despaired of detecting any such signs of docility in her niece, was further startled to observe that nothing could have been more demure than Annabella's behaviour. She seemed quite to have recovered from her sulks, curtsied shyly to the guest, and gave him her hand with the most enchanting and mischievous of smiles. Really, thought Miss Maria, watching her fondly, the child looked quite lovely!

Lord Stavely talked easily at the breakfast-table, ably assisted by both ladies. Sir Walter seemed a trifle preoccupied, and when they rose from the table, and his lordship begged leave to wander out into the sunlit garden, he acquiesced readily, and scarcely waited for his guest to step out through the long window before hurrying out of the room in his daughter's wake. He overtook her at the foot of the stairs, and peremptorily summoned her to his library. Shutting the door behind her, he said without preamble: 'Annabella, you need not be in a pet, for I have changed my plans for you! Yes, yes, I no longer think of Stavely for you, so let us have no more tantrums!'

Miss Abingdon's large blue eyes flew to his. 'Changed your plans for me, Papa?' she exclaimed.

He looked round cautiously, as though to be sure that his guest was not lurking in the room, and then said in an earnest tone: 'My dear, it is the most distressing circumstance! The poor fellow is deranged! You would never credit it, I dare say, but I found him wandering about the garden at midnight, talking of sonnets, and moonlight, and such stuff!'

Miss Abingdon lowered her gaze swiftly and faltered: 'Did you, Papa? How—how very strange, to be sure!'

'I was never more shocked in my life!' declared Sir Walter. 'I had not the least notion of such a thing, and I must say that I think Louisa Tenbury has not behaved as she should in concealing it from me!'

'It is very dreadful!' agreed Miss Abingdon. 'Yet he *seems* quite sane, Papa!'

'He seems sane *now*,' said her parent darkly, 'but we don't know what he may do when the moon is up! I believe some lunatics are only deranged at the full of the moon. And now I come to think of it, they used to say that his grandfather had some queer turns! Not that I believed it, but I see now that it may well have been so. I wish I had not pressed him to visit us! You had better take care, my child, not to be in his company unless I am at hand to protect you!'

Miss Abingdon, who, out of the tail of her eye, had seen Lord Stavely strolling in the direction of the rose garden, returned a dutiful answer, and proceeded without loss of time to follow his lordship.

She found him looking down at the sundial in the middle of a rose plot. He glanced up at her approach and smiled, moving to meet her. Her face was glowing with mischief, her eyes dancing. She said: 'Oh, my lord, Papa says you are mad, and he does not in the least wish me to marry you!'

He took her hands and held them. 'I know it. Now, what am I to do to convince him that I am in the fullest possession of my senses?'

'Why, what should it signify?' she asked. 'I am sure you do not care what he may think! I don't know how I kept my countenance! He says I must take care not to be in your company, unless he is at hand to protect me!'

'I see nothing to laugh at in that!' he protested.

She looked up innocently. 'I am so very sorry! But indeed I did not think that you would care!'

'On the contrary, it is of the first importance that your papa should think well of me.'

'Good gracious, why?'

'My dear Miss Abingdon, how can I persuade him to permit me to pay my addresses to you if he believes me to be mad?'

For a moment she stared at him; then her cheeks became suffused, and she pulled her hands away, saying faintly: '*Oh!* But you said you would not—you know you did!'

'I know nothing of the sort. I said I would not press an unwanted suit upon you. Do not take from me all hope of being able to make myself agreeable to you!'

Miss Abingdon, no longer meeting his eyes, murmured something not very intelligible, and began to nip off the faded blooms from a fine rose tree.

'I must study to please Sir Walter,' said his lordship. 'How is it to be done? I rely upon your superior knowledge of him!'

Miss Abingdon, bending down to pluck a half-blown rose, said haltingly: 'Well, if—if you don't wish him to believe you mad, perhaps—perhaps you had better remain with us for a little while, so that he may be brought to realize that you are quite sane!'

'An excellent plan!' approved his lordship. 'I shall be guided entirely by your advice, Miss Abingdon. May I have that rose?'

Sir Walter, informed by the gardener of the whereabouts of his guest and his daughter, came into the rose garden in time to see Miss Abingdon fix a pink rose-bud in the lapel of Lord Stavely's coat. His reflections on the perversity and undutifulness of females he was obliged to keep to himself, but he told Miss Abingdon, with some asperity, that her aunt was searching for her, and taking Lord Stavely by the arm, marched him off to inspect the stables.

Miss Abingdon found her aunt in a state of nervous flutter, having been informed by her brother of their guest's derangement. 'And I thought him such a sensible man! So handsome, too, and so truly amiable!'

'Oh, my dear aunt, is he not the most delightful creature?' confided Miss Abingdon, eyes and cheeks aglow. 'Only fancy his wishing to marry me!'.

Miss Maria started. 'No, no, that is quite at an end! Your papa would never hear of it! And when I think that only yesterday you were vowing you would marry Tom Hatherleigh in spite of anything your papa could say, I declare I don't know what can have come over you!'

'Moon madness!' laughed Miss Abingdon. 'Just like Lord Stavely! *Poor* Papa!'